HEX
APPEAL

ALSO EDITED BY
P. N. ELROD

Dark and Stormy Knights

Strange Brew

My Big Fat Supernatural Wedding

My Big Fat Supernatural Honeymoon

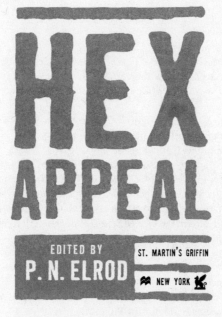

HEX
APPEAL

EDITED BY
P. N. ELROD

ST. MARTIN'S GRIFFIN
NEW YORK

These short stories are works of fiction. All of the characters, organizations, and events portrayed in these short stories are either products of the authors' imaginations or are used fictitiously.

www.stmartins.com

Library of Congress Cataloging-in-Publication Data

Hex appeal/P. N. Elrod [editor]. — 1st ed.
    p. cm.
  ISBN 978-0-312-59072-7 (trade pbk.)
  ISBN 978-1-4668-0259-9 (e-book)
 1. Paranormal fiction, American. 2. Witches—Fiction. 3. Fantasy Fiction, American. I. Elrod, P. N. (Patricia Nead).
  PS648.O33 H49 2012
  813'.54—dc23

2012004626

First Edition: June 2012

10 9 8 7 6 5 4 3 2 1

CONTENTS

RETRIBUTION CLAUSE

by ILONA ANDREWS

Adam Talford closed his eyes and wished he were somewhere else. Somewhere warm. Where cool waves lapped hot yellow sand, where strange flowers bloomed, and birdsong filled the air.

"Take off the watch! Now!" a male voice barked into his ear. "You think I am fucking with you? You think I am playing? I'll rip your flesh off your body and make myself a skin suit."

Adam opened his eyes. The three thugs who pinned him to the brick wall looked half-starved, like mongrel dogs who'd been prowling the alley, feeding on garbage.

He should never have wandered into this side of Philadelphia, not in the evening, and especially not while the magic was up. This was Firefern Road, a place where the refuse of the city hid out among the ruins of the ravaged buildings, gnawed by magic to ugly nubs of brick and concrete. The real predators stalked their prey elsewhere, looking for bigger and meatier scores. Firefern Road sheltered scavengers, desperate and savage, eager to bite, but only when the odds were on their side.

Unfortunately, he had no choice.

"You have the cash," Adam said, keeping his voice low. "Take it and go. It's a cheap watch. You won't get any money for it."

The larger of the thugs pulled him from the wall and slammed him back into the bricks. The man bent over him, folding his six-foot-two frame down to Adam's five feet five inches, so their faces were level, forcing Adam to stare straight into his eyes. Adam looked into their blue depths and glimpsed a spark of vicious glee. It wasn't about the money anymore. It was about domination, humiliation, and inflicting pain. They would beat him just for the fun of it.

"The watch, you little bitch," the thug ordered.

"No," Adam said quietly.

A muscular forearm smashed into his neck, cutting off his air. Bodies pressed against him. He felt fingers prying at the metal band on his narrow wrist. His heart hammered. His chest constricted.

Think of elsewhere. Think of blue waves and yellow sand . . .

Someone yanked at the band. The world was turning darker—his lungs demanded air. Pain shot through his limbs in sharp, burning spikes.

Blue waves . . . Azure . . . Calm . . . Just need to stay calm . . .

Cold metal broke his skin. They were trying to cut the watch off his wrist. He jerked and heard the crunch of broken glass. Two tiny watch gears flew before his eyes, sparking with residual traces of magic.

Imbeciles. They'd broken it.

The magic chain that held his body in check vanished. The calming visions of the ocean vanished, swept away by an avalanche of fury. His magic roared inside him, ancient, primal, and cold as a glacier. Frost clamped his eyebrows, falling off in tiny snowflakes. The short blond hairs rained down from his head, and pale blue strands grew in their place, falling down to his shoulders. His body surged, up and out, stretching, spilling out into its natural shape. His outer clothes tore under the pressure as his new form stretched the thick spandex suit he wore underneath to its limit. His feet ripped the cheap cloth Converse sneakers. The three small humans in front of him froze like frightened rabbits.

With a guttural roar, Adam grasped the leader by his shoulder and yanked him up. The man's fragile collarbone broke under the pressure of his pale fingers, and the man screamed, kicking his feet. Adam brought him close, their eyes once again level. The thug trembled and fell silent, his face a terrified rigid mask. Adam knew exactly what he saw: a creature, an eight-foot-tall giant in the shape of a man, with a mane of blue hair and eyes like submerged ice.

Inside him, the rational, human part of Adam Talbot sighed and faded. Only cold and rage drove him now.

"Do you know why I wear the watch?" he snarled into the man's face.

The thug shook his head.

"I wear it so I can keep my body in my tracking form. Because when I'm small, I don't draw attention. I can go anywhere. Nobody pays me any notice. I've been tracking a man for nine days. His trail led me here. I was so close, I could smell his sweat, and the three of you ruined it for me. I can't follow him now, can I?" He shook the man like a wet rag. "I told you to walk away. No. You didn't listen."

"I'll listen," the thug promised. "I'll listen now."

"Too late. You wanted to feel big and bad. Now I'll show you what big and bad is."

Adam hurled the human across the alley. The thug flew. Before he crashed into a brick ruin with a bone-snapping crunch, his two sidekicks turned and fled, running full speed. Adam vaulted over a garbage Dumpster to his right and gave chase.

Ten minutes later, he returned to the alley, crouched, dug through the refuse with bloody fingers, and fished out his watch. The glass and the top plate were gone, displaying the delicate innards of gears and magic. Hopelessly mangled. Just like the thug who still sagged motionless against the ruin.

The alley reeked with the scavenger stench: fear, sweat, a hint of urine, garbage. Adam rose, stretching to his full height, and raised his face to the wind. The hint of Morowitz's scent teased him, slightly sweet and distant. The chase was over.

Dean Morowitz was a thief, and, like all thieves, he would

[3]

do anything for the right price. He'd stolen a priceless necklace in a feat of outrageous luck, but he didn't do it on his own. No, someone had hired him, and Adam was interested in the buyer much more than in the tool he had used. Breaking Morowitz's legs would probably shed some light on his employment arrangements, but it would inevitably alarm the buyer, who'd vanish into thin air. Following the thief was a much better course of action.

Adam sighed. He had failed. Tracking the thief now would be like carrying a neon side above his head that read, POM INSURANCE ADJUSTER. He'd have to give Morowitz a day or two to cool off, then arrange for a replacement watch to hide his true form before trying to find the man again.

A mild headache scraped at the inside of Adam's head, insistent, like a knock on his door.

He concentrated, sending a focused thought in its direction. "Yes?"

"You're needed at the office, Mr. Talford," a familiar female voice murmured directly into his mind.

"I'll be right there," he promised, rose to his full height, and began to jog, breaking into the long-legged distance-devouring gait that thousands of years ago carried his ancestors across the frozen wastes of the old North.

Night was falling. Anyone with a crumb of sense cleared from the streets or hurried to get home, behind the protection of four walls, barred windows, and a sturdy door. The rare passersby scattered out of his way. Even in post-Shift Philadelphia, the sight of an eight-foot-tall human running full speed in skintight black spandex wasn't a common occurrence. He drew the eye, Adam reflected, leaping over a ten-foot gap in the asphalt. He pounded up the wooden ramp onto the newly built Pine Bridge, spanning the vast sea of crushed concrete and twisted steel that used to be the downtown.

The bridge turned south, carrying him deeper into the city.

Far in the distance, the sunset burned out, couched in long orange clouds. The weak light of the dying sun glinted from the heaps of broken glass that used to be hundreds of windows. The cemetery of human ambition.

Human beings had always believed in apocalypse, but they expected the end of the world to come in a furious flash of nuclear cloud, or in environmental disaster, or perhaps even on a stray rock falling from the universe beyond. Nobody expected the magic. It came during one sunny afternoon, in broad daylight, and raged through the world—pulling planes from the sky, stealing electricity, giving birth to monsters. And three days later, when it vanished, and humanity reeled, thousands were dead. Survivors mourned and breathed a sigh of relief, but two weeks later the magic came again.

It flooded the world in waves now, unpredictable and moody, coming back and disappearing on its own mysterious schedule. Slowly but surely, it tore down the tall buildings, feeding on the carcass of technology and molding humanity in its own image. Adam smiled. He took to it better than most.

The latest magic shift took place about half an hour ago, just before he got jumped. While unpredictable, the magic waves rarely lasted less than twelve hours. He was in for a long, magic-filled night.

The bridge split into four different branches. He took the second to the left. It brought him deep into the heart of the city, past the ruins, to the older streets. He cleared the next couple of intersections and turned into the courtyard of a large Georgian-style mansion, a redbrick box, rectangular in shape and three stories high. Anything taller didn't survive in the new Philadelphia unless it was really old. The POM Mansion, as the house came to be known, had been built at the end of the eighteenth century. Its age and the simplicity of its construction afforded it some immunity against magic.

Adam jogged to the doors. Pressure clutched him for a brief

moment, then released him—the defensive spell on the building recognizing his right to enter. Adam stepped through the doors and walked into the foyer. Luxurious by any standards, after his run through the ruined city, the inside of the building looked almost surreal. A hand-knotted blue Persian rug rested on the floor of polished marble. Cream-colored walls were adorned by graceful glass bells of fey lanterns, glowing pale blue as the charged air inside their tubes reacted with magic. A marble staircase veered left and up, leading to the second floor.

Adam paused for a moment to admire the rug. He'd once survived in a cave in the woods for half a year. Luxury or poverty made little difference to him. Luxury tended to be cleaner and more comfortable, but that was about it. Still, he liked the rug—it was beautiful.

The secretary sitting behind a massive redwood desk looked up at his approach. She was slender, young, and dark-skinned. Large brown eyes glanced at him from behind the wide lenses of her glasses. Her name was May, and in the three years of his employment with POM, he'd never managed to surprise her.

"Good evening, Mr. Talford."

"Good evening." He could never figure out if she had been there and done that and was too jaded, or if she was simply too well trained.

"Will you require a change of clothes?"

"Yes, please."

May held out a leather file. His reason for being called into the office. He took it. Priority Two. It overrode all of his cases. Interesting. Adam nodded at her and headed up the stairs.

The heavy door of the office slid open under the pressure of Adam's hand. When he joined the ranks of POM Insurance Adjusters three years ago, someone asked him how he wanted his office to look. He told him, "Like the cabin of a pirate captain," and that was exactly what he got. Cypress paneling lined every inch of the floor, walls, and ceiling, imitating the inside of a wooden ship. The antique-reproduction desk, bolted to the floor for sheer authenticity, supported a sextant, a chronometer, and a bottle of Bombay Blue Sapphire. Behind the desk, an enormous map drawn in ink on yellowed paper took up most of the wall. To the left, bookshelves stretched, next to a large bed sunken into a sturdy wooden frame, so it looked like it was cut into the wall. The bed's dark blue curtain hung open.

His nostrils caught a hint of faint spice. He inhaled it, savoring the scent. Siroun.

"You smell like blood," Siroun's smooth voice said behind him.

Ah. There she is. He turned slightly and watched her circle him, scrutinizing his body. She moved like a lean panther: silent, flexible, graceful. Deadly. Her hair, cropped short into a ragged, messy halo, framed her face like a pale red cloud. She tilted her head. Two dark eyes looked at him.

"You fought with three people, and you let them break your watch?" Her voice was quiet and soothing, and deep for a woman's. He'd heard her sing once, a strange song of murmured words. It had stayed with him.

"I was tracking Morowitz," he told her.

"Into Firefern?"

"Yes."

"We agreed you would wait for me if his trail led into Firefern."

"I did. I called it in to the office, waited, then followed him."

"The office is about four miles from Firefern."

"Yes."

"How long did you wait?"

He frowned, thinking. "I'd say about two minutes."

"And that struck you as the appropriate length of time?"

He grinned at her. "Yes."

A bright orange sheen rolled over her irises, like fire over coals, and vanished. She clearly failed to see the humor in this situation.

Post-Shift Philadelphia housed many people with something extra in their blood, including shapeshifters, a small, sad pack of humans stuck on the crossroads between man and beast. Occasionally, they went insane and had to be put down, but most persevered through strict discipline. Their eyes glowed just like that.

Adjusters worked in pairs, and he and Siroun had been partnered with each other from the beginning. After all this time together, working with her and observing her, he was sure that Siroun wasn't a shapeshifter. At least not any kind he had ever encountered. When she dropped her mask, he sensed something in her, a faint touch of ancient magic, buried deep, hidden like a fossil under the sediment of civilization. He sensed this same primal magic within himself. Siroun wasn't of his kind, but she was like him, and she drew him like a magnet.

Siroun pulled the leather file out of Adam's fingers and sat on the bed, curling around a large pillow.

Adam was possibly the smartest man she had ever known. And also the biggest idiot. In his mind, big and strong equaled invincible. It would only take one bullet to the head in the right spot, one cut of the right blade in the right place, and none of his regeneration would matter.

He went into Firefern by himself. Didn't wait. Didn't tell her. And by the time she'd found out, it was too late—he was already on his way to the office, so she paced back and forth, like a caged tiger until she heard his steps in the hallway.

Adam sat behind his desk, sinking into an oversized leather chair. It groaned, accepting his weight. He cocked his head to the side and moved the bottle of Bombay Sapphire a quarter of an inch to the left. The bright blue liquid caught the light of the fey lantern on the wall and sparkled with all the fire of the real gem.

She pretended to read the file while watching him through the curtain of her eyelashes. For sixteen years, her life was full of chaos, dominated by violence and desperation. Then came the prison; and then, then there was POM and Adam. In her crazed, blood-drenched world, Adam was a granite island of calm. When the turbulent storms rocked her inner world, until she was no longer sure where reality ended and the hungry madness inside her began, she clung to that island and weathered the storm. He had no idea how much she needed this shelter. The thought of losing it nearly drove her out of her mind, what little was left of it.

Adam frowned. A stack of neatly folded clothes sat on the corner of the desk, delivered moments before he walked through the door, together with a small package now waiting for his attention. She'd looked through it: T-shirt, pants, camo suit, all large enough to accommodate his giant body. Adam checked the clothes and pulled the package close. She'd glanced at it—the return address label had one word: Saiman.

"Who is he?" Siroun asked.

"My cousin. He lives in the South." Adam tore the paper and pulled out a leather-bound book. He chuckled and showed her the cover. Robert E. Howard: *The Frost-Giant's Daughter and Other Stories*.

"Is he like you?" Apparently they both had a twisted sense of humor.

"He has more magic, but he uses it mostly to hide. My original form is still my favorite." Adam leaned back, stretching his enormous shoulders. The customized chair creaked. "He has the ability to assume any form, and he wears every type of body except his own."

"Why?"

"I'm not sure. I think he wants to fit in. He wants to be loved by everyone he meets. It's a way of controlling things around him."

"Your cousin sounds unpleasant."

Siroun leafed through the file. Not like Adam would need it. He had probably read it on the way up. She once witnessed him go through a fifty-page contract in less than a minute, then demand detailed adjustments.

He was looking at her; she could feel his gaze. She raised her head and let a little of the fire raging inside color her irises. *Yes, I'm still mad at you.*

Most people froze when confronted with that orange glow. It whispered of old things, brutal and hungry, waiting just beyond the limits of human consciousness.

Adam smiled.

Idiot.

She looked back at the file.

He opened the top drawer of his desk, took out a small paper box, and set it on the desk. *Now what?*

Adam pried the lid open with his oversized fingers and extracted a small brown cupcake with chocolate frosting. It looked thimble-sized in his thick hands. "I have a cupcake."

He had lost his mind.

Adam tilted the cupcake from side to side, making it dance. "It's chocolate."

She clenched her teeth, speechless.

"It could be your cupcake if you stop—"

She dashed across the room in a blur, leaped, and crouched on the desk in front of him. He blinked. She plucked the cupcake from his huge hand with her slender fingers and pretended to ponder it. "I don't like a lot of people."

"I've noticed," he said. He was still smiling. Truly, he had a death wish.

Siroun examined the cupcake some more. "If you die, I will have to choose a new partner, Adam." She turned and looked at him. "I don't want a new partner."

He nodded in mock seriousness. "In that case, I'll strive to stay alive."

"Thank you."

Knuckles rapped on the door. It swung open, and the narrow-shouldered, thin figure of Chang, their POM coordinator, stepped inside. Chang looked at them for a long moment. His eyes widened. "Am I interrupting?"

Siroun jumped off the desk and moved back to the bed, palming the cupcake. "No."

"I am relieved. I'd hate to be rude." Chang crossed the office, deposited another leather file in front of Adam, and perched in a chair across the room. Lean to the point of delicate, the coordinator had one of those encouraging faces that predisposed people to trust him. He wore a small smile and seemed slightly ill at ease, as if he constantly struggled to overcome his natural shyness. Last year, a man had attacked him outside the POM doors with the intent of robbing him. Chang decapitated him and put his head on a sharpened stick. It sat in front of the office for four days before the stench prevailed, and he took it down. A bit crude, but very persuasive.

"That's a beautiful bottle," Chang said, nodding at the Bombay. "I've never seen you drink, Adam. Especially dry gin. So why the bottle?"

"He likes the color," Siroun said.

Adam smiled.

Chang glanced at the flat screen in the wall and sighed. "Things are much easier when technology is up. Unfortunately, we'll have to do this the hard way. Please turn to page one in your file."

Siroun opened the file. Page one offered a portrait of a lean man in a business suit, bending forward, looking into the dense torrent of traffic of cars, carts, and riders. A somber man, confident, almost severe. Slick lines, square jaw, elongated shape of the face inviting comparison with a Doberman pinscher, light skin, light blond hair cut very short. Early to mid forties.

"John Sobanto, an attorney with Dorowitz & Sobanto, and your target. Mr. Sobanto made a fortune representing powerful clients, but he's most famous and most hated for representing New Found Hope."

Siroun bared her teeth. Now there was a name everyone in Philly loved to despise.

New Found Hope, a new church born after the Shift, had pushed hard for pure human, no-magic-tolerated membership. So hard, that on Christmas day, sixteen of its parishioners walked into the icy water of the Delaware River and drowned nine of their own children, who had been born with magic. The guilty and the church leaders were charged with first-degree murder. The couples took the fall, but the founder of the church escaped without even a slap on the wrist. John Sobanto was the man who made it happen.

"Mr. Sobanto is worth $4.2 million, not counting his investments in Left Arm Securities, which are projected at 2 million plus," Chang said. "The corporation was unable to obtain a more precise estimate. Please turn to page two."

Siroun flipped the page. Another photograph, this one of a woman standing on the bank of a lead-colored Delaware River. In the distance, the remains of the Delaware Memorial Bridge jutted sadly from the water. He knew the exact spot this was taken—Penn Treaty Park.

Unlike the man, the woman was aware of being photographed and looked straight into the camera. Pretty in an unremarkable way that came from good breeding and careful attention to one's appearance. Shoulder-length hair, blond, worn loose, standard for an upper-class spouse. Her eyes stared out of the photograph, surprisingly hard. Determined.

"Linda Sobanto," Chang said. "The holder of POM policy

number 492776-M. She spent the last three years funneling an obscene portion of Mr. Sobanto's earnings into POM bank accounts to pay for it."

A severe, confident man on one page, an equally severe, determined woman on the other. An ominous combination, Siroun decided.

Adam stirred. "So what did Mr. Sobanto do to warrant our attention?"

"It appears he murdered his wife," Chang said.

Of course.

"Mrs. Sobanto's insurance policy had a retribution clause," the coordinator continued. "In the event of her homicide, we're required to terminate the guilty party."

"How was she killed?" Siroun asked.

"She was strangled."

Personal. Very, very personal.

"Mr. Sobanto's thumbprint was lifted from her throat. He had defensive wounds on his face and neck, and his DNA was found under her fingernails. His lawyers have arranged a voluntary surrender. He is scheduled to come in Thursday morning, less than a day from now."

"Is he expecting us?" Adam asked.

Chang nodded in a slow, measured way. "Most definitely. Please turn to page three."

On page three, an aerial shot showed a monstrously large ranch-style house hugging the top of the hill like a bear. Three rectangular structures sat a short distance from the house, each marked by a red X.

"Guards stationed in a pyramid formation, four shifts. The gun towers are marked on your photograph. The house is trapped and extensively warded. At least two arcane disciplines were utilized in creation of the wards. For all practical purposes, it's a fortress. Page four, please."

Siroun turned the page. A blueprint, showing a large central room with smaller rooms radiating from it in a wheel-and-spokes design.

"We believe Mr. Sobanto has locked himself in this central chamber. He is guarded by spells, traps, and armed men."

Siroun shifted in her chair. "The guards?"

"Red Guard," Chang answered.

Sobanto hired the best.

"Expensive to hire," Adam murmured, plaiting the fingers of his hands together.

"And very expensive to kill," Chang said. "Red Guard lawyers are truly excellent, particularly when negotiating a wrongful death compensation. We don't want additional expenses, so please don't kill more than three. A higher death count would negatively impact the corporation's profit margin. Please turn to page five."

Page five presented another image of John Sobanto, surrounded by men and women in business suits, a thin-stemmed glass in his hand. A cowled figure stood in the shadow of the column, watching over him.

Siroun leaned forward. *No, the image is too murky.*

"His reaction time suggests that he is not human. A shapeshifter operative on our staff had an opportunity to sample his scent. He found it disturbing. We don't know what he is," Chang said. "But we do know that John Sobanto made a lot of people unhappy with his latest settlement. There have been two attempts on his life, and this bodyguard kept Sobanto breathing."

Siroun smiled quietly.

"You have eleven hours to kill Mr. Sobanto." Chang closed the file. "After that, he has arranged to surrender into the custody of Philadelphia's Finest. Sniping people in police custody is bad for business. Will you require a priest for your final rites?"

Adam glanced at Siroun. She gave a barely perceptible shake of her head.

"That won't be necessary."

"Good luck. Break a leg, preferably not your own." Chang smiled and headed for the door. "Remember, no more than three Red Guardsmen."

The door closed behind him with a click.

Siroun slipped off the bed. "Disable the guards, break into a fortress, shatter the wards, disarm the traps, bust into the central chamber, kill a preternaturally fast bodyguard, and eliminate the target. Shall I drive?"

"Sounds like a plan." Adam headed for the door.

Adam sat on the floor of the black POM van and watched Siroun drive. She guided the car along the ruined, crumbling highway with almost surgical precision. She had only two modes of operation: complete control or complete insanity. Considering how tightly she clenched herself now, he was in for a hell of a night.

The magic smothered gas engines; the converted POM van ran on enchanted water. The water vehicles were slow, barely topping fifty miles an hour at the best, and they made an outrageous amount of noise. They'd have to park the car some distance from the house and approach on foot.

Adam stretched. They had had to take all of the seats, except for the driver's, out of the van to accommodate him. From where he sat, Adam could see a wispy lock of red hair and Siroun's profile. Her face, etched against the darkness of the night, almost seemed to glow.

Some things can come to pass, he reminded himself. Some things are improbable, and some are impossible.

He had to stop imagining impossible things.

Siroun stirred. "What would drive a man to kill his own

wife? Two people live together, love each other, make a safe haven for themselves."

"I saw a play once," Adam said. "It was about a man and a woman: They were in love a long time ago, but as years passed, they ended up spending their time torturing each other. The man had told the woman, 'Here is the key to my soul. Take it, beloved. Take the poisoned dagger.' Those we love know us the best. They know all the right places to strike."

She shook her head.

"If we were lovers, and I betrayed you, you would kill me." Why did he have to go there? Like playing with fire.

She didn't look at him. "What makes you say that?"

"Love and hate are both means of emotional control to which we subject ourselves. Once you were done with me, you'd want to be free of the pain of betrayal. Absolutely free."

No comment, Siroun? No, not even a glance.

He looked out the window. They had exited the highway onto a narrow country road that wound its way between huge trees. The same magic that devoured skyscrapers fed the forests. Moonlight spilled from the sky like a gauzy silvery curtain, catching on massive branches of enormous hemlocks and white pines. The woods encroached onto asphalt weakened by the magic's assault, the trees leaning toward the van like grim sentries intent on barring their passage.

Fifty years ago, this might have been a cultivated field or a small town. But then, fifty years ago, he wouldn't have existed, Adam reflected. Magic fed the ancient power in his blood. Without it, he would be just a man.

Fifty years ago, nobody would've purchased an insurance policy with a retribution clause, which assured that one's murderer would be punished. An eye for an eye, a tooth for a tooth. It had been a gentler, more civilized time.

"Strangulation contains death," Siroun said. "There's no release. It's deeply personal. He wanted to see her eyes as he squeezed the life out of her second by second. To drink it in. He must've hated her."

"The question is why," Adam said. "He was a skilled lawyer. I've looked through the file some more. He seems to have a remarkable talent when it comes to jury selection. In every case, he manages to pick a precise mix of people to favor his case, which suggests he's an excellent judge of human nature, but all of his arguments are very precise and emotionless. People have passions. He is dispassionate. He would have to be at the brink of his mind to strangle someone. Especially his wife. It doesn't add up."

"Still waters run deep," she murmured, and made a right turn. The vehicle rolled off the road, careening over roots. "We're here."

They stepped from the car onto a forest floor thick with five centuries of autumn. Adam stretched, testing his pixilated camo suit. It was loose enough to let him move quickly. The huge trees watched him in silence. He wished it were colder. He would be faster in the cold.

Siroun raised her head and drew the air into her nostrils, tasting it on her tongue. "Woodsmoke."

Adam slid the short needle-rifle into its holster on his belt. It was made specifically for him, a modern version of a blowgun made to operate during magic. Siroun stretched her arms next to him, like a lean cat. Her camo suit hugged her, clenched at the waist by a belt carrying two curved, brutal blades. She pulled a dark mask over the lower half of her face and raised her hood. She looked tiny.

Anxiety nipped at him.

"Stay safe," he said.

She turned to him. "Adam?"

Shit. He had to recover. "We're only allowed three kills. You look on edge. Stay in the safe zone."

"This isn't my first time."

She looked up, high above, where the rough column of a tree trunk erupted into thick branches, blocking the moonlight. For a moment, she tensed, the smooth muscles coiling like springs beneath the fabric, and burst forward, across the soft carpet of pine needles and fallen twigs. Siroun leaped, scrambled up the trunk in a brown-and-green blur, and vanished into the branches as if dissolved into the greenery.

Adam locked the van and dropped the keys behind the right-front wheel. The forest waited for him.

He headed uphill at a brisk trot, guided by traces of woodsmoke and some imperceptible instinct he couldn't explain. Stay safe. He was beginning to lose it. *Remember what you are. Remember who she is.* She would never see him as anything more than a partner. To step closer, she would have to risk something. To open herself to possible injury, to give up a drop of her freedom. She would never do it, and if he slipped again and showed her that he had stepped over the line, she would sever what few fragile ties bound them.

The old trees spread their branches wide, greedily hoarding the moonlight, and the undergrowth was scarce. A few times a magic-addled vine cascading from an occasional trunk made a grab for his limbs. When it did manage to snag him, he simply ripped through it and kept jogging.

Forty-five minutes later, Adam stepped over an electrified trip wire strung across the greenery at what for most people would've been a mid-thigh level and for him was just below the knee. With the magic up, the current was dead, but he took care not to touch it all the same. Beyond the wire, the trees ended abruptly, as if sliced by the blade of a giant's knife. The gaps between the tree trunks offered glimpses of the electric fence, sitting out in the open, and the Sobanto house, a dark shape beyond the metal mesh. He saw no guards, but the Red Guards didn't stroll along the perimeter. They hid.

Adam went to ground. The fragrant cushion of pine needles accepted his weight without protest. He slid forward a few feet and saw the house, sprawling in the middle of the clearing. A gun tower punctuated the roof. Two guards manned it, armed with precision crossbows.

Adam craned his neck. Judging by the moss on the trunks, he was facing west. The west guard tower would be behind the house—he didn't have to worry about it. He was at the southern edge of the house, so the north guard tower wouldn't present too much of an issue either. Adam crawled another three feet and craned his neck to look left. A blocky structure wrapped in a cage of metal bars rose a few dozen yards away—the south guard tower and his biggest problem. The bars glowed with a faint yellow sheen. Warded.

Adam reached into his camo suit and pulled a small spyglass free. He raised it to his eye and focused on the house. The fence slid closer. A standard twelve-foot-high affair, horizontal wires, coils of razor wire guarding the top edge. The space between the wires was uneven. Something was pulling the fence inward, and that something was probably a ward.

The defensive spells came in many varieties. Some were rooted into the soil, some depended on external markers, rocks, sand, bones, trees . . . The most powerful ones required blood or a living power source. Judging by the distortion in the fence, this was one hell of a ward, very strong and very potent. Definitely fed by a power source.

Adam craned his neck, looking for the pipeline. He found it twenty-five feet above the ground. A long, green shoot passed through the south guard tower and terminated in a network of thin roots. The roots hung suspended in thin air, dripping magic into the invisible spell. The makers of the ward had found some sort of way to tap into the magic of the forest and channeled it to protect the house.

Adam frowned. The closest route to the house was straight

on, through the fence, the ward, and finally through the solid-looking side door on the left end of the mansion. The fence didn't present a problem, but the ward would prevent him from getting inside. His magic was too potent. To take down the ward, he had to sever the roots, but to get to the roots, he would have to take down the ward. A catch-22.

A faint scent floated on the breeze. Siroun. She was on the edge of the woods, to his left, probably right beside the south guard tower. If she took out those guards, she could reach the roots feeding the ward, but to do that she'd have to clear a stretch of open ground in plain view of the crossbows from both the house and the tower. He had to give her a distraction, the kind that would focus both the house and the tower on him.

No guts, no glory.

He put away the spyglass, backed away, and rose to his feet. The woods grew fast, which meant they would have to cut down trees at a steady rate to keep the forest from encroaching onto the property. Adam jogged through the woods, searching. There. A two-foot-wide pine trunk lay on its side, its wide end showing fresh chain-saw marks. Just the right size.

Adam strode to the tip of the tree and pulled out his tactical blade. Two feet long, to him it was conveniently sized, more a knife than a sword. He hacked at the thin section of the trunk. Two cuts, and the narrow crown broke off the tree. That gave him a few branches near the tip. Good enough. Adam returned the blade to the sheath, grasped the trunk about four feet from the bottom, and heaved. Small branches snapped, and the pine left the ground. He shifted it onto his shoulder and strode through the nearest gap between the trees, toward the fence.

A moment, and he was out in the open. The guards on top of the house stared at him, openmouthed. Adam waved at them with his free hand, grasped the tree, and spun. The thirty-foot pine smashed into the fence. Boom!

The effort nearly took him off his feet. The wires snapped under the pressure.

Crossbow bolts whistled through the air. One sprouted from the ground two inches from his foot. The fence was in their way.

Adam pulled the tree upright and brought it down again like a club. Boom!

The second bolt sliced his shoulder, grazing it in a streak of heat.

Boom!

The third bolt singed Adam's neck.

The nearest pole careened with a tortured creak and crashed down, taking the fence with it.

Adam spun, like a hammer thrower, and hurled the tree at the house. It cleared the ward in a flash of blue and smashed into the roof guard post. Boards exploded.

A bolt bit into his thigh, a gift from the south tower.

He was completely exposed now. The next bolt would hit him where it counted. Adam braced himself. He couldn't dodge a bolt, but he could turn into it. Better take one in the shoulder than one in the gut.

The guard tower stood silent and still. No bolts sliced his flesh. He grasped the shaft of the bolt protruding from his thigh and wrenched it out. It hurt like hell, but it would heal. It always did.

The tower's door slid open, and Siroun emerged. Behind her, a camouflaged figure fell to the floor, its arms slack. Siroun leaped onto the green shoot feeding the ward and dashed along its length as if it were a wide path on solid ground.

So graceful.

Siroun reached the end of the shoot, crouched, and struck in the same smooth movement, slashing the roots. Pale liquid oozed from the cuts. She cut again, lightning fast. The ward trembled and vanished, and she dropped to the ground softly.

Adam sprinted to the house. When he got going, he was impossible to stop. His shoulder smashed into the reinforced door. It flew open with a pitiful screech of snapped bolts and shattered boards. Adam stumbled in, glimpsed the sharp end of the crossbow bolt staring at him from six feet away, and dodged to the left. The bow twanged, and the bolt fell at his feet sliced in half. Siroun leaped forward, swung her curved knives, and the guard's head rolled to the floor. Blood spurted in a thin spray from the stump of the neck, painting the wall crimson. The body took a step forward and tumbled down.

Adam exhaled.

"Death number one," Siroun whispered.

The house stank of unclean magic. Siroun ran down the hallway, light on her feet. Adam's hulking form moved next to her. It always amazed her how fast he could move. You'd expect a man of his size to shamble, but he was surprisingly agile, the way giant bears were sometimes surprisingly agile just before their claws caught you.

They had been making their way toward the center of the house, where Chang's blueprint indicated a stairway. They'd run into the guards. Both times, she avoided casualties. Now the bloodlust sang through her, slithering its way through her veins like a starving, enraged serpent. She needed a release.

Somewhere deep within the house, a knot of foul magic smoldered. It brushed against her when she stepped through the door and recoiled, but not fast enough, not before she caught the taint of its magic. It felt old, primitive, and starved, gnawed by the same hunger inside her that longed for blood and severed lives.

A faint red sheen blocked the hallway ahead. Another ward, weaker and simpler than the first. Still, it would take time.

Adam moved toward the ward, casually bumping the fey

lantern on the ceiling with his hand. The hallway drowned in darkness.

She ran up to the ward on her toes and swept her palm over its surface, close but never touching. Thin streaks of yellow lightning snaked through the red, trailing the heat of her hand. Past it, down the hall, she saw another translucent red wall.

Three men burst from the side room on their left. Adam barreled into them like a battering ram. The two front guards flew several feet and crashed to the ground in a heap of cracked bones. Siroun snapped a kick, connecting with the third guard's jaw. He went down with a low moan.

Adam bent over the fallen female guard. The woman jerked back when she saw his face. He probed her side. "You have a broken rib," he informed the woman. "Don't move."

She glared at him with remarkably blue eyes. "Go fuck yourself."

Siroun pulled the duct tape from her pack. Six seconds, and the guards lay trussed up on the floor. Adam spun toward the ward. Siroun touched his arm and pointed to the side room. He understood and charged into it. His shoulder hit the wall. The wooden boards exploded, and she followed him into the next room, bypassing the ward.

Another wall, another crash, another ragged hole in the wood. The sheer power he could unleash was shocking.

They broke through the next wall. A foul stench hit her, the lingering, heavy odor of a greasy roast burned by an open flame. Bile rose in a stinging flood in Siroun's throat.

Adam halted.

A barrier rose before them. Flesh-colored and transparent, almost gel-like, it cleaved the room in half, stretching from the left wall to the right. Long, thick veins, pulsing with deep purple, pierced the gel, branching into smaller vessels and finally into hair-thin capillaries. Between the veins, clusters of pale yellow globules formed long membranes, folded and pleated into pockets. A loose network of dark red filaments bound it all into one revolting whole. Adam stared at it in horrified fascination.

Tiny gas bubbles broke free of the capillaries and slid to the surface of the barrier to pop open. Here and there, small spherical vesicles of the yellow substance floated through the lattice of the filaments and veins, pushed by the invisible currents, bending and swiveling when they came to an obstacle.

It lived. It was a very primitive kind of life, but a life.

Her gaze traveled to the far left, drawn to the source of the vesicles, and found a gross, misshapen thickening of the yellow membranes, a bulging sack, tinged with carmine filaments. Globules of yellow matter detached from the surface of the sack and fluttered away one by one. She focused on it and found an outline of a human hand within the sack, complete with outstretched fingers. Another vesicle slid from the sack's top, allowing for a glimpse of a swollen blue-black thumb. As Adam watched, the nail broke free from the bloated digit and spun away, caught by a current.

Adam gagged and retched, spilling sour vomit onto the expensive rug.

Siroun took a step forward. She knew this intimately well. This was witch magic: not the balanced, measured magic of the regular covens, but a darker, twisted kind, born of complete subjugation to the primal things. Most witches withdrew at the first hint of their presence. This witch had embraced it, and it had gifted her with this ward.

The foul magic hissed and boiled around her, sparking off her skin. *That's right. Look but do not touch.*

Siroun thrust her hand into the barrier.

The filaments trembled.

The yellow membranes shivered as if in anticipation. Folds slid and unfolded, streaming toward Siroun's hand.

Adam moved, probably determined to pull her from the thing before it stripped the flesh from her bones.

She let the thing inside her off the chain. Blue fire burst from her skin. The pink gel around her hand shriveled and melted in a plume of acrid smoke. Adam coughed. The fire grew brighter, biting chunks from the barrier in a greedy fury. The membranes tried to sliver away, the filaments collapsed and curled, but the fire chased them, farther and farther, until nothing was left. A swollen, blue corpse crashed to the floor, one arm stretched upward. Its stomach ruptured and a thick brown liquid drenched the rug. The stench of decomposition flooded the room.

The last glowing droplets of the gel dissipated. The blue fire calmed to mere lambency, clothing her hand like a glove. She turned her hand back and forth, watching the glow. Funny how the mind tends to trick you. She never forgot that she was cursed. The constant bloodlust that burned inside her would never let her delude herself. But most of the time she managed to put that knowledge aside, skirt it somehow in the deep recesses of her mind, until she stood there with her hand on fire. Adam was looking at her, and she didn't want to look back, not sure what she would find on his face.

Siroun blew on the flames. The fire vanished.

She stepped through the ward. Pale glyphs ignited on the floor, wheels of strange arcane signs. Siroun glanced back at Adam over her shoulder. She knew bloodred fire filled her eyes, but Adam didn't flinch. For that she was grateful.

"Witch magic?" he asked.

"Yes and no. Sometimes, when a witch is very troubled, she breaks away from the coven and begins to worship on her own. She becomes a priestess of the old gods. This thing was very old, Adam. Older than your blood."

"Why is it here?"

"Because this house has been hexed. But I can tell you that

it wasn't meant for us." She pointed at the door at the end of the room. The door stood ajar, betraying a hint of the stairs going down. "It was meant to keep in whoever came up these stairs."

"It sealed Sobanto underground?"

She nodded and padded to the stairs. "Don't step on the glyphs."

The stairs brought them to another door. Siroun paused, listening. Heartbeats, one, two, three, four. She raised four fingers. Adam pulled a small cloth bag from one of his pockets. The spicy scent of herbs filled the air. A sleep bomb, very small, with a tiny radius of impact. Once released, the magic inside it would explode the herbs, and anything that breathed within the room would instantly fall asleep.

Adam passed her the bag. Siroun held her breath.

Three, two . . .

He smashed his fist into the door, knocking a melon-sized hole in the wood. She tossed the sleep bomb into the opening, and both of them sprinted upstairs.

A muffled cough, followed by a weak scream, echoed from the room. The sound of running feet, a dull thud, a throat-scraping hack, and everything fell silent. They sat together on the stairs, waiting for the power to dissipate. One minute. Two.

"Do you think our client was a witch?" Adam asked.

"That seems the only likely explanation." Siroun leaned forward, looking down the stairs. The less he saw of her face, the better.

"I thought witches didn't work on their own."

"They don't. Being in a coven is like being . . . in a place where you belong. It's like being with your family. The other witches might judge you, they might fight with you, and you might even dislike some of them, but they will be there when you need them most."

Unless they betray you. Allie's face swung into her mind's

view. "I'm your sister," the phantom voice murmured from her memories. "Don't be afraid. I would never do anything to hurt you." But she did. They all did.

"If you're a witch with power, you become aware of things," she said, choosing her words carefully. "Do you know the history of the shifts?"

Adam nodded. "Thousands of years ago, magic and technology existed in a balance. Then humans used magic to lift themselves from barbarism. Extensive use of magic created an imbalance, causing the first shift, when technology began flooding the world in waves. This began the technological age that lasted roughly for six thousand years. Now we have overdeveloped technology, and the world seesawed again—the magic has returned and wiped out our civilization once again."

Siroun nodded. "Before the shifts, before the imbalance, humans worshipped things. If it frightened them, and they couldn't kill it, they called it a god. Faith has a lot of power, Adam. Their faith influenced these entities, nurturing them, granting them powers. They are very simple creatures because the people who worshipped them were simple. Now the magic has awakened, and these things are waking up with it. Witches stand closer to nature than most magic users. They seek balance, and sometimes they come across an old presence. These old ones, they are hungry. We molded them into gods, and they want their meal of magic and lives. For whatever reason, Linda Sobanto broke away from her coven and became a priestess to one of those things."

"What drove her, do you think?"

"Anger." That was what drove her. Anger at being violated, anger at the ultimate betrayal. "The glyphs on the floor upstairs. They are a prayer."

"To whom?"

Siroun shook her head. "I don't know. But I know that what she asked of it cost her. Dealing with gods, even simple gods, never comes without a price tag. Never. They don't gift. They barter."

"How do you know all this?" he asked.

Because my sister did the same, and I paid the price. "I've seen a hex like this before," she said, choosing the words very carefully. "I once handled the case of a child. A girl. She was ten years old."

She wished she hadn't started this, but now it was too late.

"What happened to the little girl?" Adam asked.

"Her sister was a witch. Their coven was inexperienced but powerful. They came across an old god, and they tried to barter for more power. The god needed a flesh form to exist, so during a really strong magic wave, they gave the little girl to the god. The symbols used were nearly identical." She kept talking, holding the memories at bay, keeping her voice flat. "The child proved to be more gifted than anticipated. She fought the god off until technology came and ripped it out of her body for good."

"But she was never the same," Adam murmured.

"No."

Siroun read concern in his eyes. Not for Sobanto, for herself. That was the last thing she wanted.

Siroun pushed to her feet. "Time is up."

They trotted down the stairs. Adam kicked the door, splintering it. Four Red Guards lay on the carpet. She only heard three hearts beating. "Damn it."

Adam turned the closest man over, picked him up, and gently lowered him on the couch. "Dead."

"How?"

"Probably an allergic reaction. It happens occasionally."

She gritted her teeth.

"There is nothing to be done about it now."

Pointless fury boiled inside her. He wasn't supposed to die. Why the hell did he die? So stupid . . .

"We move on," Adam said.

She snarled. He took a step toward her.

"We move on," Adam repeated.

She spun on her foot, walked out of the room, and stopped. The floor of the hallway was filled with glowing glyphs.

Adam watched Siroun as she crouched, hugging the floor. Her face had this odd look, a disturbing mix of sadness, almost sympathy, as if she were at a funeral, comforting a friend. Around her, arcane patterns on the floor emitted glowing tendrils of vapor. The colored fog stretched upward a couple of feet before gently fading.

"It took her months to do this," she whispered.

The entire length of the hallway floor shimmered with magic. It was oddly beautiful.

Siroun reached out and touched a congealed dark drop on the floor. "Blood," she whispered. Her nostrils fluttered. The orange fire in her irises darkened once again to near red. "Her blood."

She rose and pointed to the middle of the hallway, where red glyphs bloomed, like poppies. "That's where he killed her."

"What's the purpose of all this?" he asked.

"An illusion." The fire in Siroun's eyes died to almost nothing. Her voice held profound sadness. "Give me your hand, Adam."

He offered her his palm and watched as her slender fingers were swallowed by his huge hand. Siroun reached out with her other hand. Her thumbnail flicked across her index finger. A single drop of blood dropped from her hand into the glyphs. The glow vanished like a snuffed-out candle. The hallways went completely dark. A single tiny spark flared at the far end and expanded into a figure of a small boy. He stood on a stool, barefoot, large eyes opened wide. A chain hung from his throat. His mouth opened, and the high voice of a young child echoed through the hallway. "Please let me go, Mommy. Please let me go. I'll be good . . ."

The stool shot out from under the boy's feet, as if knocked aside by someone's brutal kick. The child hung, on the chain, choking, his eyes bulging.

Adam lunged forward and stopped, pulled back by Siroun's hand.

"It's not real," she told him. "It's only an illusion."

The child struggled. They watched him kick and die. Slowly, one by one, the glyphs ignited. The body, the chain, and the stool faded.

Adam remembered to breathe. His chest refused to expand, as if someone had dropped an anvil on it.

"She made her husband think she had killed their son," Siroun said. "And then he killed her. She sacrificed herself. Whatever dark thing she prayed to now inhabits her body. She made a bargain, you see? Her body for revenge on her husband."

"Why?"

"I don't know. We have to keep going. We'll find answers when we find Sobanto." She pulled him gently, and he followed.

The last door loomed in front of Adam. Wood reinforced with steel. No matter. He crashed into it, and it burst open, unlocked. Adam stumbled forward, into the huge chamber. He had barely enough time to take in the domed ceiling, half-lost in the gloom, the bare walls, and the lonely figure sitting motionless under a column of blue light; and then heat seared his left hip. He saw nothing, felt nothing save for that brief fiery slice, but his leg gave, and he crashed to the floor, catching himself on his bent arms and rolling onto his side to diminish the impact.

A dark stain spread across the leg of his pants. He still felt no pain. Adam pulled back the sliced fabric, revealing a slash across his muscle. The edges of the wound fit so tightly together, it might have been made by a razor blade.

Numbness claimed his hip. He took a deep breath, and, suddenly, he couldn't feel his legs.

Poison. He was cut by a poisoned blade, coated with some sort of paralyzing agent, probably containing anticoagulant. Adam froze. His body regenerated at an accelerated rate. It would overcome most poisons, given time. But time was in short supply. The less he moved, the faster he'd heal, but prone like this, he presented too good a target.

Come on. Take a shot. I'll snap your neck like a toothpick.

Adam scanned the chamber.

Nothing. Only the gloom and a man seated in a metal chair. John Sobanto, wearing the slack expression of a man caught in some sort of spell. A ring of small pale stones surrounded his chair. He knew this spell. If he could remove the stones, the ward would disappear.

A hint of movement made him glance right. Siroun stood next to him. Her eyes glowed like two rubies.

Her lips parted. "I see you, sirrah," she whispered, her hiss carrying to the farthest heights of the chamber.

A blur struck at her from the gloom. The cloaked bodyguard attacked. She parried, blades clanging together, and the bodyguard withdrew. A shred of dark fabric fluttered to the floor.

Siroun laughed, an eerie sound that shot ice down Adam's spine. "I'm coming, sirrah. Face me!"

The blur landed on the floor at the far wall, solidifying into a cloaked man. Soundless like a phantom, he pulled off his cloak and dropped it onto the floor. Chiseled, each muscle cut to perfection, he stood nude, save for muay thai shorts. His bare feet gripped the floor, his toes bore curved yellow claws. Colored tattoos blossomed across his legs, stomach, and chest, muted against the faint green tint of his skin. A striking cobra on one arm, a crouching monkey king on the other, tortoise on the abdomen, elephant on the chest, iguana under the right collarbone, tiger under the left. Faint outlines of scales, tattooed or real, shielded his shaved skull. His eyes were yellow like amber, luminescent with cold intensity, reptilian in their lack of feeling.

The bodyguard raised a knife with a yellow blade that looked as if it were carved from an old bone.

Siroun looked at him. "You need to turn now."

He leaped across the room. They clashed and danced across the chamber, preternaturally fast, slashing, parrying, kicking, and finding purchase on the sheer walls.

Pain clenched Adam's thigh, ripping a deep, guttural moan from him. His body had finally overcome the poison. The cut was deep—the blade had grazed the bone.

Adam began dragging himself toward the spell shielding Sobanto. Fifty feet. He pulled, gripping the slick floor with his fingers, ignoring the jolts of acute pain rocking his thigh.

For the space of a breath, Siroun landed on the floor next to him, barely long enough for him to register a bloody gash across her forearm, and leaped away again, sailing across the chamber. He crawled by the drops of her blood, fixated on the blue beam of light.

Only fifteen feet.

Fourteen.

He saw the tattooed bodyguard loom before him. The man's skin burst, and a monstrosity exploded out, huge, scaled, armed with enormous crocodilian jaws and a massive reptilian tail.

A werereptile. That was impossible. Reptiles were cold-blooded. No shapeshifter could overcome that.

The werecrocodile laughed at him, the feral grin of a predator displaying nightmarish fangs. And then Siroun crashed into the bodyguard. The yellow knife struck twice, biting deep into her side. They broke free and halted six feet apart.

The shapeshifter's yellow eyes focused on crimson drenching

Siroun's side. "You're finished," he said, his voice a deep roar disfigured by his jaws.

Siroun smiled. A pale red flush crept on her cheeks and spread, flooding her neck, diving under her clothes, reaching all the way to her fingertips. Heat bathed Adam. "Not yet," she whispered, and charged, sweeping the bodyguard from the floor like a gale.

Adam focused on the blue beam. His entire side was on fire, and he clenched his teeth, clutching on to consciousness. He could feel the soft welcoming darkness hovering on the edge of his senses, ready to swallow him whole.

His fingers touched the stone. A burning pain laced his skin, as if he'd stuck his hand into boiling water. Adam clenched the stone.

The room swayed. He was losing it.

He snarled and fed his magic into his hand. Ice sleeked his skin, welcoming, soothing. Adam strained, using every bit of his strength, and yanked the stone free.

The ward blinked and vanished.

A hoarse scream ripped through the chamber. Across the floor, a body fell from the ceiling, but Siroun was faster still, and she landed a fraction of a heartbeat before it hit the ground, in time to catch the falling man. The body in her arms boiled and collapsed back into its human form.

Gingerly, she carried the prone form, as if he were a child, and lowered the bodyguard by Adam's feet. The shapeshifter's face lost its feral edge. His tattoos bled colored ink in dark rivulets, the images draining slowly from his skin.

Siroun kissed her fingertips and touched the man's forehead. Her eyes were luminescent and warm. Not a trace of bloodlust remained.

"You fought well," she whispered.

In the chair, John Sobanto drew a long, shuddering breath.

His eyelashes trembled. Sobanto's eyes snapped open. "You turned off the field and broke the wards," he said. "She is coming."

The lawyer was looking at Adam. She looked, too. He was bleeding. His big hands trembled. Breaking the ward had taken too much magic. His body didn't have enough strength to regenerate. She had to get him out of there.

"Who's coming?" Adam said. "Your wife?"

"She isn't my wife anymore," Sobanto whispered.

A sharp shriek rolled through the silence. Siroun felt the knot of foul magic at the far end of the house rip apart. A presence spilled out, the force of its fury lashing her like a splash of boiling lead. Siroun recoiled, snarling.

The entity moved toward them, slicing through the walls and doors, churning with magic and malevolence so dark she had to fight to keep clear. There was nothing they could do to stop it.

She spun to Adam. "We don't have much time. Kill him now."

"We can't. We don't know if he is guilty."

They had to follow the protocol. The case was no longer cut-and-dried. She had to buy them time. Siroun swallowed. "Hurry, Adam."

He turned to Sobanto.

She thrust her mind into the path of the entity and struck. Her blow did little damage, but it was too enraged to ignore her. Siroun fled, zigzagging back and forth, and the presence followed, chasing the shadow of her mind.

"What did you see in the hallway?" Adam asked.

Sobanto swallowed. "Our son. I saw her hang our son."

"Did you attack her?"

"Yes. I grabbed her by her throat. I tried . . . I meant to pull her off him. I didn't know. She died. I killed her. I found a note. It said she sacrificed herself and her body would now belong to a god. It said I would pay for everything."

The entity lashed at Siroun. She barely avoided it. "Why?" she snarled. "Why does she hate you?"

"I don't know. We had a good marriage, considering the circumstances."

"The circumstances?"

"Hurry, Adam." She forced the words out. "I cannot elude her much longer."

Sobanto hesitated.

"We have little time," Adam told him.

The lawyer closed his eyes. "I bought her. From the Blessings of the Night coven."

The wraith bit into Siroun's defenses. Sharp needles of pain stabbed her lungs; for a moment, she could not breathe. She ripped herself free.

"You bought her?" Adam asked.

"They needed a lawyer. They were facing criminal charges, and they had no money. I needed somebody to analyze the behavioral patterns of the jury and my opponents. We made a deal."

"Why did you marry her?"

"I wanted my children to have what she had. I'm deficient. I don't relate to people, not the way she could. And she was beautiful."

He had bought her, like a purebred dog.

"She chose the juries for you," Adam said. "She monitored them through the trial, and you claimed the credit."

"I didn't abuse her!" Desperation rang in Sobanto's voice. "I denied her nothing. Best clothes, best jewelry, the best of everything."

"Why didn't she just leave?" Adam asked.

"She was bound to me by the coven."

The entity clamped her. Pain ripped through Siroun. Emotions twisted her into a knot, echoes of a woman lost. At once she was lonely, longing, caught between the need to please and revulsion, bitter, empty, watching life passing by, unable to escape, growing tired, growing old, growing stupid, knowing she was not loved, would never be loved, would never be free . . .

She cried out and tore herself free again. She could barely stand. "He's telling the truth," she said.

"Why does she hate him?"

"Because he did not love her. He is a sociopath, Adam. He's incapable of giving her what she wanted. She thought when their son was born, he would feel something, but he doesn't. End it. We must kill him, or the thing that has her body will rip him to pieces. It's almost here."

"Kill me," Sobanto said suddenly. "I want to die. I just don't want her to have me."

Adam raised his chin, his face, blanched of all blood, strangely proud, almost regal. "We have no claim on this man. He served as an instrument in his wife's suicide. On behalf of the POM Insurance, I, Adjuster Adam Talbot, resign all rights to retribution, as specified by Part 23, paragraph 7 of the POM policy manual."

Sobanto's face finally showed emotion: stark, all-consuming fear.

The creature that used to be Linda Sobanto burst through the doorway, a boiling cloud of black, streaked with violent scarlet. The cloud churned, and a woman's face congealed from its depth. She opened her mouth. Sobanto took a step back, his hands raised before him. The cloud lunged . . .

And howled in fury.

Siroun twisted her knife, turning it all the way around Sobanto's neck. The resistance against her blade was so slight, she barely felt it.

A thick stream of blood slid across the blade to drip on the floor. Sobanto opened his mouth. Blood gushed. Siroun withdrew the blade. He stayed upright for another moment and crumpled to the floor.

The entity screamed. The crimson within her flared and streaked apart, ripping the darkness into pieces. The darkness folded on itself, sucked into a tiny point, and vanished. Quiet reigned.

Adam crashed to the floor.

She crouched by him and brushed the blue hair from his face.

"We had no claim," he murmured.

"I know," she said, and wiped a smudge of blood from his lips. "Rest now. Let your body heal. Once the wound closes, I will get you out of here."

"Why did you kill him?"

"Linda made a bargain: her body for the life of her husband. The transfer would not be complete until the creature that took her form killed Sobanto. If it took his life, it would no longer be a cloud, Adam. It would be an old god made flesh. It wouldn't harm me because of what I am. But it would kill you."

She leaned over him and kissed him gently on the forehead. "I couldn't let it kill you." *After all, you're all I have.*

★ ★ ★

Author's Bio:
Ilona Andrews is the pseudonym for a husband-and-wife writing team of Andrew and Ilona Gordon. They reside in Oregon with their two children, three dogs, and a cat. They've coauthored two series, the bestselling urban fantasy of *Kate Daniels* and the romantic urban fantasy of *The Edge*. Enjoy reading more about them at **www.ilona-andrews .com**.

BIGFOOT ON CAMPUS

by JIM BUTCHER

The campus police officer folded his hands and stared at me from across the table. "Coffee?"

"What flavor is it?" I asked.

He was in his forties, a big, solid man with bags under his calm, wary eyes, and his name tag read DEAN. "It's coffee-flavored coffee."

"No mocha?"

"Fuck mocha."

"Thank God," I said. "Black."

Officer Dean gave me hot black coffee in a paper cup, and I sipped at it gratefully. I was almost done shivering. It just came in intermittent bursts now. The old wool blanket Dean had given me was more gesture than cure.

"Am I under arrest?" I asked him.

Officer Dean moved his shoulders in what could have been a shrug. "That's what we're going to talk about."

"Uh-huh," I said.

"Maybe," he said in a slow, rural drawl, "you could explain to me why I found you in the middle of an orgy."

"Well," I said, "if you're going to be in an orgy, the middle is the best spot, isn't it."

He made a thoughtful sound. "Maybe you could explain why there was a car on the fourth floor of the dorm."

"Classic college prank," I said.

He grunted. "Usually when that happens, it hasn't made big holes in the exterior wall."

"Someone was avoiding the cliché?" I asked.

He looked at me for a moment, and said, "What about all the blood?"

"There were no injuries, were there?"

"No," he said.

"Then who cares? Some film student probably watched *Carrie* too many times."

Officer Dean tapped his pencil's eraser on the tabletop. It was the most agitated thing I'd seen him do. "Six separate calls in the past three hours with a Bigfoot sighting on campus. Bigfoot. What do you know about that?"

"Well, kids these days, with their Internets and their video games and their iPods. Who knows what they thought they saw."

Officer Dean put down his pencil. He looked at me, and said, calmly, "My job is to protect a bunch of kids with access to every means of self-destruction known to man from not only the criminal element but themselves. I got chemistry students who can make their own meth, Ecstasy, and LSD. I got ROTC kids with access to automatic weapons and explosives. I got enough alcohol going through here on a weekly basis to float a battleship. I got a thriving trade in recreational drugs. I got lives to protect."

"Sounds tiring."

"About to get tired of you," he said. "Start giving it to me straight."

"Or you'll arrest me?" I asked.

"No," Dean said. "I bounce your face off my knuckles for a while. Then I ask again."

"Isn't that unprofessional conduct?"

"Fuck conduct," Dean said. "I got kids to look after."

I sipped the coffee some more. Now that the shivers had begun to subside, I finally felt the knotted muscles in my belly begin to relax. I slowly settled back into my chair. Dean hadn't blustered or tried to intimidate me in any way. He wasn't trying to scare me into talking. He was just telling me how it was going to be. And he drank his coffee old-school.

I kinda liked the guy.

"You aren't going to believe me," I said.

"I don't much," he said. "Try me."

"Okay," I said. "My name is Harry Dresden. I'm a professional wizard."

Officer Dean pursed his lips. Then he leaned forward slightly and listened.

The client wanted me to meet him at a site in the Ouachita Mountains in eastern Oklahoma. Looking at them, you might not realize they were mountains, they're so old. They've had millions of years of wear and tear on them, and they've been ground down to nubs. The site used to be on an Indian reservation, but they don't call them reservations anymore. They're Tribal Statistical Areas now.

I showed my letter and my ID to a guy in a pickup, who just happened to pull up next to me for a friendly chat at a lonely stop sign on a winding back road. I don't know what the tribe called his office, but I recognized a guardian when I saw one. He read the letter and waved me through in an even friendlier manner than he had used when he approached me. It's nice to be welcomed somewhere, once in a while.

I parked at the spot indicated on the map and hiked a good mile and a half into the hills, taking a heavy backpack with me. I found a pleasant spot to set up camp. The mid-October weather was crisp, but I had a good sleeping bag and would be comfortable as long as it didn't start raining. I dug a fire pit and ringed it in stones, built a modest fire out of fallen limbs, and laid out my sleeping bag on a foam camp pad. By the time it got dark, I was well into preparing the dinner I'd brought with me. The scent of foil-wrapped potatoes baking in coals blended with that of the steaks I had spitted and roasting over the fire.

Can I cook a camp meal or what?

Bigfoot showed up half an hour after sunset.

One minute, I was alone. The next, he simply stepped out into view. He was huge. Not huge like a big person, but huge like a horse, with that same sense of raw animal power and mass. He was nine feet tall at least and probably tipped the scales at well over six hundred pounds. His powerful, wide-shouldered body was covered in long, dark brown hair. Even though he stood in plain sight in my firelight, I could barely see the buckskin bag he had slung over one shoulder and across his chest, the hair was so long.

"Strength of a River in His Shoulders," I said. "You're welcome at my fire."

"Wizard Dresden," River Shoulders rumbled. "It is good to see you." He took a couple of long steps and hunkered down opposite the fire from me. "Man. That smells good."

"Darn right it does," I said. I proceeded with the preparations in companionable silence while River Shoulders stared thoughtfully at the fire. I'd set up my camp this way for a reason—it made me the host and River Shoulders my guest. It meant I was obliged to provide food and drink, and he was obliged to behave with decorum. Guest-and-host relationships are damned near laws of physics in the supernatural world: They almost never get violated, and when they do, it's a big deal. Both of us felt a lot more comfortable around one another this way.

Okay. Maybe it did a wee bit more to make me feel comfortable than it did River Shoulders, but he was a repeat customer, I liked him, and I figured he probably didn't get treated to a decent steak all that often.

We ate the meal in an almost ritualistic silence, too, other than River making some appreciative noises as he chewed. I popped open a couple of bottles of McAnnally's Pale, my favorite brew by a veritable genius of hops, back in Chicago. River liked it so much that he gave me an inquisitive glance when his bottle was empty. So I emptied mine and produced two more.

After that, I filled a pipe with expensive tobacco, lit it, took a few puffs, and passed it to him. He nodded and took it. We smoked and finished our beers. By then, the fire had died down to glowing embers.

"Thank you for coming," River Shoulders rumbled. "Again, I come to seek your help on behalf of my son."

"Third time you've come to me," I said.

"Yes." He rummaged in his pouch and produced a small, heavy object. He flicked it to me. I caught it and squinted at it in the dim light. It was a gold nugget about as big as a Ping-Pong ball. I nodded and tossed it back to him. River Shoulders's brows lowered into a frown.

You have to understand. A frown on a mug like his looked indistinguishable from scowling fury. It turned his eyes into shadowed caves with nothing but a faint gleam showing from far back in them. It made his jaw muscles bunch and swell into knots the size of tennis balls on the sides of his face.

"You will not help him," the Bigfoot said.

I snorted. "*You're* the one who isn't helping him, big guy."

"I am," he said. "I am hiring you."

"You're his *father*," I said quietly. "And he doesn't even know your name. He's a good kid. He deserves more than that. He deserves the truth."

He shook his head slowly. "Look at me. Would he even accept my help?"

"You aren't going to know unless you try it," I said. "And I never said I wouldn't help him."

At that, River Shoulders frowned a little more.

I curbed an instinct to edge away from him.

"Then what do you want in exchange for your services?" he asked.

"I help the kid," I said. "You meet the kid. That's the payment. That's the deal."

"You do not know what you are asking," he said.

"With respect, River Shoulders, this is not a negotiation. If you want my help, I just told you how to get it."

He became very still at that. I got the impression that maybe people didn't often use tactics like that when they dealt with him.

When he spoke, his voice was a quiet, distant rumble. "You have no right to ask this."

"Yeah, um. I'm a wizard. I meddle. It's what we do."

"Manifestly true." He turned his head slightly away. "You do not know how much you ask."

"I know that kid deserves more than you've given him."

"I have seen to his protection. To his education. That is what fathers do."

"Sure," I said. "But you weren't ever *there*. And that *matters*."

Absolute silence fell for a couple of minutes.

"Look," I said gently. "Take it from a guy who knows. Growing up without a dad is terrifying. You're the only father he's ever going to have. You can go hire Superman to look out for Irwin if you want to, and he'd still be the wrong guy— because he isn't you."

River toyed with the empty bottle, rolling it across his enormous fingers like a regular guy might have done with a pencil.

"Do you want me on this?" I asked him. "No hard feelings if you don't."

River looked up at me again and nodded slowly. "I know that if you agree to help him, you will do so. I will pay your price."

"Okay," I said. "Tell me about Irwin's problem."

* * *

"What'd he say?" Officer Dean asked.

"He said the kid was at the University of Oklahoma for school," I said. "River'd had a bad dream and knew that the kid's life was in danger."

The cop grunted. "So . . . Bigfoot is a psychic?"

"Think about it. No one ever gets a good picture of one, much less a clean shot," I said. "Despite all the expeditions and TV shows and whatnot. River's people have got more going for them than being huge and strong. My guess is that they're smarter than humans. Maybe a lot smarter. My guess is they know magic of some kind, too."

"Jesus," Officer Dean said. "You really believe all this, don't you."

"I want to believe," I said. "And I told you that you wouldn't."

Dean grunted. Then he said, "Usually they're too drunk to make sense when I get a story like this. Keep going."

I got to Norman, Oklahoma, a bit before noon the next morning. It was a Wednesday, which was a blessing. In the Midwest, if you show up to a college town on a weekend, you risk running into a football game. In my experience, that resulted in universal problems with traffic, available hotel rooms, and drunken football hooligans.

Or wait: *Soccer* is the one with hooligans. Drunken American football fans are just . . . drunks, I guess.

River had provided me with a small dossier he'd had prepared, which included a copy of his kid's class schedule. I parked my car in an open spot on the street not too far from campus and ambled on over. I got some looks: I sort of stand out in a crowd. I'm a lot closer to seven feet tall than six, which might be one reason why River Shoulders liked to hire me—I look a lot less tiny than other humans, to him. Add in the big black leather duster and the scar on my face, and I looked like the kind of guy you'd want to avoid in dark alleys.

The university campus was as confusing as all of them are, with buildings that had constantly evolved into and out of multiple roles over the years. They were all named after people I doubt any of the students had ever heard of, or cared about, and there seemed to be no organizational logic at all at work there. It was a pretty enough campus, I supposed. Lots of redbrick and brownstone buildings. Lots of architectural doohickeys on many of the buildings, in a kind of quasi-classical Greek style. The ivy that was growing up many of the walls seemed a little too cultivated and obvious for my taste. Then again, I had exactly the same amount of regard for the Ivy League as I did for the Big 12. The grass was an odd color, like maybe someone had sprayed it with a blue-green dye or something, though I had no idea what kind of delusional creep would do something so pointless.

And, of course, there were students—a whole lot of kids, all of them with things to do and places to be. I could have wandered around all day, but I thought I'd save myself the headache of attempting to apply logic to a university campus and stopped a few times to ask for directions. Irwin Pounder, River Shoulders's son, had a physics course at noon, so I picked up a notebook and a couple of pens at the university bookstore and ambled on into the large classroom. It was a perfect disguise. The notebook was college-ruled.

I sat near the back, where I could see both doors into the room, and waited. Bigfoot Irwin was going to stand out in the crowd almost as badly as I did. The kid was huge. River had shown me a photo that he kept in his medicine bag, carefully laminated to protect it from the elements. Irwin's mom could have been a second-string linebacker for the Bears. Carol Pounder was a formidable woman, and over six feet tall. But her boy was a head taller than she already, and still had the awkward, too-lean look of someone who wasn't finished growing. His shoulders had come in, though, and it looked like he might have had to turn sideways to walk through doors.

I waited and waited, watching both doors, until the professor arrived, and the class started. Irwin never arrived. I was going to leave, but it actually turned out to be kind of interesting. The professor was a lunatic but a really entertaining one. The guy drank liquid nitrogen, right there in front of everybody, and blew it out his nose in this huge jet of vapor. I applauded along with everyone else, and before I knew it, the lecture was over. I might even have learned something.

Okay.

Maybe there were *some* redeeming qualities to a college education.

I went to Irwin's next class, which was a freshman biology course, in another huge classroom.

No Irwin.

He wasn't at his four o'clock math class, either, and I emerged from it bored and cranky. None of Irwin's other teachers held a candle to Dr. Indestructo.

Huh.

Time for plan B.

River's dossier said that Irwin was playing football for OU. He'd made the team as a walk-on, and River had been as proud as any father would be about the athletic prowess of his son. So I ambled on over to the Sooners' practice field, where the team was warming up with a run.

Even among the football players, Irwin stood out. He was half a head taller than any of them, at least my own height. He looked gangly and thin beside the fellows around him, even with the shoulder pads on, but I recognized his face. I'd last seen him when he was about fourteen. Though his rather homely features had changed a bit, they seemed stronger, and more defined. There was no mistaking his dark, intelligent eyes.

I stuck my hands in the pockets of my old leather duster and waited, watching the field. I'd found the kid, and, absent any particular danger, I was in no particular hurry. There was no sense in charging into the middle of Irwin's football practice and his life and disrupting everything. I'm just not that kind of guy.

Okay, well.

I try not to be.

"Seems to keep happening, though, doesn't it," I said to myself. "You show up on somebody's radar, and things go to DEF-CON 1 a few minutes later."

"I'm sorry?" said a young woman's voice.

"Ah," said Officer Dean. "This is where the girl comes in."

"Who said there was a girl?"

"There's always a girl."

"Well," I said, "yes and no."

She was blond, about five-foot-six, and my logical mind told me that every inch of her was a bad idea. The rest of me, especially my hindbrain, suggested that she would be an ideal mate. Preferably sooner rather than later.

There was nothing in particular about her that should have caused my hormones to rage. I mean, she was young and fit, and she had the body of the young and fit, and that's hardly ever unpleasant to look at. She had eyes the color of cornflowers and rosy cheeks, and she was a couple of notches above cute, when it came to her face. She was wearing running shorts, and her legs were smooth and generally excellent.

Some women just have it. And no, I can't tell you what "it" means because I don't get it myself. It was something mindless, something chemical, and even as my metaphorically burned fingers were telling me to walk away, the rest of me was going through that male physiological response the science guys in the Netherlands have documented recently.

Not *that* one.

Well, maybe a little.

[47]

I'm talking about the response where when a pretty girl is around, it hits the male brain like a drug and temporarily impairs his cognitive function, literally dropping the male IQ.

And hey, how Freudian is it that the study was conducted in the Netherlands?

This girl dropped that IQ-nuke on my brain, and I was standing there staring a second later while she smiled uncertainly at me.

"Um, sorry?" I asked. "My mind was in the Netherlands."

Her dimple deepened, and her eyes sparkled. She knew all about the brain nuke. "I just said that you sounded like a dangerous guy." She winked at me. It was adorable. "I like those."

"You're, uh. You're into bad boys, eh?"

"Maybe," she said, lowering her voice and drawing the word out a little, as if it was a confession. She spoke with a very faint drawl. "Plus, I like meeting new people from all kinds of places, and you don't exactly strike me as a local, darlin'."

"You dig dangerous guys who are just passing through," I said. "Do you ever watch those cop shows on TV?"

She tilted back her head and laughed. "Most boys don't give me lip like that in the first few minutes of conversation."

"I'm not a boy," I said.

She gave me a once-over with those pretty eyes, taking a heartbeat longer about it than she really needed. "No," she said. "No, you are not."

My inner nonmoron kept on stubbornly ringing alarm bells, and the rest of me slowly became aware of them. My glands thought that I'd better keep playing along. It was the only way to find out what the girl might have been interested in, right? Right. I was absolutely not continuing the conversation because I had gone soft in the head.

"I hope that's not a problem," I said.

"I just don't see how it could be. I'm Connie."

"Harry."

"So what brings you to Norman, Harry?"

"Taking a look at a player," I said.

Her eyes brightened. "Ooooo. You're a scout?"

"Maybe," I said, in the same tone she'd used earlier.

Connie laughed again. "I'll bet you talk to silly college girls like me all the time."

"Like you?" I replied. "No, not so much."

Her eyes sparkled again. "You may have found my weakness. I'm the kind of girl who likes a little flattery."

"And here I was thinking you liked something completely different."

She covered her mouth with one hand, and her cheeks got a little pinker. "Harry. That's not how one talks to young ladies in the South."

"Obviously. I mean, you look so outraged. Should I apologize?"

"Oh," she said, her smile widening. "I just *have* to collect you." Connie's eyes sparkled again, and I finally got it.

Her eyes weren't *twinkling*.

They were becoming increasingly flecked with motes of molten silver.

Cutie-pie was a frigging vampire.

I've worked for years on my poker face. Years. It still sucks pretty bad, but I've been working on it. So I'm sure my smile was only slightly wooden when I asked, "Collect me?"

I might not have been hiding my realization very well, but either Connie was better at poker than me, or else she really was too absorbed in the conversation to notice. "Collect you," she said. "When I meet someone worthwhile, I like to have dinner with them. And we'll talk and tell stories and laugh, and I'll get a picture and put it in my memory book."

"Um," I said. "Maybe you're a little young for me."

She threw back her head and gave a full-throated laugh. "Oh, Harry. I'm talking about sharing a meal. That's all, honestly. I know I'm a terrible flirt, but I didn't think you were taking me seriously."

I watched her closely as she spoke, searching for the predatory calculation that I knew had to be in there. Vampires of the White Court—

"Wait," Dean said. "Vampires of the White Castle?"

I sighed. "White Court."

Dean grunted. "Why not just call her a vampire?"

"They come in a lot of flavors," I said.

"And this one was vanilla?"

"There's no such thing as . . ." I rubbed at the bridge of my nose. "Yes."

Dean nodded. "So why not just call 'em vanilla vampires?"

"I'll . . . bring it up at the next wizard meeting," I said.

"So the vampire is where all the blood came from?"

"No." I sighed. "This kind doesn't feed on blood."

"No? What do they eat, then?"

"Life-energy."

"Huh?"

I sighed again. "Sex."

"Finally, the story gets good. So they *eat* sex?"

"Life-energy," I repeated. "The sex is just how they get started."

"Like sticking fangs into your neck," Dean said. "Only instead of fangs, I guess they use—"

"Look, do you want the story or not?"

Dean leaned back in his chair and propped his feet up on his desk. "You kidding? This is the best one in years."

Anyway, I watched Connie closely, but I saw no evidence of anything in her that I knew had to be there. Vampires are predators who hunt the most dangerous game on the planet. They generally aren't shy about it, either. They don't really need to be. If a White Court vampire wants to feed off a human, all she really has to do is crook her finger, and he comes running. There isn't any ominous music. Nobody sparkles. As far as anyone looking on is concerned, a girl winks at a boy and goes off somewhere to make out. Happens every day.

They don't get all coy asking you out to dinner, and they sure as hell don't have pictures in a memory book.

This was weird, and long experience has taught me that when the unexplained is bouncing around right in front of you, the smart thing is to back off and figure out what the hell is going on. In my line of work, what you don't know can kill you.

But I didn't get the chance. There was a sharp whistle from a coach somewhere on the field, and football players came rumbling off it. One of them came loping toward us, put a hand on top of the six-foot chain-link fence, and vaulted it in one easy motion. Bigfoot Irwin landed lightly, grinning, and continued directly toward Connie.

She let out a girlish squeal of delight and pounced on him. He caught her. She wrapped her legs around his hips, held his face in her hands, and kissed him thoroughly. They came up for air a moment later.

"Irwin," she said, "I met someone interesting. Can I collect him?"

The kid only had eyes for Connie. Not that I could blame him, really. His voice was a basso rumble, startlingly like River Shoulders's. "I'm always in favor of dinner at the Brewery."

She dismounted and beamed at him. "Good. Irwin, this is . . ."

The kid finally looked up at me and blinked. "Harry."

"Heya, Irwin," I said. "How're things?"

Connie looked back and forth between us. "You *know* each other?"

"He's a friend," Irwin said.

"Dinner," Connie declared. "Harry, say you'll share a meal with me."

Interesting choice of words, all things considered.

I think I had an idea what had caused River's bad dream. If a vampire had attached herself to Irwin, the kid was in trouble. Given the addictive nature of Connie's attentions, and the degree of control it could give her over Irwin . . . maybe he wasn't the only one who could be in trouble.

My, how little Irwin had grown. I wondered exactly how much of his father's supernatural strength he had inherited. He looked like he could break me in half without causing a blip in his heart rate. He and Connie looked at me with hopeful smiles, and I suddenly felt like maybe I was the crazy one. Expressions like that should not inspire worry, but every instinct I had told me that something wasn't right.

My smile probably got even more wooden. "Sure," I said. "Why not?"

The Brewery was a lot like every other sports bar you'd find in college towns, with the possible exception that it actually was a brewery. Small and medium-sized tanks stood here and there throughout the place, with signs on each describing the kind of beer that was under way. Apparently, the beer sampler was traditional. I made polite noises when I tried each, but they were unexceptional. Okay, granted I was probably spoiled by having Mac's brew available back at home. It wasn't the Brewery's fault that their brews were merely excellent. Mac's stuff was epic, it was legend. Tough to measure up to that.

I kept one hand under the table, near a number of tools I thought I might need, all the way through the meal, and waited for the other shoe to drop—only it never did. Connie and Irwin chattered away like any young couple, snuggled up to one another on adjacent chairs. The girl was charming, funny, and a playful flirt, but Irwin didn't seem discomfited by it. I kept my responses restrained anyway. I didn't want to find out a couple of seconds too late that the seemingly innocent banter was how Connie got her psychic hooks into me.

But a couple of hours went by, and nothing.

"Irwin's never told me anything about his father," Connie said.

"I don't know much," Irwin said. "He's . . . kept his distance over the years. I've looked for him a couple of times, but I never wanted to push him."

"How mysterious," Connie said.

I nodded. "For someone like him, I think the word 'eccentric' might apply better."

"He's rich?" Connie asked.

"I feel comfortable saying that money isn't one of his concerns," I said.

"I knew it!" Connie said, and looked slyly at Irwin. "There had to be a reason. I'm only into you for your money."

Instead of answering, Irwin calmly picked Connie up out of her chair, using just the muscles of his shoulders and arms, and deposited her on his lap. "Sure you are."

Connie made a little groaning sound and bit her lower lip. "God. I know it's not PC, but I've got to say—I am *into* it when you get all caveman on me, Pounder."

"I know." Irwin kissed the tip of her nose and turned to me. "So, Harry. What brings you to Norman?"

"I was passing through," I said easily. "Your dad asked me to look in on you."

"Just casually," Irwin said, his dark eyes probing. "Because he's such a casual guy."

"Something like that," I said.

"Not that I mind seeing you," Irwin said, "but in case you missed it, I'm all grown-up now. I don't need a babysitter. Even a cool, expensive one."

"If you did, my rates are very reasonable," Connie said.

"We'll talk," Irwin replied, sliding his arms around her waist. The girl wasn't exactly a junior petite, but she looked tiny on Irwin's scale. She hopped up, and said, "I'm going to go make sure there isn't barbecue sauce on my nose, and then we can take the picture. Okay?"

"Sure," Irwin said, smiling. "Go."

Once she was gone from sight, Irwin looked at me and dropped his smile. "Okay," he said resignedly. "What does he want this time?"

There wasn't loads of time, so I didn't get all coy with the subject matter. "He's worried about you. He thinks you may be in danger."

Irwin arched his eyebrows. "From what?"

I just looked at him.

His expression suddenly turned into a scowl, and the air around grew absolutely thick with energy that seethed for a point of discharge. "Wait. This is about Connie?"

I couldn't answer him for a second, the air felt so close. The last time I'd felt this much latent, waiting power, I'd been standing next to my old mentor, Ebenezar McCoy, when he was gathering his strength for a spell.

That pretty much answered my questions about River Shoulders's people having access to magical power. The kid was a freaking dynamo of it. I had to be careful. I didn't want to be the guy who was unlucky enough to ground out that storm cloud of waiting power. So I answered Irwin cautiously and calmly.

"I'm not sure yet. But I know for a fact that she's not exactly what she seems to be."

His nostrils flared, and I saw him make an effort to remain collected. His voice was fairly even. "Meaning what?"

"Meaning I'm not sure yet," I said.

"So what? You're going to hang around here butting into my life?"

I held up both hands. "It isn't like that."

"It's just like that," Irwin said. "My dad spends my whole life anywhere else but here, and now he thinks he can just decide when to intrude on it?"

"Irwin," I said, "I'm not here to try to make you do anything. He asked me to look in on you. I promised I would. And that's all."

He scowled for a moment, then smoothed that expression away. "No sense in being mad at the messenger, I guess," he said. "What do you mean about Connie?"

"She's . . ." I faltered, there. You don't just sit down with a guy and tell him, "Hey, your girlfriend is a vampire, could you pass the ketchup?" I sighed. "Look, Irwin. Everybody sees the world a certain way. And we all kind of . . . well, we all sort of decide together what's real and what isn't real, right?"

"Magic's real," Irwin said impatiently. "Monsters are real. Supernatural stuff actually exists. You're a professional wizard."

I blinked at him, several times.

"What?" he asked, and smiled gently. "Don't let the brow ridge fool you. I'm not an idiot, man. You think you can walk into my life the way you have, twice, and not leave me with an itch to scratch? You made me ask questions. I went and got answers."

"Uh. How?" I asked.

"Wasn't hard. There's an Internet. And this organization called the 'Paranet' of all the cockamamie things, that got started a few years ago. Took me like ten minutes to find it online and start reading through their message boards. I can't believe everyone in the world doesn't see this stuff. It's not like anyone is trying very hard to keep it secret."

"People don't want to know the truth," I said. "That makes it simple to hide. Wow, ten minutes? Really? I guess I'm not really an Internetty person."

"Internetty," Irwin said, seriously. "I guess you aren't."

I waved a hand. "Irwin, you need to know this. Connie isn't—"

The pretty vampire plopped herself back down into Irwin's lap and kissed his cheek. "Isn't what?"

"The kind to stray," I said, smoothly. "I was just telling Irwin how much I'd like to steal you away from him, but I figure you're the sort who doesn't play that kind of game."

"True enough," she agreed cheerfully. "I know where I want to sleep tonight." Maybe it was unconscious, the way she wriggled when she said it, but Irwin's eyes got a slightly glazed look to them.

I remembered being that age. A girl like Connie would have been a mind-numbing distraction to me back then even if she hadn't been a vampire. And Irwin was clearly in love, or as close to it as he could manage through the haze of hormones surrounding him. Reasoning with him wasn't going to accomplish anything—unless I made him angry. Passion is a huge force when you're Irwin's age, and I'd taken enough beatings for one lifetime. I'd never be able to explain the danger to him. He just didn't have a frame of reference . . .

He just didn't know.

I stared at Connie for a second with my mouth open.

"What?" she asked.

"You don't know," I said.

"Know what?" she asked.

"You don't know that you're . . ." I shook my head, and said to Irwin, "She doesn't *know*."

"Hang on," Dean said. "Why is that significant?"

"Vampires are just like people until the first time they feed," I said. "Connie didn't know that bad things would happen when she did."

"What kinda bad things?"

"The first time they feed, they don't really know it's coming. They have no control over it, no restraint—and whoever they feed on dies as a result."

"So she was the threat that Bigfoot dreamed about?"

"I'm getting to it."

Irwin's expression had darkened again, into a glower almost exactly like River Shoulders's, and he stood up.

Connie was frowning at me as she was abruptly displaced. "Don't know wh—oof, Pounder!"

"We're done," Irwin said to me. His voice wasn't exactly threatening, but it was absolutely certain, and his leashed anger all but made the air crackle. "Nice to see you again, Harry. Tell my dad to call. Or write. Or do anything but try to tell me how to live my life."

Connie blinked at him. "Wait . . . wait, what's wrong?"

Irwin left a few twenties on the table, and said, "We're going."

"What? What happened?"

"We're *going*," Irwin said. This time, he did sound a little angry.

Connie's bewilderment suddenly shifted into some flavor of outrage. She narrowed her lovely eyes, and snapped, "I am not your pet, Pounder."

"I'm not trying to . . ." Irwin took a slow, deep breath, and said, more calmly, "I'm upset. I need some space. I'll explain when I calm down. But we need to go."

She folded her arms, and said, "Go calm down, then. But I'm not going to be rude to our guest."

Irwin looked at me, and said, "We going to have a problem?"

Wow. The kid had learned a lot about the world since the last time I'd seen him. He recognized that I wasn't a playful puppy dog. He realized that if I'd been sent to protect him, and I thought Connie was a threat, that I might do something about it. And he'd just told me that if I did, he was going to object. Strenuously. No protests, no threats, just letting me know that he knew the score and was willing to do something about it if I made him. The guys who are seriously capable handle themselves like that.

"No problem," I said, and made it a promise. "If I think something needs to be done, we'll talk first."

The set of his shoulders eased, and he nodded at me. Then he turned and stalked out. People watched him go, warily.

Connie shook her head slowly, and asked, "What did you say?"

"Um," I said. "I think he feels like his dad is intruding on his life."

"You don't say." She shook her head. "That's not your fault. He's usually so collected. Why is he acting like such a jerk?"

"Issues," I said, shrugging. "Everyone has a parental issue or two."

"Still. It's beneath him to behave that way." She shook her head. "Sometimes he makes me want to slap him. But I'd need to get a chair to stand on."

"I don't take it personally," I assured her. "Don't worry."

"It was about me," she said quietly. "Wasn't it? It's about something I don't know."

"Um," I said.

It was just possible that maybe I'd made a bad call when I decided to meddle between River and his kid. It wasn't my place to shake the pillars of Irwin's life. Or Connie's, for that matter. It was going to be hard enough on her to find out about her supernatural heritage. She didn't need to have the news broken to her by a stranger, on top of that. You'd think that, after years as a professional, I'd know enough to just take River's money, help out his kid, and call it a night.

"Maybe we should walk?" I suggested.

"Sure."

We left and started walking the streets of downtown Norman. The place was alive and growing, like a lot of college towns: plenty of old buildings, some railroad tracks, lots of cracks in the asphalt and the sidewalks. The shops and restaurants had that improvised look that a business district gets when it outlives its original intended purpose and subsequent generations of enterprise take over the space.

We walked in silence for several moments, until Connie finally said, "He's not an angry person. He's usually so calm. But when something finally gets to him . . ."

"It's hard for him," I said. "He's huge and he's very strong and he knows it. If he loses control of himself, someone could get hurt. He doesn't like the thought of that. So when he starts feeling angry, it makes him tense. Afraid. He's more upset about the fact that he feels so angry than about anything I said or did."

Connie looked up at me pensively for a long moment. Then she said, "Most people wouldn't realize that."

I shrugged.

"What don't I know?" she asked.

I shook my head. "I'm not sure it's my place to tell you."

"But it's about me."

"Yeah."

She smiled faintly. "Then shouldn't I be the one who gets to decide?"

I thought about that one for a moment. "Connie . . . you're mostly right. But . . . some things, once said, can't be unsaid. Let me think about it."

She didn't answer.

The silence made me uncomfortable. I tried to chat my way clear of it. "How'd you meet Irwin?"

The question, or maybe the subject matter, seemed to relax

her a little. "In a closet at a party. Someone spiked the punch. Neither of us had ever been drunk before, and . . ." Her cheeks turned a little pink. "And he's just so damned sexy."

"Lot of people wouldn't think so," I noted.

She waved a hand. "He's not pretty. I know that. It's not about that. There's . . . this energy in him. It's chemical. Assurance. Power. Not just muscles—it's who he is." Her cheeks turned a little pink. "It wasn't exactly love at first sight, I guess. But once the hangover cleared up, that happened, too."

"So you love him?" I asked.

Her smile widened, and her eyes shone the way a young woman's eyes ought to shine. She spoke with calm, simple certainty. "He's the one."

About twenty things to say leapt to my mind. I was going to say something about how she was too young to make that kind of decision. I thought about how she hadn't been out on her own for very long, and how she had no idea where her relationship with Irwin was going to lead. I was going to tell her that only time could tell her if she and Irwin were good for one another and ready to be together, to make that kind of decision. I could have said something about how she needed to stop and think, not make blanket statements about her emotions and the future.

That was when I realized that everything I would have said was something I would have said to a young woman in love— not to a vampire. Not only that, but I heard something in her voice or saw something in her face that told me that my aged wisdom was, at least in this case, dead wrong. My instincts were telling me something that my rational brain had missed.

The kids had something real. I mean, maybe it hadn't gotten off on the most pure and virtuous foot, but that wasn't anything lethal in a relationship. The way they related to one another now? There was a connection there. You could imagine saying their names as a unit, and it *fit*: ConnieandIrwin. Maybe they had some growing to do, but what they had was real.

Not that it mattered. Being in love didn't change the facts. First, that Connie was a vampire. Second, that vampires had to feed. Third, they fed upon their lovers.

"Hold on," Dean said. "You missed something."

"Eh?"

"Girl's a vampire, right?"

"Yeah.

"So," Dean said. "She met the kid in a closet at a party. They already got it on. She done had her first time."

I frowned. "Yeah."

"So how come Kid Bigfoot wasn't dead?"

I nodded. "Exactly. It bothered me, too."

The girl was in love with Irwin, and it meant she was dangerous to him. Hell, she was dangerous to almost everyone. She wasn't even entirely *human*. How could I possibly spring something that big on her?

At the same time, how could I *not*?

"I should have taken the gold," I muttered to myself.

"What?" she asked.

That was when the Town Car pulled up to the curb a few feet ahead of us. Two men got out of the front seat. They wore expensive suits and had thick necks. One of them hadn't had his suit fitted properly—I could see the slight bulge of a side-arm in a shoulder holster. That one stood on the sidewalk and stared at me, his hands clasped in front of him. The driver went around to the rear passenger door and opened it.

"Oh," Connie said. "Marvelous. This is all I need."

"Who is that?" I asked.

"My father."

The man who got out of the back of the limo wore a pearl gray suit that made his thugs' outfits look like secondhand clothing. He was slim, a bit over six feet tall, and his haircut probably cost him more than I made in a week. His hair was dark, with a single swath of silver at each temple, and his skin was weathered and deeply tanned. He wore rings on most of his manicured fingers, all of them sporting large stones.

"Hi, Daddy," Connie said, smiling. She sounded pleasant enough, but she'd turned herself very slightly away from the man as she spoke. A rule of thumb for reading body language is that almost no one can totally hide physical reflections of their state of mind. They can only minimize the signs of it in their posture and movements. If you mentally exaggerate and magnify their body language, it tells you something about what they're thinking.

Connie clearly didn't want to talk to this man. She was ready to flee from her own father should it become necessary. It told me something about the guy. I was almost sure I wasn't going to like him.

He approached the girl, smiling, and after a microhesitation, they exchanged a brief hug. It didn't look like something they'd practiced much.

"Connie," the man said, smiling. He had the same mild drawl his daughter did. He tilted his head to one side and regarded her thoughtfully. "You went blond. It's . . . charming."

"Thank you, Daddy," Connie said. She was smiling, too. Neither one of them looked sincere to me. "I didn't know you were in town. If you'd called, we could have made an evening of it."

"Spur-of-the-moment thing," he said easily. "I hope you don't mind."

"No, of course not."

Both of them were lying. Parental issues indeed.

"How's that boy you'd taken up with? Irving."

"Irwin," Connie said in a poisonously pleasant tone. "He's great. Maybe even better than that."

He frowned at that, and said, "I see. But he's not here?"

"He had homework tonight," Connie lied.

That drew a small, sly smile out of the man. "I see. Who's your friend?" he asked pleasantly, without actually looking at me.

"Oh," Connie said. "Harry, this is my father, Charles Barrowill. Daddy, this is Harry Dresden."

"Hi," I said brightly.

Barrowill's eyes narrowed to sudden slits, and he took a short, hard breath as he looked at me. He then flicked his eyes left and right around him, as if looking for a good place to dive or maybe a hostage to seize.

"What a pleasure, Mr. Dresden," he said, his voice suddenly tight. "What brings you out to Oklahoma?"

"I heard it was a nice place for perambulating," I said. Behind Barrowill, his guards had picked up on the tension. Both of them had become very still. Barrowill was quiet for a moment, as if trying to parse some kind of meaning from my words. Heavy seconds ticked by, like the quiet before a shootout in an old Western.

A tumbleweed went rolling by in the street. I'm not even kidding. An actual, literal tumbleweed. Man, Oklahoma.

Then Barrowill took a slow breath and said to Connie, "Darling, I'd like to speak to you for a few moments, if you have time."

"Actually . . ." Connie began.

"Now, please," Barrowill said. There was something ugly under the surface of his pleasant tone. "The car. I'll give you a ride back to the dorms."

Connie folded her arms and scowled. "I'm entertaining someone from out of town, Daddy. I can't just leave him here."

One of the guard's hands twitched.

"Don't be difficult, Connie," Barrowill said. "I don't want to make a scene."

His eyes never left me as he spoke, and I got his message

loud and clear. He was taking the girl with him, and he was willing to make things get messy if I tried to stop him.

"It's okay, Connie," I said. "I've been to Norman before. I can find my way to a hotel easily enough."

"You're sure?" Connie asked.

"Definitely."

"Herman," Barrowill said.

The driver opened the passenger door again and stood next to it attentively. He kept his eyes on me, and one hand dangled, clearly ready to go for his gun.

Connie looked back and forth between me and her father for a moment, then sighed audibly and walked over to the car. She slid in, and Herman closed the door behind her.

"I recognize you," I said pleasantly to Barrowill. "You were at the Raith Deeps when Skavis and Malvora tried to pull off their coup. Front row, all the way on one end in the Raith cheering section."

"You have an excellent memory," Barrowill said.

"Got out in one piece, did you?"

The vampire smiled without humor. "What are you doing with my daughter?"

"Taking a walk," I said. "Talking."

"You have nothing to say to her. In the interests of peace between the Court and the Council, I'm willing to ignore this intrusion into my territory. Go in peace. Right now."

"You never told her, did you?" I asked. "Never told her what she was."

One of his jaw muscles twitched. "It is not our way."

"Nah," I said. "You wait until the first time they get twitterpated, experiment with sex, and kill whoever it is they're with. Little harsh on the kids, isn't it?"

"Connie is not some mortal cow. She is a vampire. The initiation builds character she will need to survive and prosper."

"If it was good enough for you, it's good enough for her?"

"Mortal," Barrowill said, "you simply cannot understand. I am her father. It is my obligation to prepare her for her life. The initiation is something she needs."

I lifted my eyebrows. "Holy . . . that's what happened, isn't it? You sent her off to school to boink some poor kid to death. Hell, I'd bet you had the punch spiked at that party. Except the kid didn't die—so now you're in town to figure out what the hell went wrong."

Barrowill's eyes darkened, and he shook his head. "This is no business of yours. Leave."

"See, that's the thing," I said. "It *is* my business. My client is worried about his kid."

Barrowill narrowed his eyes again. "Irving."

"Irwin," I corrected him.

"Go back to Chicago, wizard," he said. "You're in my territory now."

"This isn't a smart move for you," I said. "The kid's connected. If anything bad happens to him, you're in for trouble."

"Is that a threat?" he asked.

I shook my head. "Chuck, I've got no objection to working things out peaceably. And I've got no objection to doing it the other way. If you know my reputation, then you know what a sincere guy I am."

"Perhaps I should kill you now."

"Here, in public?" I asked. "All these witnesses? You aren't going to do that."

"No?"

"No. Even if you win, you lose. You're just hoping to scare me off." I nodded toward his goons. "Ghouls, right? It's going to take more than two, Chuck. Hell, I like fighting ghouls. No matter what I do to them, I never feel bad about it afterward."

Barrowill missed the reference, like the monsters usually do.

He looked at me, then at his Rolex. "I'll give you until midnight to leave the state. After that, you're gone. One way or another."

"Hang on," I said, "I'm terrified. Let me catch my breath."

Barrowill's eyes shifted color slightly, from a deep green to a much paler, angrier shade of green-gold. "I react poorly to those who threaten my family's well-being, Dresden."

"Yeah. You're a regular Ozzie Nelson. John Walton. Ben Cartwright."

"Excuse me?"

"Mr. Drummond? Charles . . . in Charge? No?"

"What are you blabbering about?"

"Hell's bells, man. Don't any of you White Court bozos ever watch television? I'm giving you pop reference gold, here. Gold."

Barrowill stared at me with opaque, reptilian eyes. Then he said, simply, "Midnight." He took two steps back before he turned his back on me and got into his car. His goons both gave me hard looks before they, too, got into the car and pulled away.

I watched the car roll out. Despite the attitude I'd given Barrowill, I knew better than to take him lightly. Any vampire is a dangerous foe—and one of them with holdings and resources and his own personal brute squad was more so. Not only that but . . . from his point of view, I was messing around with his little girl's best interests. The vampires of the White Court were, to a degree, as dangerous as they were because they were partly human. They had human emotions, human motivations, human reactions. Barrowill could be as irrationally protective of his family as anyone else.

Except that they were also *inhuman*. All of those human drives were intertwined with a parasitic spirit they called a Hunger, where all the power and hunger of their vampire parts came from.

Take one part human faults and insecurities and add it to one part inhuman power and motivation. What do you get?

Trouble.

* * *

"Barrowill?" Officer Dean asked me. "The oil guy? He keeps a stable. Of congressmen."

"Yeah, probably the same guy," I said. "All vampires like having money and status. It makes their lives easier."

Dean snorted. "Every vampire. And every nonvampire."

"*Heh,*" I said. "Point."

"You were in a fix," he said. "Tell the girl, you might wreck her. Don't tell her, and you might wreck her and Kid Bigfoot both. Either way, somebody's dad has a bone to pick with you."

"Pretty much."

"Seems to me a smart guy would have washed his hands of the whole mess and left town."

I shrugged. "Yeah. But I was the only guy there."

Forest isn't exactly the dominant terrain in Norman, but there are a few trees, here and there. The point where I'd agreed to meet with River Shoulders was in the center of the Oliver Wildlife Preserve, which was a stand of woods that had been donated to the university for research purposes. As I hiked out into the little wood, it occurred to me that meeting River Shoulders there was like rendezvousing with Jaws in a kiddy wading pool—but he'd picked the spot, so whatever floated the big guy's boat.

It was dark out, and I drew my silver pentacle amulet off my neck to use for light. A whisper of will and a muttered word, and the little symbol glowed with a dim blue light that would let me walk without bumping into a tree. It took me maybe five minutes to get to approximately the right area, and River Shoulders's soft murmur of greeting came to me out of the dark.

We sat down together on a fallen tree, and I told him what I'd learned.

He sat in silence for maybe two minutes after I finished. Then he said, "My son has joined himself to a parasite."

I felt a flash of mild outrage. "You could think of it that way," I said.

"What other way is there?"

"That he's joined himself to a girl. The parasite just came along for the ride."

River Shoulders exhaled a huge breath. It sounded like those pneumatic machines they use to elevate cars at the repair shop. "I see. In your view, the girl is not dangerous. She is innocent."

"She's both," I said. "She can't help being born what she is, any more than you or I."

River Shoulders grunted.

"Have your people encountered the White Court before?"

He grunted again.

"Because the last time I helped Irwin out . . . I remember being struck by the power of his aura when he was only fourteen. A long-term draining spell that should have killed him only left him sleepy." I eyed him. "But I don't feel anything around you. Stands to reason, your aura would be an order of magnitude greater than your kid's. That's why you've been careful never to touch me. You're keeping your power hidden from me, aren't you?"

"Maybe."

I snorted. "Just the kind of answer I'd expect from a wizard."

"It is not something we care for outsiders to know," he said. "And we are not wizards. We see things differently than mortals. You people are dangerous."

"Heh," I said, and glanced up at his massive form beside mine. "Between the two of us, I'm the dangerous one."

"Like a child waving around his father's gun," River Shoulders said. Something in his voice became gentler. "Though some of you are better than others about it, I admit."

"My point is," I said, "the kid's got a life force like few I've seen. When Connie's Hunger awakened, she fed on him without any kind of restraint, and he wound up with nothing worse than a hangover. Could be that he could handle a life with her just fine."

River Shoulders nodded slowly. His expression might have been thoughtful. It was too dark, and his features too blunt and chiseled to be sure.

"The girl seems genuinely fond of him. And he of her. I mean, I'm not an expert in these things, but they seem to like each other, and even when they have a difference of opinions, they fight fair. That's a good sign." I squinted at him. "Do you really think he's in danger?"

"Yes," River Shoulders said. "They have to kill him now."

I blinked. "What?"

"This . . . creature. This Barrowill."

"Yeah?"

"It sent its child to this place with the intention that she meet a young man and feed upon him and unknowingly kill him."

"Yeah."

River Shoulders shook his huge head sadly. "What kind of monster does that to its children?"

"Vampires," I said. "It isn't uncommon, from what I hear."

"Because they hurt," River Shoulders said. "Barrowill remembers his own first lover. He remembers being with her. He remembers her death. And his wendigo has had its hand on his heart ever since. It shaped his life."

"Wendigo?"

River Shoulders waved a hand. "General term. Spirit of hunger. Can't ever be sated."

"Ah, gotcha."

"Now, Barrowill. He had his father tell him that this was how it had to be. That it had to be that way to make him a good vampire. So this thing that turned him into a murdering monster is actually a good thing. He spends his whole life trying to convince himself of that." River nodded slowly. "What happens when his child does something differently?"

I felt like a moron. "It means that what his father told him was a lie. It means that maybe he didn't have to be like he is. It means that he's been lying to himself. About everything."

River Shoulders spread his hands, palm up, as if presenting the fact. "That kind of father has to make his children in his own image. He has to make the lie true."

"He has to make sure Connie kills Irwin," I said. "We've got to get him out of there. Maybe both of them."

"How?" River Shoulders said. "She doesn't know. He only knows a little. Neither knows enough to be wise enough to run."

"They shouldn't *have* to run," I growled.

"Avoiding a fight is always better than not avoiding one."

"Disagree," I said. "Some fights *should* be sought out. And fought. And won."

River Shoulders shook his head. "Your father's gun." I sensed a deep current of resistance in River Shoulders on this subject— one that I would never be able to bridge, I suspected. River just wasn't a fighter. "Would you agree it was wisest if they both fled?"

"In this case . . . it might, yeah. But I think it would only delay the confrontation. Guys like Barrowill have long arms. If he obsesses over it, he'll find them sooner or later."

"I have no right to take his child from him," River Shoulders said. "I am only interested in Irwin."

"Well, I'm not going to be able to separate them," I said. "Irwin nearly started swinging at me when I went anywhere close to that subject." I paused, then added, "But he might listen to you."

River Shoulders shook his head. "He's right. I got no right to walk in and smash his life to splinters after being so far away so long. He'd never listen to me. He's got a lot of anger in him. Maybe for good reasons."

"You're his father," I said. "That might carry more weight than you think."

"I should not have involved you in this," he said. "I apologize for that, wizard. You should go. Let me sort this out on my own."

I eyed River Shoulders.

The big guy was powerful, sure, but he was also slow. He took his time making decisions. He played things out with enormous patience. He was clearly ambivalent over what kind of involvement he should have with his son. It might take him months of observation and cogitation to make a choice.

Most of us don't live that way. I was sure Barrowill didn't. If the vampire was moving, he might be moving now. Like, right now.

"In this particular instance, River Shoulders, you are not thinking clearly," I said. "Action must be taken soon. Preferably tonight."

"I will be what I am," River said firmly.

I stood up from the log and nodded. "Okay," I said. "Me too."

I put in a call to my fellow Warden, "Wild Bill" Meyers, in Dallas, but got an answering service. I left a message that I was in Norman and needed his help, but I had little faith that he'd show up in time. The real downside to being a wizard is that we void the warrantees of anything technological every time we sneeze. Cell phones are worse than useless in our hands, and it makes communications a challenge at times though that was far from the only possible obstacle. If Bill was in, he'd have picked up his phone. He had a big area for his beat and likely had problems of his own—but since Dallas was only three hours away (assuming his car didn't break down), I could hold out hope that he might roll in by morning.

So I got in my busted-up old Volkswagen, picked up a prop, and drove up to the campus alone. I parked somewhere where

I would probably get a ticket. I planned to ignore it. Anarchists have a much easier time finding parking spots.

I got out and walked toward one of the smaller dorm buildings on campus. I didn't have my wizard's staff with me, on account of how weird it looked to walk around with one, but my blasting rod was hanging from its tie inside my leather duster. I doubted I would need it, but better to have it and not need it than the other way around. I got my prop and trudged across a short bit of turquoise-tinted grass to the honors dorms, where Irwin lived. They were tiny, for that campus, maybe five stories, with the building laid out in four right-angled halls, like a plus sign. The door was locked. There's always that kind of security in a dorm building, these days.

I rapped on the glass with my knuckles until a passing student noticed. I held up a cardboard box from the local Pizza 'Spress, and tried to look like I needed a break. I needn't have tried so hard. The kid's eyes were bloodshot and glassy. He was baked on something. He opened the door for me without blinking.

"Thanks."

"No problem," he said.

"He was supposed to meet me at the doors," I said. "You see a guy named, uh . . ." I checked the receipt that was taped to the box. "Irwin Pounder?"

"Pounder, hah," the kid said. "He'll be in his room. Fourth floor, south hall, third door on the left. Just listen for the noise."

"Music?"

He tittered. "Not exactly."

I thanked him and ambled up the stairs, which were getting to be a lot harder on my knees than they used to be. Maybe I needed orthopedic shoes or something.

I got to the second floor before I felt it. There was a tension in the air, something that made my heart speed up and my skin feel hot. A few steps farther, and I started breathing faster and louder. It wasn't until I got to the third floor that I remembered that the most dangerous aspect of a psychic assault is that the victim almost never realizes that it's actually happening.

I stopped and threw up my mental defenses in a sudden panic, and the surge of adrenaline and fear suddenly overcame the tremors of restless need that I'd been feeling. The air was thick with psychic power of a nature I'd experienced once before, back in the Raith Deeps. That was when Lara Raith had unleashed the full force of her come hither against her own father, the White King, drowning his mind in imposed lust and desire to please her. He'd been her puppet ever since.

This was the same form of attack, though there were subtle differences. It had to be Barrowill. He'd moved even faster than I'd feared. I kept my mental shields up as I picked up my pace. By the time I reached the fourth floor, I heard the noise the amiable toker had mentioned.

It was sex. Loud sex. A lot of it.

I dropped the pizza and drew my blasting rod. It took me about five seconds to realize what was happening. Barrowill must have been pushing Connie, psychically—forcing her to continue feeding and feeding after she would normally have stopped. He wanted her to kill Irwin like a good little vampire, and the overflow was spilling out onto the entire building.

Not that it takes much to make college kids interested in sex, but in this instance, they had literally gone wild. When I looked down the four hallways, doors were standing wide open. Couples and . . . well, the only word that really applied was *clusters* of kids were in the act, some of them right out in the hall. Imagine an act of lust. It was going on in at least two of those four hallways.

I turned down Irwin's hall, channeling my will into my blasting rod—and yes, I'm aware of the Freudian irony, here. The carved runes along its length began to burn with silver and scarlet light as the power built up in it. A White Court vampire is practically a pussycat compared to some of the other breeds on the planet, but I'd once seen one of them twist a pair of fifty-pound steel dumbbells around one another to make a point. I might not have much time to throw down on Barrowill in these narrow quarters, and my best chance was to put him down hard the instant I saw him.

I moved forward as silently as I knew how, stepping around a pair of couples who were breaking some sort of municipal statute, I was sure. Then I leaned back and kicked open the door to Irwin's room.

The place looked like a small tornado had gone through it. Books and clothing and bedclothes and typical dorm room décor had been scattered everywhere. The chair next to a small study desk had been knocked over. A laptop computer lay on its side, showing what I'd once been told was a blue screen of death. The bed had fallen onto its side, where two of the legs appeared to have snapped off.

Connie and Irwin were there, and the haze of lust rolling off the ingénue succubus was a second psychic cyclone. I barely managed to push away. Irwin had her pinned against the wall in a corner. His muscles strained against his skin, and his breath came in dry, labored gasps, but he never stopped moving.

He wasn't being gentle, and Connie apparently didn't mind. Her eyes were a shade of silver, metallic silver, as if they'd been made of chrome, reflecting the room around her like tiny, warped mirrors. She'd sunk her fingers into the drywall to the second knuckle on either side of her to hang on, and her body was rolling in a strained arch in time with his motion. They were gratuitously enthusiastic about the whole thing.

And I hadn't gotten laid in forever.

"Irwin!" I shouted.

Shockingly, I didn't capture his attention.

"Connie!"

I didn't capture hers, either.

I couldn't let the . . . the, uh, process continue. I had no idea how long it might take, or how resistant to harm Irwin might be, but it would be stupid to do nothing and hope for the best. While I was trying to figure out how to break it up before someone lost an eye, I heard the door of the room across the hall open behind me. The sights and sounds and the haze of psychic influence had my mental processes running at less than peak performance. I didn't process the sound into a threat until Barrowill slugged me on the back of the head with something that felt like a lump of solid ivory.

I don't even remember hitting the floor.

When I woke up, I had a Sasquatch-sized headache, my wrists and ankles were killing me. Half a dozen of Barrowill's goons were all literally kneeling on me to hold me down. Every single one of them had a knife pressed close to one of my major arteries.

Also, my pants had shrunk by several sizes.

I was still in Irwin's dorm room, but things had changed. Irwin was on his back on the floor, Connie astride him. Her features had changed, shifted subtly. Her skin seemed to glow with pale light. Her eyes were empty white spheres. Her cheekbones stood out more harshly against her face, and her hair was a sweat-dampened, wild mane that clung to her cheeks and her parted lips. She was moving as if in slow motion, her fingernails digging into Irwin's chest.

Barrowill's psychic assault was still under way, and Connie's presence had become something so vibrant and penetrating that for a second I thought there might have been a minor earthquake going on. I had to get to that girl. I *had* to. If I didn't, I was going to lose my mind with need. My instant reaction upon opening my eyes was to struggle to get closer to her on pure reflex.

The goons held me down, and I screamed in protest—but at least being a captive had kept me from doing something stupid and gave me an instant's cold realization that my shields were down. I threw them up again as hard as I could, but the Barrowills had been in my head too long. I barely managed to grab hold of my reason.

The kid looked awful. His eyes were glazed. He wasn't moving with Connie so much as his body was randomly shaking in independent spasms. His head lolled from one side to the other, and his mouth was open. A strand of drool ran from his mouth to the floor.

Barrowill had righted the fallen chair. He sat upon it with one ankle resting on his other knee, his arms folded. His expression was detached, clinical, as he watched his daughter killing the young man she loved.

"Barrowill," I said. My voice came out hoarse and rough. "Stop this."

The vampire directed his gaze to me and shook his head. "It's after midnight, Dresden. It's time for Cinderella to return to her real life."

"You son of a bitch," I snarled. "She's killing him."

A small smile touched one corner of his mouth. "Yes. Beautifully. Her Hunger is quite strong." He made a vague gesture with one hand. "Does he seem upset about it? He's a mortal. And mortals are all born to die. The only question is how and in how much pain."

"There's this life thing that happens in between," I snarled.

"And many more where his came from." Barrowill's eyes went chill. "His. And yours."

"What do you mean?"

"When she's finished, we leave. You're dessert."

A lump of ice settled in my stomach, and I swallowed. All things considered, I was becoming a little worried about the outcome of this situation. *Talk, Harry. Keep him talking. You've never met a vampire who didn't love the sound of his own voice. Something could change the situation if you play for time.*

"Why not do it before I woke up?" I asked.

"This way is more efficient," Barrowill said. "If a young athlete takes Ecstasy, and his heart fails, there may be a candlelight vigil, but there won't be an investigation. Two dead men? One of them a private investigator? There will be questions." He shrugged a shoulder. "And I don't care for you to bequest me your death curse, wizard. But once Connie has you, you won't have enough left of your mind to speak your own name, much less utter a curse."

"The Raiths are going to kill you if you drag the Court and the Council into direct opposition," I said.

"The Raiths will never know. I own twenty ghouls, Dresden, and they're always hungry. What they leave of your corpse won't fill a moist sponge."

Connie suddenly ceased moving altogether. Her skin had become pure ivory white. She shuddered, her breaths coming in ragged gasps. She tilted her head back and a low, throaty moan came out of her throat. I've had sex that wasn't as good as Connie sounded.

Dammit, Dresden. Focus.

I was out of time.

"The Council will find out, Chuck. They're *wizards*. Finding unfindable information is what they *do*."

He smirked. "I think we both know that their reputation is very well constructed."

We *did* both know that. Dammit. "You think nobody's going to miss me?" I asked. "I have friends, you know."

Barrowill suddenly leaned forward, focusing on Connie, his eyes becoming a few shades lighter. "Perhaps, Dresden. But your friends are not here."

Then there was a crash so loud that it shook the building. Barrowill's sleek, black Lincoln Town Car came crashing through the dorm room's door, taking a sizable portion of the wall with it. The ghouls holding me down were scattered by the debris, and fine dust filled the air.

I started coughing at once, but I could see what had happened. The car had come through from the far side of this wing of the dorm, smashing through the room where Barrowill had waited in ambush. The car had crossed the hall and wound up with its bumper and front tires resting inside Irwin's room. It had smashed a massive hole in the outer brick wall of the building, leaving it gaping open to the night.

That got everyone's attention. For an instant, the room was perfectly silent and perfectly still. The ghoul chauffeur still sat in the driver's seat—only his head wobbled loosely, leaning at a right angle to the rest of his neck.

"Hah," I cackled, wheezing. "Hah, hah. Heh hah, hah, hah. Moron."

A large figure leapt up to the hole in the exterior wall and landed in the room across the hall, hitting with a crunch only slightly less massive than the car had made. I swear to you, if I'd heard that sound effect they used to use when Steve Austin jumped somewhere, I would not have been shocked. The other room was unlit, and the newcomer was a massive, threatening shadow.

He slapped a hand the size of a big cookie tray on the floor and let out a low, rumbling sound like nothing I'd ever heard this side of an amplified bass guitar. It was music. You couldn't have written it in musical notation, any more than you could write the music of a thunderstorm, or write lyrics to the song of a running stream. But it was music nonetheless.

Power like nothing I had ever encountered surged out from that impact, a deep, shuddering wave that passed visibly through the dust in the air. The ceiling and the walls and the floor sang in resonance with the note and impact alike, and Barrowill's psychic assault was swept away like a sand castle before the tide. Connie's eyes flooded with color, changing from pure, empty whiteness back to a rich blue as deep and rich as a glacial lake, and the humanity came flooding back into her features. The sense of wild panic in the air suddenly vanished, and for another timeless instant, everything, *everything* in that night went utterly silent and still.

Holy.

Crap.

I've worked with magic for decades, and take it from me, it really isn't very different from anything else in life. When you work with magic, you rapidly realize that it is far easier to disrupt than to create, far more difficult to mend than to destroy. Throw a stone into a glass-smooth lake, and ripples will wash over the whole thing. Making waves with magic instead of a rock would have been easy.

But if you can make that lake smooth again—that's one hell of a trick.

That surge of energy didn't attack anything or anybody. It didn't destroy Barrowill's assault.

It made the water smooth again.

Strength-of-a-River-in-his-Shoulders opened his eyes, and his fury made them burn like coals in the shadows—but he simply crouched, doing nothing.

All of Barrowill's goons remained still, wide eyes flicking from River to Barrowill and back.

"Back off, Chuck," I said. "He's giving you a chance to walk away. Take him up on it."

The vampire's expression was completely blank as he stood among the debris. He stared at River Shoulders for maybe three seconds—and then I saw movement behind River Shoulders.

Clawed hands began to grip the edges of the hole behind River. Wicked, bulging red eyes appeared. Monstrous-looking *things* in the same general shape as a human appeared in complete silence.

Ghouls.

Barrowill didn't have six goons with him.

He'd brought them *all*.

Barrowill spat toward River, bared his teeth and screamed, "Kill it!"

And it was on.

Everything went completely insane. The human-shaped ghouls in the room bounded forward, their faces and limbs contorting, tearing their way out of their cheap suits as they assumed their true forms. More ghouls poured in through the hole in the wall like a swarm of panicked roaches. I couldn't get an accurate count of the enemy—the action was too fast. But twenty sounded about right. Twenty flesh-rending, super-humanly strong and durable predators flung themselves onto River Shoulders in an overwhelming wave. He vanished beneath a couple of *tons* of hungry ghoul. It was *not* a fair fight.

Barrowill should have brought more goons.

There was an enormous bellow, a sound that could only have been made by a truly massive set of lungs, and ghouls exploded outward from River Shoulders like so much hideous shrapnel. Several were flung back out of the building. Others slammed into walls with so much force that they shattered the drywall. One of them went *through* the ceiling, then fell limply back down into the room—only to be caught by the neck in one of River Shoulders's massive hands. He squeezed, crushing the ghoul's neck like soft clay, and there was an audible pop. The ghoul spasmed once, then River flung the corpse into the nearest batch of monsters.

After that, it was clobbering time.

Barrowill moved fast, seizing Connie and darting out the door. I looked around frantically and spotted one of the knives the goons had been holding before they transformed. My hands and ankles had been bound in those plastic restraining strips, and I could barely feel my fingers, but I managed to pick up the knife and cut my legs free. Then I put it on the front bumper of the Lincoln, stepped on it with one foot to hold it in place, and after a few moments managed to cut my hands loose as well.

The dorm sounded like a medley of pay-per-view wrestling and the *Island of Doctor Moreau*. Ghouls shrieked. River Shoulders roared. Very, very disoriented students screamed. The walls and floor shook with impact again and again as River Shoulders flung ghouls around like so many softballs. Ghoulish blood spattered the walls and the ceiling, green-brown and putrid-smelling, and as strong as he was, River Shoulders wasn't pitching a shutout. The ghouls' claws and fangs had sunk into him, covering him in punctures and lacerations, and his scarlet blood mixed with theirs on the various surfaces.

I tried to think unobtrusive thoughts, stayed low, and went to Irwin. He still looked awful, but he was breathing hard and steady, and he'd already begun blinking and trying to focus his eyes.

"Irwin!" I shouted. "Irwin! Where's her purse?"

"Whuzza?" Irwin mumbled.

"Connie's purse! I've got to help Connie! Where is her purse?"

Irwin's eyes almost focused. "Connie?"

"Oh never *mind*." I started ransacking the dorm room until I found Connie's handbag. She had a brush in it. The brush was liberally festooned with her blond hairs.

I swept a circle into the dust on the floor, tied the hair around my pentacle amulet and invested the circle with a whisper of will. Then I quickly worked the tracking spell that was generally my bread and butter when I was doing investigator stuff. When I released the magic, it rushed down into Connie's borrowed hair, and my amulet lurched sharply out of plumb and held itself steady at a thirty- or forty-degree angle. Connie went thataway.

I ducked a flying ghoul, leapt over a dying ghoul, and staggered down the hall at my best speed while the blood went back into my feet.

I had gone down one whole flight of stairs without falling when the angle on the amulet changed again. Barrowill had gone down one floor, then taken off down one of the residential hallways toward the fire escape at the far end. He'd bypassed security by ripping the door off its hinges, then flinging it into the opposite wall. Kids were scattering out of the hallway, looking either horrified or disappointed. Some both. Barrowill had reached the far end, carrying his daughter over one shoulder, and was headed for the fire door.

Barrowill had been savvy enough to divest me of my accoutrements, but I was still a wizard, dammit, blasting rod or no. I drew up my will, aimed low, and snarled, *"Forzare!"*

Pure kinetic force lashed invisibly through the air and caught Barrowill at the ankles. It kicked both of his feet up into the air, and he took a pratfall onto the floor. Connie landed with a grunt and bounced to one side. She lay there dazed and blinking.

Barrowill slithered back up to his feet, spinning toward me, and producing a pistol in one hand. I lurched back out of the line of fire as the gun barked twice, and bullets went by me with a double hiss. I went to my knees and bobbed my head out into the hall again for a quick peek, jerking it back immediately. Barrowill was picking Connie up. His bullet went through the air where my head would have been if I'd been standing.

"Don't be a moron, Harry," I said. "You came for the kid. He's safe. That's all you were obligated to do. Let it g—oh who am I kidding. There's a girl."

I didn't have to beat the vampire—I just had to slow him down long enough for River Shoulders to catch up to him . . . assuming River *did* pursue.

I took note of which wing Barrowill was fleeing through and rushed down the stairs to the ground floor. Then I left the building and sprinted to the far end of that wing.

Barrowill slammed the emergency exit open and emerged

from the building. He was moving fast, but he also had his daughter to carry, and she'd begun to resist him, kicking and thrashing, slowing him down. She tugged him off balance just as he shot at me again, and it went wide. I slashed at him with another surge of force, but this time I wasn't aiming for his feet—I went for the gun. The weapon leapt out of his hands and went spinning away, shattering against the bricks of the dorm's outer wall. Another blast knocked Connie off his shoulder, and she let out a little shriek. Barrowill staggered, then let out a snarl of frustration and charged me at a speed worthy of the Flash's understudy.

I flung more force at him, but Barrowill bobbed to one side, evading the blast. I threw myself away from the vampire and managed to roll with the punch he sent at my head. He caught me an inch or two over one eyebrow, the hardest and most impact-resistant portion of the human skull. That and the fact that I'd managed to rob it of a little of its power meant that he only sent me spinning wildly away, my vision completely obscured by pain and little silver stars. He was furious, his power rolling over me like a sudden deluge of ice water, to the point where crystals of frost formed on my clothing.

Barrowill followed up, his eyes murderous—and then Bigfoot Irwin bellowed, "Connie!" and slammed into Barrowill at the hip, using his body as a living spear. Barrowill was flung to one side, and Irwin pressed his advantage, still screaming, coming down atop the vampire and pounding him with both fists in elemental violence, his sunken eyes mad with rage. "Connie! Connie!"

I tried to rise but couldn't seem to make it past one knee. So all I could do was watch as the furious scion of River Shoulders unleashed everything he had on a ranking noble of the White Court. Barrowill could have been much stronger than a human being if he'd had the gas in the tank—but he'd spent his energy on his psychic assault, and it had drained him. He still thrashed powerfully, but he was no match for the enraged young man. Irwin slammed Barrowill's nose flat against his face. I saw one of the vampire's teeth go flying into the night air. Slightly-too-pale blood began to splash against Irwin's fists.

Christ. If the kid killed Barrowill, the White Court would consider it an act of war. All kinds of horrible things could unfold. "Irwin!" I shouted. "Irwin, stop!"

Kid Bigfoot didn't listen to me.

I lurched closer to him but only made it about six inches before my head whirled so badly that I fell onto my side. "Irwin, stop!" I looked around and saw Connie staring dazedly at the struggle. "Connie!" I said. "Stop him! Stop him!"

Meanwhile, Irwin had beaten Barrowill to within an inch of his life—and now he raised his joined hands over his head, preparing for a sledgehammer blow to Barrowill's skull.

A small, pretty hand touched his wrist.

"Irwin," Connie said gently. "Irwin, no."

"He tried," Irwin panted. "Tried. Hurt you."

"This isn't the way," Connie said.

"Bad man," Irwin growled.

"But you *aren't*," Connie said, her voice very soft. "Irwin. He's still my daddy."

Connie couldn't have physically stopped Irwin—but she didn't need to. The kid blinked several times, then looked at her. He slowly lowered his hands, and Connie leaned down to kiss his forehead gently. "Shhhh," she said. "Shhhh. I'm still here. It's over, baby. It's over."

"Connie," Irwin said, and leaned against her.

I let out a huge sigh of relief and sank back onto the ground. My head hurt.

Officer Dean stared at me for a while. He chewed on a toothpick and squinted at me. "Got some holes."

"Yeah?" I asked. "Like what?"

"Like all those kids saw a Bigfoot and them whatchama-calits. Ghouls. How come they didn't say anything?"

"You walked in on them while they were all still trying to put their clothes back on. After flinging themselves into random sex with whoever happened to be close to them. They're all denying that this ever happened right now."

"Hngh," Dean said. "What about the ghoul corpses?"

"After Irwin dragged their boss up to the fight, the ghouls quit when they saw him. River Shoulders told them all to get out of his sight and take their dead with them. They did."

Dean squinted and consulted a list. "Pounder is gone. So is Connie Barrowill. Not officially missing, or nothing. Not yet. But where are they?"

I looked at Dean and shrugged.

I'd seen ghouls in all kinds of situations before—but I'd never seen them whipped into submission. Ghouls fought to the grisly, messy end. That was what they did. But River Shoulders had been more than their match. He'd left several of them alive when he could have killed them to the last, and he'd found their breaking point when Irwin had dragged Barrowill in by his hair. Ghouls could take a huge beating, but River Shoulders had given them one like I'd never seen, and when he ordered them to take their master and their dead and never to return, they'd snapped to it.

"Thanks, Connie," I groaned as she settled me onto a section of convenient rubble. I was freezing. The frost on my clothes was rapidly melting away, but the chill had settled inward.

The girl looked acutely embarrassed, but that wasn't in short supply in that dorm. That hallway was empty of other students for the moment, though. We had the place to ourselves, though I judged that the authorities would arrive in some form before long.

Irwin came over with a dust-covered blanket and wrapped it

around her. He'd scrounged a ragged towel for himself though it did more to emphasize his physique than to hide it. The kid was ripped.

"Thank you, Irwin," she said.

He grunted. Physically, he'd bounced back from the nearly lethal feeding like a rubber freaking ball. Maybe River Shoulders's water-smoothing spell had done something to help that. Mentally, he was slowly refocusing. You could see the gleam coming back into his eyes. Until that happened, he'd listened to Connie. A guy could do worse.

"I . . ." Connie shook her head. "I remember all of it. But I have no idea what just happened." She stared at River Shoulders for a moment, her expression more curious than fearful. "You . . . You stopped something bad from happening, I think."

"Yeah, he did," I confirmed.

Connie nodded toward him in a grateful little motion. "Thank you. Who are you?"

"Irwin's dad," I said.

Irwin blinked several times. He stared blankly at River Shoulders.

"Hello," River rumbled. How something that large and that powerful could sit there bleeding from dozens of wounds and somehow look sheepish was beyond me. "I am very sorry we had to meet like that. I had hoped for something quieter. Maybe with music. And good food."

"You can't stay," I said to River. "The authorities are on the way."

River made a rumbling sound of agreement. "This is a disaster. What I did . . ." He shook his head. "This was in such awful taste."

"Couldn't have happened to nicer guys, though," I said.

"Wait," Connie said. "Wait. What the *hell* just happened here?"

Irwin put a hand on her shoulder, and said, to me, "She's . . . she's a vampire. Isn't she?"

I blinked and nodded at him. "How did . . . ?"

"Paranet," he said. "There's a whole page."

"Wait," Connie said again. "A . . . what? Am I going to sparkle or something?"

"God, no," said Irwin and I, together.

"Connie," I said, and she looked at me. "You're still exactly who you were this morning. And so is Irwin. And that's what counts. But right now, things are going to get really complicated if the cops walk in and start asking you questions. Better if they just never knew you were here."

"This is all so . . ." She shook her head. Then she stared at River Shoulders. Then at me. "Who *are* you?"

I pointed at me, and said, "Wizard." I pointed at River. "Bigfoot." I pointed at Irwin. "Son of Bigfoot." I pointed at her. "Vampire. Seriously."

"Oh," she said faintly.

"I'll explain it," Irwin told her quietly. He was watching River Shoulders.

River held out his huge hands to either side and shrugged. "Hello, son."

Irwin shook his head slowly. "I . . . never really . . ." He sucked in a deep breath, squared off against his father, and said, "Why?"

And there it was. What had to be the Big Question of Irwin's life.

"My people," he said. "Tradition is very important to them. If I acknowledged you . . . they would have insisted that certain traditions be observed. It would have consumed your life. And I didn't want that for you. I didn't want that for your mother. I wanted your world to be wider than mine."

Bigfoot Irwin was silent for a long moment. Then he

scratched at his head with one hand and shrugged. "Tonight . . . really explains a lot." He nodded slowly. "Okay. We aren't done talking. But okay."

"Let's get you out of here," River said. "Get you both taken care of. Answer all your questions."

"What about Harry?" Irwin said.

I couldn't get any more involved with the evident abduction of a scion of the White Court. River's mercy had probably kept the situation from going completely to hell, but I wasn't going to drag the White Council's baggage into the situation. "You guys go on," I told them. "I do this kind of thing all the time. I'll be fine."

"Wow, seriously?" Irwin asked.

"Yeah," I said. "I've been in messier situations than this. And . . . it's probably better if Connie's dad has time to cool off before you guys talk again. River Shoulders can make sure you have that time."

Outside, a cart with flashing bulbs on it had pulled up.

"River," I said. "Time's up."

River Shoulders rose and nodded deeply to me. "I'm sorry that I interfered. It seemed necessary."

"I'm willing to overlook it," I said. "All things considered."

His face twisted into a very human-looking smile, and he extended his hand to Irwin. "Son."

Irwin took his father's hand, one arm still around Connie, and the three of them didn't vanish so much as . . . just become less and less relevant to the situation. It happened over the course of two or three seconds, as that same nebulous, somehow transparent power that River had used earlier enfolded them. And then they were all gone.

Boots crunched down the hall, and a uniformed officer with a name tag reading DEAN burst in, one hand on his gun.

* * *

Dean eyed me, then said, "That's all you know, huh?"

"That's the truth," I said. "I told you that you wouldn't believe it. You gonna let me go now?"

"Oh, hell no," Dean said. "That's the craziest thing I've ever heard. You're stoned out of your mind or insane. Either way, I'm going to put you in the drunk tank until you have a chance to sleep it off."

"You got any aspirin?" I asked.

"Sure," he said, and got up to get it.

My head ached horribly, and I was pretty sure I hadn't heard the end of this, but I was clear for now. "Next time, Dresden," I muttered to myself, "just take the gold."

Then Officer Dean put me in a nice quiet cell with a nice quiet cot, and there I stayed until Wild Bill Meyers showed up the next morning and bailed me out.

★　★　★

Author's Bio:
Jim Butcher enjoys fencing, martial arts, singing, bad science-fiction movies, and live-action gaming. He lives in Missouri with his wife, son, and a vicious guard dog. You may learn more at **www.jim-butcher.com**.

HOLLY'S BALM

by RACHEL CAINE

AUTHOR'S NOTE: Andy and Holly also appear in a short story entitled "Death Warmed Over" in the anthology Strange Brew (2010).

You have to have a strong stomach if you're a witch—especially one who deals in potions, because potions in general are not made out of, say, sweet herbs and baby's breath. But still, as I opened my front door and stepped in, and dropped my bag on the chair, the smell hit me like an iron skillet to the face.

I gagged, covered my mouth and nose, and fought down an overpowering impulse to turn around and leave.

But that wouldn't do because it was my house, and besides, there was no way I was going to let on how bad that stench actually had hit me. I was a *professional,* dammit.

Although it was, in fact, *really* bad. I blinked, wiped tears away from my eyes, locked the door behind me, and took several self-abusing deep breaths before my gag reflex subsided and my body adjusted to the new, foully odorous reality. It was all the worse because I had a great house. It should have smelled like vanilla and cinnamon, maybe, not like rotting corpses and cancer, with a high note of ancient, sweaty armpits.

"Honey?" I tried to sound concerned, but positive, which was somewhat spoiled by my holding my nose. "Um . . . what died?" I followed the smell into the big open kitchen, where Andrew Toland, dressed in my best apron, the one with red lace trim, was stirring a gigantic pot on top of the stove. Andy has a wicked sharp smile that was balanced by warm, disarming brown eyes; it's a face that's young in years but has lines of character that speak of the hard times and experiences. Shaggy brown hair that I couldn't convince him to trim into a more modern style.

"That had *better* not be our dinner," I said. "Or you are a dead man."

He smiled even wider. "That seem at all redundant to you, Holly Anne?"

He was right, it was redundant, because Andy Toland was, fact, already dead. He'd died back in the Old West days, fighting the world's worst zombie war; he'd rested in peace for a long time after that, before a resurrection witch—me, in fact—brought him back to help find a ruthless killer, one with the same powers of life and death that I had. I was moderately powerful, I supposed, but Andy was, and always had been, in a class by himself.

Which was why he was standing here in my kitchen, brewing up some foul concoction, instead of resting in peace in his grave. He was powerful, and he was determined, and he was in love. With *me*. God help me, I was crazy in love with him, too. Somehow, that was a stronger magic than any potion I'd ever brewed because it kept him alive in defiance of all the laws of resurrection magic. The supernatural rules said that someone brought back would get weaker exponentially the longer they stayed—that they'd be overtaken by pain and dragged back into the dark no matter how much a resurrection witch struggled to keep them alive. I'd never been able to sustain anyone I'd resurrected for longer than a couple of days.

Andy had been alive now for almost three months, and although he regularly brewed himself up a maintenance potion, he wasn't declining. Not at all. He'd never shown a moment of pain, weakness, or distraction.

It was a nine days' wonder in the magical world. I was

surprised we weren't besieged by researchers, but Andy's reaction to the first few who's buttonholed us had been swift and decisive enough to drive them off—or, more accurately, to send them circling like vultures. They could afford to wait. He wasn't going anywhere. That was kind of the whole point.

"Hi, pretty lady," he said, and kissed me lightly on the nose I was still holding closed. "How was your day?"

"Miserable, but what else is new? It's the same office job as yesterday, only fifty percent more boring now that everyone avoids me." I'd always tried to keep my day job separate from what I did in my off-hours—translation, witchcraft—but now that the word was out, I was treated like a pariah. Not that it was much of a change, actually.

"That'd be their loss, Holly Anne. Never met anybody less worth avoiding than you."

I couldn't help it. I let go of my nose and kissed him back, on the lips. "You know I have to ask," I said. "What the hell *is* that stench?" When I looked down into the stockpot, I saw a thick red potion threaded with veins of silver. He was stirring with a long-handled silver spoon, so it had a ritual component as well as the basic magical chemistry. Close-up, the smell was so thick, it was like dense London fog. Even though I held my breath, I could taste it heavy in my mouth.

"Damn, I was hoping it'd be done before you got here," he said, and checked his watch—not a wristwatch, an old-fashioned pocket watch, on a chain, although he'd finally stopped wearing a vest around the house and stuck the timepiece in his jeans pocket instead. "Sorry. I promise, it gets better."

"It couldn't get any worse," I said miserably. It came out muffled and indistinct because I had both hands clapped over my nose and mouth. My eyes were watering. I honestly couldn't understand how he could stand so close to that awful stench and not collapse. Maybe it was a sturdiness one acquired after death, but my knees were getting weak already. "I'll never get the smell out of here! Andy, sweetheart, this is where I *cook food!*"

"I know. Trust me?" He gave me the look I could never resist—puppy dog eyes and an endearingly vulnerable smile. "Here, how about we let this cook a while? I want to welcome you home proper."

"Can you leave it?"

"Well—for a bit, anyway."

I didn't wait for a second invitation to run away, and escaped out into the relatively clear air of the living room, where I gulped down breaths and wiped tears from my cheeks. Andy followed me at a more dignified pace. He overlooked my quiet gagging and let me get my bearings before he hugged me, then kissed me, and oh, that was nice. It almost made up for what he'd done to the house.

That might have gone to sweetly intimate places, in fact, except that, just then, my cell phone rang.

We both froze because my number was strictly private— only a few people had it, and one of them was my call screener, who qualified jobs for me. Her name was Melaine, and she was a brisk, funny, no-nonsense woman who seemed to regard taking messages for doctors and for witches as being pretty much the same thing. That was a rarity in Texas—even in Austin, which prided itself on diversity and tolerance for the most part. Witches were never going to be welcome in most Bible Belt towns, what with the scriptural death sentence and all.

I flipped open the cell, and said, "Melaine?"

"Hey, Miss Caldwell," her bright, calm voice said on the other end. "I got an urgent call for you from a Detective . . . Prieto? He says you know him."

I knew Detective Prieto, all right. A chill settled over me and quickly deepened to artic levels. "Go on," I said. Next to me, Andy watched, waiting and still.

"Here's his number—" She read it off slowly, making sure I had it before moving on. "He says that he needs you to look at a crime scene, right away. He gave me the address."

I scribbled down the information on a sheet of paper. "Did he say anything else?"

"Not really." Melaine paused for a moment, then said, "He sounded a little weird, actually."

My pencil stopped midnote. "Weird, how?"

"Shaky. And I'm married to a cop. I've never heard a police officer sound like that. He seemed—spooked."

That didn't make my bad feeling go away. In fact, it intensified. "Okay," I said. "Please call him back and tell him I'll meet him there in twenty minutes."

"Will do." Melaine rang off.

Andy was watching me, and he was still holding my free hand. "You look like it's something nasty."

"Probably," I said. "I'm sorry, honey. I have to go." Normally, I would have asked him to accompany me, but if he had a potion on the stove, there was no way he could. "You *did* say that will smell better, right?"

"Cross my heart," he said, and kissed me again. I stepped back and straightened my shirt, which had somehow gotten a little rumpled, then checked my office skirt and sensible low-heeled shoes. They looked approximately crime scene appropriate.

"You look just fine," he assured me, and gave me that crooked, intimate smile that made the thrill set in much deeper. "Better out of all that getup, but—"

"Mind your manners, you roughneck heathen."

"Yes, ma'am, I won't embarrass you in public. But in private, I'll be happy to make you blush all you want, anywhere you want. You just say the word."

Oh, how I wished I could. Instead, I said, "The call was from Detective Prieto. He's got a crime scene."

Andy's smile disappeared, and his body language shifted in

subtle, dangerous ways. Old West gunfighter kind of ways. He suddenly looked loose-limbed, rangy, and very dangerous. "How's that old dog?"

"Still hunting," I said. "And I think he might have caught something bad he needs my help with."

Andy nodded slowly, eyes gone dark and far away. "Wish I could go with you, sweetheart. I don't like sending you off alone, something like this."

"That's nice, but you know, I did get along just fine for years on my own without being chaperoned by a big, strong man."

That got me a small grin. "Still don't like seeing women go running off into the dark unescorted," he said. "I know it's a more civilized time, but that don't mean there ain't wolves out there."

Oh, I knew that, almost as well as he did. "Chauvinist," I said.

"I'll have you know I was raised Lutheran, missy."

That made me laugh, then cough, because the smell coming from the kitchen had, if anything, intensified. "I think something's burning," I said, and Andy gave me another peck on the cheek and went back to his stirring.

I got out my own go-bag, which I kept stocked for emergencies. Nothing but basic supplies, because if I was asked to do any kind of full resurrection, it would take days of time and effort to complete brewing up the necessary potions anyway.

In the bottom, I had tucked a legal-to-carry Smith & Wesson semiautomatic pistol.

Welcome to Texas.

I had no doubt that if Andy had joined me, he'd have had guns in his bag as well. And knives. And probably high explosives. Even in Texas, though, some of that wasn't legal to carry around, so we usually just left it as an ignorance-is-bliss kind of thing.

I was, unexpectedly, feeling a little vulnerable without him at my side.

"Holly Anne?"

He was watching me from the kitchen doorway, spoon still in his hand. He looked adorable in that apron.

I looked into his face and saw the concern. I managed a faint smile. "I'm fine," I said. "Honest. No worries, okay?"

"All right," he said. He didn't sound convinced, but then, I didn't feel too solid about it, either. Resurrection witches were not the first call from detectives on any police force, not since the laws had changed banning the testimony of the deceased. So it took something powerfully wrong for Detective Prieto to be speed-dialing me.

I was heading into something awful. I could just smell it, just like the stuff Andy was cooking on my stove.

"When you come back here, I promise, I'll have all this cleaned up," he said.

I kissed him again, quickly, and escaped the smell . . . but I had a grim feeling that it was going to be the least of my problems this evening.

The address Melaine had given me was in an industrial area of Austin; industrial areas have a certain sameness to them no matter where you are in the world. Little in the way of nature had survived here, except in the artificially maintained entrance to the business park. My headlights caught the name on the sign as we turned, and I felt a startled shock of recognition.

HIGHLAND LAKES INDUSTRIAL AND BUSINESS COMMUNITY. Yes, I'd been here before. I'd seen that dour-looking Scotsman in a kilt on the sign before. When had I . . .

Oh.

Yes, that was a bad feeling sinking through my chest, very bad indeed. I completed the turn and headed for where I saw a whole carnival of flashing red and blue lights in the distance, reflecting off the side of a building.

I'd been here before, all right; it was one of my most vivid, horrible memories.

Maybe it's a coincidence, I thought.

I should have known better.

As I pulled up to the police barricade blocking off the area, I spotted Detective Prieto. He waved away the uniformed officer who was trying to stop me and leaned in the car window. Prieto had that hard, world-weary air that many detectives sported, coated with a thick outer shell of cynical realism. "So. You're alone? Isn't your dead boyfriend still lurking somewhere?"

"Why, does it bother you?" I asked him, and couldn't control a chill in my tone.

"Won't keep me up nights."

"You asked *me* here, Detective. We're not getting off to a good start."

He shrugged. "It's that kind of night. Drive around the corner. Park next to the meat wagon."

As I pulled to a stop, the sense of familiarity deepened. It wasn't just the same industrial park and building. It was the same damn *spot.* That was just too weird to be coincidental. I turned off the engine and sat in silence for a few seconds, thinking. I wanted to get back into the car and drive away, but the fact was, I couldn't turn down a request from the police. Witches had a tough enough time as it was, with the Bible thumpers trying to get us hanged, burned, or drowned in a dunking chair. We *needed* the cops to like us. Even Prieto.

So I got out, shivering a little in the evening chill, and grabbed my bag out of the back.

Prieto caught up with me, slumped and tired but still walking fast. "Thanks for coming," he said, not as if he in any way meant it. "According to the files, you were involved in the last one. Figured we could get your take on what was going on here."

"Last one?"

"You'll see."

Up ahead, a knot of people were working—most of them crime scene technicians, collecting microscopic evidence, photographing, bagging, tagging. We stopped at the edge of the taped-off area, and Prieto waved over one of the team.

"Tell them, Greg," he said. He made the rest of them step away to give us a clear view. Once I had it, I didn't really need the update because illuminated by harsh floodlights, the scene told me everything.

What I faced was . . . monstrous.

And it was like having the worst case of déjà vu in the world . . . a traumatic flashback made real, flesh and blood, so much blood. I'd been here before, stood here before, seen this *before.*

I don't know how I managed not to throw up, or faint, or at least turn away, but I forced myself to look at all the details, searching for something, *anything,* that would break me out of the nightmare.

But it was all the *same.*

The forensic tech studied me curiously for a second before shrugging off his questions about why he'd be talking to me at all. "Well, I'm sure you can see most of it. Victim is about eighteen years old. Pretty nasty, even for this kind of thing. You can see the mutilation from here; blood evidence tells us it was mostly done while she was still alive. She's been dead about four hours, best we can ballpark it right now. No ID yet. Not much in the way of trace evidence, either. This is real similar to a case we had about a year ago. Same location. Same age of victim."

"No." I said it softly, my gaze fixed on the pale, blood-spattered face of the girl. "Not the same age as that victim. She's the *same* victim."

Prieto was staring at me, and I knew he'd been thinking the

same exact thing but had wanted confirmation. "I thought maybe it was just a close resemblance."

"It's not. DNA will confirm. It's the *same girl*, Daniel," I said. Prieto nodded.

The crime scene tech frowned. "Well, obviously, that can't be the case," he said. "That isn't possible."

I took in a breath. "Yes, it is. She's been brought back by a resurrection witch, then killed again. The same way. In the same place." I felt sick but oddly steady. I understood this now. I understood why I was here. Prieto hadn't known, but he'd at least had a suspicion. "My God. He killed her all over again."

The tech—Greg?—seemed to go still for a moment, as if he was running that through his head a few times for clarity. "I'm . . . sorry. And how exactly would you know that?"

"Because I consulted on the first case," I said. *Consulted* was a euphemism, of course; I'd brought back this victim from the dead myself. I'd asked her who'd killed her, but she'd been so traumatized and hysterical that it hadn't worked at all. I'd had to let her go without an answer. "They never caught him," I said. "Detective . . . I think he's found a way to relive his kills in a brand-new way—not just with trophies or memories or recordings. He's found a way to actually repeat them."

Prieto had gone pale because he knew what I was talking about now, and the enormity of it was starting to hit him like a falling wall. "If it's the same man, he has six kills on his list."

The world was spinning around me, wobbling like a top, and I had to focus hard to avoid feeling sick with it. "He just realized that it was safer to do it this way," I said. "There's no law against torturing and killing the dead. No law at all. As long as he can get a resurrection witch to go along with it, he can keep on going, and there's nothing we can do to stop him. Nothing legal, anyway."

"Fucking *hell*—" Prieto suddenly turned away, overcome and unwilling to let me see it. I waited for it to hit, too, but all I felt was a black sense of betrayal and inevitability. As if I'd known, deep down, that something would never rest safely in the grave about this case, this murderer, these victims.

Prieto paced, head down, then swung back on me. "It's a fucking witch working with him," he said. "One of yours. No, two of yours, right? One to create the shell, the avatar—that's a different skill set. Then a resurrection witch to put the life back in."

"Maybe this isn't what it looks like." I said that, but my heart wasn't in it. I just didn't *want* it to be true because no matter who did it, we all had a share of that kind of guilt.

"Don't try to tell me this isn't on one of *you*. It's *witches* doing this shit. What the hell is this, eh? Legal murder?" Prieto was about one second from shoving me, from the wild, angry glitter in his eyes. "Necrophiliac sons of bitches! What kind of sick fucking sadists *are* you tweaks?"

I was glad Andy wasn't with me. He'd have punched Prieto for using language like that in front of a lady, but I didn't care; he was right. Sickeningly right.

I found that the words just came, all on their own. "I'm the kind that stops *that* kind," I said. "Or dies trying."

Prieto had pulled the case files, and he had them in his car. Not a stupid man, by any means. He'd assumed it was a copycat killing, but his forward thinking saved me valuable time, and it might even save a life, although the legal system wouldn't quite see it that way.

"They're wasting their time, your forensic people," I said. "It isn't a crime to kill the dead."

Prieto sent me a scorching-hot glare. "No," he finally said. "Resurrected people don't have any rights, you know that. So it wouldn't be murder to kill them, no matter how sick it is."

"And whoever this is, he's counting on that," I said. "He's a serial killer who's discovered a way to get his thrills without nearly as much risk." I felt sick again and had to swallow hard to control myself. "The victims will remember, you know," I said. "Dying before. All the pain and terror. It would only be worse this time because they'll know it's coming."

"You ever heard of anything like this before? People bringing back the dead for their own version of fun?" Prieto asked. I shook my head, but it was a silent lie. The resurrection business, like the mortuary business, attracted its share of mentally and emotionally broken people. The witch community generally policed its own, and as those kinds of offenders were noticed, they were dealt with. Quietly. With prejudice.

I'd heard of one or two rapists who revived the dead to attack them before letting them slip away again. A few who got their kicks torturing. I'd never heard of one turning serial killer, or someone enabling one. How had he—or, God help us, she—slipped through the cracks? And if you counted the witch who'd created the shell, that made *two* of them who were guilty and keeping their silence.

Sickening didn't really cover it.

"So how do we start?" Prieto asked. "Do we go back to the parents?"

I shuddered. "No. The last thing we should do is let them know about this," I said. "Bad enough they lost a daughter so horribly in the first place, but to know she went through it *again,* just as horribly . . . we'd be continuing their torture, not relieving it."

Prieto looked even sicker as he ran it through his head. "Okay. So where's our starting point?"

I held up a file. "We could try working it from the burials. An avatar witch needs a piece of the real person to make the physical body—bone, hair, flesh, blood. You start exhuming them and see if any of the bodies have been tampered with; I'll bet you find they've all had samples taken. If I understand forensic rules properly, he—or she—should have left some trace evidence behind in the process—digging up a body is a messy, sweaty business."

"And what will you be doing?"

"Tracking avatar witches. There aren't more than a few dozen of them in this state; it isn't a common skill in our circles, and they all have to be licensed."

"Couldn't it be somebody out of state? Somebody brought in just for this purpose?"

"Sure," I said, and shrugged. "But we're a close-knit community. Someone will know something about it, even if it's just the supply shops who furnish what we need."

"How am I supposed to get bodies exhumed? I need family consent," Prieto said. "What kind of excuse am I supposed to use for that?"

"The serial killer's struck again, but you have a revolutionary new scientific technique that wasn't available before," I said. "As far as I can tell, most people don't understand science any better than they understand resurrection magic. Families will give you permission for the exhumation, almost certainly, if you tell them it will help us catch him."

"You mean, if I lie my ass off to them."

"Do you want this stopped, or not?" I thought about it for a few seconds, and continued, cautiously, "There's a third thing we can do. We can keep an eye on the dump sites. He reused one, he might reuse others. These places mean something to him."

"Well, that's a problem," Prieto said. "This isn't officially a crime, and overtime's not something we can throw around like confetti; our budget's stretched so thin it squeaks. There are five other dump sites. Can't cover them all, especially not during the night."

"I'll take the one that comes next in the series," I said. "Just in case he sticks to the pattern."

"Not by yourself, you're not," Prieto said.

"Andy could—"

He made a sharp movement and cut me off. "I want one of mine in on it," he said. "I'll find a volunteer. You want to bring Toland along, that's on you, but I need somebody who isn't on the side of the witches."

That was insulting, but I understood his position, really. He didn't trust witches in general, and if he sometimes, grudgingly accepted me, that was only a temporary thing.

"Fine," I said. "You put whoever you want with us. But I'm definitely going."

Prieto nodded, got out of the car, and began giving orders to break down his investigation.

Andy and I would find these people.

And when we did . . . hell would descend if Andy had anything to say about it.

I braced myself at the front door for the smell. On top of the trauma of the evening, I wasn't sure that I could really face it, but I needed to see Andy. I needed to talk to him about all this, pour my heart out, tell him just how awful I felt. He was the only one I *could* tell.

I unlocked the door and came inside, locked it, and realized that I was holding my breath, dreading the moment . . . but I forced myself to relax.

And the smell that washed over me was nothing like what I'd been imagining. It was unbelievably sweet and clean and lovely, and I found myself closing my eyes in an explosion of sensual ecstasy. I moaned in utter satisfaction and sank bonelessly into the nearest chair as it rolled over me and through me, taking all of my day's frustration and exhaustion along with it.

The ultimate aromatherapy.

"Wow," I said dreamily.

"See?" Andy said. I opened my eyes—I hadn't even realized that I'd closed them—and saw him standing in front of me, arms folded, smiling. "I promised it'd get better, didn't I?"

"Wow." It was all I could really manage. The only thing I could compare this feeling to was that of waking up safe in his arms in the hush of the early morning after a fantastic night of sex and sleep. "That is—wow." I was a pretty fair potion maker, but this—this was a master class, and it was beyond amazing.

Andy helped me stand up, then he put his arms around me and kissed me, and for a man wearing a girly apron he kissed with a lot of authority and great skill. It took awhile before I was able to get my head together enough to murmur, "What *is* that stuff?"

"I damn sure hope you don't mean what I just did with my lips because I thought I gave it a real good effort, and it was pretty clear—"

"The potion, Andy."

"Little something I developed back in the day. I made it mostly for you," he said, meeting my eyes and holding them. "Just wanted you to not feel so damn bad every day you come dragging home from that office place. It's not right that you work so hard like that."

"I know, I know, you can earn money, I'm sure it's against your Old West code to have your girl out working for living. But I—we—need the paycheck. The resurrection business isn't what it used to be. The last job I had barely covered a month's mortgage after I paid for supplies."

"Don't you mock my code, ma'am, it was the way I was brought up. It rubs me raw not to take care of a good woman the way I should." He hesitated, then said, "I've got something for you."

"Something more than this? Because this is *amazing*." I inhaled that intoxicating aroma again. It was the human equivalent of catnip, that smell.

"I've been taking on some side jobs," he said, and dug something out of his pocket. "Here."

It was a roll of cash. A huge roll. I blinked, weighed it, and focused on the numbers that showed at the front.

That was a *hundred-dollar bill.* "Andy . . ." I took the rubber band off and fanned the cash out. It was all hundreds. At a quick estimate, I was holding at least five thousand dollars. "Oh my God. How—?"

"Told you. Side jobs." He smiled and kissed my nose again. "Make you feel any better?"

"My *God.* That's just—" I blew out a breath, searching for some word to describe how I felt, and failing miserably. "Amazing. Thank you."

His dark eyes were intent on me, a little wary, but mostly pleased. "So I did all right?"

"You didn't have to do this." I put my hand gently against his face, and he kissed my palm without breaking eye contact. "We don't know how much energy you can expend without hurting yourself. Doing anything magical without me . . . that's dangerous, Andy."

He shrugged. "Spent most of my life on the edge, sweetness. Ain't like dangerous is new territory to me."

That frightened me. I loved Andy, and I knew he loved me, but the little voice in my head kept insisting that I not get too comfy. All of this between us, it was so tenuous, so fragile, so essentially *wrong* according to the laws of magic. Everyone who was resurrected was eventually drawn back into the dark; he'd lasted so much longer than the others, but . . . I knew it would happen. And I dreaded it.

I'd have to let him go someday. I knew it.

"Hey," Andy said, and tapped me on the nose again. "Stop woolgathering. What's eating at you? I thought the money would make it better."

"It does." I took in another calming breath of potion and smiled at him. "You said the potion was mostly for me, and believe me, I appreciate it . . . who's it for after me?"

He shrugged. "Folks," he said. "I figure since they're bound and determined to make me into some kind of hero, I might as well make a nickel from it. It's a nice potion, real safe, too. Do some good, maybe. It wouldn't hurt me none to make some more to help out with the accounts, either."

More of his wounded pride, I realized. And the fact that just maybe, he was feeling a wee bit useless in this modern world of ours, where his skills weren't so much in demand—although they almost certainly would be as soon as word got out about this singularly spectacular potion. Which led me to ask, "What's it called?"

He grinned. "Holly's Balm."

That was such a delicious notion that for a moment I actually forgot what I had to talk to him about . . . but it came back, insidious and dark, and not even the beautiful gift he'd made for me could hold it back.

I took his hand, and said, "Sit down a minute."

He did, never taking his gaze from mine, and said, "I should have asked you what Prieto called you out for. I'm guessing it ain't even half as good as bad."

"Awful," I agreed. "Last year, there were a series of murders of young women, and it was . . . gruesome, Andy. Really nasty. I was asked to bring one back, but she—there was too much trauma."

He didn't say anything, but I saw the muscles tighten in his jaw. He knew what I meant. Bringing someone back meant breathing your own essence into them, mingling with them, becoming—at least for a time—part of them. The trauma hadn't been only hers, of course. I'd been heavily medicated, after. That kind of crime took a special toll on a witch.

"I'm guessing that's not the end of it," he said, "bad as that is."

"The crime scene I was called out to tonight . . . it was the same one."

"Same killer?"

"Same victim," I said. "Killed all over again. Resurrected. She was *resurrected,* Andy. Just so he could do it again to her."

I'd never seen that look before, not on Andy–not on anyone, really. I didn't even know what it *meant,* except that it shook him all the way to the bones.

He dropped my hand as if it had caught fire, then he stood up and paced away—just a few steps, but enough to put a world of distance between us. "Somebody brought her back," he said. "One of us. Even if the witch didn't know what would happen up front, it was damn clear once it got started."

"Someone got paid to participate," I agreed. "To hold that soul there while he did it. Why else would a witch let that happen?"

"Unless the witch is the killer."

That was disturbing. *Really* disturbing. I didn't honestly want to think that far . . . bad enough someone would have taken money and stood by while something like that was done, but I just didn't want to believe in that next step. "It gets worse," I said. "Somebody had to make the avatar."

Andy slowly turned around. He leaned his back against the wall, folded his arms over his chest, and said, "So we'll be on the hunt," he said. "Ain't no crime, is it? Killing a dead girl."

"No, it's not a crime, technically. Prieto can't do much. So it'll be up to us to make this right."

"Let me make some calls," he said.

"Andy. I want this one destroyed," I said softly. "No prisoners."

He didn't look at me, and there was a tension in his body that wasn't usual for him. "We find this resurrection witch, we burn him right down to the ground and piss on his ashes. I don't hold with this. I don't hold with it at all." And from the unforgiving look on his face, I knew he meant every word. "And then we find this killing son of a bitch and do him hard."

I noticed, although I wasn't sure why, that he hadn't mentioned the witch who created the shell.

Not at all.

* * *

I slipped into the kitchen chair across from Andy as he studied a black notebook—his own contacts, written in some strange shorthand he'd used over a hundred years ago. He'd donned a pair of reading glasses that he'd found lying around. They were hot pink, with little fake diamonds sparkling in the corners. It woke a wan spark of amusement in me. As with the apron, it took a real man to wear those and not look uncomfortable.

"You're calling your people?" I asked. He stretched, and one of the pearl snap buttons on his shirt popped loose, revealing a well-defined but scarred chest.

"Yeah, I thought I'd best. I made some these last few months that probably ain't in your formal books." I could believe that; Andy seemed to slide into the underbelly of our witch-world with alarming ease. He'd probably made friends with shady characters who'd never even think of talking to me—or that I'd dare call up, either. "You want to make your own calls down here?"

"Best if we don't distract each other," I said. "I'm going to use a falsehood potion. You want some?"

"Day I can't tell if one of these bottom-feeders is lying to me is the day you ought to put me back in the ground," he said. "No thanks."

He sounded all business. There was a dark, angry edge to him that made me feel . . . oddly excluded.

"Okay," I said. "I'll stay out of your way. Give me five minutes for the potion."

While the potion brewed, I pondered my approach. It was a delicate business; witches were licensed by the state, but we were also secretive and protective of each other because in many places, there had been trouble: cross burnings on lawns, arson, beatings. We weren't a friendly, close-connected bunch. I'd have to work hard to get to those who might have information to share.

Andy was silent, flipping through his book. I kissed his cheek as I filled up my teacup with the potion, and he nodded in distraction. I walked toward the stairs.

"Holly Anne," he said. I glanced back. "I'm sorry. This got to me pretty hard."

"Me too," I said. "No apology necessary. I'll see you in a bit."

I sat at my desk and sipped potion for about ten minutes; it wasn't unpleasant, sort of like a milky version of chamomile tea. The magic would give me an unmistakable signal if someone lied to me . . . and I had every expectation that someone would.

I made thirty calls in an hour and got two vague falsehoods out of it; they were probably nothing, but I made notes by the names anyway. My circle of contacts included resurrection and potion witches, but the witches who made the avatars . . . the bodies that we poured life back into . . . they were a different story altogether. Very hard to find. There were three listed contacts in the state for those with that particular skill set, available only through the witches' network; I spoke with all of them and hit a brick wall. Two hung up on me without speaking.

"I'm so sorry," said the last one—no name, but a brisk female voice that sounded grandmotherly, with a hint of Eastern Europe in her accent. "Client requests are confidential. You understand how this must be."

"It's possible that avatar are being used for . . . criminal reasons," I said. "You don't want that kind of attention, trust me."

"No, we definitely do not. But the fact remains, *if* one of our technicians created the body you're speaking of, what was made of it later has nothing to do with us. We do not restore life. We only create flesh."

"I know," I said. "But I also know that sometimes the bodies you create go for . . . other purposes."

"What other purposes?" She sounded scornful, but already, the lie-detector potion was tingling its warning message over my skin. "I do not know of these."

"Oh, come on. It's common knowledge in the trade that

some of the less scrupulous witches create bodies for use by, uh, men with unusual appetites. Or for medical use. Right?"

"Rumors. Nothing more."

"Well, this goes far beyond that," I said. "This is a body being used to house a restored spirit. One who was murdered. One who was murdered *again,* made to feel the same horror and torture *again.* And this time, she would have known it was coming. Can you even imagine that?"

She was silent for a long, long moment. "That is a great sin. A great betrayal."

"Yes. Yes, it is. I need your help, ma'am. I need to find out who hired this body to be made. He's probably asking for others, too. They'll face the same fate unless we can stop him."

She hesitated, then said, "There are other kinds of justice. Older kinds."

"Yes, ma'am. And we're going to do that, but I need a lead. Something. *Anything.*"

She fell silent. I listened to her breathe, and waited, biting my tongue because I wanted to sell her harder but knowing that it was the wrong move. She'd do it, or she wouldn't. I couldn't force it.

"I will think on this," she said. "Perhaps you will receive a call back, but it won't be from me." She hung up with a soft click, and I stared at the phone for a moment. I didn't have any contact information for her, not even a place to start; the number she was using went through a privacy exchange, and that would take a lot more firepower to crack than I could bring to bear.

With nothing left to do, I carried my empty teacup downstairs and rinsed it out in the sink. Andy had left a half-full cup of coffee there on the counter, and most of a sandwich, but there was no sign of him. Even his notebook was gone. I called his name, but got no reply.

And then I saw the note on the table. *Gone to check a lead,* it said, in his careful, flowing script, the kind nobody really teaches kids anymore. *Keep the doors locked tonight. Be back in the morning.*

I would have expected him to actually *tell* me this since I was upstairs, but then again, I'd had the door shut, and he'd have known that getting distracted when using a lie-detecting potion is bad. Well, at least he'd left me a note.

I felt abandoned, nevertheless. I'd wanted to talk to him about all this, really talk . . . and I needed to be held, too. It bothered me how much I missed him; I'd always been self-sufficient before I'd met him.

Now, I thought of *me* as part of *us.* Was that a good thing? I really wasn't sure, but the idea of voluntarily walking away from Andy and just being me, solitary, again . . . that wasn't what I wanted, either.

I just wanted us to *talk,* and evidently I wasn't going to get what I wanted tonight.

Tonight. Oh God, I'd forgotten to tell him about Prieto, and what we'd agreed about the stakeout on the next dump site. I checked my cell phone, which I'd left in my purse in the other room, and found two calls from the policeman, and one voice mail. The recording cussed me out and told me to call if I still intended to do this thing, dammit.

Andy had told me to stay in and lock the doors, but *he'd* gone off following a lead. There was no reason I couldn't do the same. Besides, I'd have company—*police* company at that. It was like having my own personal bodyguard.

I dialed Prieto. He answered on the second ring, tired and surly as usual. "Sorry," I said. "I was following up on potential leads."

"Anything?"

"Not really. I have to wait for someone to get back to me."

"Still want to do the stakeout tonight?"

"Yes," I said. "It's just me. Andy won't be available."

"Neither am I," Prieto grunted. "Got other cases I gotta work. Greg said he'd take a shift with you overnight, he's off tomorrow."

"Greg . . . ?"

"Crime scene geek, you met him. Greg Kincaid. You want him to swing by and pick you up?"

"Yes, I guess so. Anything I should bring?"

"You want anything to eat or drink, bring it. I don't trust anything those CSI freaks bring out of their lab fridges; you don't know what's been sitting next to it. You got my number if anything happens."

"Thanks," I said, then hesitated before saying, "Do you think we'll get him?"

"Doubt it," he said. I'd never heard Prieto sound quite that dour. "I can't throw any real resources at this. If he gets got, it'll be your witches, probably."

That was depressing because I wasn't feeling a lot of love from the witch community for this, and Andy . . . well, Andy would do his best, and his best was incredible, but it was just the two of us, so far.

Maybe the stakeout would be lucky.

I hung up with Prieto and changed into comfy clothes, packed snacks and water, and was ready and waiting at the door when a dark blue late-model sedan pulled up at the curb. The passenger window rolled down, and the driver leaned across the seat to look out at me.

"Miss Caldwell?" he asked. I remembered him now, from the crime scene. He wasn't especially, well, anything . . . a pleasant, rounded face, and a nice smile. He was probably in his late twenties. "Sure hope you brought snacks."

"Greg, right?" I opened the door and got in, putting the bag on the floor between my feet as I strapped myself in. "Do you like potato chips?"

"Who doesn't? Bonus points if you brought dip."

"Ranch," I said, and returned his smile. "And just what are you bringing to the table?"

"A fearless sense of adventure," Greg said, "also, beef jerky. Aren't we waiting for your boyfriend? Prieto said something about him tagging along."

"He can't make it. Guess you're stuck with me."

He flashed me another of those warm, comfortable smiles. "Not a problem, trust me." It wasn't *quite* flirting . . . there was a little something more than just being sociable, but not enough that I'd feel hit on. Masterfully done. He reached over and punched some buttons in the dash, and the GPS lit up. "You know, even if he does do this again tonight—which personally I kind of doubt—he doesn't have to keep the same order of dump sites. I wouldn't, if it were me. So don't get your hopes up that we're going to heroically save somebody tonight."

"I'm not," I said. "He doesn't kill them where he dumps them, anyway. By the time we see him—if we do—the victim will already be past saving."

Greg nodded as he drove down my residential street. He took a right at the main intersection. "Of course, you could say they're sort of past saving anyway," he said. "I mean, from what Prieto said . . . these are his previous victims, right? He's sort of reliving his greatest hits. Technically, it's not even murder. I guess you could argue improper disposal of a body, but . . ."

"It's murder," I said flatly. Greg's ability to blithely reduce these young women to objects—to *corpses*—without value chilled me, even though I knew that he was right, from the standpoint of legalities. "They still feel everything he does to them. How can it be anything *but* murder?"

He cast me a sideways look, raised his eyebrows, and said, "Sorry. I didn't mean anything by it. I was just talking about—"

"The law," I said. "Yes, I know. But these girls never got any

law on their side, did they? Nobody was ever caught and punished, and now to say that he can just do it all over *again* . . ."

"Maybe it's not the same guy at all. Maybe it's a, a groupie or
something."

That was yet another sickening thought, but I doubted it;
there had been too close a similarity in the small details of the
crime scene. That wasn't the work of a copycat unless the copycat had been given access to all of the police's data.

We'd strayed pretty far from the otherwise pleasant talk about
potato chips and ranch dip, and I already missed the comfort of
that, even if it was false. As if he sensed that, Greg started a running monologue about the neighborhoods we were passing—it
was entertaining, if still a bit morbid, since he'd only been around
here on official business, and business was apparently pretty good.
By the time the GPS's stern feminine voice announced we'd
arrived at our destination, he'd given me a whole new appreciation for the ghosts that haunted even this relatively benign section
of Austin.

The second dump site was an empty, overgrown field, which
in this time of year meant lots of dry, tangled weeds grown up
to about knee height. It was dark, and the streetlights only cast
a vague suggestion in the lot's direction. We parked down the
street in front of a small bodega that advertised homemade
tacos and tortillas, and Greg turned off the engine.

"That's it," he said, and nodded toward the vacant lot. "The
body was found there almost exactly twenty-four hours after
the first victim was discovered. Forensics were pretty much a
dead end; vacant lots are hell for working any trace evidence,
and there was nothing of any use on the body itself."

"Did you work the case?" I asked.

He shook his head. "Before my time," he said. "I joined about
seven months ago. I read up on it since Prieto told me what was
going on." He settled back in his seat with a sigh and unbuckled
the safety belt. "Better get comfortable. We may be here a while."

"Shouldn't we check the lot first?" I asked. "Just to make sure it hasn't already happened?"

Greg stared out the windshield for a moment, unmoving, and then said, "Yeah, I guess that's probably a good idea. Want to go with me?"

"I'll wait here." I was happy to let him go tramping off in the dark. I had my cell phone out, just in case, but Greg's expedition—aided by a flashlight—was evidently unsuccessful. As he came back, I got the cheerful chime for a text message, which almost startled me into dropping the phone.

Andy had texted me, which was odd; I didn't think he was comfortable enough with the technology to actually type out messages. But it came from his number, and read, KEEP DOORS LOCKED WILL BE HOME BY 8 AM.

Well, technically, I wasn't breaking the rules. I had the *car* doors locked though I thumbed the control to let Greg back in. He took his seat, stowed the flashlight again, and said, "Nothing out there but the usual trash, condoms and crack vials."

That was a relief, but it also made it that much more imperative we stay awake and alert. I broke out the water first, then the chips and dip. Greg didn't say much for a while, and I was okay with that. I was busy worrying about where Andy was, and what he was doing. Surely, it was a lot more dangerous than this.

"Can I call you Holly?" Greg suddenly asked, as I scraped up the last of the ranch dip onto a scrap of chip from the bottom of the bag. "Sorry, that was sudden, wasn't it? Calling you Miss Caldwell all night just seems awkward. Like I'm back in school."

"Holly's fine," I assured him.

"I was just wondering how you got into all this. Not this, meaning the stakeout, but—"

"The witch business?" I smiled a little. "What's a nice girl like you doing in a thing like that?"

"Something like that."

I shrugged. "I was studying for a degree in chemistry when I discovered that I had kind of a gift—I could combine chemicals, and they didn't exactly follow the normal rules of engagement that they did for other people. My professor finally said that I had an unusual talent and gave me the name of a counselor who could tell me something about it. It wasn't that I started out to be one. It just happened."

"Sounds like what I do," Greg said, in the same quiet tone as before. "It just kind of happened."

"So what got you into forensics?" I asked.

Oddly enough, he smiled a little, as if I'd said something funny. "Oh, I've always been interested in stuff like that," he said. "You know, true crime. I read a lot of books, watched a lot of movies. Looked glamorous the way they show it on the screen. In real life, though, it's boring. Lots of waiting around for results. Lots of painstaking tests. And not nearly as many pretty girls hanging around the crime scenes as you'd think."

That was almost certainly true. Most detectives I'd ever worked with, male or female, were grim, tired, and not exactly model material. "Still. With all the glamorous forensics dramas on TV, I imagine it helps you out with meeting people."

This time, he laughed outright, and it had a funny, tinfoil edge to it. "Oh yeah," he said. "It helps. The problem is, they never hang around. I mean, I'm really just a glorified lab monkey. They're looking for some kind of super secret agent with cool toys." He shifted in his seat and turned his head to look at me. I waited for him to say something—anything—but he just stared for so long that I began to feel a little uncomfortable.

Then Greg said, "Hey, check the alley on your side."

I whipped my head around so fast I nearly pulled a muscle. Beside the bodega was a standard industrial-type alley, wide enough to drive a garbage truck through, with room for big rusted Dumpsters. I caught sight of a shadow ducking between the containers. "Homeless, maybe?" I said. My throat had gone suddenly dry, and I took another pull from my water bottle to combat it. "Did you get a good look?"

"Not really. Could be a vagrant, a mugger . . . could be our killer checking out the area." Greg reached down for the flashlight. I reached out and put my hand over his, and he quickly pulled back.

"I think we should wait," I said. "Either way, it's not safe going in there after him. Chances are it's nobody we need to worry about, right?"

"Right," he said. "Sorry if I freaked you out."

"You didn't," I said, but it was a lie. I'd felt goose bumps shiver all over me, just for a moment, but now rational thought was coming back. The only real danger we were facing at the moment was a dire lack of snack food and a growing bladder problem. The bodega was open all night, and I'd seen a few people come and go; they'd probably let us use the restroom if it was an emergency. Greg had some kind of credentials as a law enforcement officer, anyway. Surely that counted toward bathroom privileges.

Greg seemed content to let the silence lie. He turned on the car radio to an oldies station, and for the rest of the long night, we found neutral, pleasant things to chat about while taking turns visiting the bodega's narrow, not-terribly-sanity facilities.

We passed the night without incident. The sun came up, and the vacant lot we'd staked out still looked empty. No sign of a body.

Greg got out and walked the lot, just in case, but came back with a discouraged look on his face. "Nothing," he said as he started the car. "He's hit somewhere else, or he took the night off. Sorry, Holly, I guess this one's a bust. Time for bed."

I caught myself yawning. Even though I'd dozed a bit while Greg kept watch, I felt achy and light-headed from the lack of real sleep and unpleasantly buzzed from all the coffees. "I can't sleep," I mumbled, and yawned again, popping my jaw in the process. "Got to shower and go to work."

"You're kidding. You'll be dead on your feet."

"Aren't you going in?"

"Not me," Greg said. "I have the day off. If you're smart, you'll call in sick. C'mon, is the world really gonna stop turning if you don't turn in some spreadsheet nobody really reads?"

I almost laughed; he was quoting me almost verbatim about my own day job. And he had a point, really. I was so exhausted that I wasn't sure I wouldn't fall asleep on my keyboard, even if I could make it in to the office. Maybe calling in a sick day wasn't a bad idea after all.

"Huh," Greg said. "I guess your boyfriend's home."

I opened my eyes—when had I closed them?—and saw that I'd dropped off again during the ride; he'd pulled the sedan up in the driveway of my house, and Andy stood on the porch, arms folded. He looked tense and a little bit dangerous, and I realized that unlike his note to me, I'd totally forgotten to write a note for *him*. It had never occurred to me that I might not be back first.

"He doesn't look happy," Greg said.

"He's not," I said. I gathered up my empty snack bag and water bottles, and opened the door. "Thanks, Greg. I appreciate you giving your time to do this even if it didn't work out."

"I'm in forensics," he said. "We're used to null results. The ones where you actually find the killer—those are pretty rare. Well, anyway, I'm happy to have gotten to know you a little. Hope to see you again, sometime."

I nodded and watched him back up and drive away. He didn't look nearly as tired as I felt.

Andy did. He stayed where he was, standing on the porch with his arms folded, as I walked up the steps toward him. "Friend of yours?"

"His name's Greg," I said. "He's a forensic tech. Prieto arranged for us to cover one of the dump sites last night, just in case the killer was following the same pattern."

"Doesn't seem likely."

"You'd be right about that since nothing happened." I covered a yawn. "I'm sorry, honey. I should have told you, but I forgot, then you were gone. Did you find out anything?"

"Not as much as I'd hoped," he said. He opened the door for me and stepped aside to let me go first—unconscious chivalry, something ingrained in him so deeply, I doubted he even knew he was doing it. "It wasn't safe for you to be out there on your own."

"Wasn't safe for *me*? Andy, you didn't even tell me where you'd gone! And you know I don't like it when we're apart."

He locked the door behind us. "Don't you even tell me to be careful. I fought a zombie war, in case you forget. I'm not made from spun sugar."

"It's not that," I said softly. "But what if—what if the longer we're apart, the thinner the connection between us? I can't help but think that it's dangerous for you to be out there without me. Not physically dangerous. Magically dangerous."

He was already shaking his head. "You need to stop worrying."

"I know, but I just don't understand how you're still here. Still . . . alive. It defies all the laws of magic I understand, and it scares me that you could just be . . . gone one of these days."

That made him look at me, and some of the tension eased out of his face. He reached out and took me in his arms—not holding me close, just . . . holding. "Sweetness," he said softly, "I thought you'd guessed by now that there's only one person in this life who can undo what brought me back. You."

"Me?"

"You stop loving me, and that connection will spin right out of my control," he said. "The dark will have me. It's always there, waiting, but you keep me here. The minute you don't want me, the minute you turn your back on me, that's the minute I start to die again." He sounded casual, but there was something serious about the expression in his face, the tightness around his eyes and mouth.

He was afraid of that, at least a little.

"Never happen," I said. I felt crazily better, and this time, I almost laughed. "Never, ever, *ever* happen, Andrew. Thank God. If *that's* all we have to worry about, we've got nothing at all to worry about."

He kissed my fingers, and that was the end of that, at least from my perspective. My heart felt warm and peaceful, but when I looked over, I saw that he still had that drawn, tight expression. What he'd just said had eased my mind, but it hadn't eased his. I didn't know why, or how to fix it. Sometimes, there were black chasms of misunderstandings between us; we came from different eras, different beliefs, different lives. And I wondered if, way down, he might not believe that I really did love him, all evidence to the contrary.

"I think I'm going to call in sick," I told him, and that got a smile, a slow and very wicked one.

"Works better if somebody calls in for you," he said. "Being all concerned. Which I am."

"I'm not so sure that's a—"

It was too late. Andy picked up the phone and dialed; he knew my work number by heart. Ten seconds later, he must have gotten an answer. "Yes, ma'am, I'm calling for Holly Anne Caldwell . . . no, I know she's not there, ma'am, she's here with me. Yes, she's sick. Got some terrible fever. I'm putting her to bed right away. I figure it's contagious, too, she's coming out in red spots. May need a doctor. Me? I'm her minister. Reverend Toland." He fended off my attempts to get the phone away from him; when he was really trying, butter wouldn't melt in Andy Toland's mouth, and he sounded utterly convincing. "Yes ma'am, thank you, I'll let her know. Hope she's better tomorrow. Thanks."

He hung up and spread his hands in a gesture that made me smack him on the arm. "Seriously! They're going to send me a fruit basket now! You couldn't just tell them I had a cold?"

"Had to make sure they let you off, didn't I? Now, you need to do what I said. Go right on to bed."

I was still caught between outrage and delight, and delight finally won. "All right," I said. "You want to come with me?"

He gave me a crooked smile, and said, "Ma'am, I am a minister, you heard me say it on the phone. I minister to your needs just as often as I can, but I promise, not today. You crawl in and sleep, and I'm going to go talk to those two resurrection witches you said weren't telling you the truth."

That drove away the cobwebs for a moment. "Andy—"

He kissed me—sweet and light and undemanding, this time. "You go on," he said. "I'll get you up for lunch. Then we'll see what we do about making up for lost time between the two of us."

He was right, I did need the rest; I was asleep practically from the moment my head hit the pillow.

When lunchtime came, I woke up to Andy's kissing me awake, and the delicious warmth of that gave way to a rumble of real hunger as he stepped back and put a bed tray over my lap. "There," he said. "Grilled ham and cheese sandwich, just like we used to make it back in Amarillo, when the streets were paved with cow chips. Only difference is I used presliced bread instead of having to hack it off the loaf."

He plunked himself down on the other side of the bed as I dug into the meal; when Andy cooked, it was always with a down-home enthusiasm that denied the existence of cholesterol, and damn, it was great. I tried not to think about the calories, which was actually a lot easier than normal since I'd skipped two meals in a row.

"Did you eat?" I asked after I'd swallowed the last delicious, buttery piece of the sandwich. He picked up the remote control and flipped on the television mounted on the wall across from the bed.

"Yep," he said. "Ate, cleaned up the kitchen, waited until I was sure you'd had at least six full hours. How you feeling?"

"Great," I said. "You're not seriously going to watch TV now."

He'd tuned it to a show that featured drunk people wandering around screaming at each other. Reality television. "Can't help it," he said. "Don't really want to watch it, but I still do. Don't seem right, people putting their personal business out like this, for everybody to gawk over. In—" He caught himself, and grinned. "I was about to say *in my day,* but that'd make me feel about two hundred years older than I actually am in body. But in my day, folks kept their private lives private."

"I guess it's a different way of looking at things," I said. "Maybe as connected as everybody is now, there's no way to keep your business all that private anymore. And not as much need."

He put the remote aside, moved the remains of the lunch tray, and kissed the side of my neck. It felt warm, comfortable, and seductive at the same time. "I have no mind to share any of you with an audience, Holly Anne. I want to keep you all to myself."

I knew that we ought to be talking about the case, or about what we were going to do to find the killer, but as his arm went around my shoulders, as I curled into his warm body, I felt no real desire to spoil this. *We need this,* I thought. *We need this time.*

Because there would never be enough time. I knew that. All lovers faced a ticking clock, but ours was loud, and close, and inevitable, and we both knew it. Andy was strong, but his strength couldn't hold, it *couldn't.*

"Hey," he said, and tilted my chin up to meet my eyes. He had deep, richly brown eyes, full of secrets. Full of warmth, too. "You're thinking too dark, you know that? Leave it out there."

"I can't," I said. "I keep thinking about those girls. We failed last night. We didn't get him. You really didn't find anything, either?"

"We really going to talk about this now?"

I nodded silently, and he sighed and settled back against the pillows, staring at the flickering TV screen again. "I had some knowledge of someone who'd hired an avatar witch. Not through the network."

I sat up and stared at him, but he didn't meet my eyes. "*What?*"

"It's a dead end," he said. "I mean that exactly, 'cause when I tracked the son of a bitch down who handed over the money, he was dead and buried in a ditch out behind his house." There was something unnatural in the focus he was giving the stupid reality show, and I knew he wasn't really seeing it. What he was seeing was far worse. "Didn't have time to do a real resurrection, so I took some shortcuts."

"What do you mean, *shortcuts*?"

"There are things I know you don't, Holly Anne. Things it's better you don't, and this is one of 'em."

"What are you talking about, Andy?"

"There's a way to pull a soul back over into his own ruined body and hold it there, long as you're not too particular about what it takes to get it done." He paused a moment, then said, "I got a couple of questions answered, once he stopped screaming. Couldn't hold him long. Your killer wasn't too kind to that body."

I swallowed hard. From the stony look on Andy's face, it was worse than he was willing to tell me, which made it *way* worse than I could imagine. "Oh God," I said faintly. "Why didn't you tell me?"

"Just did. No reason to give you nightmares, wasn't your doing. Anyway, I found out who gave him the money to hire the witch. Name was a dead end."

"You should still tell Prieto," I said. "Maybe the witch he hired has more information . . ."

Andy was already shaking his head. "Nothing more to be learned. Believe me, your police friend ain't gonna get any more out of this than I did."

"It's not just about the information. It's about justice."

He looked at me, suddenly. His eyes were unreadable. "Justice."

"That witch is guilty. Maybe guilty after the fact, but she ought to be charged and her license to practice taken away, at the very least. If you don't want to go to the police, we need to report her to the network."

"I will," he said. He settled back against the pillows, still watching me. "Holly . . ."

I slowly stretched out, facing him. We were close together now, close enough that I could feel the warmth of his breath stirring my hair. I held out my hand, and he took it, and our fingers twined together.

"Going to be staking out that place again tonight?" he asked.

"Probably."

"Mind if I tag along?"

"Not at all." I smiled, and it felt sad. "I love spending time with you, Andy. I wish there were all the time in the world to spend with you."

"Hush, now. Don't let what's sad take away what's beautiful." His fingertips touched my cheek, lightly, and my lips parted in unbidden response. "*You're* beautiful."

"We're beautiful," I said, and kissed him. He tasted like apples and wine, sweet and crisp and clean, and his mouth opened with a wordless groan under mine. The wet, slick dance of our tongues made my skin tingle, melted warmth from the rest of my body to trickle and pool between my legs, and I didn't resist as he shifted his weight and eased me back to the pillows

A sharp tug was all it took to pull loose the snaps on his plaid shirt, and he smiled as he straightened up to take it off. I loved the way light slipped golden over his skin, catching on his muscles and glistening on the hair on his chest; it even gilded the scars, the ones that his avatar had carried out of the resurrection even though he ought to have, by all logic, been fresh and unmarked. The scars had a kind of beauty to them—living badges of the kind of courage I couldn't really imagine.

Andy stood up and shed his jeans, and stood there looking down at me; and then he sat on the edge of the bed and trailed his fingertips lightly over my stomach. His touch made me tremble, and my breath come faster. "It seems disrespectful to those dead girls to want you this much right now," he said. "But want you I do, Holly Anne. This minute. And I think you want me just as much. Right?"

I deliberately pulled down the sheet, never looking away from those deep, shadow-haunted eyes. His hand moved slowly over the bunched fabric, then up my inner thigh. He grasped the thin elastic band of my panties and pulled them off. He slowly caressed and kissed my bare leg, moving up into the shadows. I gasped and arched against him as he stroked me in wet, deep, aching places. His mouth, lips, and tongue bathed my nipples in heat, and I was well on the way to a bright and shattering climax even before Andy shifted his weight and slowly, relentlessly filled me.

It took my breath away, and he held there for a moment, staring into my eyes. "All right?" he whispered, and I nodded and wrapped my legs around him, pushing him deeper, arching against him. "God *damn*, Holly . . ."

"Stop talking," I whispered, and kissed him as he lost the fine edge of control to which he'd been clinging.

Our lovemaking was swift and hot and hard, different from

the times before; it seemed to go on forever, one breathless deep thrust after another. No words, just indrawn breaths and gasps and whispers that had no meaning other than what we felt.

He'd never been more real to me. More *alive*. And he drove me to a shattering, gasping pinnacle with my nails digging into his skin, leaving marks. He came a few deep, fast strokes later, and collapsed against me, shuddering with the force of it.

When he stirred, his kisses were sweet and soft and slow—a silent gift. We lay together, linked, for a long time before he heaved a deep sigh, and said, "Didn't mean it to go quite that way."

"I did," I said, and touched his lips gently with mine. "I needed it."

"Ah. Well, I wouldn't want to disappoint a lady."

"That was *not* what a lady would have done."

"I'll have you know that I've known me a good number of ladies, and a fair number of them . . ."

I put my fingers on his mouth, stopping him. "Really not the time for your back-in-my-day reminiscences, Andy."

He kissed my hand. "I know that."

There was a ring from somewhere in the direction of his pants, which were on the floor, and both of us sighed. Andy touched his forehead to mine for a few apologetic seconds, then said, "I was hoping to hear from somebody on another lead . . ."

"Take it," I said. He kissed me gently and slipped out of bed to grab up his pants and find the cell. He didn't put the pants *on*, which I could only appreciate; he was breathtaking, for all his scars—or because of them. I couldn't imagine not having him here, with me, always, and now the gnawing fear came back that this was the last time I'd have this, the last night we'd be together.

Life was so fragile, sometimes.

He said hello, listened, then cast a glance at me and left the room to talk. I got up and gathered my scattered clothes, got fresh ones from the closet, and turned on the hot water in the bathroom.

Andy popped his head in. "Sweetness, I've got to go meet a man about a horse."

"Knowing you, I'm afraid you mean that literally. Want to shower? It'll only take about ten minutes."

He smiled, a slow and wicked expression that made my blood warm, again. "Maybe twenty," he said.

"You're such a gentleman."

That made him shrug. "Not so's you notice."

It was about fifteen, truth be told, but fiercely sweet, then he was dressed and gone, with his hair still shining and wet. I took my time, relaxing in the spray and the calming scent of the lavender soap.

My cell was ringing when I stepped out. I toweled off hastily, wrapped my hair, and grabbed the phone just before the call flipped over to voice mail. "Hello?" I sounded cross, and I was. I hoped it wasn't my day job calling, because if it was, I didn't sound *nearly* enough out of it.

Instead, I got a male, totally unfamiliar voice. "You were asking questions about a witch who'd made an avatar recently."

"That's right." I felt a quick burn of excitement. "Do you have a name?"

"I do," the voice said. "But understand, I don't like doing this."

"I appreciate that. I won't ask. All I need is a name, and I won't tell anyone where I got it. I'm not asking *your* name, either."

There was a long hiss of silence, as if the caller was debating hanging up, then the man said, "You know him. I've seen you with him."

I frowned, racking my brain for all of the witches I'd met with in the past few months. There were at least fifteen, about a third of them male . . .

"It's the one you brought back," the voice said. "The one who won't die. Toland."

"What are you—" Silence settled cold inside. I was aware of the whisper of traffic outside on the road, of wind in the tree by the window, of the rattle of the air-conditioning kicking in, the warmth of the sunlight on the towel over my legs.

But the world had stopped. Just . . . stopped. For me.

"You're wrong," I said. I didn't even mean to say it, but the words came bubbling up, out of control. "He didn't. He's a resurrection witch, not—"

"He can do both. He's the *only* one who can do both. Didn't you know that?"

And the caller hung up without waiting for an answer.

I pulled the phone away from my ear and stared at it, numbed and empty. *No.* No, it wasn't true. It couldn't be.

But I remembered. He'd brought home five thousand in hundred-dollar bills. Cash. The way that illicit transactions were done all over the world.

He wouldn't. He couldn't.

But he'd thrown himself into this with a furious intensity— been gone all night—interrogated a murdered man for information . . . was that the action of someone trying to help me, or someone trying to cover his own guilt?

Oh God, God, God . . .

Deep breaths, Holly. Give him a chance to explain. You can't believe this, you can't just think he would do something like this. You know him.

Did I? I'd seen Andy grow more and more frustrated over the past few weeks, feeling useless to contribute toward our money problems. Feeling less of a man for not finding his chosen employment in this vastly changed world. He was used to simpler times, direct actions, clear rules.

I suddenly knew . . . *knew*, with a sick wave of despair. He was guilty. Guilty of making the shell of the dead girl, at least. It sickened me, but I could believe that. He hadn't resurrected her, though. I knew him better than that he'd coldly looked on as she was tortured, mutilated, killed.

Still, there was something bitterly disappointing about this . . . not just that he'd taken money from a serial killer, but that . . .

That he hadn't trusted me enough to confess it.

Oh God.

I dropped the phone on the table, leaped out of the bathroom, and pulled on clothes as fast as I could. I was shaking and panting with panic, because I knew, *knew* that he'd lied to me. It wasn't just asking questions, not anymore.

Andy was out there tracking down a killer, and he was probably closer than anybody knew. Close enough to be in real danger.

I dialed his cell phone. It rang, and rang, then finally he picked up and said, "Bad time, Holly." He was panting, and I could tell he was running

"Where are you?"

"Can't tell you."

"Andy, please—I *know*. I know you made the shell. I know you're taking this personally. But you *need help*. This man— he's not like anything you've come up against before."

"Dammit!" He spat it into the phone, then heaved a big sigh, and said, "Not you, Holly, I'm sorry, but he made it to his car. Son of a *bitch*. I had him. I *had him*."

"Did you see a license plate?"

"No. Couldn't even make out the car real clear; all them things look alike to me anyway. Was blue, that's all I can tell you." His breathing eased a little, and he said, in a much different tone, "Holly Anne, I never meant to lie to you. Not for a second. I just couldn't tell you. Not that. I let you down. I let that gal down, and if I could take it back, I would."

"The killer didn't hire you."

"No. Money and job came by courier. Courier's the man I found dead. He couldn't tell me nothing."

"So who were you following?"

"Got a tip about the witch," Andy said. "He drove off afore the killer went for his car. I got the name of the witch; he ain't getting away. Killer's still a mystery, and I damn sure want to solve it."

I heard him starting up an engine. "Andy, did you take my car?"

"Yeah," he said. "Sorry about that. Needed to move fast. Look, I may still be able to pick up his trail. We'll talk about all this later, and I'll explain proper."

"Andy, it's serious, what you did. You know that, don't you?"

"Dead girl brought back to torture and murder? I know it is." He sounded grim and quietly heartsick. "Ain't the first time I made a mistake, but this one hurts. Hurts bad."

"You didn't make any others . . . ?"

There was a short silence, then he said, "Gotta go, Holly Anne. Please forgive me."

And then he hung up, without telling me where he was, or what he was planning to do.

It was a long couple of hours before the phone rang again. I grabbed it up in relief, but it wasn't Andy, after all.

"Got another crime scene and another dead-again," said Detective Prieto. He sounded tired and harassed. "Get a piece of paper. I'll wait here for you."

My heart was pounding painfully. "Is Andy—?"

"Is Andy what?" he snapped back. "Ain't seen him, and do me a favor, don't bring him. The son of a bitch creeps me out."

Oh, thank God. It wasn't Andy he'd found, then, which had been my instant and horrifying fear. "I—I don't have a car."

"Well, take a taxi, then, but don't expect the city to be picking up the tab. Hurry it up if you're coming. I can't keep this place secure for long." He read me the address, which I wrote down, then called a taxi for pickup.

I tried calling Andy's phone, but it went straight to voice mail. The sound of his recorded voice, so awkward and uncomfortable with this newfangled messaging, made my heart break all over again.

He'd already broken it in two by lying to me, even if it was a lie of omission, and now, there was the horrifying possibility that he'd created *more* bodies to be filled with sleeping souls. More girls to wake to torture and death.

No wonder he didn't want to talk to me. He had to stop it. I knew that he wouldn't let go until he'd accomplished that, at any cost.

The taxi honked about five minutes later, and I felt sick as I opened the cabinet to retrieve my go-bag . . . and found it missing. I'd left it in the car, which Andy was driving. Not that I had the heart, or the stomach, to try to resurrect one of these poor, tortured souls, but it was habit to have it with me. A bit of constancy and comfort that I'd have to do without.

I gave him the address, and the taxi driver struggled with GPS coordinates until he finally said, "Lady, that's some kind of park. You sure—?"

"Yes," I said. "I'm sure."

He shrugged and put the car in gear. Just another twenty-dollar fare to him.

Unlike the first crime scene, this time there was no uniformed police presence, no warning tape. Just Prieto's big brown car, a shining dark blue one beside it, and an empty parking lot with a thin line of trees at the back of it.

There was one lonely crime scene technician photographing the scene: Greg. I waved at him, and he looked over and nodded. He waved back before continuing to snap pictures.

Prieto looked me over as the cab that had brought me drove away. "Here I thought you and Toland were joined at the hip. That's two times you've shown up without him."

I avoided the whole topic of Andy Toland because it hurt too deeply. "Where are the other crime scene guys?"

"I didn't call them in. Legally, the worst we got here is illegal disposal of a body, and nobody wants to waste crime scene dollars on this thing, not in a budget-cutting economy. Hey, Greg, hang back for a minute. I want her to get the full impact of what her damn witch friends did."

Greg stepped back and waited, watching me curiously as I walked forward. I immediately identified her: the second victim. Her dark eyes were open, staring up at the clouds as they passed overhead; they had filmed over but hadn't dried out completely. Her full lips were parted. She had a look on her face I couldn't quite define—surprise, and something horribly close to relief.

She'd been happy to die, at the end. Happy the suffering was over.

I thought about the cash sitting in the bureau drawer at home, waiting for a trip to the bank, and shivered; that was blood money—no, worse than that. I could never bring myself to touch it again.

"This dump site wasn't on the original case files. It's new. He's changed it up to reduce his risk, which means we're screwed halfway to hell on stopping him unless you and the undead boyfriend run down that resurrection witch."

"Andy has a name for you. He may have information about the killer, too." I said. Standing there, staring at the torn evidence of another girl's horrible, violating death made me angry at Andy, really and painfully furious. He could have confessed. *Should* have confessed. If he'd made the shells, he could have told me and Prieto about it, and immediately handed over the courier who'd paid him; that would have made it at least partly right again. I knew why he'd tried to go it alone . . . it was in Andy's Old West nature. But it was wrong this time.

No. This . . . this was beyond wrong. There was no mending it.

"Holly?"

Prieto's voice was quiet, and unlike his usual dismissive tone. It honestly seemed . . . compassionate. I looked up to see him standing on the other side of the body, watching me. Behind him, the tech was staring, too. After a few seconds, he went back to work, but Prieto's focus remained.

"Something you want to talk about?" he asked. "I can tell by the look on your face that you're hurting."

I shook my head. I *did* want to tell him, I wanted to blurt it out and be free of the dreadful pressure of this secret, but I couldn't. Instead, I dialed Andy's phone again. Got voice mail.

In the background, as distant as another world, the click of Greg's strobe sounded like the dry scrape of claws on cement.

"All right, but there's something you're torn up with guilt about. Something to do with Toland. What is it?"

Prieto was maneuvering me into talking, and he was frighteningly good at it. I could see now why he was such an excellent detective; he had a calm, gentle manner toward suspects, one that made me want to confide in him. Unburden myself and relieve the boiling internal pressure.

I sucked in a deep breath, turned, and walked away toward the street. I'd dismissed the cab, and now I was sorry I had; I'd expected that Prieto would offer a ride back home, or have one of the uniformed officers do it, but the last thing I wanted was to be stuck in a car with him now. I was frighteningly fragile, and he'd know just where to push to collapse my thin, wavering wall of resistance.

"Holly Anne," he said from behind—closer than I thought he should be. "Is he off looking for the killer? Because that's not his job. That's mine. You have to tell me what you know. He could be in a lot of danger if he goes off and tangles with this cold bastard."

Good. That came bubbling up from the black, angry depths of my soul, and I tried to push that down, tried to excuse it as temper. "He'll be fine," I said. "He's strong." God, I was so disappointed in him now. And angry. And frustrated.

And then I felt it.

My stride faltered a little, as if I'd hit an unexpectedly soft patch of ground, but it wasn't a physical blow, it was a feeling that swept over me, like a stinging black rain.

Weakness. Disconnection. *Loss.*

I knew that feeling, I'd been dreading it all this time, every day, every hour. It was the other shoe dropping.

It was Andy Toland losing his iron-hard grip on life and sliding back into the darkness from which he'd come.

I stopped and wrapped my arms around my stomach, shocked by the depth of the desperation ripping through me. *No, no, no . . .* I wasn't sure if it was me feeling that, or Andy, or both of us, a tangled knot of despair and pain and anguish. *Oh, mercy, please . . .*

"You all right?" Prieto touched my shoulder, but I couldn't respond. I panted for breath, and there were tears shimmering in my eyes. Bright, harsh tears that bent the light and broke it into twisting black shadows. Death was coming.

Death was *here.* I was losing him, and I didn't know why, or how, or how to stop it.

I heard an engine roaring, and looked up to see a car round the corner and pull into the parking area, skidding and sliding in a greasy veil of smoke. My car. A shadow behind the wheel.

Before the momentum was burned away, the driver's side door snapped open, and a body tumbled out in a loose-limbed heap.

Andy.

He rolled over on his back, gasping, arching in the struggle to resist the touch of the darkness that was welling up inside. I could feel it drenching his cells, drowning the life out of him.

I wasn't even aware of falling on my knees beside him on the cracked surface, but the touch of his skin was the most real thing in the world to me. "Andy—Andy, no . . ."

He grabbed for my hand and squeezed it tight. His eyes were wide and blank with concentration. I could see that the whites of his eyes were coloring over with blackness. Death was coming, and coming fast.

"Found the resurrection witch. He's dead," he gasped out. "Holly, Holly, I damn sure didn't mean for this to happen. I never meant to cause suffering. You believe that?"

"I do," I said. It was hard for me to see his expression now, through the bright veil of my tears. "You made the shells. You didn't know what they'd be used for."

"Should have," he whispered. "Should have fucking well known. I killed that witch, but he gave up his black-hearted son of a bitch boss first. Gave him up and he's here, Holly, he's right here with you, and I had to make it back to you, I had to . . ."

I didn't know what that meant. I looked over my shoulder; Prieto stood nearby, watching us with a confused expression. His cell phone was in his hand, but I could see that he didn't know who he could call for help. Not for this. "He dying?" Prieto asked.

I was afraid to tell him, but there was no doubt of it, not now. I could sense the relentless tide of it growing inside him. "*No,* Andy, stay with me," I begged. "God, *please,* stay with me, I'm sorry, I'm sorry I doubted you . . ."

"Holly, listen," he said. His voice was faint, but there was a note of urgency in it, a raw edge of insistence. "*He's right here.*"

Prieto. *No.* I didn't believe it, I couldn't, but I turned to look at him. He frowned back. He hadn't heard what Andy had said. "That doesn't make sense," I said. "Why would he call us in, why would he if he knew—"

"Not him!" Andy forced the words out, and squeezed my hands so hard I felt bones shift. "*Other one.*"

The blue car.

Greg.

I didn't register the sound of the gunshot immediately; it took a long, confused second to penetrate as anything but a sharp, alien noise. By then Prieto was falling, the cell phone dropping to shatter on the pavement before he did. Half of his face was gone in a red ruin of bone and blood and brain, and, for a numbed instant, I thought his head had actually exploded in some kind of freak accident . . .

And then I realized that someone had shot him, as a bullet ricocheted off the door of the car and dug a raw gouge in the pavement not a foot away from me.

I screamed and ducked. Andy tried get up, to put himself in front of me because that was who he was, what he had always been.

I'd given up on him. I'd let myself doubt, and doubt had set him adrift just when he needed me most. And still he'd fought his way back out of the dark to come here. To warn me.

I wrenched open the back door of my car, and there, in the back floorboards, were two bags. Andy's, and mine. I threw myself inside and grabbed both. I thumped Andy's down on the pavement next to him.

He didn't reach for it. In fact, he didn't move at all. I still felt the connection between us, but it was pulling at me like a razor-sharp hook in flesh, and I was gasping from the agony of it. Death was dragging him away, and he was fighting it with every single ounce of magic and courage he possessed.

I didn't dare try to get to him, there wasn't time. Instead, I dumped the contents of my own bag on the floorboards.

The gun tumbled out, solid and reassuring, and I got it up and aimed just as a shadow stepped in front of the driver's side door.

Greg. So damn *normal*. I'd spent an entire evening sitting in a car with him, laughing at his jokes, sharing chips and ranch dip and discussing the merits of the original *Star Trek* with the follow-ons. I'd liked that Greg, but now, as I saw his face, I realized that the man I'd gotten to know had been a ghost. A mask.

What was behind it was something not really human—full of cruel anticipation and dark pleasure and a particularly soulless kind of glee that held no hint of joy.

He pointed his weapon straight at me and smiled. "Drop it," he said. "I already killed Prieto, and this guy's gone, too." He nudged Andy with his foot, and Andy's head lolled bonelessly. He was pale and lifeless as a rubber doll. His eyes were open, but blank as glass. "Drop it."

I squeezed the trigger, but he was faster. My shot went wide. His hit my shoulder and slammed me back against the upholstery in a bright red spray of blood. It must have hurt, but my brain skipped a beat, then it was just numb, as if I'd been asleep on that side of my body for too long. Shock, clamping down to preserve my life.

I'd dropped the gun. I bent forward to try to pick it up, but he grabbed my foot and dragged me out, flailing, leaving a thick wet trail of crimson behind. He kept dragging, past Prieto's corpse, onto the grass. I tried to get up when he released his hold, but he put a knee in the center of my chest as he put his gun away and drew a knife. "Never shot a woman before," he said. "It's not as much fun as I'd hoped. You didn't scream enough, but we can fix that. We'll have to make this quick, though, Holly Anne; it's kind of public around here. Exciting, though, isn't it?" His grin was loose and wet and horrifying. "I sat there all night with you in that car, you know, wondering if I should take you over to that field and do you there for your friends to find. If you'd followed me out there, I don't think I could have stopped myself."

I shut my eyes because there was nothing I could do now. I was wounded, and he had the knife, I had nothing at all. Not even hope.

Andy. I love you, I always loved you, I am so sorry I even doubted it . . .

At least we could be together, somewhere beyond all this. Somewhere far from the pain and the sharp bite of the blade as it touched my arm, widening the bullet wound. Cutting my life away. I heard myself scream, but I focused on retreating into a place of silence, of peace, of *Andy*.

I love you. I'm so sorry for hurting you. You're the only thing that ever really mattered to me, the only man who ever touched me in my heart, and I love you, I will always . . .

"I know," Andy Toland said. I thought it was in my head, I really did; reality had come undone. I opened my eyes. It wasn't Andy crouching over me, it was the killer, Greg, with his totally normal blue golf shirt underneath, and his totally normal face with a wolf's eyes and a shark's smile like some horrible accident of nature . . .

But it *had* been Andy speaking. He was standing right behind Greg. Pale as death, stark as an ink drawing, built of flesh and blood and bone and *rage*.

And below all that, there was love, oh God, so much love it mended my shattered heart into an unbreakable whole.

He pumped his shotgun one-handed and put it to the back of Greg's head. For a second, Greg froze; his predator's eyes turned frightened, and his smile faltered. Then he dropped the knife and held up his hands. "Please don't shoot," he said. "I surrender. I won't give you any trouble."

He must have thought that would do it. I could have told him different because Andy Toland was never a policeman, was never a lawyer; he grew up in a world where, sometimes, the only judge, jury, and justice was to be had in the flash of a gun.

And this was personal.

I turned my head just in time before he fired the shotgun. Both barrels.

Andy had angled the shot up, but some of the blood and . . . other things . . . fell on me. I expected to feel Greg's lifeless corpse sprawl across me, but Andy had hold of his collar, and he pitched him off to the side like trash. Then Andy dropped to his knees and clamped both hands on my shoulder.

I still felt the pull of the dark, but this time I realized that it wasn't Andy fighting that tide. It was *me*. "Holly Anne," he said. "Holly, you listen to me. *Listen*. You're not leaving. I ain't allowing that. You just *listen*."

"I'm sorry," I said. I felt vague and distant now. "I was angry you didn't tell me. You understand? I didn't mean to let you go."

"All done now," he said in his most smooth, soothing voice. His buttery voice, the one he used to lie to my boss to get my day off. Oh Jesus, I was going to die on my day off. That was just sad. And I hadn't gotten my reports finished.

Andy cursed in a soft, trembling voice, and fumbled in his pocket for his cell phone. He punched 911, but I didn't hear the conversation. I was busy thinking how odd it was to be looking at him from so great a distance. He had a nice nose after all, even if it had been broken once. I couldn't understand why he was crying. "Did you have a shotgun in your bag?" I asked. "Because that must have been really heavy."

"Shut up, my love, please *Jesus*—"

"I love you," I said. It was important to say it.

And then I closed my eyes and with a great sense of relief, let go.

And Andy Toland held me, hovering there, suspended in the dark, tethered to him by the unbreakable chain of our love.

It took two surgeries and three weeks in the hospital to put my arm back together properly, and Andy never left my side. I think there might have been some violence involved in his defiance of visiting hours, but by the time I was conscious enough to really know, he and the medical community had achieved a cautious truce.

The police chief showed up to formally shake my other hand and present me with a certificate of appreciation, which was nice. There was a check for my services, too, which was even better. My boss sent flowers.

Andy looked good on the evening news, telling all them reporting sons of bitches to go to hell. I almost choked on my chicken broth.

But the best thing . . . the best of all . . . was going home with Andy, and being carried over the threshold, and smelling the astonishing scent of his potion brewing in its final stage. "I made sure it wasn't so smelly for you," he said. "Got a surprise, too."

I breathed in Holly's Balm and rested my head against his shoulder. "No more surprises," I said. "Promise me."

"All right then." He smiled, put me on the couch, and pulled up a chair. He pulled from his pocket a thick sheaf of papers, which he unfolded. "You need to sign these."

"What is it?"

"Company papers."

"Company for *what*?"

"Holly's Balm," he said. "You own it, and I just got the first check for agreeing to let this company sell it. All I got to do is give 'em the recipe, and they'll hire on the potions witches to do it. Us included. Should make us a tidy sum in paychecks, plus this signing bonus for you."

Oh, there was a check. He held it in front of me.

That was a *lot* of zeroes. Six of them, with a respectably large single digit in front of them.

"Andy—I can't take all this . . ."

"It's only half," he said. "The other half's gone to Detective Prieto's family. They won't want for nothing, I promise you that. And—and to the families of them girls. I sent it without signing the note." A quiet, shy smile spread over his lips. "Did good this time, didn't I?"

I took the check, put it and the papers aside, and kissed him, long and sweet. He tasted like the potion, like every good thing that had ever happened in the world and nothing bad.

"Yes," I said. "You did good."

The potion was called Holly's Balm, but the fact was . . . he was all the balm I'd ever need.

★   ★   ★

Author's Bio:

Rachel Caine is the *New York Times* and internationally bestselling author of the Morganville Vampires series, the Weather Warden series, the Outcast Season series, and the new Revivalist series. She lives and works in Fort Worth, Texas. Her website is **www.rachelcaine.com**.

SNOW JOB

by CAROLE NELSON DOUGLAS

Everyone wondered why a Sin City bigwig like Christophe performed twice nightly as "Cocaine" with his own rock band at his Inferno Hotel venue. That was like "the Donald" leading a fifties doo-wop group nightly at the Trump Las Vegas, although that very thought was more shuddersome than a pack of feral zombies invading a tea party.

Everyone was dying to know, in a 2013 Vegas packed with supernatural moguls, just what flavor of paranormal the Seven Deadly Sins' lead singer, Christophe, aka Cocaine, aka Snow, was. Rumor whispered that he was an albino vampire, but Snow maintained that was way off base.

Except for the albino part, obviously.

One night between shows, the rock-star mogul stepped firmly out of character.

"Get me Delilah Street," Snow told his security chief, Grizelle, even though he knew that the formidable shapeshifter hated Delilah Street almost as much as Delilah Street claimed to hate him.

"You've never asked me to provide you with a woman before," Grizelle observed.

"I'm not asking now. She's a paranormal investigator."

"She's a self-advertised paranormal investigator. I find her annoying. I thought you did, too."

His colorless lips sketched the shadow of a smile. "I do."

"She's a bloody amateur," Grizelle went on, "and she's the Cadaver Kid's girlfriend, or hadn't you noticed?"

"She's going to be *my* bloody amateur next. And, Grizelle, I notice everything, including when you're jealous."

"Jealous? Who's got your back with tooth and claw?"

"You do."

His pale hand stroked the top of her gleaming ebony hair, which was styled into shoulder-length braids. She was a tall, handsome woman with watered-silk skin, a moiré pattern of black and deepest gray that outshone her emerald green silk sheath dress and metal-heeled gladiator sandals.

As Grizelle leaned into his fond gesture, her moiré skin sprouted black-and-white fur, and the green gown dwindled into the concentrated gleam of feline irises. Now that Grizelle had shifted into a huge black-striped white tiger, her platter-sized paws rested on the broad shoulders of Snow's white leather jumpsuit, and her emerald eyes were slitted with devotion as one furred cheek rubbed her scent on him.

Her gesture almost dislodged the black sunglasses he always wore to shield his presumably pink eyes from the light.

"I'm going to need a human investigator in my corner very soon, Grizelle," he whispered into her large, tufted ear.

The white big cat eased down onto all fours before rising in her human form, shaking her stripes into velvety black skin and satiny black hair. Her flashing emerald eyes evoked the glitzy green costume of Envy in the Seven Deadly Sins band.

"I'm your security chief," she reminded her boss. "Tell me what's wrong."

"I told you. Delilah Street isn't here." His voice held the sharpness of command now.

"She doesn't like you," Grizelle half growled, sounding cattier than a soap-opera diva. "It might be difficult to convince her to jump at your call."

"I'm sure you'll devise a plan. Don't wait. Something wicked this way comes."

You'd think a girl could get a peaceful night's snooze in a cozy Enchanted Cottage. Sleeping Beauty managed it for decades in a drafty old castle.

My bedroom isn't located in any fairy-tale joint, but in a replica of a 1940s honeymooner's nest from a movie named *The Enchanted Cottage*. Inside it, the film story line went, true love had overlaid movie star looks on a plain old maid and a disfigured war hero.

I awoke to the sound of repeated gunfire and sat up, blinking like a gothic heroine in my filmy-curtained four-poster bed, and immediately scanned for intruders.

One of my two casement windows was open and banging against the wall. The light sweat of alarm on my skin didn't detect so much as a breath of night air, never mind a window-sash-crashing wind.

Checking the bedroom floor, I saw no sign of my devoted rescue dog. Quicksilver was known to enter and exit the cottage windows at night, though discreetly and without drama, but never on the second floor.

Next I noticed that the creepy "bugs-moving" feeling along my thighs wasn't my nightshirt riding up. It was the crocheted bedspread slowly ebbing to the bed's foot.

Since this is post–Millennium Revelation Las Vegas and not your father's Sin City, but one crawling with supernaturals, I had immediate suspects. The first were the often unseen domestic "helpers" that came with the Enchanted Cottage. The second most likely suspect was a first on my list—a genuine ghost.

I grabbed the absconding coverlet with both hands and jerked it up to my waist again.

It jerked back down.

I leaned forward to jerk harder.

Something grabbed my T-shirt front and tugged even more. I fell facedown on the foot of the bed as that unseen "something" outflanked me to pinch my now-exposed rear.

This indignity ruled out a disembodied ghost, but not the mischievous pixies, gnomes, and poltergeists that abound in the borders between the paranormal and natural worlds. My house "spirits" so far had been as good as two-thousand-dollar-an-ounce gold. Something you could count on.

They'd never resort to anything as crude as this spectral horsefly bite.

I rolled over and off the bed, my slender ankle bracelet thickening as I went into uproot-and-expel mode. In seconds, my silver familiar had migrated to my rear and transformed into a really heavy and cold metal fanny pack.

That form was Vegas-appropriate, sure, but not helpful. Nothing would pinch my butt again, but I didn't need a rear anchor right now either.

My yell and karate kick were meant to clear my immediate space.

Instead, the unseen Something grabbed my extended ankle and jerked again.

I would have gone belly-down on the floor if I hadn't caught hold of a bedpost, spun around it, and kicked my legs back onto the bed to crawl over the crumpled coverlet and jump off the other side.

"Show yourself, coward," I shouted from the floor as a diversion.

I launched myself at the wall near the door, hoping to run into my invisible visitor. I detected a momentary brush with something so elusive, I ended up plastered against the wallpaper, a floral design with blossoms bigger than my hands.

I heard a high-pitched, self-satisfied . . . giggle.

"Little Miss Muffet sat on her tuffet," a crazy voice sing-songed.

It came from the open, gently tapping window.

I charged the sound. When I got there, something lifted my hips so only my toes touched the floor. A forceful push could catapult me past whoever or whatever was there, through the open window to the flagstones below.

My unseen dancing partner released the dangerous grip with a patronizing pat on the fanny pack that had me cursing. I'd already curled my fingers around the closing window frame and swung inward with it to the wall. Once my feet were flat on the floor again, I slammed the window shut and held it closed with my back, sealing in my tormenter.

". . . and she began to cry," the disembodied voice taunted.

By now I was panting hard but hardly tearful. The silver familiar had finally got the message that I could defend my own rear better than eight pounds of solid sterling (would that my glutes were that pumped). It looped around my bicep as a funky designer cuff . . . a lariat-in-waiting.

I surveyed the room. Everything was dead still, even my airy bedpost curtains. The shut window was no longer a point of entry or exit.

My glance fell on the stainless-steel water bowl against the opposite wall, kept in my bedroom for Quicksilver's midnight security rounds when he was home. It was ten inches across because I'm talking a 150-pound dog, part wolf, part wolfhound. I sometimes thought his nights out might be spent chasing his own tail.

Great! Just when I could use him guarding *my* besieged tail here at home.

I caught a glimmer of something in the mirror over my dresser. Mirrors have been doors for me ever since I came to Las Vegas, so I see more in them than most people. Is it me or Sin City? Or a combustible combination of both? Watch this space.

Right then, I realized my filmy bedpost curtain was gathered into a fan of folds about . . . five feet six inches above the floor. Something clutched the fabric.

I jumped onto my bed again—most solo fun I've ever had on it—bounced and caromed off the opposite wall, bent to grab the dog's water dish . . . and flung the contents at the empty space between me and the bedpost.

For an instant, a wet figure took weird negative shape, like a strip of old-time camera film soaked in developing fluid.

"Strip" is the word. I ripped the coverlet from my bed and leapt on the being playing peekaboo behind the bedpost. My pounce encountered, and drove back, a solid form. I pushed forward until I pinned it to the wall.

"Ow! My eye," the voice howled. "Jack put in a thumb and pulled out a plum—"

"Enough with the nursery rhymes! *If* I wanted a naked man in my room," I told my unseen prisoner, "it wouldn't be the Invisible Man. Now, get decent, then explain yourself."

Releasing mushy biceps—mad scientists aren't much for working out—I folded my arms under the message on my sleep T-shirt—KICK SASS.

"Nice pecs," Dr. Jack Griffin, aka the Invisible Man, commented on my posture with another giggle.

Where's Fabio when you finally think you need him?

I stepped back a stride to watch a reverse strip show.

My abused crocheted coverlet, probably made by pixies, or possibly even Madame Defarge, began to elevate like a cobra from a basket. It twisted around and around as it went higher, making my visitor seem to be donning a Roman toga.

"Here." I tossed a rhinestone-banded fedora from my dresser top to his approximate middle. "Put this on. I like looking people in the face, even when they're invisible."

"Snazzy hat," he cooed, giggling as my hat levitated over the room scenery between the togaed shoulder and his forehead.

My uninvited guest was no threat to anything but my patience. He was a rogue Cinema Simulacrum, or CinSim. Old black-and-white movie characters filmed on silver nitrate could be overlaid on illegally smuggled zombies from Mexico. The mysterious Immortality Mob leased them to Vegas attractions, where they were chipped to remain in suitable settings. My personal affinity for silver made me their champion. They, in turn, were my best confidential informants in town.

"Say, Miss Street," the Invisible Man cajoled. "I just had to have a little fun with you. Can't you take a joke?"

"Why now? And how'd you escape the Inferno Hotel on the Strip to get all the way over to Hector Nightwine's Sunset Road estate and my digs on it?"

"I'm an invisible man of mystery."

"You'll be unseen chopped liver if you don't start talking."

He adjusted the hat to the jaunty angle I used when I wore it. Ruin it for me, why don't you?

"I'm the only unchained CinSim in Vegas, darlin' girl. I can go where I want because nobody can see me."

"Why would a major Vegas mogul like Snow let one of his valuable leases go wandering so far?"

"I'm not as visibly valuable as the Inferno Hotel's other CinSims. Nick and Nora Charles are chipped to the Inferno bar with that darn dog, Asta. The noir CinSims have their own custom sets on the Limbo level. The bordello CinSims like Errol Flynn and Marilyn Monroe inhabit the Lust level right below."

Mention of Limbo and Lust "levels" didn't faze me. The Inferno sat atop a re-created Nine Circles of Hell.

"I'm just an off-balance oddball," Dr. Jack said, "as I was in my film life. Mr. Mad Scientist, always considered more smart and crazy than sexy. An invisible CinSim gets no recognition. *You,* at least, put up with me. I thought you even really liked me."

He sounded pouty now.

"I like you fine. *At* the Inferno Hotel, not in my bedroom."

"That's what I broke even my long-distance bonds to come and tell you. Things *aren't* fine at the Inferno Hotel. It's haunted."

"The house muscle, Grizelle, is tiger enough to handle it."

"My dear lady. Grizelle is . . . no longer . . . what she was. No one or nothing at the Inferno is."

"What's new about that? Snow is just doing his usual control-freak act."

"*Snow's* no longer in control. Look at me!"

"I can't."

"Oh, sure, Miss Street, I like to give girls at the bar the occasional fanny pinch, but when did I get into serial assault on asses? Tonight. Then, heading here, I almost ended up way down the freeway in Laughlin. All us Inferno entities are possessed. Haywire. Any minute, the news will hit the thousands of tourists trekking in and out of the hotel. And now Snow's nowhere to be found."

"Small loss," I muttered, shaken despite myself. "Since when am I backup security for the Inferno?"

"It's all so horribly wrong, Miss Street. The slot machines are spitting out razor blades. At the Inferno bar, your white-chocolate Albino Vampire cocktails are pouring out as dead dark as Black Russians. The 'perfect film wife,' Nora Charles, has runs in her silk hose, and hubby Nick Charles is out of gin!"

Dr. Jack's last complaint alarmed me the most. Thirties booze-hound detective Nick Charles running out of Boodles was like the film *Casablanca* running out of doomed lovers. Sheer travesty.

While I stood there wondering what suit of armor I should wear to a cursed Las Vegas hotel, my casement window slammed open again. This time the cause was all too visible.

A huge wolfhound-wolf-cross dog with vampire hearing and fangs and a bloodhound sniffer—wanted to know who'd been tipping over his water dish and messing with his rescuer from a fate worse than death . . . euthanasia. I grinned approval at his superdog two-story jump. No need to play nice and use the first-floor doggie doors tonight.

Quicksilver's bounds abused my bedspread again. He landed by the upended bowl, skidded through the spilled water, and scented the unseen intruder. As I stepped away from confining Mr. Elusive, Quick leapt with paws extended at the exact shoulder height to pin the Invisible Man to the wall.

"Thanks, partner. Keep him busy while I get 'decent.' And no peeking," I warned Jack Griffith, "even if you are a doctor."

"I'm not that kind of a doctor and Rin Tin Tin here seriously needs a manicure. *Ouch!*"

"I know. He likes his nails long, and I don't ever argue with that muzzle."

Living in an Enchanted Cottage has its benefits. I slipped into my endless closet, still wondering what to wear to an unspecified widespread haunting, and closed the door. A hovering pixie made herself into Tinker Bell so I could see in the dark.

I sighed. Deeply, madly, truly. Snow and I had cherished a heavy-duty mutual loathe-hate relationship since I came to Las Vegas several months ago in search of my double, my possible sister, Lilith Quince. She was my mirror image, and mirrors had turned out to be my medium after the Millennium Revelation pulled back the curtains on the supernaturals coexisting among us.

Call me one weird sister, but I wasn't high on bailing out the Inferno, or its owner. I've never been into male sex symbols. I'm not talking about the planet Mars with the provocative little arrow. Blatant onstage booty calls for screaming female fans and profit insult my intelligence. Elvis would have swiveled in vain. Justin Timberlake would have to get his screams and squees from some other chick.

Cocaine, aka Snow, played Pride incarnate as lead singer in his Seven Deadly Sins band. He ended each show by enslaving his mosh-pit groupies with a post-concert Brimstone Kiss that had them swooning and coming back again and again—and never getting another smooch.

What a racket to sell tickets. The least he could do was sleep with the poor lovesick fans, but he never did, just teased them and left them panting.

Jerk!

This was not about Snow, I reminded myself while squirming into the steel-studded vampire-fighting catsuit I owed to the Inferno security wardrobe. The shiny black fabric was supernatural Kevlar, suppler and stronger than leather and up to facing down any unknown but wayward supernatural capable of turning an entire hotel and all its contents . . . well, upside down.

My silver familiar, a souvenir of my ongoing war with Snow, left its default position as a thin hip chain under the James Bond–ish wet suit and eeled down a tight sleeve. It emerged clamped on my left wrist as a pair of handcuffs locked onto the same arm.

Cool look. I hoped the familiar would schedule a rerun the next time I was out for dinner with my investigative partner and dead-dowsing significant other, Ric. That would keep his mind on dessert.

I stuffed my feet into Ed Hardy motorcycle boots and emerged through the closet door as the pixie winked out. The Invisible Man, a learned scientist in his day, gave a piercing wolf whistle.

"Quicksilver, *leave kitty!*" I called my dog off just as his very visible fangs neared Dr. Jack's very invisible throat.

"Toss me my fedora," I told Dr. Jack. "I like to look professional going to a job."

"My work here is done." His voice was a rasp. "May you and the very big doggie live long and prosper."

Quick let his forelegs click to the floor. He picked up one wet paw and wrinkled his muzzle.

"Not your mess," I told him. "we're walking into a much

bigger one. What's your position on anyone or anything who mucks with our CinSim friends?"

He lifted a rear leg and did nothing more.

I nodded. "That's right. You took out that Kansas weather witch's TV tower with one well-placed piss during her electrical storm. Let's go see what's shaking at the Inferno Hotel and find out who needs pissing on now."

I looked around. My bedspread was a pyramid of folds on the floor, topped by my slightly used fedora. I decided I could leave home without it.

Just driving up to the Inferno in my vintage Cadillac convertible, Quicksilver riding shotgun in sunglasses, almost shocked the catsuit off me . . . not that anybody on the Vegas Strip would much notice a naked woman these days.

They sure couldn't miss the hotel's drastically altered façade. I parked on the curved driveway well before the entrance canopy, so I could gaze up. Neon was busting out all over up and down the Las Vegas Strip.

Not at the Inferno. Tonight it was less the Technicolor erupting volcano and more the smoldering ruin. The usual exterior fireworks had faded to cold, colorless flames the shades of ashes . . . the gray and black and white of a vintage film, like the CinSims inside.

Tourists elbowed in and out of the massive front doors, eyes on free-offer flyers, oblivious to the racket, bustle, and anyone else, as usual.

So I was only secondarily shocked almost out of my butt-stomping booties when my parking valet pal, Manny, opened my Caddy's driver's side door.

Good grief! Manny's usual vibrant orange demon scales were dolphin blue-gray instead, and his mood was as subdued as his color.

"Dolly's looking a bit lackluster, Miss Street," he said.

"Well, sure. Her paint job isn't reflecting the neon-bright flames ringing the hotel for sixty stories up. You look a bit down in the forked tongue and tail yourself."

Manny shrugged as he slid into her red leather upholstery. "Something's different about the hotel? You got me."

Beside me, Quicksilver whimpered his suspicions.

"You're right," I told my dog. "The Invisible Man wasn't wrong."

We left Manny punked out behind the steering wheel as we hoofed it along the crowded sidewalk. I looked back to see the speed-demon valet putt-putting Dolly's three hundred horses up the parking ramp. I'd never let Manny floor it like the regular leadfoots, but that exit was seriously lame.

Every hair on Quicksilver's body stood on end the moment the hotel's entry doors whooshed shut behind us. My studded wet suit felt warm and cozy, but the skin of my exposed face and hands tightened as if plunged into ice water.

The usual over-air-conditioned casino atmosphere had gone even more arctic.

Quick clung to my left hip, Mr. Service Dog incarnate.

I plunged through any crowd openings, heading straight for the Inferno bar, where my favorite tipsters hung out. I was relieved when a tall, dark-haired man in white tie and tails caught my eye.

Nick Charles, the famous detective, was still at his CinSim post. My relief trickled out in a sigh. If Nick Charles was on duty at the Inferno bar, all was right with the post–Millennium Revelation world.

He turned to greet me, a quizzical eyebrow arched toward his receding hairline of wavy hair. "Miss Delilah Street, as I *don't* live and breathe. Aren't you a treat to see in your upscale long johns?"

He hoisted his constant prop, a martini glass that was perpetually half-empty or half-full, depending on your life philosophy.

"I'm so glad to see you." I actually gushed I was so relieved to find Nick being his normal self.

"That goes double for me, as my vision often does. I have a mystery to solve that has me hammered." He uttered a puzzled complaint. "There is swill in my glass."

"There's always expensive swill in your glass," I pointed out.

"This stuff is undrinkable, and from me that's saying something."

I leaned forward to sip from the rim that swayed to and fro with his well-oiled sense of balance. We could have been on the *QE II*. A wavelet washed into my mouth.

"Oh, Nicky. This won't hurt you. It's just . . . water."

Nick's dapper shoulders shuddered. "Poison! Nora." His voice lifted to summon his wife. "I'm being poisoned."

"Hang on for a minute, Nicky dear," she trilled from the other side of bar. "I'm coming, but Asta is being a perfect *beast!*"

Quicksilver was not an Inferno bar regular, but he sensed when things were awry. He gave his yard-troll-at-the-cottage-door growl that was half-inquisitive and half-desirous of a snack.

Nora came jerking around the bar's other side in all her willowy high-fashion glory, up to an impudently tilted and veiled hat overshadowed by a large gray ostrich feather.

Quicksilver leapt forward with a pounce and growl that indicated prey.

I had no leash but my voice. *"Leave kitty,"* I ordered. It worked in Sunset Park, and here he'd stopped on a whisker although his discontented growl kept going and growing until the sound of a squalling baby rose to my ears.

How odd for Quicksilver to carry on like a coyote pup.

I looked down. Quicksilver was silent, but his blue-eyed gaze also fixed on something . . . a critter the size of a wire-haired terrier but with huge-clawed paws that churned the carpeted floor while a sound like an angry monkey grated through its fangs.

My jaw dropped, then stood to attention again in amazed speech. "That's . . . not . . . Asta."

"Of course it is," Nora cooed fondly. "He's just throwing a tantrum. Isn't he, dear?" she asked Nick.

No, it was a real "kitty," sort of. And not a *he*. I recognized the white-and-black-striped coat of Grizelle's white-tiger form, but now she was just a . . . baby, a fifty-pound cub with demonic green eyes staring straight at me as if ready to tear my heart out.

For an instant, the fuzzy-wuzzy adorable black-and-white baby-tiger stripes morphed into short frothy white petticoats and blouse under a full-skirted black apron. The long gray claws became dark Mary Jane shoes on white-stockinged feet, and the cub's face was surrounded by petite black pigtails tied with poison green ribbons. So cute it was scary! I stamped my Ed Hardy tattooed motorcycle boot at her, and Grizelle's fierce, but truly "girly," expression returned with a snarl to a tiger-cub likeness with the rest of her.

What was going on here?

Nick's martinis turned to tap water? Awesome security chief Grizelle reduced to a leashed tiger cub? Nick and Nora not noticing the major family pet switch? What else was wrong at the Inferno Hotel?

"Why didn't you tell me Miss Street is trespassing again?" asked a resonant baritone that could strike twenty-five thousand people silent . . . or set them screaming mindlessly.

I turned fast. The Inferno owner, operator, and rock-star mogul stood so close I almost got leather burns from *his* black jumpsuit. We could have gone on the Inferno stage with his cub and my dog as an animal act.

Curiouser and curiouser, with neon on it.

The suspected albino vampire's skin and shoulder-blade-brushing hair were both as white as white could be, but he was not the usual milky monovision with a blindfold of dark glasses the only off-color note. Gone was his bleached-leather stage costume. Instead, his jumpsuit was dead black, as black as those signature sunglasses.

"It's our bar," Nick's voice came over my shoulder in a grumpy slur. "We were leashed here first."

"You tell him, Nicky." Nora struggled to untwine the tiger cub's lead from around her gray silk hose. Major snags to match the unsightly existing runs were in their future.

"I believe you mean 'leased,'" Snow corrected Nicky.

I tried not to ogle Snow's skintight Elvis-comeback black leather outfit although doing so came with my job as a paranormal investigator. As with his usual white leather jumpsuit, also borrowed from Elvis, this one was open to his navel like a red-carpet starlet's dress.

The black outfit was how I knew we were dealing with a CinSim of himself that Snow had commissioned. Simple for an albino. He was all white to begin with. The perpetual sunglasses that protected his light-sensitive irises were always black.

He only had to have himself shot on a bit of rare surviving silver nitrate film.

Then the image was impressed onto a fresh zombie 3-D body canvas through the Immortality Mob's so-far-secret process. Las Vegas was the cusp where cutting-edge science and paranormal-fueled magic met . . . and was turned into pure old-fashioned profit. But only vintage silver nitrate film would work. Get ahold of a precious piece of it and . . .

Prest-O Change-O, you had an exact reproduction, on cue, on tap, at Snow's command. He'd bought and manufactured his dark double. He hadn't grown his own in the mirror, as I apparently had with Lilith.

Cheater.

I wondered what immortal bit of lost vintage filmmaking had been sacrificed to Snow's desire for a double and his deal with the Immortality Mob, not to mention what poor dead schlub got to power the mogul's needs.

You might get the idea that I didn't like Snow, but you'd be wrong.

I *despised* his cheesy rock-star appeal to the "weaker sex" and myself for having to deal with him. If he wasn't an albino vampire rumor made him, he was some variety of potent supernatural. Finding out exactly what was number one on my bucket list.

There was no arguing that Snow wasn't the Darkside darling and an American idol. His pale skin was also as muscular as Michelangelo's major-hot statue of a naked David duplicated at Caesars Palace. I could see why, when Snow's pelvis was on-stage working his white Fender Stratocaster guitar like a giant screaming electric fig leaf, mosh-pit groupies swooned.

But why was the CinSim Snow coming out to play when Snow was still in town?

Was this part of the Inferno "haunting"?

Meanwhile, Nick was showing off for Nora by wobbling up to Snow's black cowboy-booted physique and going nose to nose. Nick's film-white finger tapped Snow right between the pecs, dead center of the Jack Frost scars etched like lace and lightning bolts on his bare chest that were either souvenirs from the finger of God casting him down from heaven or souvenirs of some evil entity shocking him back to life in the heart he didn't have. My theory anyway.

"Those 'leases' that confine all us CinSims are leashes," said Mr. Charles. "And we don't like it. We've got a right to roam, like any Micky Mouse cell phone."

Snow's broad shoulders and schooled torso-twist literally shrugged off Nick.

"How you can stay drunk on plain water I'll never know, Mr. Charles," he said. "Your lovely wife is having trouble controlling the family pet, as usual, only the pet in question is a juvenile version of my security chief, which is *not* as usual."

CinSim Snow knew the score, yet no one noticed but me. He turned my way. Wearing bootheels, I was almost Nick Charles's six-foot height. Snow still towered.

"You're the investigator, Miss Street. May I suggest you do your job?"

He walked away from the bar area, the crowds parting as if sensing the passage of the Invisible Man. Once offstage, Snow's secret mojo allowed him to move around the hotel-casino floor unrecognized by the masses. I looked up at the jumbo HDTV high above. The Seven Deadly Sins were rocking out in an instrumental frenzy, no lead singer/guitarist in sight.

The sound was muted, but they were performing live.

I think.

Back to the family Charles. "You've changed your ensemble tonight," I told Nora.

"Of course." Her voice lilted with good humor. "Snow purchased the rights to my extensive wardrobe as well as me." She did a fashion-model twirl. "Otherwise, my bar duty would get boring, for me and for the clientele."

"But why the hat obscuring your sophisticated-lady face?"

"Can you keep a secret?" Nora turned her back on me, encouraging me to come around for a girlfriend conference.

When I faced Nora and her several-layered veil again, she lifted it for a sneak peek.

Gasping, I saw that Nora's elegant pencil-thin eyebrows had blossomed into furry Brook Shield caterpillars. Her mascara had run, giving her eyes the spiked, drawn-on look of a circus clown.

"It's a surprise new look," she said with a winsome smile.

"Are you girls done?" Nick peered over Nora's shoulder while she hastened to lower her veil. "I have a phenomenon to report, dear ladies. My keen suspicions have been raised. Would you care to look where I direct, Miss Street?"

I turned again to face the bustling casino with the jumbo

HDTV screen high above. The Seven Deadly Sins were rocking out with *Black* CinSim Snow in place as their lead singer.

"Just look there." The contents of Nicky's martini glass almost overran one rim as he pointed.

"All the groupies are going nuts. So?"

"Exactly my opinion of 'groupies,'" Nick declared. "We didn't have them in my day. They sound like a variety of aquarium fish," he said carefully, "fish" being a difficult word to enunciate in his perpetual but charming sloshed condition.

The ace detective tattled on. "I saw our mutual friend, Mr. Snow."

"Friend? Speak for yourself."

"I am trying to, Miss Street, if you will deign to listen. At the end of the earlier show, I saw Mr. Snow bend down to present the groping groupies with handsome white silk neck scarves of the type that go so well with my tux."

I didn't need more CinSim wardrobe notes, or to know about Snow's throwaways to his fans now that he no longer bestowed the notorious Brimstone Kiss for some mysterious reason.

"I saw," Nick Charles went on, "less than an hour ago, the entire mosh pit and our mutual sponsor, dressed all in white like a bride, as usual. I saw the whole k-k-kit and ka-Boodles disappear in a f-f-flash of fire.

"I swear." He held his bare right palm upright like a witness in court.

I held up a hand for Nicky's martini glass. How weird to see the clear glass and the liquid inside take on subtle colors as the object left CinSim possession for my custody. I sipped.

Still just water. Flat, dull water. Nick Charles's vision of mosh-pit hell had not been the Boodles talking.

But if the "real" Snow and his closest fans had been kidnapped, where were they? And how would I get there? Things were so truly topsy-turvy here at the Inferno that it gave me a bold new idea.

"Nora, will you watch Quicksilver while I take 'Asta' for a walk?" I held my hand out for the dog leash.

She seemed startled by the idea, but the writhing tiger cub actually rubbed its furry sides back and forth on my calves as I took custody of its lead.

Luckily, my body suit prevented any touchy-feely contact between me and Snow's shape-shifting security chief now stuck in baby white-tiger form. Grizelle and I would only touch each other if it was hand-to-claw combat, and once, recently, it had been.

"Asta is chipped to stay here at the bar," Nick warned me.

Grizelle sure wasn't. From the loud purr that ended in a squall like a human infant's, I knew she badly wanted out of here and onto the real Snow's trail, too.

I nodded at Quicksilver to tell him he was the Asta substitute for now. Since he and Grizelle had tangled, too, I knew he'd enjoy supplanting her. He adored CinSims.

Just then, a drunken tourist wearing a Michael Vick T-shirt hurtled toward Nora, reaching for her veil.

"Let's see the famous face, pretty lady."

Uh-oh. Wrong logo. The tipsy tourist saw the whites of Quick's fangs instead. Quicksilver had far more guardian chops than the missing Asta.

Meanwhile, I had a case of hotel haunting to solve.

On the huge screen, the camera panned across the jumping, squealing groupies. One wasn't moving, so I focused on the still center of the mayhem. Oh. I was targeting my exact image— Lilith, my double-trouble sister from mirror-world. I spun to face the mirror behind the bar that reflected the exact same scene. For only this split-second moment, I could use it.

"I don't know if shapeshifters can survive breaking the mirror barrier," I muttered as I leapt toward the image of myself, my hand curled tight around the tiger cub's leash.

Grizelle answered with a fierce growl. She bounded through

the mirror, turning into liquid quicksilver ahead of me, a circus tiger breaking through a paper drum-skin.

I hated to perform my disappearing act in public, but most tourists were eyeing the HD screen, and the CinSims would never betray my trade secrets.

How does a quantum leap through a quicksilver mirror backing feel? Imagine passing through oily dark lightning. Then four paws and two feet landed hard on the black floor of what seemed an empty soundstage.

Not quite empty.

In the farthest darkness, a disturbing spotlit tableau boiled with motion three hundred feet away. If you've ever seen a close-up of maggots infesting a corpse on a crime forensics TV show, which I can guarantee you have, that's what the brilliantly lit postage-stamp-size scene recalled.

I started forward at a gallop, baby Grizelle leaping alongside me like a . . . well, like a gazelle. I had to wonder how a major beast felt being so totally downsized, and could understand the shapeshifter's fury. The distant mob scene disturbed me, too.

As we closed on the action, I realized we were viewing the dark backs of about fifteen young women shoving, pushing, even climbing each other to make contact with a . . . white marble statue set against a black stone wall.

The obscured figure we neared was not all white now. Telltale blots of red dappled the object of the assault. My emotions sickened to see a rerun in progress of what I'd only witnessed at the bitter end . . . my partner Ric Montoya's multiple fang-marked body after a whole freaking vampire empire, including vampire tsetse flies, had feasted on him. I had to stop this.

Closer still, a frantic Grizelle and I bounded, our charging footsteps muffled by the tiger's pads, my ridged-rubber boot soles, and the attackers' deafening shrieks.

Now I was close enough to read the backs of the attackers.

Backs? *Read?* What were they? Living billboards? What was I missing? Oh, the women were wearing T-shirts with messages that echoed their shouted words. And those words were becoming clear and scarily familiar.

"You can't whip us up, then just stop," peeved female voices taunted.

"How does it feel to be 'snowbound'?"

"Yeah. Like *we* were, Cocaine."

"We want what's coming to us . . . the Brimstone Kiss."

I skidded to a stop. *Oh, no.* The figure pinned by the ravenous horde was no hunk of unfeeling marble. It had to be Grizelle's boss and my so-unfavorite Vegas mogul.

The seething, clawing harpies using the real Snow for a climbing wall shouted "Come on, Cocaine, give," and "Snow up a storm for us," as well earthier online endearments I also recognized, like "Ice Prick." Or so the rumor went.

Only my hard grip on the leash kept fifty pounds of snarling tiger cub from scaling the T-shirted human torsos ahead of us. Now I knew what these attackers were, not the relentless ancient tormenters who'd savaged Ric but modern fangirls gone bad. Even fifteen women, crazed enough, can make a mob.

Groupies were indeed Nick Charles's schooling "fish" . . . if you thought "piranha."

"Grizelle," I ordered, "velvet paws and fangs *only*. They're paying customers and fans. The boss would not want them hurt, no matter what. Got it?"

The tiger cub's white muzzle lifted in grudging acknowledgment. I hoped she didn't take it out of my skin later, when we were all back to normal, which I swore we would be. All of us, even Snow and the groupies.

Was I still missing something? Maybe I was being naïve, and Snow *liked* this scene. I had no time to overthink anything. Even my silver familiar jumped ship, abandoning its cool double-handcuff bracelet form. It split to rocket up one arm, across my shoulders, and down to the other wrist so fast I hoped I'd just *sensed* hot metal burns.

When I looked, my wrists were circled by cuff bracelets. The pair was etched with serious monster designs, snake-pit-tangled shapes I couldn't name. Sea monster, kraken, giant squid? Both cuffs trailed silver-chain tentacles—more than the average octopus—say nine per wrist.

I was literally "armed" with my own matched set of heavy metal cat-o'-nine-tails. Could I whip community ass now . . .

The familiar had become such an intuitive part of me, I'd almost forgotten it had been spawned by my unintentionally touching a lock of Snow's albino hair, and he might be murderously goaded to revenge at the moment.

Would the familiar, no matter how lethal the form, still obey my "prime directive," think first and do no harm unless about to *be* harmed? Yeah, I'm a pacifist kick-ass chick. So sue me, but expect to pay court costs.

My only option was wading into the frenzied fans' midst, jerking anonymous arms and shoulders away from the prey while Grizelle nipped the heels of their churning feet.

Only Grizelle and I knew the worst part of this assault scene, a damning secret that made me squirm with sympathetic pain for a man, or whatever, I despised.

Only we knew the mauling groupies were pressing Snow's eternally wounded back—damaged because of me—to the hard stone. He was bound between pain and humiliation like a mythical demigod in Tartarus, the Greek abyss below even Hades, and the mother of all hells.

Whatever breed of immortal Snow was, I knew he was vulnerable—or even human enough—to bleed. I'd never seen but often envisioned the raw, meaty mess my driving compassion for my lover, Ric, had made of his back. I hadn't known it, but every lash scar my lips fresh from an extorted Brimstone Kiss had erased on Ric's skin had appeared as a fresh welt on Snow's several hotel stories away.

Vegas after the Millennium Revelation was the kind of naughty world where one good deed would exact at least another bad one in exchange. Ugly speculations were occurring to me in fractured seconds.

My God. What if these spellbound women were no longer just berserk groupies, what if this sinister hotel-wide change also had made them into *vampires*?

Above the feeding frenzy loomed Snow's profile, ghost white face and long hair turned sideways, neck cords strained, albino eyes shut, denuded of the ever-present sunglasses.

By then I'd jerked a pathway through the clawing groupies so eager to close ranks and fight off rescuers. My arms lashed out, the tentacles of silver chains cutting slashes in their black Seven Deadly Sins and snowsluts.com T-shirts, other tentacles wrapping their necks and bare forearms.

The swinging metal stingers left silver comet trails in the air . . . and streaks of glitter on the black knit and the flesh beneath the raw-edged rips, on the women's arms, lifting to defend now, not assault. Their fevered demands became moans as I slashed them into stumbling away, cradling their arms and mumbling.

"That hurts . . . burns . . . stings."

Only then did I realize what the monsters engraved on my silver cuffs were . . . jellyfish.

Most jellyfish stingers were not homicidal, but protective. So far, no major harm had been done. Grizelle, that intractable . . . huntress . . . had used her formidable baby teeth to snag jeans legs and T-shirt sleeves, dragging the groupies away over and over, until they clustered in a supine moaning clot.

Now I had to face—how it pained me to attach this word to Snow, but it was true—the victim. Not only did I dread the sight of the bloody rock idol . . . this was my deepest personal trauma, a Ric rerun, only with Snow instead, my worst nightmare starring my best enemy.

I approached, taking in the man manacled against a towering black basalt wall. Way too much Samson for this Delilah.

Bloodsucking lip prints covered Snow's pristine white skin and bleached leather like a graphic design and his bare face . . . I'd never before seen those semicircles of white eyelashes innocently curved along his eyelids. They reminded me of severed snowflakes.

Something winked from the floor at his feet: his shiny black sunglasses, torn off and tossed down. He was an albino, no matter what else he was. Even Snow didn't deserve to be crucified by his idolaters, his weak vision identified and their protection cast away. His pale blue-veined eyelids still danced to the REM mode, barely visible yet jerking in that unmistakable tic of nerves on edge. Genetically defenseless.

I bent to retrieve the fragile sunglasses.

"Hey, leave that! It's ours," a groupie shouted.

A couple rose to charge again, trying to topple me from performing my one good deed, but Grizelle protected me during my ass-out moment.

I elbowed away any still-upright groupies with my flailing glitter whips, climbed Snow like a Sherpa, and placed the sunglasses over the rock god's spotlight-blinded eyes.

I let myself slide down the marble sculpture of his form, back to the obsidian floor of this place, satisfied his eyes were open again and hidden behind the same tiny, gleaming reflection of me I faced every time we met.

With his full persona in place, he struck me as way too cool and invulnerable again. I'd never seen his back flinch after he'd inherited Ric's boyhood beatings, and at the moment he even seemed a bit amused by my race to his rescue.

"So," I said to Snow. "Are we good now?"

His head bowed toward my presence. "*You're* good," he said. "But you could be better."

If he wasn't hurting, I wasn't feeling merciful . . . more like had, and mad.

"Let's consider," I said, "the thousand cheesy films of women chained and mauled. Maybe you 'asked for it,' rock star. Not that I'd ever tell that to the Pussycat Dolls." Who maybe had, too. Sex objects could be so obvious.

Why couldn't we all just keep our kinks in the bedroom closet?

Because they made money.

"It's my job, Miss Street." He made it sound more like a vocation.

I'd noticed that two of the snaps beneath his costume's gem-studded fly had popped open during the struggle among his frenzied fans to claim a piece of him. I mean, who could miss that bling? I was able to get my fingers, uh, down under to press the snaps decorously shut.

"And doing that isn't yours," he finished.

Interesting, though. Snow was obviously not getting off on this mass grope scene any more than I was . . . or . . . wait . . . not until I appeared in the neighborhood.

What to do? If I stepped away, I'd leave him even more exposed to the fanimals, so I stayed put as a barrier and nervously rubbed a bloodred stain on his torso, managing only to smear it.

His hair brushed my embarrassed pink face as his head bent to watch me, knowing what I didn't until my fingers touched the sticky dab of red, retreated, and I inhaled the scent of perfume, not coppery blood.

No wonder Snow had suffered this apparent feeding frenzy so stoically.

Instead of bloody sucking marks, these "vampire" groupies had left . . . lipstick kisses on almost every inch of exposed flesh, which Snow had a lot of. He was a bloody Andy Warhol canvas. Oh, blessed Bela Lugosi! I hadn't prevented a physical ravening; I'd interrupted a rave, a rainbow party gone bad.

"It's only lipstick, Delilah." Snow so loved stating the obvious when I'd missed the boat. My moral outrage only got me a ticket on Roll-Your-Eyes line. My time here had been wasted, and I looked like an idiot.

"I see that. Now," I admitted.

"Even you wear lipstick sometimes."

That was true. My Snow White coloring made most makeup unnecessary. I was your natural woman, until I ran into unnatural situations. Like this.

"Just a little light lip *gloss*," I said between clenched teeth.

"Even better."

I was *not* going to flirt with a guy whose fly I'd just locked down. I was tempted to leave him here to free his own ass. Except . . .

"Your back—?" I asked.

His long hair shook with his head. "—is my eternal unhealing wound, thanks to your innocent meddling. Forget that. I need to be free, not pain-free."

Still, Snow's sensitive white skin had turned scarlet under his wrist manacles. My hands fretted at the bonds that imprisoned him. The dark metal was so cold and slick, my fingers iced at the touch. The familiar twined around my wrist as a bracelet dangling only one edged charm, a four-inch diamond-grit jeweler's saw on a chain. The miniaturized shark's teeth no more nicked the black metal than the same saw or an acetylene torch could impact my silver familiar.

"Black-moon tarnished silver, Delilah," Snow said. "I thought your silver talent could counter any supernatural traps, but I see you can't. Get the hell out while you can. Protect the Inferno CinSims."

"From what?"

Then I remembered a pretty damning lost detail in this whole misunderstood mess. "Why did I spot Lilith among the groupies upstairs? She only manifests outside my mirror when things are really wrong."

"Don't you know?" he asked. "She's your shadow, not mine."

The black lenses reflected me eyeing them suspiciously. "She's been yours, too, Snowman! She's not here now. Why not? Everyone I know has been sucked one way or another into this hell, haven't they? These fevered groupies are just the Greek chorus, not the female lead . . ."

Oh. I realized that the current cast of characters was missing a powerful key figure I had spotted earlier but might not have truly recognized.

"And *I'm* not the female lead either," I said aloud. "I wasn't even supposed to be here. It all began with . . ."

I focused on the Grizelle cub stalking back and forth between the lines of now-cowed women nursing their stinging glitter wounds. Only in Vegas. But the glitter-whip marks were another element that looked worse than it was. We were all being *played*.

I surveyed the vast soundstage from polished floor to the blackest, emptiest most opaque heights above us all.

I'd always teased the Lilith in my mirror that Mom, if we'd had one, had named us after shady ladies in biblical times. Delilah was an Old Testament seductress and spy who brought Samson to the same plight Snow faced, blinded and chained, only by a single vengeful woman instead of a hen party.

"Lilith?" I asked myself. Maybe not *my* Lilith. Now I wasn't sure *who* I'd seen in my own image upstairs in the mosh pit. I sure wasn't invoking my double, because there was no silver-backed mirror here to magnify my few powers, only darkness.

Still, a terrifying theory had me by the throat. *Something* had possessed these groupies to assault Snow instead of worship him from afar. Or someone.

"Lilith," I repeated, scared now of an answer.

Maybe I was looking for a Lilith who dated back before Eden, back before the Fall and even maybe before Satan's Fall from heaven. Maybe I was going for the east-of-Eden sweepstakes, the woman reportedly kicked out of Eden like Cain, the font of all feminine evil from what some believed were myths and tales banned from the Old Testament, or maybe she was just one vastly misunderstood mama . . .

I named her and Named her beyond any duplicate of me in the mirror.

"*Lilith!*" Lilith, *the* Lilith. I called, and therefore conjured her.

Whew. Wind came screaming through this empty time tunnel, reaming the hell out of Hell.

Planting my boots and my purely human will, I stared past the wind-tossed black veil of my hair and found a giant sister image flashing on and off in the surrounding darkness. She was ghostly of skin, with long, long dark tresses mirroring the toss of mine in the windstorm of her manifestation.

Not my double, but my enemy. Everything's enemy. Lilith Unplugged.

She'd appeared in human form but was still the crimson-pupiled demon succubus of legend. Even I had to admit she looked particularly fetching in an iridescent snakeskin gown with a mermaid fishtail train that matched her chartreuse irises.

The Grizelle cub, recognizing that a really serious player had joined the game, leapt to rip its front claws down Lilith's green gown. The claw marks sealed as fast as Grizelle could make them, the cub snarling with greater rage every time the damage of her attacks came undone.

Lilith's lithe white arms, pale as a serpent's underbelly, spread to welcome the cowed groupies into her devouring, almost maternal, gesture and proximity. They came stumbling atop each other in a rush, slavering over their new idol, madness resurfacing in their eyes.

I glanced over my shoulder. Lilith's deep contralto croon was hynotizing the agitated groupies. Their eerily green irises seemed to reflect emotions of lust and envy. What a rock star wannabe she was.

"I know when you pissed *me* off," I told Snow. "When did you piss off the mother of all demons?"

"Millennia ago. I didn't suspect you'd have the smarts, guts, or power to call out a major demon. Her distraction won't last long. She'll want to expand her presence now that you've called her here. Leave me to deal with her. Escape while you can."

Well, thank you. Nothing like an employer who'd tricked you into ending an involuntary bondage scene between a sex idol and his adorees . . . and then considered your outing a major monster a screwup on your part. Trouble is, I can't abandon any living being in trouble, human or paranormal, even Snow. Tell me life is hard and not fair. Tell me death is a tango dancer, and I'm naïve and old-fashioned, but do not tell me I can't do what I need to.

Even against Grizelle.

Even against my sister Lilith.

Even against the Lilith who was kicked out of Eden for being the world's first and best bad girl. But why did she have it in for Snow?

"I know what Lilith has done to you lately. What did *you* do to Lilith?" I demanded.

Snow's face turned away again, my angry image fading in the sunglasses with the gesture. "Not what I did. What I didn't do. It's what *she* wanted to do with *me*."

Ah. Hell hath no fury like a female demon scorned. So she'd cursed him. How?

"We all want to undo you, Snow," I told him dryly. "Now, listen up. This is not just any Lilith, right? This is not my mirror-me. This is really Lilith, Adam's first wife, who was driven from Eden for wanting to be on top?"

The sunglasses tilted down toward my face. "Yes, but it's me she's cursed, not Adam."

"And the curse is . . . ?"

His second of hesitation felt like an eon knowing Lilith's sick interlude with the groupies was likely to end at any moment.

"Spill it."

"I can only give pleasure, not receive it."

Wow. I processed that. It sort of explained the Brimstone Kiss. It didn't explain why he'd stopped giving them after he'd forced me to accept one. He'd said I'd failed the test, but maybe it wasn't *his* test, maybe it was Lilith's.

"No wonder," I told him, "she's mad as hell and won't take it anymore, like the groupies. You cheated on her."

With me.

As much as I hated to admit it, I'd just seen I could get a rise out of Snow. If that wasn't a symptom of pleasure, I don't know what was with a man.

He smiled. "So you can't spare any more empathy time for me, Delilah?"

"Hell, no. I tend to side with the girls."

I turned as a snarling Grizelle took a guardian post at Snow's feet and advanced on Lilith. She'd settled into mere life-size form and was awaiting me like a headmistress with a wayward pupil.

"You confront as well as conjure me?" She stepped away from the demon-drugged, smiling groupies pulling their hair out a single filament at a time. "Do you know who I am now, feeble interloper? How powerful I am?"

"As a matter of fact, I do."

"Do you know who or what *he* is?"

"Snow, International Supernatural of Mystery? Nope, but I intend to find out in my way on my own time."

"I know what you are, Delilah. You must be pleased to see your enemy bound at the mercy of such trifling fools as these enamored human females."

"No, Lilith, I am not. *I* don't care to use intermediaries."

Her lurid eyes glittered hotter, the green haloed with scarlet. "Are you *daring* to refer to me?"

"Yup. Oh, you're a gorgeous demon witch with a lot of revenge due you. God's first and final mistake, made from the same human clay as Adam, his equal, not his wimpy rib. Your successor, Eve, took the apple and lost paradise, but you played the serpent for the Fall, didn't you? Hell hath no fury like *a first wife* scorned," I paraphrased, "and you have a minor immortal fury on. So . . . Snow is Adam?"

"Snow is more than mere man."

"Snow is . . . Satan?"

"He's more than mere devil."

Loved the new slant on Snow, but that wasn't my main goal.

"Maybe he is, but *you* are tiresomely predictable, Lilith. You suck the life from children born and unborn, the blood from the human, the soul from the eternal. You haunt men's dreams and drain them to death. You can only be banished by the uttering of eight hidden names . . ."

"So you *do* know me. You don't know my names."

"Wikipedia knows your secret names nowadays, Lil. You are outdated."

Behind me, Snow gave a short, taunting laugh. "Guess she's got your number, Lilith. You need to get on Facebook, drum up some fans besides my gullible groupies."

I knew one thing else about her, one so-egocentric weakness. And that I *could* use.

While Lilith glared at Snow, her expression cold and her eyes burning hot, I bent to trace a large pattern with my forefinger on the obsidian floor, watching the silver-familiar chains run liquid down my fingernail to pool and spread and sink into the blackness.

I heard Snow's smothered cry of pain and guessed that the black-moon metal was searing his skin at Lilith's command.

He'd spoken to distract Lilith, and the last thing I wanted was owing him for more pain incurred on my behalf.

My forefinger moved fast to contain the widening mercurial puddle by scribing the fanciful curlicue form in my mind . . . the frame of Snow White's wicked stepmother's mirror that reflected me in the Enchanted Cottage's upper hall.

Even Lilith sensed my actions and looked down to see what I was doing, a fatal mistake.

There was a mirror here now, with the silver familiar providing the reflective backing. We were unveiling Disney under glass, for obsidian is a polished black stone, a dark mirror, and we were both standing on it.

Lilith stared unblinking into her own reflection—pale white face, long dark hair, glittering green gown—a wavering writ on water.

Some old texts said Lilith had been enamored of staring into a mirror. I'd ensured that her own image would seduce her yet again. That weakness momentarily drained her demon powers and made her just another shallow mean girl simpering in a high-school girls' room mirror.

Lilith screeched as she realized I'd made her trap herself, then she fled with a Wicked Witch of the West meltdown into the reflected image at her feet.

After she vanished, I spotted my own image resolving on the wind-riffled oil-slick surface left behind and dove down after her. An icy plunge from this dark empty abyss brought me into a soaring arrival in dark, overpopulated chaos, teeming with enough sound and fury to make my ears bleed. In the mosh pit, groupies were swaying hypnotically, screaming for the Brimstone Kiss.

Around me, Lust and Envy and Greed, oh my, rocked out. Was this me or Lilith joining the Seven Deadly Sins on the Inferno concert stage, and was I really doing a hip-banging boogie with . . . Lust?

That busty, redheaded wench on backup electric guitar had more moves than a corkscrew. Lust's color-enhanced green eyes went supernova while I glimpsed Lilith inhabiting the performer's succubus soul. The withering contact shorted out even Lust. Her leering, lascivious face grew blow-up-doll blank. Lust froze into a mannequin position, then her limbs began lifting like a puppet's.

What a vindictive witch Lilith was. If she shut down the Sins into motionless zombies, the band's rep would be ruined.

Oh, yeah? The show must go on.

I heard and saw the audience screaming and whistling like a tidal wave under a thousand spotlights. Made me want to give them their money's worth. I grabbed the flame-fronted guitar from Lust before Lilith got the performer's hands in gear, noticing that the silver familiar was now a pair of wrist cuffs, both bearing flashing ovals of mirror.

My more-than-air-guitar act flashed the Lilith eyes out of Lust, leaving her standing with hands as currently empty as her dazed irises.

Where was Lilith? I edged downstage next to Greed. From the back, the bass guitarist glittered with gilt braid and the green-orange colors of paper money. As I came abreast, a fading green glint in his robotic gaze said Lilith had scavenged his soul, as she had those of so many others long before this joint concert date of ours.

Lilith was no longer physically present. She was soul-hopping to keep ahead of my two-wristed mirror punches. If every Sin had worn my mirrored kick-demon accessories, she'd be gone for good. I still didn't know what kind of supernatural Snow was, and I sure didn't know who or what sang and stomped and strummed in his onstage band. Whatever they were, they were taken unawares. Lilith could keep systematically possessing the Sins band members' bodies to avoid a showdown with me and my mirrors.

The only way I could exorcise her from this stage and place and time was to leave her nowhere to hide. We were the same physical type—dark hair, pale skin—so I was her walking mirror image, but I needed more than a serial soul-chase, I needed a coup de gras. The lost chord, the final karate chop, the worst-case scenario for an egocentric demon with a bloodthirsty edge.

The stage floor throbbed to the earthshaking thumps, and human hearts, including mine, were fibrilating all over the place. Lilith was amping up the vibration and sound system into heart-attack mode.

I'd made my way downstage until I was behind Dark Snow, who was bumping and grinding to beat the band with his '57 Custom Les Paul Black Beauty electric guitar. Could I have ever dreamed I'd think Snow was the Super in the white hat and way more wholesome than this hell-bent CinSim doppel-gänger?

As the groupies starting boosting each other up to climb onto the stage and reenact the bad scene from below the Inferno, Quicksilver came loping in from stage right. An oversize wolf at full power run, silver fur riffling in the spotlights, is a vision to behold.

The audience screamed encouragement when Quick spotted Anger in his sequined flame-covered costume, Lilith's green eyes just starting to inhabit his while he beat the hell out of the drums.

It felt like we were all tumbling around in a thunderstorm.

Like lightning, Quick took them both down, Anger and Lilith. His ferocious leap set the percussion instruments rolling off the stage into the overexcited audience. Entering with a shrill chorus of *arfs* behind Quicksilver came . . . Asta, gray all over with black markings. As in his movies, the noisy canine turned coward and dove for shelter among the scattered drum set, ass-up and tail down.

What an animal act!

Where had Lilith shifted to? The possession-drained band was losing its force, and I was running out of Sins to expel Lilith from. Wait! Envy, with her green dress on, was a natural for Lilith's next victim. The rocker's eyeballs were looking like kiwi-jam-slathered toast when a huge white tiger took her down with velvet paws before she could make another move.

Me, I'd had no idea how powerful my rock-star black leather and silver-studded catsuit could be. I hip-butted Sloth into the mosh pit with my wrist mirrors flashing—leftovers of Lilith's possession dying in his eyes at first physical contact—and surveyed who . . . and what . . . was still standing.

Grizelle. Huge again? And Asta onstage? They couldn't both occupy the same space, unless . . .

Before my wondering eyes, Light Snow appeared from stage right to riotous applause and shouting. He grabbed a guitar from the rack in front of the upset drums and strode straight toward Dark Snow, rocking into a dueling guitar act.

Of course. Lilith now occupied the CinSim Snow.

The crowd was ecstatic. Man, that was way too much demonic possession, hard-rock leather and shaking going on. The frenzy generated by the Seven Deadly Sins battling an ancient soul-sucking demon would be a sure sellout ticket on any tour.

Grizelle, again her own formidable human self, was pacing the stage's rear, awaiting the chance to pounce on Lilith/Dark Snow.

I squinted beyond the houselights, trying to spot my friends at the Inferno bar.

No luck.

Wait a minute.

We had me, Quicksilver, Grizelle, and Real Snow onstage.

Light Snow was playing his white Stratocaster as if he were alone in the universe engaged in a duel with the devil. Maybe music was his magic. It was sure almost deafening me even though the Sins had gone quiet.

I glanced at the mosh pit. All the ravening groupies from below were back in place, squeeing and screeching and jumping up and down but staying put, competing for the black scarves Dark Snow lofted into their midst . . . scarves that were turning whiter than snowflakes as they fell.

Was it all reverting to normal? Did Lilith finally have no handy soul to possess next? Grizelle and I were not easy take-over options. Even as I watched, I again spotted *my* Lilith mirror image, my badass but so far purely human double almost crowded out and lost among the groupies. I'd first seen her there from the Inferno bar. She'd led me into the mirror and this control-freak battle with her big bad namesake.

As the possessed Dark Snow bent to commune with screaming groupies, my Lilith's white hands grabbed and climbed the color-changing scarf, her own freaky living black tattoos doing the kind of silver-familiar jig up her forearms I experienced.

Lilith was boosted from the shoulders of the fans right onto the stage.

I zeroed in on Dark Snow's black leather back, wondering if the same whip wounds were now tormenting Lilith. Something was. The CinSim's entire figure stiffened, then demonic Lilith's head and face came swiveling around to face me, a whirlwind of long black hair whipping her savage features.

Oh. So *Exorcist*. And me with only a Catholic school education to deal with her.

And a mirror-twin sandwich.

I tried to wrench off a mirror wrist cuff to toss to my Lilith, but the demon snarled to show an *Alien* maw striking snakelike from her icy cover-model features.

Too much horror-movie imagery. I angled my arms and wrists into a tortured configuration that bounced a reflection of my Lilith into my other wrist mirror and zinged the demon right between the eyes. Don't it make your green eyes bloodred?

Blinded by the light, the demon screamed as she deserted

Dark Snow to the piece of animated vintage film he was, and turned her seductive femme fatale form toward the mosh pit, fleeing to the ever-easy groupies.

Not now.

Her mirror-me namesake stood there, a solid barrier between the demon and her enchanted flock, leaving the demonic Lilith totally on her own, without a home, like a rolling stone . . . and not the rock-band sort.

The demon's screaming female form undulated like a sound wave until it flickered off and out.

Lil and I faced each other across a void that didn't involve a mirror for only the second time in our so-far-separate lives. My soul sister winked, and winked out, too. Onstage, Dark Snow was fading to black as Light Snow's screaming guitar and onstage charisma overpowered Lilith's recent CinSim plaything. Behind me, the Seven Deadly Sins were shrugging off the Lilith drug and reassembling, recovering their grooves and rocking out like the usual maniacs.

I did not belong here, nor my big dog.

We slunk offstage with Grizelle. Maybe we were an exiting backup group. Once in the wings, Quicksilver *arfed* and streaked back to the Inferno bar, Asta on his tail, to check on the Cin-Sims. Something slapped my impenetrable catsuit on the butt.

"Great show," Dr. Jack whispered in my ear as he breezed by.

Grizelle eyed me hard, her iridescent snake-belly eye shadow gleaming like Lilith's irises. "Forget what just went down, or you'll be cat kibble tomorrow."

The familiar had become a harmless charm bracelet, dangling tiger heads, guitars, and demon horns.

"Nice work," Snow said.

He'd ducked into the wings before an encore. The lipstick marks were history, along with the reddened skin under the wrist manacles. Those manacles were no longer tarnished black-moon silver but platinum or white gold, nothing so common as my silver familiar. My silver abilities hadn't freed him, but once I'd outed and distracted Lilith from keeping him bound, he'd been able to invoke some conversion magic of his own.

"So the curse of Lilith is gone?" I asked.

"No, but she is. For now."

"She must have possessed your groupies. What does the curse have to do with them?"

"You have to know?"

"I deserve to know."

His sunglasses eyed the stage, not me. "Why did I offer no more than the Brimstone Kiss to the mosh pit? Maybe there's nothing more."

Snow pleading impotency? That stopped me cold.

"That's really true? Must hurt worse than your back," I said.

Maybe I'd imagined my effect on him, or that it had fueled Lilith's jealous rage, my own form of arrogance. Maybe the heat I thought I'd been picking up had just been frustration.

He nodded. "You have no idea, Delilah."

"No satisfaction for eternity? Kinda mean. All because of Lilith?"

"What do you expect from a bitch goddess?"

"Those groupies," I pointed out, "gave their all for your after-concert Brimstone smooch. Then you stopped doing it. You can't blame them resenting your going cold kiss on them."

"I know you encouraged them into 'recovering' from an addiction to the hope of the kiss, but it did deliver more than they ever imagined."

"Multiple orgasms from a single kiss that they can never get again? You never kiss the same groupie twice. A vibrator is a lot more reliable."

"And here you came to Vegas just months ago an old maid."

"Twenty-four isn't old." He had me grating answers between my teeth, as usual.

"It is for a virgin."

"Ex-virgin. So you got nothing from all the Brimstone Kisses you handed out to the groupies for so long but an ego boost and the sadistic pleasure of knowing they'd eventually remain in the same condition as you, unsatisfied."

"According to their signature song, it worked for the Rolling Stones."

"*You* sent Dr. Jack to my bedroom . . . You hired me on the sly. Why?"

"Not me directly."

"Grizelle doesn't count. She loves you. She hates me. Yet she rolled over and let me lead. It's not like we were dancing here. Why?"

"You're right. I ordered her to."

"Why?

"Maybe because I knew you're the only woman in Vegas who wouldn't be distracted by the opportunity to maul me."

I snorted. "You so flatter yourself, but you're right there."

"Maybe because you're the only woman in Vegas with still a streak of mercy in her soul."

That I couldn't answer. Guilty as charged.

"I know what you despise, but what do you want, Miss Street?" His colorless fingertips reached out to the familiar around my wrist. "I'm momentarily the grateful mogul. You have me at your mercy, like Samson under the spell of Delilah. Extort me."

Now, did the *un*merciful minority of my soul feel like taking him up on that offer? Did some taint of Lilith's jealous, demonic fury linger with me, wanting an eternal piece of him, too? Nothing personal.

"Damned white of you," I said. "You've run up quite an unpaid tab at my little Darkside Bar. I'll take what you owe me out in IOUs as needed."

"That's pretty vague coming from a hard-boiled dame like you."

"So suffer for a while longer. You're apparently used to it."

As I walked away, I considered the endless options of a future with Snow in my debt.

Maybe my mercy could temper our loathe-hate relationship, but how little did I love him? Let me count the ways.

*　*　*

Author's Bio:
Carole Nelson Douglas's sixty novels include S.F./fantasy, mystery, and romance bestsellers. Her cozy-noir Midnight Louie, feline PI mysteries number twenty-four. Delilah Street, Paranormal Investigator, began prowling 2013 Vegas-from-Hell in *Dancing with Werewolves* and was last seen in *Virtual Virgin*. Carole collects vintage clothing and homeless animals and does dance. Visit her website: www.carolenelsondouglas.com.

OUTSIDE THE BOX

by P. N. ELROD

To paraphrase a line from the movie—it wasn't in the book—vampires are like chocolates; you don't know what you get until you open the box.

Not that I was going to dig up a coffin stuffed with a newly made and hungry vamp. My partner and I would watch from a safe distance, the fresh grave bounded by my heavy-duty holding spell. How the vamp got free from its burial would tell us what breed we had on our hands. They were all dangerous, but some more than others.

My name is Marsha Madinia Goldfarb, occupation/vocation/inclination: witch. I register the post-dead and help with the orientation to their new lifestyle. Think you can escape bureaucracy by dying? That would be a no. Sooner or later, however badass a bloodsucker you might be, you will deal with someone from the Company, like me, armed with a clipboard and forms to fill out.

So here I was, my butt parked on a folding campstool in an old cemetery next to an abandoned wreck of an old country church, the sun gone and the darkness thickening.

Meh. It's a living.

I gave a jump when the custom sound system in the Type III ambulance behind me came to life, blasting the air with the *Peter Gunn Theme*.

My partner, a vampire named Ellinghaus, began to appear, fading in like old-school special effects: ghostly at first, then forming up and taking on color and solidity. No streaming mist for this guy, he was there or not-there. He timed the fades and formings to the beat of the music. It was his party trick. Not all of them had that kind of control.

Like the rest, his breed of vamp had a special Latin name with the Company geeks, but the informal designation was "Chicago Special." It coincided with his personal style. He dressed and acted as you might expect from a guy obsessed with the Blues Brothers, complete down to the hat and sunglasses. He even had the accent. On him, it worked. Other vamps ribbed him about it, often not in a good-natured way, but outside the Company people liked him on sight, thinking he was with some nightclub show.

Considering his choice of prime Mancini as his waking-up number for tonight, that was close enough.

Pop-culture packaging aside, Ellinghaus was tough, just couldn't get around during the day like some of the Dracs could. No shape-shifting, either, but I'd never heard him complain. He'd been in a long, lightproofed storage bench in the back of his home on the road for at least eleven hours and somehow managed not to look rumpled. I could admire that.

His occupation: keeping an eye on the witch so she doesn't get damaged.

Vamps are a dime a dozen, but true spell-slingers are rare, though you wouldn't think so with my pay scale. More and more, I'd been giving thought to going indie, usually on Friday, when the amount on the check left after Company deductions was only enough to cover basic living expenses. I'd signed a seven-year contract, though. Two more to go for either renewal (and a significant raise) or resigning with the usual confidentiality spell in place for life.

"Good evening, Miss Goldfarb," Ellinghaus said. He leaned in through the open window of the cab and shut off the player. He'd made his entrance.

"Hey, Ell." I'd tried for five years to get him to call me Marsha or even Mars, but he liked calling me "Miss Goldfarb." Whatever made him happy.

"Where are we this fine night?" Used to waking up in a different place than where he'd gone to bed, he was only mildly curious.

"Still in Texas."

"Where in Texas, if I may inquire?"

"About two hundred miles west of HQ. We've been knocked back to the Stone Age. No phone, no Internet. Sorry."

He took that pretty well. I hadn't. "Anyone else joining us?"

"I don't think so. No mentor called this one in."

His solid form went ghostlike, and he rose straight up like a slow balloon. I should be used to that, but it's cool to watch and just never gets old.

"Anything?" I asked when he came back to earth after a good look around.

"Lots of nothing. No cars on the road. I am thinking this is an orphan case, Miss Goldfarb."

"It has that dump-site vibe, yes."

He stalked over to the grave, stopping short of the barrier marked by the salt I'd put down, his head tilted, listening for activity. "Must be too soon," he said.

Post-death incubation varied, anything from twenty-four to forty-eight hours. More than that, and it's assumed the change failed. Then we back off and call an investigation team to process as a questionable death, possibly a murder.

We don't get many of those these nights, but it happens.

Most of the time the vampire's maker is standing by ready to mentor the newbie. In those cases we just fill out the paperwork, hand them a brochure about the benefits of working for the Company, and get out.

Then there are the orphans who, for one reason or other, don't have anyone to show them the ropes. It's shameful and wrong, like the casually cruel mouth-breathing morons who love playing with a new puppy, then abandon the grown dog on the side of the road to starve, go wild, or get killed in traffic.

When the Company finds the vamps who do that, there are penalties, severe ones. The CEOs take the Stan Lee trope of "with great power comes great responsibility" seriously. It's the second-most-important rule in the greater community; ignore it at your peril. You make 'em, you take 'em.

I'd dealt with only a few orphans and counted myself lucky not to be around when the Company caught up with their makers. Word was that it got noisy.

Responsible vampires don't pick out-of-the-way, long-neglected graveyards for their protégés. Some brainless jerk had dumped his or her table scraps.

Tonight's case was going to be a bitch, I thought.

The wind kicked up, hot air sweeping through the long, drought-dry grass, making it hiss. The old church creaked like something trying to wake up. It must have been a tidy gathering place once upon a time, but a century of Texas weather had baked it to death. The structure leaned in the direction of the prevailing wind. The front door was on the ground and rotting, and I could see through to where the altar had been. No pews, perhaps those had been carted away to a newer, larger church.

This place was just sad. How many weddings, christenings and funerals had it seen? All that life past and gone, nothing to show for it but an ugly wreck and pale tombstones for people forgotten by time.

I've been in older cemeteries, scarier ones, ones that closed down the club for Gothic atmosphere, but there's a special bone-dust creepiness to the ones in Texas. I don't know if it's the way the wind hits the lonely tilted markers or the fire ants, but I don't like them.

"Should have brought more lights," I muttered. I scrounged

in my backpack for a flashlight but didn't flick it on, else it would mess up my night vision. It felt good having a hunk of metal in my hand, especially one that doubled as a stun gun. I'd bought it on the Internet. Nifty toy.

Ellinghaus heard, of course. He could pick up the stirrings of a groggy neo with six feet of earth between. He gave a neutral grunt. "May I suggest a campfire and s'mores?"

He might have been kidding, it was hard to tell when he wore sunglasses, which was all the time.

"Maybe later."

He grunted again, and I felt less creeped out. He'd reminded me that he had my back. The only danger I was in was from the insect life and my imagination.

Ellinghaus opened the back doors of the ambulance, checked the mini fridge and snagged a plastic sports bottle that would have his preferred beverage in it. I never asked whether it was animal or human blood, as that's considered to be a social faux pas in the community. If he wanted me to know, he'd say—if he even thought it was important. For instance, he'd never asked whether the sandwiches I stacked next to his blood supply were turkey or ham. What did it matter?

He took a deep swig, gave a long, soft sigh, and I pretended not to hear. That was also something I should be used to by now, but it was less cool than his ability to float around or go invisible at will.

Word had passed down to the bullpen from one of the Company seers that there was to be a return case on this date and at this particular spot in the great state of Texas. That was all she could give, and we'd not gotten a corresponding call from any vamp about registering his or her offspring. Some actively hated the red tape, but their "kids" got registered, like it or not, because they couldn't hide their rebirth from the seers. I don't know why some vamps kicked up such a fuss. It's just paperwork and not like we put microchip trackers under the skin.

At least I don't *think* we do.

Most flashes of the future that come to seers are not reliable. It's to do with theoretical physics and how things are constantly in flux because people are constantly in flux. Michio Kaku's multiple universe stuff is involved, and it all works to effectively neutralize specific predictability. That's why you don't find seers winning the lottery. If they could, they would, but they can't, so they work, same as anyone else. Some still buy tickets, you never know.

Prediction rules are different for the undead, though. Their passing and return somehow creates a short-term stability point for seers to pick up on with—what else—uncanny accuracy. That's their story, and they've stuck to it for centuries. It's easier to call it magic than to try explaining the equations to a liberal arts student who flunked algebra. (I'd not lost sleep over that one, having had no use for the subject. We can't all be academically well-rounded.)

Anyway, when the word came, my gut gave a strange flutter, and I said I'd take the job. I don't have psychic gifts in league with seers, but I never ignore that feeling. I wanted to tackle this one even if I didn't consciously know why.

Five hours later I was in the ambulance the Company assigned permanently to Ellinghaus, who was on duty that week. The big Type III was his traveling home, and I tried to take it easy for the last mile as we lurched over a bad road, heading for, not unexpectedly, a cemetery next to the remains of a wood-frame church. I pulled up a few yards away, set the brake, and got out. There was an hour of sunlight left. Ellinghaus was still dead—I refused to think about it—leaving me on my own, so I made the most of it.

It didn't take more than a minute to find the fresh grave. No effort had been made to tamp down the soil or conceal it, but why bother? No one had been out here for years. I wouldn't put it past the maker vamp to have picked this isolated spot for no other reason than knowing it would inconvenience a Company employee.

I got my spell stuff together, nothing much, just sea salt in a five-pound container with a handle and perforations on the lid to make it into a giant shaker. Next, a small ice chest containing cold packs and a sports-drink bottle full of fresh bovine blood, then a change of clothes for whoever had been buried. Not knowing the sex wasn't a problem, everyone started out with gender-neutral gray sweats. I opted for extra large and put them and some hospital scuffs neatly on the ice chest next to the grave.

Then it was time to focus and chant, pacing around the site, sprinkling the salt as I went. Three circuits did the trick; gotta love those prime numbers.

Vamps, being supernaturals, are subject to magical influences to a degree not shared by ordinary day-walking humans. For instance, if I put a holding circle around a regular person, he'd walk right through and not know it was there. But a vampire is held fast, unable to leave until I take it down. It's a necessary precaution; most new vamps don't wake up well and need a short adjustment period to get themselves together.

Ellinghaus, finished with his breakfast or whatever he called it, put the bottle back in the fridge, then rummaged in a vertical storage locker where he kept a number of weapons behind a trick panel. He had the usual peacekeepers that vamps respect: stakes, fully charged Tasers, police-grade stun guns, a hickory baseball bat (no shape-shifting jokes, please), and several types of firearms—including a real machine gun from the 1920s—all with special ammo made from wood, silver, and garlic-smeared lead. One pistol fired tranq darts with enough drugs to stun a charging rhino. Two shots worked for most.

My favorite, because it wasn't lethal to humans, meaning I could use it without damaging myself, was a custom-made toxic green plastic pistol that could shoot holy water twenty feet. Some of the really rare Euro-breeds and a few old-school Dracs reacted to a squirt of that as though it were acid. Other breeds were immune, and the Company geeks were still trying to figure out why. For some reason, volunteers for experimentation were hard to find.

The Company prefers to avoid violence, of course, but if things went very wrong, then Ellinghaus had to be prepared to deal with an organic killing machine every bit as fast, strong, and deadly as himself. He liked having the advantage several times over.

Not all newborn vamps want to stick around to answer questions, even if their mentors insist; they want to cut loose and see if the hype's true about their condition. (It is.) But there are rules to follow when you wake to the big change.

The number one rule for *all* of us: stay off the human radar.

It is inviolable.

If one gets noticed, we all get noticed. So don't get noticed.

That's hard to remember when you're anxious to prove that you are the coolest apex predator on two legs.

But really, it's just not allowed. Break the rule, and you *will* be staked.

The greater supernatural community has a zero-tolerance policy for grandstanding idiots. Ellinghaus was in charge of making sure the newbies knew there was policing and strict enforcement.

Of course, there are plenty who attempt to challenge that. The sense of entitlement some of the Dracs and Euro-breeds have is almost childish, but they get nobbled. It's that or be killed.

The nobbling is magical, of course, buried in the registration process and quite painless.

The rule's been around (more or less) since Polidori blew the whistle on Lord Ruthven. Back then, if a vamp made a village too hot to plunder, he just hopped a horse or flew his shape-shifted batty ass twenty miles over to find some other place to misbehave.

No more. The bad old days of rocking mayhem without consequences are gone. Since the Industrial Revolution, the whole subculture's gone conservative to survive.

That's okay with most because no one wants to end up in an experimental lab with inquisitive types vivisecting former humans down to their DNA. Or staked by fanatics who've seen one too many Hammer films—that's a biggie on every vamp's learning-experiences-to-avoid list. That sort of thing still happens, along with witch burnings, in third-world countries. I try not to think about it.

Standard operating procedure is for someone like me to lay a complex restraining spell on new vampires before they know what's happened. They *have* to obey the directive of the magic. Spell details are proprietary to the Company, but it works.

Usually. I'd heard rumors of epic fails, but the real-deal reports were above my pay grade.

On my initial look around, I found faded tire tracks. I pointed them out to Ellinghaus, and we agreed that whoever had buried the body had gone back up the pockmarked road I'd taken to get here. There was a small hope that the maker-vamp had just split to find shelter for the day, but with the sun long gone, I gave up on that.

We had an orphan (or a body), and the maker, possibly killer, had a laughably long head start.

"Movement," said Ellinghaus. He shouldered his baseball bat and returned to the grave. He went still in a way only his kind can when they're not pretending to breathe and listened.

Not a body down there. That was something.

I boosted from the campstool (ow) and dug out my clipboard from the backpack. I was dressed in generic EMT clothes: khaki pants, crisp white shirt, the logo for a medical transportation company on the left pocket that matched the one on the sides of our vehicle. The business was a real one; our recovery/registration division is kept separate.

It's protective coloration on the road and intended to reassure new vamps who are understandably traumatized by their resurrection experience. Most initially think they've been in an accident, so an ambulance and kindly faces telling them everything's going to be okay can help settle them down.

Sometimes, it even works.

"Female," he added, his voice tight. "She's screaming."

"I don't like this part, either. Better give her some space."

He backed away, and I moved forward, clipboard in hand for something to hold; I'd have preferred the flashlight in my pocket. My heart rate went up though I couldn't hear anything of the woman's struggles below in the dark. I took my cues from Ellinghaus, who looked grim and even flinched.

"What?" I asked.

"Something snapped. Must be breaking through the coffin. That might make her a—" He rattled off the Latin name of a Euro-breed that can't vanish and filter up to the surface like the Dracs or Chicago Specials. They have to dig themselves out.

I was surprised about the coffin. Some mentors just wrap their neos in a blanket or body bag, bury them shallow, and wait. If this was an orphan, then why bother putting her in a box?

"She went quiet," he said.

Whoever was down there might have gone into shock or heard us. I spoke clearly, addressing the mound of earth. "Hello! Please remain calm."

In my own defense, I did not come up with the Company-approved greeting. I'm certain they stole it from some airline's lame emergency protocols.

"My name is Marsha, and I'm here to help. Please follow the

sound of my voice as best you can. Please remain calm and come to me . . ." I paused and looked at Ellinghaus, who gave a nod.

"I think she heard."

I kept up the patter, halfway expecting to see a dirt-caked arm thrusting up from the earth. The instinct is to run like hell, but we're trained to tough it out. My new instinct is to reach forward to help, but that would negate the holding spell, so I hung back, waiting.

She abruptly appeared, naked and bruised, on top of the grave. Not a Euro-vamp after all, she had figured out how to dematerialize. She'd used up what air had been in her lungs and hadn't drawn in more; her mouth hung wide in a soundless scream.

At heart, Ellinghaus was an old-school gentleman and took his hat off, holding it in front of his face to block the view.

It took a minute to get her attention; I told her my name and that I was there to help her.

"Who are you?" she husked, breathing in so she could speak.

I repeated my name and asked for hers.

"Where am I?" Her voice rose high, and she suddenly realized she was naked and tried to cover herself. She made a terrible, keening sound: raw fear. It would escalate to sheer panic if I didn't snap her out of it.

"*Hey!*" I used my no-nonsense sergeant-major bellow.

She twitched and went still, staring at me.

I pointed at the folded sweats atop the cooler. "There are some clothes; put them on."

She hesitated.

"*Now!*" I roared.

That made her jump. Ellinghaus, too, a little. You can try a kindly, soothing approach, but in some situations it's just going to prolong things. Most people respond to a direct order, at least until they pull themselves together enough to start asking questions. When they do, I go from bear to teddy bear.

"What's your name?" I asked after she pulled the top on. It hung halfway to her knees. The pants would be too long and big in the waist, but she could roll the legs and hold the rest up until I found a better size.

"You first," she snapped.

Anger was good, much better than panic. We were close enough that I got a clear look at her in the light spill from the back of the ambulance. She was strangely familiar, though I was certain I'd never met her before. It's that out-of-context recognition where you know the face, just from some other location. I told her my name again and repeated my question.

"I'm—I'm Kellie Ann Donner. Have I been in an accident?"

Oh, crap.

I glanced at Ellinghaus. He put his hat on and took off his sunglasses. He *never* takes off his sunglasses.

"What's going on?" she demanded, tears beginning to tumble. "Who *are* you people?"

I hate being off the grid. There was no way to let HQ know about the volatile situation we'd gotten into. Not that they'd change procedure, that was set in stone, but at least someone back in the bullpen could pass word up to management so they could start figuring out what to do.

That flutter in my gut came back. Why me? I wondered. Perhaps I'd had an inkling of this way back in my head, inspired by the news reports.

A week ago, Kellie Ann Donner, a night clerk at a roadside gas stop in Alabama, had inexplicably walked off her job and vanished. While it is a rage-making and horrible fact that many young women go missing and are never found again, this one caught the public imagination due to the efforts of the franchise owner, who raised holy hell with the media about his missing employee. He insisted she was a bright, responsible girl and posted a half-million-dollar reward for her safe return, no questions asked. The hometowners beat the bushes for her, and hoards of private investigators, pseudo-psychics, reporters, and other helpful crazies wanting a crack at that cash were on the case. It was like the community shark-hunt scene from *Jaws*—the movie, I'd not read the book.

CNN and other networks picked up and ran the story, that lady lawyer needled the Alabama authorities nightly on her show for not trying hard enough to find the girl, and the blurry video showing her departure had gotten more than a million hits on YouTube.

I'd seen it. From a high angle, the camera recorded the store's door opening, Kellie Ann seemed to speak to someone coming in, only no one was in front of her. For exactly twenty-two seconds she stopped moving, staring at something unseen, then left her spot at the counter and went outside. An exterior security camera caught her walking up to a plain white van, no plates visible, and getting in. Its door seemed to slam shut on its own, and the van drove off. You couldn't see the make or who was driving.

Poof, gone.

The store, lights bright on the side of a lonely two-lane, stood empty for an hour until a patrol car pulled up, and the officer, seeking his usual coffee-and-donut break for his shift, radioed in the first report of the mystery.

The Company was keeping a close eye on this one. We were certain in the bullpen that a rogue vamp was behind it since he wouldn't show up on camera. The twenty-two seconds of blank staring would be when he'd hypnotized her. She'd be docile, under his complete control, perfect for a living blood bank. But *who* would be that stupid?

For a week now, Kellie Ann Donner's face had been impossible to avoid. Moderately pretty, a birthmark just off the right corner of her mouth, she smiled at America from her high-school prom picture while friends and family put on a brave front and wore yellow ribbons. Bunches of flowers were left before an improvised shrine at the gas station. Dozens, perhaps hundreds of other people went missing that week in America, but this was the one that caught the public imagination—along with that half-million-dollar reward.

And now she was a vampire.

The inviolable rule was about to be shot to hell and gone.

Soon as the Company CEOs got my news—well, there had to be protocols in place. The simplest solution came to me, and I wanted to be wrong and hope they'd not go there. It wasn't Kellie Ann's fault. She was a *victim*. No need to make it worse.

In the meantime, I was in charge of getting her safely to our HQ in Dallas.

"Yes, Miss Donner, you've been in an accident. I'm here to help you." I held hard to my professional patience.

Again, she wanted to know who we were, and I told her. Disorientation and short-term memory loss are normal. The latter usually includes how they died. The geeks think it's a protective mechanism that kicks in because no one wants to remember that sort of thing.

"What *is* this place?" Clothes on, slippers on, she shuffled forward and bumped into the invisible barrier surrounding the grave. For a second, she looked like a street mime doing that stuck-in-a-box routine. Those magically powered walls were as solid to her as brick ones were to me.

It took time to get her past that shock, then introduce the idea (again) that she'd been in an accident, that we were not kidnappers, psychos, or part of some twisted reality show and would explain everything soon. That's a lot for anyone to take in, especially when they've not been prepared. Neos and their mentors have usually been together for years and adjust faster. Even orphans will have some inkling of what's happened to them and catch on sooner or later. It's usually because they've lived on the fringes of the supernatural community and pick up hints by osmosis. Just because we stay off the human radar doesn't mean people don't notice and wonder.

But Kellie Ann didn't have any of that. This was completely outside her tiny pocket of a sheltered world. She didn't remember anything, didn't know of the greater supernatural community, and she had no clue that she'd been murdered.

So how did she get from Alabama to an abandoned cemetery in Texas?

The vamp drove her. She was his food for the trip, perhaps kept locked in a trunk for the day. There were cases like that on the books. The supernatural community was no more immune to crime than the day-walking world. We punished the perps when we caught them.

This one had finished her off but didn't do a proper job of it, enabling her to come back. It's a mixed blessing. She was in the world again, but not all victims are able to make the adjustment.

Kellie Ann paced the boundaries I'd put up, trying to find a way out, too agitated to listen. That was also normal and the reason why she had to be confined. The fever that would drive her toward her first feeding was kicking in, and she wouldn't be responsible for her actions. You might as well tell a newborn not to cry.

I ordered her several times to open the cooler chest. With shaking hands, she finally did, fumbled with the plastic drink bottle, snapping the lid off and, madly thirsty, gulped the contents.

Ellinghaus watched this with close attention, then relaxed a little. So did I.

A new vamp's initial taste would influence the rest of their existence. They will stick with the kind of blood they got at their first meal. If it's cattle blood, then it's easier to follow the rules. If it's human, it gets complicated in ways I try not to imagine. In the bad old days, human blood (often drained from a hapless victim) tended to be what some breeds craved unless the potential vamp knew to prepare and had himself interred near a livestock pen. Don't laugh. It worked.

The Company has a deal going with a number of meat-processing plants—God knows what story they gave; for all I know, the vamps ran the slaughterhouses—and thoughtfully provided a month of free blood to orphan newbies. After that, they were expected to get gainful employment and buy it same as the rest.

With a quart of bovine in her, Kellie Ann settled down enough to focus, and I began making headway. Just not for long. Her eyes, flushed an alarming red from the feeding, soon dulled, then she sat on the cooler, blinking at me, nodding agreement at whatever I said. With a strange, drunken smile, she pointed at Ellinghaus.

"I know you, you're that guy."

He touched his hat brim. "Yes, ma'am. Close enough."

"That. Guy." She waved a hand around. "My dad loves your movies."

"Very kind of him." He shot me a look. "I believe she is ready to go, Miss Goldfarb."

I needed a prop for this part and got a metal rod about a foot long and as big around as my thumb from my backpack. Nothing like cold iron to take the juice from a spell. I prodded the invisible wall, felt the energy thrum and dissipate, then the holding mechanism was gone, like popping a balloon.

Ellinghaus stepped forward and asked Kellie Ann for permission to help her to the ambulance.

I know. But it worked. She took his arm, made two unsteady steps, then her legs wobbled. He swept her up, hardly breaking stride, and got her in, stretching her flat on the rolling gurney clamped to one wall. I came up behind with the cooler and discarded bottle, stowed them, and went back for the stool and backpack. One more chore: fill a few plastic zip bags up with a quantity of dirt from her grave. Without it, she'd not be able to rest during the day. The geeks were still working on the why behind that one, too. I dropped the bags into an equipment drawer with the folding shovel and had a last glance at the horrible place. I hoped she wouldn't remember it.

My partner had buckled her in under a blanket and gone through to the cab of the bus.

"You going to change?" I asked.

"Is it necessary?" He really liked his black suit; the look had proved to be disarming and distracting to Kellie Ann, as intended.

We'd be going the speed limit, and medical transport vehicles drove all hours, day and night, so there'd be no reason for a cop to bother with us. Sure, Ellinghaus could hypnotize us out of a situation, but why take chances? We could *not* be caught with a missing person. "I think you should. If we get pulled over . . ."

"I see your point. One moment."

While he went outside to trade the hat, black coat, and tie, for a white shirt to match mine, I swabbed Kellie Ann's face with a damp wipe and told her to relax, we were taking her to a doctor.

"But I feel fine," she said dreamily.

With the drugs dissolved in that bottle of blood, she'd be feeling just wonderful for hours to come. It's better this way. Really. Maybe she'd have been calm enough to cooperate and come willingly, but if not, then even Ellinghaus wouldn't have been able to hold her for long. She'd vanished once to escape her grave and could do so again by accident. Not a good idea when you're booming down the road at sixty-five.

I couldn't raise a holding spell inside the ambulance, so a

strong cocktail with lots of Xanax in it would keep her happy and her body solid until specialists could take charge. They'd treat her the same as any rape victim. Hopefully she'd be able to adjust to her new life.

If she was allowed to live it.

The simple solution, the one that didn't bear thinking about, was to disappear her.

I said her name a few times, and she gave me a tired smile. "We're going to need your consent to help you," I said. "I need you to sign a standard release form."

"I don't have insurance."

"It's all right, this is on the county. You don't have to worry about that. Sign here, and I'll be able to treat you."

"I feel *fine*," she insisted.

"I know you do, but you have to sign. It's a formality."

"Need to read it first."

"Of course." I held the clipboard, and she must have read the simple agreement several times, unable to take any meaning from it. I fitted a marker-type pen into her hand and held the board firm as she scrawled her name at the bottom. She dotted the "i" with a little heart.

Thank God that was done. She might not have felt it, but I did, the tiny crackling of power that told me the spell that would compel her to obey the number one rule had taken hold. When she sobered up, she might not recall much of this, but she would adhere to the agreement. I'd have loved to meet the designer of that crafting; it was elegant and simple and powerful—like Hepburn's little black dress in *Breakfast at Tiffany's*. Was I envious? You bet.

Things like that temped me to renew my contract when the time came. I'd get the big pay raise and truly advanced training in my craft. Right now I was a good, if limited, spell-slinger. I could slam a holding spell in my sleep and read auras in the right light, but there were others to be learned.

I ran the signed agreement through a portable laminating machine. The plastic would keep the ephemeral parchment preserved pretty much forever if it was properly stored, and the Company had excellent facilities. There. Most of my job was done. I heaved a huge sigh and felt ravenous. Spell work and therapy on the fly are exhausting.

Kellie Ann seemed to doze. No vitals like a heartbeat or pumping lungs, but no problem. It just meant she was a Chicago Special, a Drac, or another Euro-breed I was too tired to recall. I grabbed a double-thick turkey sandwich and Coke from the fridge, dragged my weary carcass to the cab, and belted into the passenger seat.

Ellinghaus still had on his sunglasses but otherwise looked like an EMT. Between bites, I gave him directions, and he got us clear of the bumpy road, onto a two-lane, and more than an hour later a four-lane heading in the right direction for home. The GPS began working again, along with my cell and laptop, but I told him to pull into the next gas station. We needed a fill-up, and I wanted to phone this one in on a landline.

He found a busy truck stop, pulled up to one of the diesel stations, and took care of the bus while I kept an eye on Kellie Ann. Regs demanded there always be someone with the patient though she was still out of it. Once Ellinghaus was done, I fled to a washroom. His ambulance has a potty, and I could pull the curtain divider shut behind the cab for privacy, but sue me, I prefer the kind with running water.

The phones were by the facilities. I used a Company card for the charges.

The night shift was the busy time at HQ, like Monday morning anywhere else, but there was some kind of old-country holiday with an unpronounceable name on. The phone rang and rang before someone finally picked up. I got an audible gasp—not common when dealing with people who don't breathe all the time—when I asked to speak to Ms. Vouros. She was second only to God in authority so far as I was concerned. She was upper, *upper* management, and I doubted she knew my name. I'd never spoken to her directly. She relied on e-mails and underlings. Speculation ran that she learned her management style from Elizabeth Báthory, but that was ridiculous because old Liz had been a narcissist psycho, not a real vampire.

Which did not preclude Vouros from being a narcissist psycho, so I was very polite and stuck to the bare-bones business when she got on the line. I gave her my location, who I was with, and shared the joy about Kellie Ann Donner.

It was significant that Vouros did not ask me to repeat anything. I took it to mean she'd grasped the situation.

"Oh, *crap*," she said, confirming.

I refrained from asking what to do next; she'd tell me if it deviated from the usual drill. She shot a few questions, getting an overview of the situation, and I gave her my best guess about what breed might be involved.

"Never mind that. Is she under control?"

"Yes, ma'am."

"I'm sending a team to the gravesite to process it. The forensics crafter should be able to find maker traces. You two get straight back here, no stops."

What did she think, that Ellinghaus and I would take in a movie? Good luck with that. There were hardly any drive-ins left. Only on the way to the truck did it hit me how rattled she must be.

The trip was routine from this point; Ellinghaus had his music plugged in from his iPod, and I tried to get some shuteye stretched out on the padded bench in the back. The storage area under it was where he slept during the day with a bag of his soil, but I wasn't bothered by that anymore. I belted in and wrapped tight under a blanket, fending off the A/C.

Of course I didn't sleep. Who could?

I checked on Kellie Ann for the umpteeth time. Okay, *she*

could sleep, or whatever it was vamps did. She made me want to have soothing drugs of my own. I couldn't stop wondering what would happen to her once we got inside the gate.

If she disappeared permanently, it would solve everything for the Company. It would be hell on her family, but Company's rules outweighed their right to know her fate.

If Kellie Ann was allowed to live and be a part of the greater community, she'd have to get a whole new ID, maybe relocation to another country. She wouldn't like that. There was a kind of magic that could compel her to accept, but that sort of crafting is dangerous. When it goes completely against the will of the subject, they either throw it off or go nuts or both. None of those options is a party.

Or—with certain kinds of bounding spells in place so she could not share about being vamped—Kellie Ann could return to her family. She'd be primed to give them a tale of an abductor who'd drugged her, then let her go in a fit of conscience. The mystery around her disappearance would fade, and she could go back to most of her former life, with some dietary changes in place.

While it wasn't anything I could influence, I would recommend it in my report and at my debriefing.

She would be closely questioned by experts. Spell work would be involved to pick her memory. Company investigators would want every detail to find out the name of the moron vampire behind this PR headache.

I wouldn't feel sorry for him, either.

I gave up trying to sleep and returned to the cab. Ellinghaus was easy to hang with, no need to talk if we didn't feel like it. He let a few miles pass before pulling out his ear buds and speaking. His voice was low, conversational. The general noise of the bus would prevent our patient from hearing him.

"Did you, by chance, notice her hands, Miss Goldfarb?"

"Can't say that I did, no."

"They were not messed up as one might expect, given her circumstances."

Trying to claw your way from a coffin was hard on the manicure. "It just means she healed up when she vanished. You do that."

"Yes, I do that. But it takes longer when the injury involves wood, and I heard wood snapping."

"Okay."

"I just thought I should mention that, is all."

"Put it in your report. The geeks love details."

"Indeed they do."

I told him that Vouros was sending out a forensics crafter to process the grave.

He grunted approval.

That department had serious magical talent. Never mind about wearing gloves and being careful not to leave behind any DNA, they could get a fix on a vamp by magical means. It was also proprietary spell work, and scary efficient. Too bad they couldn't apply it to human murder cases, only to supernaturals.

"I've been wondering about some things, too," I said.

"Such as what, if I may inquire?"

"Such as how the hell did she get way out there? Who would even know about that place?"

"I have given some thought to that, as well. Perhaps the perpetrator was originally from the area and thought he could hide his crime, thinking no one would ever visit. He must not have expected her to revive."

"He's in for a shock."

"Deservedly so."

Ellinghaus hates them, the ones he calls crash-feeders. Since the Company got itself truly organized (at about the same time as the FBI), there'd not been many of those cases. He's a stickler for rules, and when a crash-feeder comes along, it makes the rest of the vamps look bad. They resent anyone who caves to the crave.

"I suppose I could ask around, maybe look into genealogy records for that area," he said. "I made note of the family names on the stones."

"As good a place to start as any."

"Might you consider initiating an online records search?"

"Glad to, but not right now. I'm tired and don't want to get carsick."

A grunt of understanding. Some vamps forget how tough it is to be human and subject to fatigue. Ellinghaus didn't seem to be among their number. Not for the first time I wondered how old he was; I'd never asked, and he's never brought it up. He could be fifty or five hundred, no way to tell. But he was comfortable to be with and always professional. I hoped he found those same qualities in me.

"Would you like to listen to some jazz, Miss Goldfarb?"

"Smooth?" I wasn't in the mood for anything fast and raucous.

"And dark as chocolate."

"The best kind."

The music did its own magic to the point that I nodded off long enough to feel rotten when I snapped awake. Ellinghaus was on the exit for HQ; we were two minutes out with a long, comfortable margin before dawn. I was rumpled and soggy of brain, but if I had another Coke, it would leave me too wired to sleep later. Just have to tough it out minus chemical help.

Company grounds were intentionally deceptive. The buildings looked to be typical light industrial on the outside, with lots of security lights and cameras, nothing unexpected. However, the cyclone fence was extra tall, topped with razor wire and electrified. That was for human intruders. For everyone else, there was a boundary spell in place like the one I'd cast around Kellie Ann's grave, but this one was on steroids with a crack chaser. My hat was off to the witch who had crafted it. He or she had created a vast domed perimeter, and no vamp could get in or out without magical help.

When dealing with people who can go invisible, people who might not agree with Company policies, you can't overdo the locks.

The guard's blockhouse in front was always manned. A vampire and witch pairing, as usual, to watch the gate. They recognized us, and Judy, the vamp, asked about the newbie.

"Orphan case," said Ellinghaus. He knew better than to share our bombshell before management had a meeting on the subject.

"That sucks," said Rosa, the witch. She was straight-faced, clearly not chasing a bad joke.

"I hate when that happens," added Judy. I went in the back, opening the doors so she could make sure only three people were going in. Vamps can see others of their kind even when they're vanished. She didn't find unauthorized intruders in El- linghaus's storage locker and hardly glanced at the dozing Kel- lie Ann. Judy hopped out and called to Rosa to pass us in.

Rosa had a glass rod that would shift, rather than dissipate, power and waved it in a wide pattern that was too fast and subtle for me to follow, combining the action with a chant un- der her breath. The barrier that would have crushed Ellinghaus flat into his seat back had he tried to gun forward ceased to be there. Rosa nodded him in, working the wand and chant until our taillights were clear, then ceased, and things thumped back into place. I felt the power like a tangible echo. It would be so cool to know how to craft that kind of magic. Architecturally, the ones I raised were like a box made from Lincoln Logs. The one around HQ was comparable to a Renaissance cathedral in artistry and staying power.

However much training I got, I'd never be able to design anything like that. I had talent, but it was journeyman, not genius.

We braked again at another gate and guardhouse fifty feet along. It marked the second boundary wall. If the outer gate was ever compromised, then this one would hold, the guards protected within the compound. If that sounds military, it is. A lot of the vamps had served through the ages, and the Company made use of their experience.

We passed through, and the witch on duty chanted the gate back into place. I relaxed internally now that we were home.

The parking lot was almost empty, which was unusual for this time of night.

"Think it's the holiday?" I asked after pointing it out.

"Security measure. Ms. Vouros won't want this generally known yet."

She'd probably given everyone the night off, using the holiday as an excuse. The fewer people, the fewer witnesses. They'd have happily grabbed at the free time, no questions.

Whatever was in store for Kellie Ann would be in place by now, and perhaps had been within minutes of my phone call. She was in for close questioning soon. I decided to stay with her. I'd be a familiar face, and she'd need a friend in her corner.

I told Ellinghaus to take it easy on the turns and made my way to the back, glad of the grab bars. Kellie Ann was awake, looking more alert.

"Where are we?"

"Almost there." I rummaged in a drawer and got a package of sweatpants in a small and tore it open. "Here, these will fit you better. I'll help you sit up."

"Um . . ." She glanced at the opening to the cab.

The lightproof privacy curtain was fastened to one side. I undid it and pulled it across. "Okay, it's just us girls now."

"I wanna call my momma," she whispered.

"This first." I pulled the oversized pants off her and shook out the replacements.

She lurched up, swinging her legs around, facing me. "I *said* I wanna call my momma."

"I heard you, Kellie Ann, but we have to—"

She grabbed my hair strongly and made me look into her eyes. "Do you not hear me? Give me your phone."

I fumbled it from a pocket and handed it over. Some freaked-out part of my mind panicked, but the rest accepted this as perfectly normal and reasonable.

"Sit down and keep quiet," she ordered, still whispering.

This also happened though I wanted to do the opposite. The internal conflict between what I wanted and the blunt, powerful orders set my heart thumping fit to burst.

Kellie Ann smiled soothingly. "Relax, Marsha. I'm your friend. You like me and want to help me."

Like hell, I thought, but felt my face smiling back. It hurt.

She broke eye contact and tapped a number into my phone. "I'm in. Get moving."

The ambulance slowed. We'd be pulling into the guest-processing wing of the main building. Ellinghaus couldn't have heard anything, not over the motor noise with the curtain in the way.

Kellie Ann pulled on the smaller pants, pushed back the long sleeves of her top, and eased open the tall locker with the hidden weapons. She'd had plenty of time to sneak a search during the long drive back when I'd napped. She went for two pistols with extra long magazines filled with mixed ammo. Whether she faced a human or a vamp, she could take out just about anyone she liked.

As soon as he cut the motor, she slammed the curtain back and shot Ellinghaus, pressing the muzzle into the top of his shoulder and firing three rounds angling down into his trunk.

He jerked, grunted, and slumped, and inside I screamed and screamed and could not move a muscle.

She left the bus and hustled into the main building. I don't know what she did next, but I imagined the worst and that she would be swift and efficient. First the receptionist, then whoever was manning the bullpen, then perhaps Vouros herself. Kellie Ann wouldn't show up on internal cameras. Our security people would have no clue.

I'd not been spared out of kindness. She'd want me to take down the inner gate. Whoever she'd phoned would deal with Judy and hypnotize Rosa into doing the same, and HQ would be wide open to . . . what?

Just about anything. There were plenty of vamps who hated the Company. They'd be glad to see it gone, along with every-one in it.

The fear of that, the rage, the grief for Ellinghaus washed through me—negative emotions full of power. Some crafters trained to avoid them, but I saw them as another kind of survival mechanism and embraced their dizzy chill. I shut my eyes, re-membering Kellie Ann's face in front of me, her words burrow-ing into my brain like worms.

Not hard. The real difficulty was replacing the image with something else. Visualization training was basic to all spell-slingers. The better you see what you want in your head, the more success with the magic.

Sweat crept over me as I made that memory fade, the color seeping away until her face was gone, and I was surrounded by dense white fog. I could hold it only for a few seconds, being badly out of practice. Like others, I tended to rely too much on props and chanting.

But when I opened my eyes, I'd shaken off the worst of it. I could stand and did so, struggling on wobbly legs to get to El-linghaus.

His white shirt was covered with blood, and he was utterly

slack. I pushed up the sunglasses. His eyes were rolled into his skull, just the whites showing. With no vital signs, I couldn't tell if he was truly dead or alive and just unable to respond.

Terror and grief for him had me moving past the panic, forcing my sluggish limbs to obey me, not some bitch vamp's forced influence. I stumbled to the mini fridge and grabbed a drug-free drink bottle and got it to him. Tipping his head, I squeezed blood down his throat, not knowing if that would choke him or not. What if it went into his lungs?

You don't have time for this.

She'd be back any minute, and I had to do something.

Fight a *vampire*? Who was I kidding? Even throwing down a holding spell to keep her out of the vehicle wouldn't be enough, she could shoot through it. I wasn't absolutely necessary to taking out the inner gate; she could use the hapless crafter on duty there after shooting her partner.

Screw that.

That bloodsucking bitch had shot *my* partner.

Rage tipped things, scattering logic and common sense. I went to the locker and hauled out the machine gun. The damned thing scared the hell out of me; maybe it would do the same for Kellie Ann.

Almost a yard long, with the fifty-round drum attached, it weighed a ton and was too awkward for the confines of the ambulance, but I'd have to deal. A long time ago, Ellinghaus had shown me how it worked. In a spectacularly noisy rush, he'd emptied the drum in seconds. I didn't want to do that.

Just above the trigger on the left . . . okay, safety off, set it for single rounds. Keep the muzzle pointed away from me, aim for the thickest part of her body, and brace for the recoil.

Damn, the thing was *heavy*. I couldn't charge out and go after her. Better to wait until she came back and attempt a bush-whacking. Get her to approach from a specific direction, and I'd have a chance.

I opened the back doors and slipped out, the gun's leather strap looped over one shoulder, taking the weight. I steadied it with one hand; the other grasped my container of sea salt.

It was the fastest shield I'd ever done and crude, but it would keep her from coming in the front. I worked out from the right side, shaking the salt in a wide spray around the truck. The wall would be thick, brittle, and full of gaps, but would stop her, I hoped. I chanted the energy into place, finishing on the left side, having formed a giant C-shape around us, the walls of the back opening about ten feet thick and five wide, making a short passage to the doors.

That would be my kill box. I'd heard the term on a TV documentary.

What was happening at the front gate? Were her friends there? Had they breached it?

Ellinghaus groaned.

I was next to him just that quick. He looked bad, his reddened eyes dazed and face showing pain. His fangs were out, but it was a good sign. The wooden slug had to have missed his heart. The others were still in him, preventing him from vanishing so he could heal, but he wasn't lost yet. I got him to drink more blood. It's the universal first aid for vamps.

"Radio?" he mumbled.

I clicked it on and tried to raise someone, anyone, but nothing. Next, I got his phone and punched the Company version of 911, but again, nothing. The battery was charged, what the—

"Jamming," he said. "They're organized."

"Who?"

"Newbies, old Dracs with short memories, who knows. That dame is no rookie . . . oh, this hurts."

It had to be perdition made solid to drag that out of him.

"Gotta hold on, Ell. I have a blocking up. I'm going to stop her."

He squinted at me, alarm in his eyes when he noticed the

Thompson dragging on my shoulder. "Mars, you gotta be kidding."

Now was not the moment to notice his lapse into using my nickname for the first time. "Okay, I'm kidding, you get better right now and take over."

He winced and looked past me, even more alarmed.

Kellie Ann strode from the building toward us, a pistol in each hand and blood spray on her oversized top. I dragged Ellinghaus from his seat, hoping the vehicle's motor would shield him from fire. He couldn't move much yet. I peered over the dash in time to see her smash right into my half-assed wall about ten feet out.

That pissed her off. When she recovered, she tried a single shot that put a star in the windshield. I ducked and crawled toward the back. Just had to cower for a bit until she circled around and into my trap, then shoot first.

Only she didn't do that.

A running jump, a second of invisibility making her weightless, then she thudded down on the top of the bus. I'd been in too big a hurry to think of capping my wall with a roof.

I fell back and sent two wild shots straight up. Good thing I was already on the floor; the gun's kick wasn't as bad as I'd thought but would have still knocked me there. So that's why you had to hold this monster on all three contact points and brace.

I sorted myself out and fired three more rounds through the aluminum skin, taking out the overhead light. Glass dropped, and the empty brass flew.

"Marsha!" Her voice . . . not above, she'd slipped away to the right side, perhaps feeling out the barrier for an opening as I'd hoped. "Marsha, listen to me. You *have* to *listen* to me."

I'd seen the training vids. That was the favorite phrase of vamps the world over, the one that led into the hypnotic process. If they'd put you under once, you were more vulnerable to their voice. I fired through the wall, the crack and kick of the gun distracting me and cutting her off. Couldn't keep this up all night, I'd run out of bullets. Why didn't the bitch come around to the back?

Oh, hell, there she is.

I fired. The bullet passed harmlessly through her mostly transparent form. She smiled, a beautiful, winning, friendly smile, her eyes sparkling.

I made myself look away and shot again. Another wasted bullet.

She kept coming forward. Damn it, what a stupid, stupid trap. She'd hold herself in that state, get close, go solid, and put me under and—

Custom sound system cranked to max, the *Peter Gunn Theme* boomed through the air like a physical thing.

It hurt my ears, but Kellie Ann, with a vampire's sensitive hearing, went straight into agony mode. She recoiled and vanished altogether.

Ellinghaus was still on the floor, sitting up just enough to reach the buttons on the dash. He had his iPod buds in his ears; they would mitigate the sound somewhat. He gave me a thumbs-up, settled his shades back into place, and swigged more blood.

The racket wouldn't stop her forever, but it would keep her voice out of my head for the moment. I needed a Plan B.

I signed to Ellinghaus, making a spinning motion with one hand.

He got it and hit the siren.

Oh, yeah, that was good, annoyingly good. Combined with the shots I'd fired, the noise finally got the attention of the vamp guard at the inside gate. He came running at double speed around the main building.

Soon as he saw her—there's a reason for the gray sweats on newbies—he concluded she needed to be disarmed and restrained. That was fairly impossible with an enemy who can

go incorporeal and levitate, even filter through brick walls if
need be.

She tried to take him out with pistol fire. He had the same
advantage of being able to fade and return. While she might
have gotten others by surprise, he was trained for just this kind
of fight.

They went at each other like tigers in a tornado, much of it
too fast to follow as they faded in and out, sweeping over the
parking lot, trading shots and blows. She was no newbie, that
was evident. He'd need an edge. We all did. I slipped off the
machine gun and scrounged in the locker and seconds later left
the relative safety of the bus.

Ellinghaus croaked something, but the music and siren blotted it out. Neither the guard nor Kellie Ann could hear me; I
hoped they'd be too involved with each other until I got close
enough.

I cut loose with the oversized toxic green water gun, soak-
ing her (and the guard when I missed) with holy water. Neither
reacted to it, except for some cursing from the spray. Their
immunity didn't matter, though. I dropped the empty gun and
pulled out a Taser. I figured the salt in the holy water would
add to the impact of its shock.

I'm too much of an optimist. It screws me over every time.
Just as I made my range, Kellie Ann pulled a blurringly fast maneuver and caught the guard with a bullet the instant he went
solid to attack. I couldn't tell if it was wood, but he dropped and
stopped moving.

Before I took another step, she was behind me, one strong
arm around my neck, pulling me up and back. She slapped the
Taser away; I'd had no chance from the start, just adrenaline
and high hopes. I froze for an instant, feeling my ear tickle as
she whispered into it to put me under again, but I couldn't hear
over the siren and Henry Mancini's frenzied bass and horns. As
she dragged me backward, heading toward the inside gate, I

glimpsed Ellinghaus emerging unsteadily from the ambulance. With metal and wood in him, he'd never be able to vanish. The stuff short-circuited things. She'd kill him for sure.

Give him an edge, then.

She'd gotten the Taser, but missed the stun-gun flashlight in my pocket.

When I hit her with the business end, there was a hellish crack and zap as the voltage slammed through her. It couldn't pass to me because of the limited distance between the contact poles, but she convulsed, muscles jumping, and fell forward.

Vamps are a lot heavier than you'd think. Something to do with changes to their muscle and bone density. She knocked the breath out of me as we slammed flat against the concrete.

It was a bitch, but worth it if it stopped her.

I lay helpless as her body bunched and twitched, her bare nails gouging the pavement like iron hooks.

Then she stubbornly pushed off, rolled to her feet, and staggered in an unsteady circle. If she tried to vanish, it didn't work. The jolt was as good as a bullet for disrupting that ability.

She crouched and flipped me over, snarling. Her fangs were out. I was to be first-aid fodder.

Then Ellinghaus suddenly loomed over us, his prized machine gun cradled in his arms. Damn, he *owned* it. He lashed out with a sideways martial arts kick that knocked her clean off me. She landed yards away but managed to get upright, her feet under her for a sprint.

He cut loose, the gun in full-auto mode, firing in short, controlled bursts.

I couldn't see much from my angle. Just as well.

Three rounds at a time he emptied the drum. The brass rained, and the smell of cordite and hot metal filled the air.

Out of bullets, but not out of fight, Ellinghaus lunged forward, and I missed whatever came next, for which I was grateful.

When he came back into view, there was a lot more blood on him.

He rolled his head a little to work kinks from his neck and shoulders, then said, "That disagreeable person is no longer a problem, Miss Goldfarb."

The ambulance siren wailed and whooped; *Peter Gunn* ended, and the next track began.

Aretha Franklin told the whole compound about *R-E-S-P-E-C-T*.

The rest of the bad guys had breached the outer gate after wounding Judy and forcing Rosa to take it down, but the inner gate stalled them. They couldn't get Rosa to open it because it was a different spell sequence. She just didn't know the right chant. They shoved her out of the way, forced to wait for Kellie Ann, their own special Trojan horse, to complete her part of the invasion.

Which did not go to plan.

Rosa, who was a lot better at visualizations than I, threw off their hypnotic influence faster and fled back to her guard shack. She wasn't so terrified as to forget to put her part of the gate up again, trapping two SUVs full of pissed-off Dracs in the space between. Once they realized what had happened, some of them shifted into bats and attempted to fly free only to hit the outer dome head-on. Others tried vanishing, sinking into the earth, hoping to sieve down far enough to get under the barrier. That was an epic fail, too. The designer, anticipating such ploys, had put in a foundation barrier. They either didn't know about it or had forgotten that detail.

A sense of entitlement does not guarantee brains, just the arrogance to think having one plan to get in and destroy HQ would be sufficient.

Once other members of Company security arrived—many

were witches with specialist magic I could only dream about—the whole lot of Dracs was rendered neutral and taken away. I didn't know where and had no mind to find out.

In the aftermath—and there was a hellish amount of paperwork—we figured out their plan.

The vamp we'd brought in was not Kellie Ann Donner but did look like her, right down to the mole off the corner of her mouth. She'd searched far and wide for a patsy and found her working the night shift in that franchise gas station.

The vamp had kidnapped the poor girl, forced the change on her, and buried her deep in a box in that old cemetery. The box was big enough for two. The vamp had doubled up for the day with Kellie Ann's corpse, waiting for her to revive, knowing that somewhere a Company seer would pick up on it and send a registration/recovery team.

The media frenzy and the reward money? All backed by the Dracs. The intent was to get the Company so worried about the number one rule being breached that they'd miss the real goal.

Those SUVs were stuffed with explosives. With them, plus the fake Kellie Ann and other Dracs killing or incapacitating anyone they found, they'd inflict enough damage on this branch of the Company to virtually wipe it out. Computer records would have survived in backup form, but all those signed registration agreements down in the vaults would have been wholly destroyed.

Free of magical restraint, any vamp who felt like cutting loose would be able to do so.

Not smart. Humans in the twenty-first century are infinitely more dangerous than their ancestors, though some of the really old vamps like to think otherwise.

Morons.

Ms. Vouros and others in the skeleton crew in the main

building had a bad time of it from the fake Kellie Ann's assault. She was a good shot but hadn't stuck around to finish them off properly. They'd been hurt but eventually recovered. Most, including Ellinghaus, had to have surgery to get the slugs out, but it was done during the day while they were dead and unaware. A quick vanishing, and they were ready to get back to kicking rogue Drac ass and taking names.

The forensics team that had been sent out to process the burial found the real Kellie Ann Donner. The fake one had snapped her neck right after revival; that was the sound Ellinghaus had taken for breaking wood.

But even young Dracs are tough as hell and hard to kill a second time. The team tried standard first aid, and damned if it didn't work. Her first accidental vanishing healed her up physically, but they had their hands full calming her down and getting her back.

To my surprise, Vouros did not take the easy way out and disappear her. Rogue vamps were behind the disruption and damage to Donner and her family, and Vouros felt a responsibility to try to patch things back together. She used the penitent kidnapper story, and eventually it worked. Post processing and orientation (with ongoing therapy), Kellie Ann went home. She and her family refused offers of book and movie deals, though I heard she accepted a job at the Company's Birmingham branch.

Ellinghaus and I got the Jekyll and Hyde treatment: We were unfairly blamed for bringing in the fake Kellie Ann but also hailed as heroes for stopping her.

After that ear-shattering maneuver, no one ever again gave my partner flack about his favorite obsession.

I asked for a raise. Nothing unreasonable, just something in keeping with cost-of-living expenses.

Better believe I was pissed off when Vouros turned me down,

citing from memory the clause in my contract that covered the limits of pay to apprentices. In turn, I cited my brilliance while under pressure in slowing down the fake Kellie Ann, so she could be stopped; and then I asked for a promotion.

Vouros said she'd think about it and said no in the next breath she drew.

"It's just another two years to automatic promotion and a doubling of your check," she reminded me.

Being a vamp, she had quite a different view of time than I, a short-lived human.

Grumbling, I went to the staff cafeteria and, in a fit of self-destructive rebellion, grabbed one of their infamously bad-for-your-figure desserts. It was a tower of chocolate brownies layered with chocolate ice cream, chocolate chunks, and hot chocolate syrup on top and as many cherries as you liked. As a coping mechanism for job frustration, it did the trick.

I was halfway through it when Ellinghaus came by and sat opposite me in the booth. He was back in his favorite black suit, tie, and hat, shades firmly in place. He sat straight up, hands clasped neatly on the table.

"Good evening, Miss Goldfarb." He'd said that to me countless times, but tonight it seemed tinged with an uncommonly cheerful tone that made me want to brain him one. "Are you ready to get back to business as usual?"

I shot him a suspicious glare. "Were you listening outside when I talked to Vouros?"

"That would be completely unprofessional, Miss Goldfarb."

"Don't avoid the question."

But he made no response. I mined ice-cream-soaked brownie from the bowl, and he watched, apparently fascinated.

"What?" I asked.

"My ambulance has been judged to not be up to Company standards because of the bullet holes."

"Sorry about that."

"But rather than get a replacement, I have opted to buy it from them. They'll paint out the logos, of course."

"Okay."

"Once I get the holes patched, it will make a dandy home on the road."

"I'm happy for you. Wait—are you leaving?"

"I've asked for and been given a sabbatical. Thought I'd go up north and check out the music."

"Oh." I felt a strange and heavy letdown at the news. "How long a sabbatical?"

"A few years."

By the time he got back, I'd be locked into another contract. In the meantime, they'd team me with some other vamp. Ellinghaus was eccentric, but I was used to him. He was a positive distraction from the routine, and I knew for a fact I could trust him with my life.

"Well, we'll keep in touch on Facebook."

"Actually, I was hoping you might consider something else. I would be pleased and honored if you would come along. Nothing improper, just two coworkers taking a sabbatical in the same place."

I dropped my spoon.

"We could watch each other's backs, same as usual."

"But I . . . two more years . . ."

"If I may be allowed to ask a personal question, are you happy here, Miss Goldfarb?"

"Uh . . ."

"Do you see yourself advancing as far as you'd like on your current career path?"

"Um . . . when you put it that way . . . no and no. But if I left I'd need a job."

"There are excellent opportunities to be had for a crafter of your talents."

Work was available for those with magical training, but you

had to have connections or a really good résumé. I lacked both. "Oh, Ell, I'm a one-, maybe two-trick pony with the bounding spell and aura-reading."

"Which has it all over the ponies who have no tricks." He tilted his head. "Your heartbeat's gotten very fast. May I take that to mean you might be interested in discussing this further?"

"Maybe. This is a big thing."

"Indeed it is, Miss Goldfarb."

To my shock, he took off the glasses. I wasn't used to him without the shades. He seemed almost naked.

Damn, but he had beautiful eyes.

★ ★ ★

Author's Bio:
P. N. Elrod is an award-winning author and editor, best known for her ongoing urban fantasy series, *The Vampire Files*. She's sold more than twenty novels to various publishers with translations into several languages. A hopeless chocolate addict, she's hard at work on a new Steampunk series. More info on her toothy titles may be found at www.vampwriter.com.

HOW DO YOU FEEL?

by SIMON R. GREEN

It's not easy having a sex life when you're dead.

I was sitting at the bar in Strangefellows, the oldest pub, night-club and supernatural drinking hole in the world; smoking and drinking and popping my special pills . . . Trying to feel something, anything at all. I don't need to drink or eat, any more than I need to breathe, but I like to pretend. It makes being dead easier to bear. Without my special pills and potions, I don't feel much of anything. And even with the pills, only the most extreme sensations can affect me.

So I drank the most expensive Napoleon brandy and smoked a thick Turkish cigar threaded with opium. Still, all I felt was the barest shadows of sensation, pinpoints of pleasure flaring briefly in my mouth, like stars going out. I was on the last of my pills, and my body was shutting down again.

I looked at myself in the long mirror behind the bar; and Dead Boy looked back at me. Tall and adolescent thin, wrapped in a heavy deep purple greatcoat with a black rose at the lapel, over black-leather trousers and calf-skin boots, the coat hung open to show a pale grey torso, pock-marked with bullet-holes and other wounds, old scar tissue, and accumulated damage. Including the Y-shaped autopsy scar. Stitches, staples, superglue, and the odd length of black duct tape, held everything together. A large, floppy hat, crushed down over thick, curly, black hair. A pale face, dark fever-bright eyes, and a colourless mouth set in a flat, grim line.

Dead Boy.

I toasted myself with the brandy bottle. I like brandy. It doesn't mess about, and it gets the job done. With the pills to push it along, I can almost get drunk; and, of course, I never have to worry about hangovers. I indulge my senses as much as I can, for fear of losing them. I sometimes wonder whether my human emotions might start to fade, too, if I didn't remember to exercise them frequently. I may be dead; but there's life in the old carcass yet.

I put my back to the unpolished wooden bar and looked around me. The place was packed, and the crowd was jumping. All the flotsam and jetsam of the Nightside, that dark and magical hidden heart of London, where the night people come out to play. Lost souls and abandoned dreamers, gods and monsters, golden boys and red-lipped girls, all of them hot in pursuit of pleasures that might not have a name but most certainly have a price.

It seemed like there were lovers everywhere that night, and I looked on them all with simple envy, jealous of the everyday joys I could never experience. A young man sat smiling happily while a female vampire chewed hungrily on the mess she'd made of his neck. If he could see past her glamour, and see her as I saw her, he wouldn't be smiling so easily. Any vampire is just a corpse that's dug its way up out of its grave to feast on the living.

Not far away, a couple of deeply butch ghouls in bondage gear snarled happily at each other over a finger buffet, playfully snapping at each other's faces with their sharp, sharp teeth. Two lesbian undines were drinking each other with straws and giggling tipsily as their water-levels rose and fell. And a very ordinary young couple, with Tourist written all over them, were drinking a glass of something expensive through two heart-shaped straws, lost in each other's eyes.

Young love, in the Nightside. I wanted to shout at them, to

tell all of them: do something, do everything, while you still can . . . Because at any time, any one of you can be snatched away. And then it's too late to do and say all the things you meant to say and do.

Off to one side, my gaze fell upon an off-duty rent-a-cop, still wearing his gaudy private uniform. Huge and stocky, he'd clearly been using knock-off Hyde extract to bulk up his muscles. He was having a good time yelling at his girl, a slender blonde upper-class, up-herself, business-woman type. She finally shook her head firmly; and the Hyde slapped her. Just a casual blow, but more than enough to wrench her head right round and send blood flying from her mouth and nose.

The Hyde looked around, daring anyone to say anything; and then his gaze fell upon me.

"What are you looking at, corpse face?"

I wasn't going to get involved. I really wasn't. But there are limits.

I got up and strolled over to his table. People and others hurried to get out of my way, and a kind of hush fell over the bar. Followed almost immediately by an expectant buzz, as everyone started placing bets. The Hyde looked uneasily around him. He was new here. But he still should have known better. I stood over the Hyde and smiled slowly at him.

"Say you're sorry," I said. "Doesn't matter what for. Just say you're sorry, and you can still walk away."

The Hyde lurched to his feet. His size made him awkward. He snarled some pointless obscenity at me and punched me in the head. The blow had a lot of weight behind it, but not enough to move my head more than an inch. There was a sound like a fist hitting a brick wall, and the Hyde yelled in surprise as he hurt his hand. I sneered at him.

"You'll have to do better than that if you want me to feel anything."

The Hyde hurled himself at me, hitting me again and again

with fists the size of mauls. I let him do it for a while, just to see if he could hurt me. When you're dead, one sensation is as good as another. But the pills were wearing off, and the blows were as distant to me as the sounds they made, and, soon enough, I got bored. So I hit him, with my dead hands and my dead strength, and he started screaming. His bones broke, and his flesh tore, and blood flew thickly on the smoke-filled air. We crashed back and forth among the nearby tables, and other fights sprang up along the way. With cries of "You spilled my drink!" and "You're breathing my air!" the bar regulars cheerfully went to war with each other. Chairs and bodies flew through the air, and all through Strangefellows, there was the happy sound of fisticuffs and people venting.

And behind me I could hear the Hyde's girl screaming at me, "Please! Don't hurt him!" Which was typical.

The Hyde hung limply from my blood-soaked hands. I shook him a few times to see if there was any life left in him, then lost interest. I dropped him carelessly to the floor and went back to my seat at the bar. The business woman crouched, crying, over the broken Hyde. You just can't help some people. The bar fight carried on without me. I couldn't be bothered to join in. It's hard to work up the enthusiasm when you can't feel pain or take real damage.

I drank some more brandy, and it might as well have been tap-water. I drew cigar-smoke deep into my lungs, and they didn't even twitch. The pills' effects never last long. Which is why I always make a point of enjoying what I can, when I can. I was just getting ready to leave when Walker came strolling casually through the bar towards me. Walker, in his smart City suit and his old-school tie, his bowler hat, and his furled umbrella. The Voice of the Authorities, those grey background figures who run the Nightside, inasmuch as anyone does, or cares to. Walker moved easily through the various fights, and not a single hand came close to touching him. Even in the heat of battle, everyone there had enough sense not to upset Walker. He strode right up to me and smiled briefly; and if my heart could have sunk, it would. Whenever Walker deigns to take an interest in you, it's always going to mean trouble.

"Dead Boy," he said, perfectly calmly. "You're looking . . . very yourself. But, then, you haven't changed one little bit, since you were murdered here in the Nightside, more than thirty years ago. Only seventeen years old, mugged in the street for your credit cards and the spare change in your pockets. Left to bleed out in the gutter, and no-one even stopped to look; but then, that's the Nightside for you. Very sad.

"Except, you made a deal, to come back from the dead to avenge your murder. You've never said exactly who you made this deal with . . . It wasn't the Devil. I'd know. But anyway, you should have read the small print. You rose up from your autopsy slab and went out into the night, tracked down, and killed your killers. Very messily, from what I hear. So far, so good; but there was nothing in the deal you made about getting to lie down again afterwards. You were trapped in your own dead body. And so it's gone, for more than thirty years. Have I missed anything important?"

Walker does so love to show off. He knows everything, or at least, everything that matters. In fact, I think that's part of his job description.

"I killed the men who killed me," I said. "They didn't rise up again. And after all the terrible things I did to them before I let them die, Hell must have come as a relief."

"Well, quite," said Walker. "Except . . . they weren't your everyday muggers. Your death was no accident. Someone paid those three young thugs to kill you." He smiled again, briefly. "You really should have taken the time to question them before you killed them."

I stared at him. It had never even occurred to me that there had been anything more to my death than . . . simply being in the wrong place at the wrong time.

"Who?" I said, and my voice sounded more than usually cold, even to me. "Who hired them to kill me?"

"A man called Krauss," said Walker. "Very big in hired muscle, back in the day. You'll find him at the Literary Auction House, right now. If you hurry."

"Why?" I said. "Why would anyone have wanted me dead? I wasn't anyone back then."

"If you're quick, you can ask him," said Walker.

"Why are you telling me this?" I asked him, honestly curious.

He gave me his brief, meaningless smile again. "You can owe me one."

He tipped his bowler hat to me, turned away, and looked at the mass of heaving, fighting bodies before him, blocking his way to the exit. They were all well into it now, too preoccupied with smiting the enemy to pay attention to Walker. So he raised his Voice and said, "Stop that. Right now." And they did. The Authorities had given Walker a Voice that could not be denied. There are those who say he once made a corpse sit up on its slab to answer his questions. Everyone stood very still as Walker strolled unhurriedly through them and left. And then they all looked around and tried to remember what it was they'd been fighting about.

I sat at the bar, pondering the nature of my dead existence, and my past. I've been dead a lot longer than I'd been alive, and it was getting harder to remember what being alive had been like. To have a future, and a purpose, instead of just going through the motions, filling in the time. Had it really been more than thirty years since anyone had said or even known my real name? Thirty years of being Dead Boy? I'd never made any attempt to contact my family or friends. It wouldn't have been fair on them. They all thought I was dead and departed; but they were only half-right.

I had come to the Nightside looking for something different; and I found it, oh yes.

It's hard for me to feel anything much, being dead . . . But with the right mix of these amazing pills and potions I have made up for me specially, by this marvellous old Obeah woman, Mother Macabre, voodoo witch . . . my dead senses can be fooled into experiencing all the sweet moments of life. I can taste the spiciest foods and savour the finest wines, ride the lightning of the strongest and foulest drugs, and never have to pay the price.

I even have a girl-friend.

I do still feel emotions. Sometimes. They are what make me feel most alive, when I can be prodded into experiencing them. Good or bad, it makes no difference. I savour them all, when I can. And avenging old hurts is still at the top of the list of the things that make me feel most alive.

There was music playing in the bar, clear again now the sounds of battle had died away; but it was all just noise to me. I can't appreciate music any more; and I do miss it. I have to wonder what else I've lost that I haven't even noticed. I don't shave, or cut my fingernails, or my hair. I had heard they go on growing after you're dead, but that turned out not to be the case. I wear brightly coloured clothes to compensate for my dead look, and I act large because I've lost my capacity for subtlety. I go on though I often wonder why.

I left the bar, walking unconcerned and untouched through the still-touchy crowd. Everyone gave me plenty of room, and many made the sign of the cross, and other signs, to ward off evil. I do try to be good company, but my people skills aren't what they were. I made my way out onto the street, and there, waiting for me, was my very own brightly gleaming, highly futuristic car. A long, sleek, steel-and-silver bullet, hovering above the ground on powerful energy fields because it was far too grand to bother with old-fashioned things like wheels or gravity.

The door opened, and I got in. I announced our destination, and the car purred smoothly away from the curb. I settled back in my seat. I knew better than to touch the wheel. My car always knows where it's going. I opened the glove compartment and rooted around in it hopefully. And, sure enough, there was just one special pill left. An ugly bottle-green thing, which left a chalky residue on my pale grey fingertips. I washed it down with a few swallows of vodka from the bottle I always keep handy. I like vodka. It gets the job done. My dead taste buds started to fire and flutter almost immediately, and I opened a packet of Hobnobs. I crammed a biscuit into my mouth and chewed heavily, the thick chocolate taste sending a warm glow all through me.

"So, Sil," I said, spraying crumbs on the air. "How's it going?"

"Everything's going down smooth, sweetie," said Sil. My car's very own artificial intelligence has the rich and smoky voice of a very sexy woman. I never get tired of hearing it. She came to the Nightside through a Timeslip, falling all the way from the twenty-third century. She found me, and adopted me, and we've been together ever since. We're in love. My lover, the car. Only in the Nightside. Nobody else knows; she only ever speaks to me.

"You really shouldn't spend so much time in bars, sweetie," said Sil. "All that booze and brooding; it does you no good, physically or spiritually. Especially when I'm not with you."

"I like bars," I said, finishing the packet of biscuits and tossing the empty wrapper onto the back seat. "Bars . . . have food and drink, atmosphere and ambience, bad company and good connections. They help me feel alive, still part of the crowd. And it's not like I need to work. I only ever work to keep busy. To keep from brooding on the bitter unfairness of my condition."

"You mustn't give up," said Sil. "You have to keep looking. There has to be a way, somewhere, to break your deal and come alive again. This is the Nightside, after all. Where dreams can come true."

"Especially the bad ones," I said. "What if . . . all I find is how to become completely dead, at last?"

"Is that what you want?" said Sil.

"It's been so long since I could rest," I said. "I've forgotten what sleep's like, but I still miss it. Just keeping going . . . can be such an effort. Sometimes, I think of just how good it would feel . . . to be able to put down the burden of my continuing existence. If that was all I could find, could you let me go?"

"If that's what you want," said Sil. "If that's what you need. Then yes, I could do that. That's what love is."

I perked up as Sil bullied her way into the main flow of traffic. All kinds of cars and other vehicles, from the Past, the Present, and all kinds of Futures, thunder endlessly back and forth through the Nightside, never slowing, never stopping, intent on their own unknowable business. I'm one of the few people who actually enjoys navigating through the deadly and aggressive Nightside traffic because you can be sure that Sil and I are always the most deadly and aggressive things on the road.

A lipstick red Plymouth Fury sped by, with a grinning dead man at the wheel, followed by a stretch hearse, with two men in formal outfits and top hats in the rear, struggling to force something back into its coffin. A car with far too much chrome and truly massive tail fins, and a highly radioactive afterburner, slammed bad-temperedly through the slower-moving traffic, occasionally running right over smaller vehicles that didn't get out of its way fast enough. And something that blazed fiercely with an unnaturally incandescent light flashed in and out of the traffic at impossible speed, laughing and shrieking and throwing off multi-coloured sparks.

While I was busy watching that, an oversized truck pulled in behind Sil, sticking right on her tail. She drew my attention to it, and I looked in the rear-view mirror just in time to see the whole front of the truck open up like a great mouth, full of row upon row of rotating teeth, like a living meat-grinder. The truck surged forward, the mouth opening wider and wider, to draw Sil in and devour her. And me, of course.

Sil waited till the truck thing was right behind us, then opened up with her rear-mounted flame-throwers. A great wave of harsh yellow flames swept over the truck, filling its gaping mouth. The whole truck caught fire in a moment, massive flames leaping up into the night sky. The truck screamed horribly, sweeping back and forth across the road as though trying to leave the consuming flames behind, while the rest of the traffic scattered to get out of its way. The truck thing exploded in a great ball of fire; and, after a moment, chunks of burning meat fell out of the sky. I lowered the side-window and inhaled deeply, so I could savour the smell. Take your fun where you can find it; that's what I say.

Sil finally drew up outside the Literary Auction House, in the better business area of the Nightside, and pulled right up onto the pavement to park. Secure in the knowledge that absolutely no-one was going to dispute her right to be there. She opened the door for me, and I got out. I took a moment to adjust my purple greatcoat fussily, and be sure my floppy hat was set at just the right jaunty angle. Making the right first impression is so important when you're about to march in somewhere you know you're not welcome . . . probably make a whole lot of trouble, and almost certainly beat important information out of people.

The Literary Auction House is where you go when you're

looking to get your hands on really rare books. Not just the *Necronomicon* or the unexpurgated *King in Yellow*. I'm talking about the kind of books that never turn up at regular auctions. Books like *The Gospel According to Mary Magdalene, The True and Terrible History of the Old Soul Market at Under Parliament,* and *101 Things You Can Get for Free If You Just Perform the Right Blood Sacrifices*. All the hidden truths and secret knowledges that They don't want you to know about. Usually with good reason.

I swaggered in through the open door, and the two guards on duty took one look at me, burst into tears, and ran away to hide in the toilets. Not an uncommon reaction where I'm concerned. Inside the main auction hall, the usual unusual suspects were standing around, enjoying the free champagne and studying the glossy catalogues while waiting for things to start. I grabbed a glass of champagne, drained it in one swallow, and spat it out. I never bother with domestic. Even my special pills can't make that stuff interesting. There were platters of the usual nibbles and delicacies and flashy foody things, so I filled my coat pockets for later. And only then did I peer thoughtfully at the crowd, pick out some familiar faces, and head right for them. Smiling my most disturbing smile, just to let them know I was here for a reason and wouldn't be leaving till I'd got what I wanted.

Deliverance Wilde was there, fashion consultant and style guru to the Fae of the Unseelie Court, tall and black and loudly Jamaican in a smartly tailored suit of eye-wateringly bright yellow. Jackie Schadenfreude, the emotion junkie, wearing a Gestapo uniform and a Star of David, so he could feed on the conflicting emotions they evoked. And the Painted Ghoul, the proverbial Clown at Midnight, in his baggy clothes and sleazy make-up. Chancers and con men, minor celebrities and characters for pay: the kind of people who'd know things and people they weren't supposed to know. As I approached, they all moved to stand a little closer together, for mutual support in the face of a common danger. It would probably have worked with anyone else. I stopped right before them, stuck my hands deep in my coat pockets, and rocked back and forth on my heels as I looked them over, taking my time.

"You know something I want to know," I announced loudly. "And the sooner you tell me, the sooner I'll go away and leave you alone. Won't that be nice?"

"What could we know that you'd want to know?" said Deliverance Wilde, doing her best to look down her long nose at me.

"You want a book?" said the Painted Ghoul, smiling widely to show his sharpened teeth. "I've got books that will make you laugh till you puke blood. All the fun of the unfair, with cyanide-sprinkle candy-floss thrown in . . ."

He stopped talking when I looked at him, the smile dying on his coloured mouth. Jackie Schadenfreude screwed a monocle into one eye.

"What do you want, Dead Boy? Please be good enough to tell us, so we can thrust it into your unworthy hands and be rid of you."

"Krauss," I said. "There's a man here called Krauss, and I want him."

"Oh him," said Deliverance Wilde, visibly relaxing. "Don't know why you'd want him, but I'm only too happy to throw him to the lions. Take him, and do us all a favour."

"Why?" I said. "What is he?"

"You don't know?" said Jackie Schadenfreude. "Krauss is the Bad Librarian. A booklegger. Specialises in really danger-ous books, full of dangerous knowledge."

"The kind no-one in their right mind would want," said the Painted Ghoul, sniggering. "All the terrible things that people can do to people. Usually illustrated. Heh heh."

I nodded slowly. I knew the kind of book they meant. After I came back from the dead and found I was trapped in my body, I did a lot of research on my condition, in many of the Nightside's strange and curious libraries. I know more about all the various forms of death, and life in death, than most people realise. I'd acquired some of my more esoteric research materials from men like Krauss.

"Krauss is bad news," said Deliverance Wilde, mistaking my thoughtfulness for indecision. "He deals in books that show you how to open dimensional doorways, and let in Things from Outside. Books that can teach you to raise Hell. Literally. The book equivalent of a back-pack nuke."

"Books full of the secrets of Heaven and Hell," said Jackie Schadenfreude. "And all the hidden places in between."

"Pleasures beyond human comprehension," said the Painted Ghoul, licking his coloured lips. "Practices to make demons and angels cry out in the night. Heh heh."

"Knowledge of the true nature of reality," said Deliverance Wilde. "That drives men mad because reality isn't what we think it is and never has been. Take him and be welcome, Dead Boy. It's bookleggers like Krauss that give people like us a bad name."

"Where is he?" I said.

All three of them pointed in the same direction. None of their hands were particularly steady.

I headed straight for Krauss, and everyone along the way fell back to give me plenty of room. Krauss was a nondescript, elderly man in a tweed suit with leather patches on the elbows, wearing an old-school tie he almost certainly wasn't entitled to. He was so immersed in his auction catalogue, circling things and making notes, that he didn't even see me coming till I was right on top of him. He looked up abruptly, alerted by the sudden silence around him, and peered at me over the top of a pair of golden pince-nez.

"Hello," he said, carefully. "Now what would the low and mighty Dead Boy want with a mere booklegger like myself? Can

I perhaps be of service, help you locate something? Some suitable tome on the pleasures to be found in dead flesh, perhaps? Something explicit, on the delights of the damned? Satisfaction and complete discretion guaranteed, of course."

"You don't even recognise me, do you?" I said.

"But of course I do, my good sir! You're Dead Boy! Everyone in the Nightside knows Dead Boy."

"You only think you know me," I said. "But then, it has been thirty years and more since you paid three young thugs to mug and murder me, down on Damnation Row."

His jaw actually dropped, and all the colour fell out of his face. "That was *you*? Really? I can't believe it . . . I helped create the legendary Dead Boy? I'm honoured!"

"Don't be," I said.

Krauss chuckled a little, relaxing now he thought he knew what this was about. "Well, well . . . I can't believe my past has caught up with me, after so many years . . ." He tucked his catalogue neatly under one arm and looked me up and down, studying the results of his work. "I haven't been involved in the muscle trade for . . . well, must be decades! Yes! That was a whole other life . . . I was a different person, then."

"So was I," I said. "I was alive."

His smile disappeared. "But you can't blame me for what I did, all those years ago! I'm a changed man now!"

"So am I," I said. "I'm dead. And I'm not happy about it."

"What . . . what do you want from me?" said Krauss. "I didn't know . . . I had no idea . . ."

"Who paid you?" I said. "Who hired you to have me killed? I want to know who, and why. I wasn't anybody back then. I wasn't anyone special. I was just a teenager."

Krauss shrugged quickly. There was sweat on his face. "I never asked why. Wasn't any of my business. I hired out muscle; that was what I did! I never asked her why, and she never said."

"She . . . She who, exactly?"

"Old voodoo woman," said Krauss. "Called herself Mother Macabre. Spooky old bat. Not the kind you ask questions of."

He had more to say, about how he shouldn't be blamed for someone else's bad intentions, that he just supplied a service, that if he hadn't done it, somebody else would have; but I wasn't really listening. Mother Macabre was the name of the old Obeah woman who'd been supplying me with all those special pills and potions, for more than thirty years. Could it really be the same woman? Why would she pay to have me killed, then help me out? Guilt? Not likely; not in the Nightside. It didn't make sense; but it had to be her. She was why Walker had pointed me in this direction. I looked Krauss in the eye, and he stopped talking abruptly. He started to back away. I dropped one heavy, dead hand on his shoulder, to hold him still. He winced at the strength in my hand and whimpered.

"I helped make you who you are!" he said desperately. "I helped make you Dead Boy!"

"Let me see," I said. "How do I feel about that?"

I closed my hand abruptly, and all the bones in his shoulder shattered. He screamed. I hit him in the head. The whole left side of his face caved in, and his scream was choked by the blood filling his throat. I hit him again and again, breaking him, watching dispassionately as pain and horror and blood filled Krauss's face. Because the last pill had worn off, and I didn't feel anything. I thrust one hand deep into his chest, closed my cold, dead fingers around his living heart, and tore it out of his body. He fell to the floor, kicked a few times, and lay still. I looked at the bloody piece of meat in my hand, then let it drop to the floor.

I'd killed the man who arranged my death, and it didn't touch me at all. I sat down on the bloody floor, picked up Krauss's body, and held it in my arms, cradling it to my chest. I still didn't feel anything. I let him go and got up again. I looked around me. Even hardened denizens of the Nightside were shocked at what I'd done. Some were crying, some were vomiting. I smiled slowly.

"What are you looking at?"

I didn't really care; but I had a reputation to maintain.

Outside, Sil was waiting patiently. She opened the door for me, and I took a rag out of the inner compartment and scrubbed the blood off my hands. There was more blood soaked into the front of my greatcoat, but that could wait. My coat was used to hard times. I got into the driver's seat, the door closed, and Sil set off again.

"Where now?" she said.

"Just drive for a while," I said. "And hush, please. I have a lot to think about."

She drove on, cruising through the hot, neon-lit streets, while I looked at nothing and tried to make sense of what I'd learned. Mother Macabre, my trusted old Obeah woman, who'd helped me hang on to what was left of the real me for more than thirty years. Why would she have wanted me dead? I wasn't anybody then. Nobody special. What . . . purpose could my poor death have served? The thoughts went round and round in my head and got nowhere. I'm not a great one for thinking. No. Much better to go to the source and ask some very pertinent questions, in person.

"Sil," I said. "Take me to Mother Macabre. Take me to the Garden of Forbidden Fruits."

You can find the Garden of Forbidden Fruits not far from the main business centre of the Nightside. It's where you go when you want something a bit alternative to all the usual sin and sleaze. Just the place to buy an inappropriate gift, like a killer plant that will sneak up on the recipient while they're asleep. Or seeds that will grow into something really disturbing. And very special drugs, to give you glimpses of Heaven and Hell or rip the soul right out of you. If it grows, if it fruits and flowers in unnatural ways, you'll find it somewhere in the Garden of Forbidden Fruits.

I told Sil to wait for me and entered the Garden through its ever-open doors. It was just a long hallway, which seemed to stretch away forever, lined on both sides with the kind of shop or establishment you only ever enter at your own risk. I'd been here many times before, to pick up my special pills and potions from my old friend, Mother Macabre. The withered old black crone, in her pokey little shop, the traditional image of the voodoo witch, who smiled and cackled as she made up my packages with her clever, long-fingered hands, and only ever charged me what I could afford. That in itself should have been enough to tip me off that something was wrong. You just don't get that, in the Nightside.

I strode past The Little Shop of Horticulture, with its window full of snapping plants, past The Borgia Connection (for that little something he'll never notice in his food) and Mistress Lovett's Posy Parlour (Sleep without dreams . . .). I ignored the hanging plants outside shop doorways, which hissed at me as I passed, or sang songs in languages I didn't recognise. I ignored the familiar, hot, wet smells of damp earth and growing things, the powerful perfumes of unlikely flowers, and the underlying stench from the bloody earth their roots soaked in. I looked straight ahead, and everyone and everything in that long hallway shrank back from me as I passed. Till, finally, I came to the only shop-front I cared about, the one I'd visited so many times before and never thought twice about. Mother Macabre's Midnight Mansion.

I stood outside the open door. It wasn't any kind of mansion, of course. Just a shop. Dark and dingy and more than a little pokey. There was never anything on display, and the only window was blank. Mother Macabre's patrons liked their privacy. I put my shoulders back and lifted my chin. Never let them know they've hurt you. I strolled into the shop with my hands buried deep in the pockets of my coat, so no-one could see that my hands were curled into fists.

It looked just as it always did. It hadn't changed because I was seeing it with new eyes. The familiar four walls of shelves, tightly packed with tightly sealed jars and bottles, full of this and that. Some of the contents were still moving. There was High John the Conqueror root; and mandrake root in sound-proofed jars; vampire teeth, clattering against the inside of the glass; all kinds of raw talent for sale, with colour-coded caps, so the assistant could tell them apart at a glance; and a whole row of shrunken heads, with their mouths stitched shut to stop them from screaming. All the usual tat the tourists can't get enough of. And behind the counter, as always, a tall, young, strong-featured black woman dressed in the best Haitian style, with an Afro and a headscarf, speaking in broad patois for the middle-aged tourist couple dithering over their purchases. Her name was Pretty Pretty, and woe betide anyone who ever raised an eyebrow at that. She had always been very kind to me; but I wasn't sure if that would save her now.

I waited patiently, until she was finished with the tourists. They left happily enough, with their jar full of something that glowed with a sour, spoiled light; and I shut the door behind them and turned the sign to read CLOSED. Pretty Pretty looked at me curiously and started to say something in the patois. I raised a hand, and she stopped.

"Please," I said. "I'm not a tourist."

"Never said you were, darling," said Pretty Pretty, in the polished voice of her very expensive finishing school. "Now what on earth are you doing here? You can't have run out already, surely? I mean, honestly darling, you do get through those things at a rate of knots . . . You're not supposed to pop them back like sweeties . . ."

And then she stopped, her voice just trailing away. There must have been something in my face, in my eyes, because she stood very still behind her counter. She must have had defences there, but she had enough sense not to go for them. I smiled at her, and she actually shuddered.

"Mother Macabre," I said. "I want her. Where is she?"

"She just left, darling," said Pretty Pretty. She swallowed hard. "Maybe half an hour ago? You just missed her . . . Is it important?"

"Yes," I said. "Stay out of the way, Pretty Pretty. I'm prepared to believe you're not involved. Keep it that way."

I strode past the counter and kicked in the door that led to Mother Macabre's private office. The lock exploded, and the heavy wood cracked and fell apart. I pulled the pieces out of the broken frame and threw them to one side. There must have been magical protections, too, because I felt them run briefly up and down my dead skin; but they couldn't touch me. Pretty Pretty made an unhappy noise but had enough sense to stay behind her counter.

The private office looked very ordinary, very business-like. I tried the computer on her desk, but it was all locked down. And even I can't intimidate passwords out of a computer. I tried all the desk drawers, and the in-tray and out-tray, but it was all just everyday paper-work. Nothing of interest. So I trashed the whole office, very thoroughly. Just to make a statement. Pretty Pretty watched timidly from the doorway. When I tore the heavy wooden desk apart with my bare hands, she made a few refined noises of distress. When I'd finished, because there was nothing left to break or destroy, I stood and considered what to do next, picking splinters out of my unfeeling hands. I looked sharply at Pretty Pretty, and she jumped, only a little.

"Where would Mother Macabre be? Right now?"

"I suppose she could be at her Club," Pretty Pretty said immediately. Anyone else she would have told to go to Hell, and even added instructions on the quickest route; but I wasn't anyone else. "She owns this private club, members only, called the Voodoo Lounge. Do you know it?"

"I know of it," I said. "I can find it."

"Should I . . . phone ahead? Let her know you're coming?"

"If you like," I said. "It won't make any difference. I'll find her wherever she goes."

"Why?" said Pretty Pretty. "What's happened? What's changed?"

"Everything," I said.

I'd heard of the Voodoo Lounge. Not the kind of place I'd ever visit but very popular with the current Bright Young Things, keen to throw away their inheritance on the newest thrill. Voodoo for the smart set, graveyard chill for those old enough to know better. Very expensive, very exclusive, very hard to get into, for most people. I told Sil to take me there, and she didn't say a word. We drove in silence through the angry traffic, each of us lost in our own thoughts. I was getting close now. I could feel it. Close to all the answers I ever wanted, and one final act of vengeance . . . that even I was smart enough to realise I might not be able to walk away from.

Sil pulled up outside the Voodoo Lounge. I got out and told her to wait for me. She didn't answer. She wasn't sulking, or even disapproving; it was simply that she knew better than to speak to me when I was in this kind of mood. The risen dead don't have many positive qualities, but stubbornness is definitely one of them. There were two guards on duty outside the black-lacquered doors that gave entrance to the Voodoo Lounge. Very large black gentlemen, with shaven heads and smart tuxedos. I put on my best worrying smile and strode right at them. They knew who I was, probably even knew why I was there; but neither of them did the sensible thing and ran. You have to admire such dedication to duty. They looked at me expressionlessly and moved to stand just a little closer together, blocking my way to the entrance.

"Members only, sir," said the one on the left.

"No exceptions, sir," said the one on the right.

"We have orders to keep you out."

"By whatever means necessary."

"On your way, Dead Boy."

"Not welcome here, zombie."

I let my smile widen into a grin and kept on going. One of them pulled a packet of salt from his pocket and threw the contents into my face. Salt is a good traditional defence against zombies, but I've always been a lot more than that. The other guard produced a string of garlic and thrust it in my face. I snatched one of the bulbs away from him, took a good bite, chewed on it, and spat it out. No taste. Nothing at all. And while I was doing that, the first guard produced a gun and stuck the barrel against my forehead.

"When in doubt," he said calmly, "go old school. Shoot them in the head."

He pulled the trigger. The bullet smashed through my forehead, through my dead brain, and out the back of my head. I rocked slightly on my feet, but I didn't stop smiling. The guard with the gun actually whimpered as I snatched the gun out of his hand and tossed it to one side.

"That's been tried," I said. "I'll have to fill the hole in with plaster of paris again."

I punched the guard in the face, smashing his nose and mouth and jaw, and then back-elbowed the other guard in the side of the head. They both went down and didn't get up again. Normally, I would have taken the time to do them both some serious damage, to make a point, but I had more important things in mind. I stepped over the broken guards, kicked in the black-lacquered doors, and strode into the Voodoo Lounge.

★ ★ ★

"Hello!" I said loudly as I strode into the entrance-hall. "I'm here! Come on, give it your best shot! Do your worst! I can take it!"

And the next level of defence came running silently down the hallway towards me. A short, stocky Chinaman, the tattoos down one side of his face marking him as a combat magician. A very powerful and frightening figure—to anyone else. He waited till he was almost upon me, then he gestured sharply and snatched a blazing ball of fire out of nowhere. Vivid green flames shot up around his hand, and he stopped dead in his tracks to thrust them at me. Emerald fires blasted me like a flame-thrower. But I was already turning, putting my back to him; and the searing flames slammed against my deep purple greatcoat. A terrible fire roared over and around me; but the flames couldn't touch me. In my dead state, I couldn't even feel the heat. And when the flames finally died out, I straightened up, turned around, and smiled at the combat magician.

"I had my coat fire-proofed long ago, on the quiet, for occasions just like this," I said.

And while I was saying that, holding his attention, I surged forward, snatched the jade fire amulet out of his hand, and beat him to the floor. I heard his skull crack and break under the blows, but I hit him a few more times anyway, to be sure. I stood over him, listening to the bloody froth bubble in his mouth and nose, and felt nothing, nothing at all. I studied the fire amulet, a simple jade piece with a golden cat's-eye pupil at its heart. You can buy them at any market in the Nightside, though learning the proper Words of Power to make them work costs rather more. I turned the amulet back and forth, admiring the quality of the workmanship, then I said the right Words, and set fire to the combat magician. His screams, and the sound of the consuming flames, followed me down the hall as I walked away.

* * *

The interior of the Club had been painted all the shades of red and purple. It was like walking through the interior of someone's body. The air was thick with the scents of burned meat and spilled blood, and all kinds of illegal smoke. Smells so heavy even I could detect them. The air was hot and damp, and heavy beads of condensation ran down my face. I couldn't feel the heat or the moisture, only noticed them when they fell down to stain my coat. There were doors on either side of the hallway, leading to very private rooms, for very private passions. I considered them thoughtfully. It might make me feel better, to kick the doors in and see what was going on behind them. It might make me feel . . . something. But then a voice came to me, through some hidden speaker, saying, "This way. Walk straight ahead. Come into my parlour, Dead Boy, and we'll talk. I've been waiting for you."

A calm, confident, female voice. Didn't sound like my Mother Macabre. I walked on, into the belly of the beast, into the trap that had been prepared for me. And the cold in my dead heart was the cold of dark and righteous anger.

Didn't take me long to reach the door at the end of the hall. It was standing just a little open, invitingly. I slammed right through it, almost taking the door off its hinges, and there she was, in her parlour. Mother Macabre's sweet little home away from home was more than comfortable, full of every luxury and indulgence you could think of, and some you never even dreamed of. Tables full of drinks, bowls full of pills and powders, toys and trinkets to suit the most jaded sexual palates—decadence on display. All for the Bright Young Things . . . as they sat in chairs, or sprawled on couches, or lay giggling happily on the deep pile carpet. Young ladies and gentlemen from rich and powerful and well-connected families, still young enough to believe money could buy you satisfaction, or at the very least enough pleasure to convince you that you were happy.

Spending Daddy's money and influence on the very latest thing, the newest kick, on something dark and dangerous enough to make them feel they were important, after all. They stared at me with blank eyes and meaningless smiles, and limited curiosity. And the dozen or so naked men and women, standing around the parlour to serve the young people's every need or whim, were all quite obviously dead. Well-preserved, even pleasant to the eye; but you only had to look into their faces to know there was no-one home. They weren't dead like me; they were nothing more than animated bodies, moved by some other's will.

I wasn't interested in them. I fixed my gaze on the parlour's mistress: proud and disdainful on her raised throne, like a spider at the heart of her web. Mother Macabre, sitting at her ease on a throne made of human skulls. Bone so old it had faded past yellow ivory into dirty brown, stained here and there with old, dried blood. There was a cushion on the seat, of course. Tradition and style and making the right kind of impression are all very well, but comfort is what matters.

Mother Macabre looked as she always had, a withered, old, black crone, in tattered ethnic clothes. Deep-sunk eyes, and a wide smile to show off the missing teeth. Very authentic. But I didn't believe that any more. I concentrated, looking at her with the eyes of the dead, because the dead can see many things that are hidden from the living. And just like that, the illusion snapped off. And underneath the glamour, she was just an ordinary middle-aged black business woman, neat and tidy in a smart business suit, her well-manicured hands folded calmly in her lap.

"Took you long enough to work it out," she said. "Mistress Macabre is just a trade name. Handed down through the generations, along with the trade and the look, because that's what people want when they do business with a voodoo witch. There were many Mother Macabres before me, and no doubt there will be many more after. It's a very profitable trade. Because there will always be a need for women like us. But . . . this is the real me. You should feel flattered, Dead Boy. Not many are privileged to see the real me."

"Flattered," I said. "Yes. That's how I feel, all right. Tell me: who did I really make a deal with?"

"And you've worked that out, too! Well done, Dead Boy. Yes, I'm afraid your memories of what happened after you died are as much a fake as anything else. You thought you made a deal with one of the voodoo loa, Mistress Erzulie; but everything you saw and experienced came from me. A show I put on to distract you while I did the many vile and nasty things necessary, to raise you from the dead. It was all just an illusion, another mask. Just me. It's always been just me."

"Why?" I said.

And there must have been something in my voice because everyone in the parlour stopped smiling and looked at me. Even Mother Macabre on her throne of skulls took a moment before she answered me. I fixed her with my unblinking eyes, and she actually squirmed uncomfortably on her throne.

"Why?" said Mother Macabre. "Because I needed someone to experiment on! Didn't matter who. Could have been you, could have been anyone. I was just starting out in the Mother Macabre trade. I inherited it from my mother—after I killed her. She was so old-fashioned, couldn't see the potential in the business I saw . . . Anyway, I had all these marvellous ideas for new pills and potions, but I needed someone to test them on before I introduced them to a wider audience. I needed someone young and strong and vital, new to the Nightside, without friends or protectors. I picked you out entirely at random and paid to have you killed. And then I brought you back again, to be my test subject. You took everything I gave you, every new drug and concoction I came up with, and never once questioned any of it. And because it was my lore that brought you back, your body had no secrets from me. I've studied you, from a safe distance, for all these years . . . And, oh, the things I've learned from you! You have no idea how much money you've made me down the years!"

"All the things I've been, and done," I said. "And all along I was nothing but your lab rat."

"Actually, no," said Mother Macabre. "You're a lot more than I ever intended you to be. I was just interested to see what would happen when I trapped a living soul inside a dead body, but you have made yourself into the legendary, infamous Dead Boy! You should be proud of what you've achieved!"

"Proud," I said. "Yes. That's what I'm feeling, right now."

Mother Macabre looked at me uncertainly, unable to read my dead face or my dead voice. "You really shouldn't take it personally, Dead Boy. It was only ever . . . business."

"It was my life!" I said loudly.

She smiled. "It wasn't as though you were doing anything important with it."

"All the things I could have done," I said. "All the people I might have been; and you took them away from me."

"None of them would have been as important, or as interesting, as Dead Boy." Mother Macabre sank back on her throne as though she were getting tired, or bored, with the conversation. "What does your life, or your death, matter, where there were fortunes to be made? I had a business to run! It's all about the pleasures of the flesh, you see. Control them, and you have control over the living and the dead." She looked fondly at the young people scattered around her parlour. "My lovely ladies and gentlemen. I give them what they think they want and take everything they have. And when they die . . . I raise them up again, to serve me. The dead always make the best servants.

No back-talk, no days off. And the dead make the very best lovers because they can go forever . . ."

She gestured to a naked man and a naked woman, and they came forward to caress her face and neck with their cool, dead hands. She smiled happily.

"They feel nothing. The only pleasure is mine. But then, I never was big on sharing. I knew you were coming after me, Dead Boy. Knew it the moment you killed poor old Krauss. I could have had you destroyed anywhere along the way; but I wanted to have you here, so I could watch it happen right in front of me. I have the right to destroy you because I made you. You belong to me. You always have. And after you've gone, I'll make another Dead Boy."

She snapped her fingers, and all the dead men and women in the parlour turned their heads to look at me. And then they started forward, cold and implacable as death itself. All of them just as strong as me and as capable of taking punishment. They reached for me with their dead hands, and the young ladies and gentlemen laughed and pointed, enjoying the show. I looked around me. The way to the only door was blocked, and I was clearly outnumbered. So, when in doubt, cheat.

I reached into my pocket and took out the jade fire amulet I'd taken from its previous owner. I said the right Words, and set fire to all the dead men and women. They burst into bright green flames, burning with a fierce heat that consumed their flesh in moments. They kept coming as long as they could, reaching out blindly through the flames, bumping into the furnishings and fittings and setting them alight, too. They even set fire to the clothes of the Bright Young Things. Most of them just sat where they were, watching as the flames ate them up, and laughing. Giggling happily as they died, as stupidly as they'd lived.

Mother Macabre ran for the door the moment her servants started burning, but I was there before her. I took her in my dead arms, and held her to me, almost tenderly. She beat at me with her fists, but I couldn't feel them, and she wasn't strong enough to do me any damage. I held her with all my dead strength, and she couldn't get away. The whole parlour was on fire now, burning the living and the dead alike, and the air was full of thick black smoke.

"You have to let me go!" shrieked Mother Macabre. "If we stay here, we'll both die! This fire's enough to destroy even you!"

"You say that like it's a bad thing," I said. "I'm tired. I want to rest. It will be worth it, to die here, as long as I can be sure I'm taking you with me. Thanks to you, I can't feel any of the things the living feel; but dead as I am, I can still feel some things, even without your special pills. I'm watching you die, Mother Macabre, and that feels . . . so fine."

"I can make you new pills, new potions!" Mother Macabre said desperately. "I can make you feel all the things you felt before!"

"Perhaps. But what have I got that's worth living for?"

And then we both looked round as a series of explosions shook the front of the building. There was the sound of energy weapons firing, and repeated sounds of something large and heavy and very determined crashing through the walls between us, heading right for us. And I began to smile. I looked at the door, still holding firmly on to the fiercely struggling Mother Macabre; and my futuristic car came smashing through the door and into the parlour, bringing half the wall with her. She slammed to a halt before me, her gleaming steel-and-silver body entirely untouched by all the destruction she'd wrought. And as I watched, smiling . . . as Mother Macabre watched with wide-stretched eyes and mouth . . . my car rose and transmogrified, taking on a whole new shape, until my Sil stood before me. A tall, buxom woman, in a classic little black dress, cut just high enough at the hip to show off the bar-code and copyright notice stamped on her magnificent left buttock. Her frizzy steel hair was full of sparking static, and her eyes were silver, but she was still every inch a woman. My woman.

"Nothing to live for, sweetie?" said Sil. "What about me?"

"You were listening in," I said, just a bit reproachfully.

"You were taking too long," said Sil. "I became . . . concerned. You always go over the top when you go too far into the dark. You forget there are other feelings, other pleasures, than revenge."

"Of course," I said. "You're quite right. You always were my better half. I never needed pills to feel the way I feel about you."

"What the hell is that?" said Mother Macabre, staring at Sil with horrified fascination.

"I am a sex droid from the twenty-third century," Sil said proudly. "With full trans-morph capabilities!" She shot me a smouldering look. "I have always loved my job. It took more than one man to change my name to Silicon Lily. But I never met anyone like you, my sweet Dead Boy. And I won't let you die with her. She isn't worth it."

"You're right," I said. "You're always right. You're worth living for, inasmuch as I can. But . . . I can't go on, I can't just walk out of here and let her get away with what she did to me."

"You don't have to," said Sil.

She raised one hand and morphed it into a glowing energy weapon. She shot Mother Macabre in the face and blew her head apart. I let go of the headless body, and it crumpled to the floor, still twitching. I swept blood and brains from my face and shoulder with one hand, then nodded briefly to Sil. She's always been able to do the things I can't do. She swept forward, discarding her human shape, melting into a wave of metallic silver that swept right over me. She wrapped herself around me like a suit of armour, covering me from head to foot. Embracing me, and protecting me, all at once. And, together, we walked out of the burning building.

Outside, Walker was waiting for us, watching the building burn. He barely twitched an eyebrow as Sil peeled herself off me, and resumed her human shape. She stood beside me as Silicon Lily, while I nodded politely to Walker. He tipped his bowler hat to both of us.

"Mother Macabre was getting a little too big for her boots," Walker said easily. "But I couldn't go after her, because of her . . . connections. So I pointed you at her. Well done, Dead Boy. Excellent work."

"How long have you known?" I said. "How long have you known the truth about me, and Krauss, and Mother Macabre?"

"I know everything," said Walker. "Remember?"

He smiled again, very politely, and walked off. Sil and I turned away, to watch the Voodoo Lounge burn.

"What am I going to do now, for my special pills and potions?" I said.

"There's always someone," said Sil. "This is the Nightside."

"True," I said. "If you're going to be damned, this is a pretty good place for it." I looked at her for a long moment. "Even with my pills, it takes more than an everyday woman to light the fires in my dead flesh."

"Good thing I'm not an everyday woman, then," said Silicon Lily. "I am a pleasure droid; and I do love my work! And it's good to know I can even raise the dead . . ."

"How can I love you?" I said. "When I don't have a heart any more?"

"I don't have a heart either," said Sil. "Doesn't matter. Love comes from the soul."

"Do we have souls?" I said.

She put her arms around me. "What do you think?"

It's not easy, having a sex life when you're dead. But it is possible.

"How do you feel?" said Sil.

"I feel . . . good," I said.

★   ★   ★

Author's Bio:

Simon was born in Bradford-on-Avon, Wiltshire, England where he still resides. He obtained an M.A. in Modern English and American Literature from Leicester University, studied history and has a combined Humanities degree. His writing career started in 1973, when he was a student in London. He's the author of the bestselling SF/Space Opera series: *The Deathstalker Saga,* a series of eight books, of which he himself admits that it kind of got out of hand, since it was supposed to be three 500-page books . . . His website may be found at **http://simonrgreen .co.uk.**

THERE WILL BE DEMONS

by LORI HANDELAND

I'd been out all night shooting trolls with salt—straight through the heart; it's the only thing that kills them. So when the knock came on my motel-room door before I'd even had a chance to wash their ashes out of my hair, I should have ignored it.

Except no one knew I was in Minnesota, which made me nervous. Though why, I have no idea. Demons rarely knock.

However, when I peered through the peephole and saw a wide expanse of nothing, I whirled to the right expecting, the imminent arrival of a shotgun-sized hole through the door. Not that a shotgun filled with anything but rowan or iced steel would kill me, but getting shot hurt.

Every single damn time.

The knock came again—louder, more insistent. Housekeeping or management would announce themselves. They also wouldn't stand out of sight of the peephole. Only someone who didn't want me to see them would. Unless it was someone I *couldn't* see.

I didn't like that scenario any better that the first one. But since I couldn't stay where I was, listening, hiding, practically cringing—it wasn't my style—I flung open the door and spewed fairy dust from my fingertips, even as my mind formed the words *reveal* and *freeze*.

No demon materialized in front of me. That was good. Then someone coughed, and I jerked my head to the left.

"This is bad."

His face was covered in silvery particles that stuck to his long, dark lashes like goo. His ebony hair appeared to have been dusted with snow. His face sparkled as if he'd been doused in glitter.

He *should* be frozen like a gargoyle. Instead, he lifted one hand and wiped at the mess, staring first at his palm, then lifting his dark eyes to mine.

A shudder ran through me. I'd seen those eyes before.

Every night in my dreams for the last few thousand years.

"What *are* you?" he asked.

"What are *you*?" I returned.

My hands shook. I stuck them behind my back so I wouldn't have to explain why. I wasn't sure I could. I'd been dreaming of him for so long, I'd begun to think he wasn't real, that maybe what I'd seen wouldn't happen, that what I'd done wouldn't matter. I should have known better.

"Name's Sanducci," he said. "Jimmy."

I noticed he hadn't really answered my question, but then I hadn't answered his either.

I might have dreamed of him until I knew his face, and his body, even better than I knew my own, but I'd never learned his name or figured out what, exactly, he was.

Despite being tall, at least six feet of rangy muscle, and owning eyes that were haunted with things he would much, much rather forget, he seemed young.

Of course, to someone like me, Methuselah was a toddler. Or at least he had been when I'd met him. By the time the old guy expired, right before the flood, he'd been wrinkled, white, and bent like a question mark, while I'd still looked exactly as I did now—blond, petite, annoyingly perky, and forever twenty-one.

"How old are you?" I asked.

Jimmy's chin came up. "Old enough."

"For what?"

"I was sent to meet another DK."

"Another?" I got that shiver again. "You're a DK?"

DK. Short for demon killer.

I'm not sure why I was surprised. In my dreams of Jimmy Sanducci, he'd fought demons of many kinds, and they'd killed him in many, many ways. Subsequent dreams revealed that his death tipped the scales in that eternal war between good and evil. Without this man fighting on the side of good, evil began to win. I'd have promised anything to avoid that. Even before I'd started having the dreams of him and me together, the ones where I loved him.

"Are you?" he asked, and at my blank expression, continued. "A DK?"

I nodded. "Summer Bartholomew."

"She said I'd find you here, and that we should—"

"She?" I murmured, and then I understood. Who else would be able to track where I was but—"Ruthie."

"She's my seer."

Mine too. And she knew that I worked alone. I especially could not work with him. That, however, she didn't know.

"We're supposed to—" I held up my hand, and Jimmy flinched. I guess he didn't want to get socked in the face with fairy dust again.

When the dust hadn't worked on him, I should have known right away what he was. My magic doesn't apply to those on an errand of mercy. Since saving humanity from the demon horde was the life of a DK, twenty-four/seven, my enchanted dust was useless on them.

"You better come in," I said. "I'm gonna have to call Ruthie."

He stepped into the room, then stared, openmouthed.

On the outside, this place resembled a two-story Bates Motel. But in here . . .

White plush carpet, French provincial furniture, thick white quilts and huge, cushy pillows on a king-sized bed. Through the open bathroom door, a palatial hot tub was visible, surrounded by tropical plants and gold-tipped white tile.

I clapped my hands, and all of it disappeared, leaving behind orange carpet that I didn't want to walk across in barefeet—I could swear something was crawling in it—a bedspread that smelled like dead moths, one lumpy full-sized mattress and even lumpier pillows.

"What are you?" Jimmy asked again.

"Ruthie didn't tell you?" He shook his head. "Then I'm not going to."

I snatched the TV remote off the chipped, unvarnished wooden dresser and tossed it in his direction without warning. He snatched it easily—most DKs were freakishly nimble and quick. We had to be in order to fight demons. Which meant most of us were at least part demon, too. I wondered what his part was.

"No porn," I said.

"I'm not a kid." He pointed the remote at the TV. "I haven't *been* a kid since I killed my first Nephilim."

Nephilim. The offspring of the fallen angels and man. Behind their human facade, they were the beings of legend—werewolves, vampires, shape-shifters, and more. My life has been devoted to killing them. Sometimes, I think I'll never be able to stop.

"When was that?" I asked.

Jimmy didn't even look away from the screen. "I think I was eight."

"You were *eight?*"

His dark gaze flicked to mine, then away. "Guy came at me all tooth and claw. What was I supposed to do?"

"Drink your juice box and let your parents handle it."

"Never met 'em. I was on the streets when I was—" He paused, shrugged. "I was always on the streets. Until Ruthie."

Ruthie Kane—seer, Leader of the Light, mother to all in need of a mother. For a price.

She and I needed to have a little talk.

I grabbed my cell phone from the nightstand and escaped into the bathroom, locking the door behind me before turning the shower on full blast for cover. Although—

If the kid was something special—and I was pretty sure he was—he could hear a pin drop at Niagara Falls. I could.

I left the water on anyway. It dispelled the scent of mold that the closed door enhanced. I could conjure money and stay at a better hotel. However, I'd found over the centuries that the creepy, crawly creatures I hunted usually lived far from the amenities. So I stayed wherever I found a place and magicked that place to my liking.

I hit number one on my speed dial, and five rings later, the phone was picked up in Milwaukee.

"He there already?" Ruthie asked before I could even say hello.

Ruthie didn't have caller ID. Ruthie didn't need it.

"What the hell were you thinking?" I demanded.

Silence settled over the line, broken only by the distant wail of a child. Ruthie ran a group home on the south side of Milwaukee, where she took in all the kids no one else wanted. What the powers that be didn't know was that the kids no one wanted—the ones that trouble followed—were usually the ones Ruthie was searching for.

"I don't think I heard that quite right."

Ruthie's voice was soft, but there was steel beneath. Cold steel. She'd see me dead if I didn't watch myself. Ruthie might look like everyone's favorite African-American granny, but she wasn't. Ruthie led the group of seers and demon killers known as the Federation, and she hadn't gotten to that position by being kind.

"I can't work with him, Ruthie," I whispered. "I just can't."

"I know you like to work alone. But I don't wanna send him out solo just yet. You don't gotta worry. Fact is he's scary good. One day, he might even be better than you."

From what I'd seen in my dreams, he would be. And yet, still, according to those dreams, he would die.

"I can't," I repeated.

At last Ruthie heard what I wasn't saying. "What did you see?"

I might be a demon killer, but I also had the sight. This should have put me in the seer line. However, instead of seeing demons, I saw the future—or at least possible futures.

I'd come to understand that free will fucked up everything. Everyone had it, which meant they could choose to turn left instead of right, take a bike instead of a car, sleep five extra minutes that morning, leave work five minutes late that night, and every choice altered my visions.

"He'll die," I said.

"Jimmy? How?"

"I don't know. I've seen it happen a hundred different ways. But it always happens."

"Why didn't you tell me?"

"I didn't know who he was. Even *if* he was. I do actually have dreams that are just . . . dreams."

And the other ones I'd had—of Jimmy and me all tangled in the sheets, sweaty and panting, my pale skin glowing like pearls sliding just beneath dusky water as he touched me in ways that just had to be wrong, even though nothing had ever felt so right . . .

Those I was never going to tell anyone about. Especially Ruthie.

"Doesn't matter," she said at last.

"He's your soon-to-be best boy, and his death doesn't matter?"

"If you've watched him die a hundred different ways, that

only means he's continually changing his fate. I bet he avoids it entirely."

Considering what I'd done for him, I would bet he did, too.

"What you've seen don't change why he's there. In fact, now I understand why I was told you should go with him. If you recognize somethin' from one of your dreams you'll be able to warn him, protect him, save him."

As Ruthie's orders came from God himself, or so she said, I stopped arguing. I'd learned long ago that arguing with the boss only got you stranded on the wrong side of the Pearly Gates.

"What's the assignment?" I asked.

I could almost hear Ruthie's smile. "Ask Jimmy," she said, then she was gone.

Since the shower was on, and I still had the grit of a dozen trolls in my hair, I lost the robe I'd tossed on to answer the door and stepped beneath the water.

I could get Jimmy to tell me the assignment, fly there myself—I didn't even need a plane—leave him behind, hope he'd go home. But I wouldn't.

If I was supposed to be with him, I needed to be with him. Bad things happened when DKs ignored their seers' orders. Yes, we had free will, in theory. In practice, we did what we were told, or people died.

I shut off the water, waved my hand, and I was dry, dressed, and ready. I hadn't really *needed* a shower. I just liked them.

When I stepped out of the steamy bathroom, Jimmy's eyes widened.

"What?" I glanced at my usual outfit—tight jeans, a white, fringed, leather halter top, white cowboy hat, and boots. Not a smudge on them.

"You . . . uh . . . from Texas?" he asked.

I frowned. "I'm from Heaven."

He laughed. "I suppose you've heard that line a thousand times." At my deepening confusion, he added: "Did it hurt?"

"What?"

"When you fell from Heaven?"

"I don't like to talk about that."

His laughter died. "That was a pickup line. A bad one. As in, you're so gorgeous, you must be a fallen angel."

I sat in the chair next to the dresser. "You do know what the fallen angels are, right?"

He'd better, or we were in a lot more trouble than I'd thought.

"Grigori," he answered, then something flickered in his eyes. He moved so fast, I barely saw it. The switchblade—pure silver, I could smell it—cleared his pocket as he came off the bed, opening with a single blurring motion of his wrist when he stepped toward me.

I tossed magic dust, and this time it stopped him. Planning to slit my throat was *not* an errand of mercy.

"I'm not a Grigori," I said. "They're all in the pit. Sit." Another swish of my hand, and he sat, just catching his ass on the edge of the bed. "Tell me what you know."

"God sent angels to watch over the humans," he recited robotically, which was what I got when I used the enchanted dust. "But some of them lusted instead and were confined to the deepest, darkest level of hell."

"Tartarus," I murmured. An extremely unpleasant place. I'd been lucky.

Jimmy gave a jerky nod. "Their offspring—the Nephilim— were left behind to challenge the humans. They are what we fight."

"And the fallen angels that didn't succumb to temptation?"

"Too good to go into the pit, too tainted by earth to return home, they became fairies." Jimmy blinked, and reason returned to his eyes. "That's you?"

"Me," I agreed.

"Besides that sparkly gunk"—he waved at my hands—"what else can you do?"

"Fly without wings. Glamour."

See the future.

I left that last talent out. It always gave rise to more questions than I wanted to answer, and with Jimmy, there'd be questions I *couldn't* answer.

"If you can practice glamour, then why do you look like that?"

I tilted my head, allowed what I knew to be perfectly proportioned pink lips to curl. "You don't like how I look?"

With his olive coloring, it was hard to tell, but I was fairly certain he blushed. Which was one of the reasons I looked like this.

"You look great," he blurted. "It's just . . . well . . . You seem kind of helpless and—"

"Flighty?" He shrugged. "The more helpless I appear, the dumber I act, the harder they fall." My smile widened. "Or maybe I should say, the quicker they turn to ashes."

Understanding blossomed. "It's camouflage."

"What else is glamour but that?"

"What do you really look like?"

Something he would never, ever see.

I stood. "You can tell me where we're going and what we're killing in the car."

I headed for the door. When he didn't follow, I glanced back to find his gaze scanning the room. "You don't have a suitcase?"

I wiggled my fingers. "Everything I need is right here."

The late-March sun rose through smoky Minnesota skies, casting dim rays across the still-snow-strewn parking lot. I hoped we were headed south.

"I thought you could fly," Jimmy said.

"I can, but you can't." I cast him a quick glance. "Can you?"

Jimmy hunched his shoulders. "No."

He never had answered my first question: *What are you?* I decided to rephrase. "What can you do?"

"Enough," he said.

I wondered if he knew all he was capable of, or if he was still finding out. Some DKs were late bloomers, their special talents latent until puberty and beyond. Those were usually the most dangerous ones, too, as if all the years spent growing into a power made that power practically explode once it was ready to come through.

"You need to be more specific," I said. "I'm not going into battle with an unknown weapon."

He scowled, but he answered. "I'm faster, stronger, and damn hard to kill."

"So am I."

He looked down. "I'm a dhampir."

"Son of a vampire," I murmured. He didn't seem happy about it, but then, who would be? Vampires sucked.

Ha-ha.

"I sense them," he continued, still not looking at me. "I'm extremely good at killing them."

"Okay," I said. "So we're going after a vampire?"

His head came up. Something flickered in those incredible eyes before he glanced away again. He was hiding something, but what could it be?

"We should probably take a plane," Jimmy said, the words an obvious attempt to change the subject. I let him. I knew what I needed to know. For now.

"I don't do planes." The one time I'd tried it, the controls had whirled and whirled until a few of them exploded. I'd never get in one of those tin cans again. Instead—

I lifted my chin toward the powder blue '57 Chevy Impala. "We'll take that."

Jimmy's lips curved. "Can I drive?"

"No."

He didn't take offense. Instead, his smile deepened as he slid into the passenger seat. He ran his hand along the dash, the movement causing something to shift in my stomach as I had an image of him running that hand along me.

To stop that line of thought—remembering Jimmy's touch when he'd never touched me gave me a shimmering sense of déjà vu that caused my stomach to pitch and roll—I started the engine. The sweet rumble soothed me as little else could. I loved this car. It was the only thing I had to call my own.

After backing out, I headed for the street. "Which way?"

"South," Jimmy said.

"Hallelujah."

"And west. New Mexico."

Hadn't been there in decades. Or was it centuries? Time got funny once you lived through the first millennium—or ten.

"Where in New Mexico?"

"Navajo reservation."

"Pretty big area."

"Twenty-six thousand square miles." At least he'd done his homework. "Ruthie said we should go to the foot of Mount Taylor."

What were the odds that I'd need to head to the same place I'd headed to the last time? You'd think pretty damn slim, but when dealing with supernatural entities, the opposite was true. Certain creatures could be found in certain places, and Mount Taylor had always been special. Sacred to the Navajo, but sacred often arose out of spooky.

"You know where that is?" Jimmy asked, and I nodded. "How long will it take?"

"Do I look like I have Google Maps in my brain?"

"You look like you could have just about anything in there."

He sounded impressed, and a place right between my C-cups went all gooey and warm. No one had ever been impressed by me before.

Scared of me? Horrified by me? Pleased I'd done my job? Sure. But impressed? Nope.

I kind of liked it.

"We'll be there in twenty-three hours, give or take."

He sat back. "Quicker if you let me drive."

"Fat chance."

"You gotta sleep."

I snorted. One good thing about being a fairy—I only slept if I wanted to. Considering what I saw when I closed my eyes . . . I didn't often want to.

"What are we after at Mount Taylor?" I asked.

"Sorcerer."

I frowned. He'd graduated from vampires to sorcerers? That was kind of a big leap. This entire situation made me uneasy.

"What kind of sorcerer?"

"Does it matter?"

"The only way to kill something is to know exactly what it is that needs killing."

"Ruthie said you'd know."

"Great," I muttered. I was starting to wonder if Ruthie wanted me dead. "She said this guy—?"

I glanced at Jimmy for confirmation—technically, a woman should be called a sorceress, but it was best to be sure—and he nodded.

"This guy was a *sorcerer*." I emphasized the word. "Not a witch or a warlock, a wizard or a magician?"

"No. She said 'sorcerer.' What's the difference?"

"There are two kinds of magic. White is given; black is taken."

"Given by who? Taken from what?"

The entrance ramp for I-35 loomed ahead, and I waited to answer him until I'd merged into traffic. It was early yet; the road sparkled with the remains of the salt used to prevent vehicles from winding up in a ditch during every snowstorm.

"White magic is learned," I began. "Given by another devotee. Sometimes inherited through families. In theory, a human can practice white magic. In practice, for magic to be powerful enough to be of any use, it can't be contained by them for very long. They burn out."

And wind up gibbering in the corner of their nice, cozy asylum.

"You're saying anyone practicing magic is a Nephilim?"

"Or the offspring of a Nephilim and a human." Evil spirits liked to propagate all over the place. It was kind of their thing.

"A breed," Jimmy spat.

I lifted a brow. Considering he was one, that was an interesting reaction.

"Also fairies," I pointed out. "I use white magic."

"So the white and the black have nothing to do with the good or the evil of the magic itself but with the way the magic was received?"

"Anything good can become evil if it's used in an evil manner."

"By an evil being."

"Right. And evil can be used for good."

"No way."

I thought of my dreams, the whispers, a promise.

"You'd be surprised." Before he could question me further, I continued. "A sorcerer, by definition, takes his magic."

"How do you take magic?"

"By killing someone you love."

Jimmy flinched. "No one who's human would do that."

I wasn't so sure. I'd met some humans who rivaled the

Nephilim for evil. We weren't supposed to kill them, but . . . accidents happened.

"Which is why we need to know what kind of sorcerer we're dealing with so we know how to kill him. Some are part shifter, part vampire—Well, basically anything that creeps can take some magic and become a being that's even harder to kill."

Now that I thought about it, Ruthie's sending Jimmy after a sorcerer alone would have been a very bad idea. As it was . . . not knowing what kind of murdering magician we were dealing with was a very bad idea. Once again, I got that prickle at the back of my neck.

"Tell me exactly what Ruthie said."

"She sent me to get you."

I glanced sideways. "Why me?"

He stared out the front window as if the never-ending highway that disappeared into the flat, soon-to-be Iowa plane was beyond fascinating. "I didn't ask."

"No?" That smelled like a lie, but I couldn't see why he'd bother.

"Ruthie says 'jump,' I say 'how high?' Don't you?"

Not in exactly those words, but yeah, pretty much.

"What else?"

"That we should go to the foot of Mount Taylor, where we'd find a sorcerer, and you'd know what to do."

I'd had better instructions. Then again, I'd had worse. And if Ruthie'd said I'd know what to do, I had to believe I would. No doubt whatever sorcerer we'd find there would be a type I'd found, and eliminated, before.

I began to tick them off in my mind. The Nagual, a Mayan Jaguar shaman, he'd died by silver dipped in blood.

The Aghori, a Hindu cannibal that ate magicians in order to ingest their magic. I'd used hemlock on him.

While I doubted we'd find a Hindu sorcerer in New Mexico—I'd found stranger things in stranger places—I *did* carry hemlock in the trunk.

I also carried knives made of every metal known to man, bullets in the same colors, crossbows, arrows, assorted poisons in solid and liquid form, animal and human blood, as well as ropes, chains, and whips. It paid—usually in lives—to be prepared.

"Killing what they started out as won't kill them?" Jimmy asked.

"Once they're a sorcerer, you've gotta kill that, too."

"How?"

"You know why they burned witches?"

Jimmy shrugged. "Why?"

I tightened my fingers on the steering wheel, then focused on the distant horizon.

"Because it worked."

Mount Taylor loomed large from the flat, arid land like a pyramid in the midst of Egypt. As we rolled closer, the ponderosa pines that dotted the foothills turned what had appeared from a distance to be a gigantic blueberry snow cone into Tso dzilh, the sacred mountain of the south.

Mount Taylor was one of four mountains that marked the boundaries of Navajo land, known as the Dinetah, or the Glittering World. Strange things happened there—always had, always would.

Jimmy stirred. He'd been sleeping since we hit the New Mexico border. You'd think his being unconscious would have made the trip easier. Unfortunately, it only meant my gaze kept flicking to him, cataloging memories I'd retained from my dreams.

Like the way his lashes lay on his cheeks, thick and dark, reminding me of how they fluttered against my belly in the wake of his lips.

Or the supple length of his fingers, which could leave me gasping, straining, begging with just one stroke.

When the wind whistled through the tiny crack he'd cranked in the passenger window, ruffling across his skin, stirring his hair then flicking the scent of cinnamon and soap into my face, my whole body tingled with the memory of things that hadn't even happened.

Jimmy sat up, staring at the huge blob of land that filled the windshield. "Needle? Haystack? Hell," he muttered.

"I know where to go."

He cast me a quick glance. "You *are* good at this."

"I am," I agreed, though again, his praise warmed me. "But you see that?" I pointed to the billowing cloud of smoke that trailed toward the excruciatingly blue sky. "We should probably check it out."

"Where there's smoke, there's fire?"

"Where there's destruction, there's usually a Nephilim. That looks like more than a campfire." It looked like half a town was burning. "If that isn't the work of our sorcerer, it's probably the work of something else we need to kill."

Jimmy's hand went to his pocket, where he traced the outline of his switchblade. "Fine by me."

When we reached the blaze, we discovered enough pickup trucks and old, dusty cars to fill a honky-tonk parking lot and a pyre surrounded by at least a hundred people, who stared at the leaping, dancing flames as if mesmerized.

"Zombies," Jimmy whispered.

In our world, they might be.

I got out of the car, opened the trunk, grabbed a few machetes, and tossed one to Jimmy. He lifted his brows, and I shrugged. "If parts of them start falling off and they try to bite you?" I made a chopping motion. "Off with their heads."

I didn't think they were zombies—I doubted the walking dead would be hanging around so close to a fire since it was one of the few things, along with decapitation, that killed them—but I wasn't going to bet Jimmy's life on it.

As we approached, a few of the observers turned. They were all Navajo, and quite obviously alive—no decaying eyes, moldering arms, putrefying thighs, or gangrenous tongues. Lucky us.

Hell, lucky them.

I paused and laid a hand on Jimmy's arm. The ripple of awareness when my palm touched his skin made me shiver despite the steady beat of the sun on the crown of my hat.

He cast me a curious glance, and I lowered my voice to a range that no human could hear. "The Navajo still believe in monsters. We haven't had to dust anything out this way in ages. They do it for us."

"You mean . . . ?" Jimmy let his gaze trail back to the massive, billowing bonfire. "We should just walk away?"

"Well . . ." I hesitated. "Why don't we make sure it works, then walk away?"

The Navajo whispered among themselves.

He walks in darkness.

He is the night.

Born of smoke.

Death.

Beasts.

Magic.

I think we'd found our man.

We stood there for hours, waiting for the fire to die. We couldn't see anything through the thick, choking smoke. We also didn't hear anything but the crackle of the flames, and we didn't smell anything but burning wood and acrid fumes.

That should have tipped me off right away. Nothing burns without screaming. Nothing dies without moving. Nothing turns to ashes without one hell of an unpleasant smell.

Eventually, the Navajo climbed into their vehicles and drove away. They didn't seem concerned about us. Considering the lack of evidence left behind, they didn't need to be.

When the last dusty pickup disappeared into the sun that hovered just above the western horizon, Jimmy spoke. "Now what?"

"Now we douse that fire, then bury whatever's left in at least four different places."

Jimmy's shoulders slumped on a sigh. "Okay."

"Disappointed?"

"I wanted to kick some ass."

Behind him, the ashes rippled. The red embers glowed brighter and brighter, then gave a subtle *whoosh*.

"We might have to," I murmured.

Jimmy spun as the pyre reignited, shooting as high as some of the oldest trees. The flames themselves became a man, then the man became a wolf, a mountain lion, a writhing snake. Every time I blinked, the image re-formed—now a hawk, next a tarantula, and, once again, a man.

"Shape-shifter." Jimmy's silver blade sliced the heated air.

"Worse," I said, as the blazing man walked out of the inferno completely unharmed. "He's a skinwalker. That fire only pissed him off."

As he stalked toward us, his long, dark hair streamed back, the coming night air causing the flames that still licked at the ends to extinguish with an audible *poof*. He glistened in the dying sun, the tattoos that graced nearly every inch of his body seeming to dance as muscles rippled beneath his skin.

He wasn't tall; he didn't need to be. The power, or maybe it was the fury, cascaded off him with such force the grass beneath his feet curdled and died.

"Should we run?" Jimmy asked.

The man approaching us smiled. The expression frightened me. But Sawyer always had.

I stepped in front of Jimmy, my arm lifting to make use

of my magic. Sawyer flicked his hand. He was still five feet away; he never touched me, yet I flew off my feet and landed fifty yards south. If I'd been human, the force of the fall would have fricasseed my brains. Instead, I was up and running almost instantly.

I was too late. I'd known even while I was still airborne that I would be.

Jimmy plunged the silver switchblade into Sawyer's chest. When Sawyer didn't burst into ashes, Jimmy took a step back, but he didn't run. Maybe he should have.

Except Sawyer could shift in an instant; he could move faster than the eye could track. There was no point in running. Jimmy's fate had been sealed long before now.

Sawyer lowered his head to look at the knife. He seemed calm enough, but the pyre behind him suddenly ignited all the way to the sky. Then, as quick as the lightning he commanded, Sawyer yanked the knife from his own chest and plunged it into Jimmy's.

Even as I shouted, "No!" I was wondering—

Of all the times I'd seen Jimmy die, why hadn't I ever seen this?

Jimmy collapsed to his knees, then tumbled onto his side. Sawyer tilted his head like the hawk tattooed at the base of his spine, staring at the dying man before him. Blood trickled down his bare chest, glistening in the glow of the dancing flames. But there was less blood than there should have been. His wound had already begun to heal.

I fell to the ground, tugging Jimmy onto his back. Someone was chanting, "No, no, no." I think it was me.

His eyes were closed, his face more gray than pale, his lips white. All the blood in the world seemed to be darkening his once mint green shirt.

The panic in my head, the utter devastation in my heart was

the same panic and devastation that had swamped me upon awakening from every dream where Jimmy had died.

Sawyer's hand appeared, reaching for the knife, and I sprayed glitter dust without thought, coating him from knuckle to neck.

"Don't touch him," I said, and beneath my usual voice, rumbled a beast of my own. I was going to kill him. As soon as I figured out how. "Never touch him again."

Sawyer squatted on the other side of Jimmy's body. "If you want him to heal," he said in a voice that was so deep it rumbled the mountain, "you need to take out the knife."

I lifted my gaze. My magic still clung to his skin, but it did nothing to stop him from snatching the blade and yanking it out. He stuck his fingers into the hole the knife had left in the shirt and yanked, exposing Jimmy's chest, slick with blood, and the two-inch slice in his skin, which had just begun to close. Not as fast as Sawyer's—his was nearly gone—but fast enough.

"Who is he?" Sawyer asked. "From the way you were keening, I'd guess him to be your long-lost love."

I kept my gaze on Jimmy's face, but I felt my own burn. "I just met him yesterday."

"Sure you did."

"Ruthie sent him." I frowned. "To kill you."

"I doubt that."

"You don't think Ruthie would kill you?"

Sawyer laughed, and the sound seemed to flow from those mountains and not his mouth. "If only she knew how. If only anyone did."

"But he—" I began.

"He's a dhampir," Sawyer interrupted. "And a vampire I am not."

"I know what he is."

Jimmy's face was less gray but still pale. The knife wound continued to knit together slower than I'd like. Of course, I'd like never to have been there in the first place, but I'd learned, way back at the Fall, that what I liked meant nothing at all.

"If that were the case, you would have known better than to think a simple knife to the chest would end him."

I blinked. He was right. But I'd seen Jimmy die so many times in so many ways, I'd panicked.

"I still don't understand why Ruthie would send him to kill you."

"She didn't," Sawyer said slowly, as if I'd hit my head when he'd tossed me. Maybe I had. Because none of this was making any more sense now than it had before. Unless—

I tilted my head, eyes narrowing. "This was a test?"

Sawyer lifted his bare shoulder—the one where a black wolf howled.

Seemed like a fairly easy test to me. Although Ruthie probably hadn't expected Sawyer to be on fire when we arrived.

Jimmy's eyes fluttered, then opened. I smiled. "Hey," I began.

A spark of red flared at their center, and he reached out quick as any beast, grabbing Sawyer's ankle and yanking him to the ground. An instant later, he landed on Sawyer's chest, wrapped both hands around his throat, and began to squeeze.

Sawyer just looked bored.

"Jimmy." I pulled on his hands. I was strong; he was stronger. So I hit him with a faceful of fairy dust, and whispered, "Stop."

He did.

Sawyer shoved him off and stood.

"What'd you do that for?" Jimmy wiped the sticky sparkles from his eyes. "And why'd it work?"

"He's—" I paused. What Sawyer was had always been a mystery.

"I'm one of you," Sawyer finished.

"No way in hell," Jimmy returned as he climbed to his feet.

"Her magic made you stop. Would it have if I were evil? If

you were actually supposed to kill me? Not that you could, but if I have to keep flicking you off, I might hurt you."

"Nothing can hurt me."

"Wanna bet?"

"Let's see what you got."

"No." I stepped between them again, setting one hand on Jimmy's chest, ignoring the dual sensations of "ick" from all the blood and "yum" from all the muscles. "He's dangerous.

Jimmy lifted his chin. "So am I."

"Not like him."

Jimmy stared Sawyer up and down—which was pretty easy considering he still wore nothing but tattoos—sneering a bit at the snake inked on his penis. "Is that a joke?" he asked.

Sawyer smirked.

"He's a skinwalker," I repeated.

"A shifter. So what?"

"If he was just a shifter, he'd be ashes. He can change into anything with the use of his robe."

"Robe?" Jimmy gave Sawyer another scornful once over. "Did it burn off?"

"My skin is my robe," Sawyer murmured. And he could become any of the beasts that he wore there.

"He was created in fire, birthed of smoke," I continued. "He controls the lightning. He can bring the storm."

"How do we kill him?" Jimmy asked.

"He's one of the most powerful sorcerers ever known. There is no killing him."

Jimmy's eyes widened. "Everything that breathes can die."

"Everything but him."

"Why would Ruthie—" he began.

"She didn't," Sawyer interrupted. "This was your test, boy. You failed."

"Failed?" Jimmy waved at Sawyer's still-bloody chest. "I got you."

"Not as good as I got you."

Honestly. I gave a mental eye roll. Men. Boys. Ancient supernatural creatures. The only difference was the size of their—

Jimmy's switchblade suddenly appeared once more in his hand. He must have palmed it while still on the ground. I was impressed. Annoyed as hell. But also impressed.

He flicked his wrist, and the dying sun sparked off the edge as it opened. "Let's go again."

"No," I said, and when Jimmy moved, I growled, the sound surprising him enough to make him pause. "Do *not* make me spray you."

"You're taking his side?"

"We're on the *same* side."

"If that's true, then why were all those people . . ." Jimmy curled his lip, "*his* people, roasting him? He must have done something to set them off."

"It makes them feel better to burn me every generation or so." Sawyer shrugged. "I let them."

"You *let* them?" Jimmy snorted. "Sure you did."

"You think mere humans could capture me?" Sawyer gave a delicate snort of his own. "They've seen me become my animals, watched me turn humans to ashes—"

"Why did they see you?"

Sawyer spread his hands. "Why not?"

"It adds to his legend," I said. "Makes people fear him. Probably *keeps* them from burning him more than once a generation."

"When they watch me *die,* then they see me a day, a week, a month later unharmed . . ." Sawyer didn't exactly grin—I doubt he could—but his oddly light gray eyes sparkled. "It's one of the few things that amuses me after all these years."

"How many years?" Jimmy asked suspiciously.

"Sawyer's as old as I am," I said. "Maybe older."

"This is *Sawyer*?"

Something in Jimmy's voice made me turn, but he was already past me. I should have taken away that damn knife when I had the chance.

The blade descended, headed straight for Sawyer's eye, but while Jimmy was fast, Sawyer was faster, and he snatched Jimmy's wrist, giving it a quick, vicious twist. The sound of the bone snapping warred with the thud of the knife against the ground and my own startled gasp.

Jimmy let his injured hand flop at his side as he stepped in close. "She sobs your name in her sleep, you son of a bitch. What did you do to her?"

"What didn't I?" Sawyer whispered, then flicked one hand through the air as if batting a fly.

By the time Jimmy landed, and I'd run to him, Sawyer was gone. I don't know if he shape-shifted, or ran off on his own bare feet. Maybe he just went *poof*—with him, anything was possible. In truth, I didn't care how he'd gone, I was just glad *that* he'd gone.

"You okay?" I asked, but Jimmy was already getting up.

He stared at the place Sawyer had recently stood; the only indication that the man had been real and not a mirage was the imprints of his toes in the dust.

"I don't care what he is." Jimmy retrieved his knife. The wrist Sawyer had broken still hung limply at his side, but the fingers had begun to move, curling into a fist I wasn't even sure he knew he'd made. "I'm gonna kill him someday."

Only one thing could make men—even those who weren't completely men—behave like this.

"Who is she?" I asked, proud when my voice didn't break even though my heart was.

Stupid to feel betrayed. I might have known Jimmy Sanducci intimately for eons, but he'd only met me yesterday.

And, from the way he'd said *she,* another had already captured his heart.

"No one," he murmured in a voice that clearly said *the* one.

He walked to the car and got in without glancing my way at all.

I pulled into the first motel I saw, a small, single-wing, once-white place with a neon sign that announced SLEEP EAP. It wasn't until I parked beneath it that I saw that the C and the H had burned out.

"Why are we stopping?"

Those were the first words Jimmy had said in the hour we'd been on the road.

"I'm tired."

"I'll drive."

"If a cop sees you behind the wheel like that . . ." I waved at his torn and bloody shirt, his even bloodier chest.

"You'll magic them, and we'll keep right on going."

"It's easier to stop here, take a shower and a nap, start fresh in the morning." Besides, I'd magicked so many people today, my hands hurt.

I figured he'd argue, so when he laid his head against the seat and closed his eyes, I palmed the keys and got us a room. There was no way I was letting Jimmy out of my sight until he was back under Ruthie's thumb. I wouldn't put it past him to sneak away in the middle of the night and try to kill Sawyer again.

Unfortunately, Jimmy didn't wait for the middle of the night. By the time I got back to the car, he was gone.

"Fuck!" I kicked the tire. I should have put a leash on him.

I looked up and down the road, but in the middle of nowhere, even with fairy eyesight, the highway disappeared into a black maw of nothing after a few hundred feet.

I honestly had no idea which way to go, or even if I *should* go. Jimmy was a big boy. He wasn't my responsibility.

No matter how much I might want him to be.

I turned toward the motel and got a shimmy of déjà vu so hard I staggered. I'd dreamed this.

The Impala right there, the hotel in front of me. Jimmy was gone. I was worried. Everything was the same, right down to the ache in my fingers, except . . .

The sign had been off—black and still—not flickering like it was now.

In the next instant, the neon died with a sizzling *phzaat*. Darkness settled over me like a cool spring mist. I held my breath and waited for reality to catch up with the dream.

The animal-like shriek rent the night, and I lifted into the air without benefit of wings.

I flew toward the scream, already knowing what I would find.

A cottage miles away from the nearest neighbor, at the end of what would have passed for a decent road in the year 2, the night so dark the figures that surrounded it were mere wisps darting in and out of the light that shone from the windows.

One man battled a multitude of hunched and decrepit crone-things, with tails like dinosaurs and bony, bald heads. Despite their ancient appearance, they moved fast, and they had very sharp teeth. It wasn't until one of them bleated like a goat that I remembered what they were.

Chupacabras.

Mexican vampires. The stench of rancid garlic was so strong, my eyes watered. Jimmy had probably smelled them from the car.

He seemed to be doing just fine on his own. Ashes flitted through the dim light. He whirled and jabbed, plunging a wooden stake into chest after naked, scaly chest.

However, I'd been here before, and I knew what happened. The king chupacabra—a much bigger, badder vampire, with spikes down his spine and gigantic bat wings—would swoop from the sky and drive first his right talon, then his left, through Jimmy's throat.

I snatched up a likely sliver of wood from the pile next to the cottage and began to watch the sky.

Something bleated, and I lashed out, my stake sinking into the chest of the creature that had rushed me. Instead of bursting into ashes, the thing bleated again, a long, hiccoughing expulsion that sounded like laughter, then sank its fangs into my wrist.

I cursed and cuffed the chupacabra upside its bony, bald head. Instead of releasing me, it began to suck.

And from the east, the slow *thunk* of wings.

Panic threatened. How would I kill the beast coming for Jimmy if I couldn't even end one of its minions?

Think, Summer! What kills a goatsucker?

If Ruthie had sent me here, she'd have given me more info, or I'd have found some on the way. But Ruthie hadn't sent me. My dream had.

So I tried to bring that dream to mind, but all I could see when I closed my eyes were the talons going through Jimmy's throat.

"Cross!" Jimmy shouted.

I opened my eyes, just as the clouds parted enough to reveal a thin sickle of a moon, the light fluttering off and on as the wings of something large and deadly hovered.

Using my free hand, I yanked the stake from the chupacabra and plunged it across to the other side of his chest.

Nothing happened, except that he laughed again, this time the sound not much more than a gargle of my blood in his throat. I threw some dust in his face, and said, "Release me."

When he did, I retrieved my stake and flew. I'd throw myself in front of Jimmy. Maybe during the time the king goatsucker was trying to kill me, Jimmy could kill him.

But as I flew, another idea of what *cross* might mean occurred to me. I used my thumbnail to carve one into the wood.

I reached Jimmy as the gargantuan chupacabra materialized from the night. His talons went through my chest as my stake went into his.

He burst into ashes.

I passed out.

I came to inside the cottage. I lay in a bed; a fire blazed in the fireplace. I could still smell the distant aroma of garlic. All I wore were bandages at the wrist and chest.

Somewhere, a shower ran. Even as I turned my head, the water went off, a curtain rattled. Steam and a sliver of light slithered through a crack in the door. A shadow moved beyond the light, beyond the door, then the door opened.

Naked to the waist, his hair slick and shiny, Jimmy wore only a towel that threatened to drop from his hips with every step. His eyes went to the bed, and when he saw I was awake, they widened.

"You okay?" He crossed the room and sat at my side. Reaching out, he brushed back my hair. The warmth of his fingers against my chilled skin made me want to curl into him like a cat.

I opened my mouth, but all I could do was nod and stare at the single drop of water sliding down his smooth, olive chest, glistening like oil. I wanted to touch it. I wanted to taste it. Now.

I squeezed my eyes shut.

"Summer?" His hand cupped my face; his thumb traced my cheek. "What can I do? How can I help?"

He shifted, and his thigh bumped my breasts. I moaned.

"Sorry." He fell to his knees next to the bed. "Does it hurt?"

I gazed into his eyes and thought: *It's never going to stop hurting. I'm going to love you forever, and you'll never be able to love me back.*

Because of her.

I didn't know who she was, but already I hated her.

"I'm okay," I said.

"You saved my life."

"Right place, right time."

He tilted his head and his hair, nearly dry already from the heat of the fire, tumbled across his brow. "You knew that thing was coming, didn't you?"

No point in lying.

"Sometimes I do." I shrugged, then winced when my still-healing chest protested.

He reached for the coverlet. "Let me see."

The flames flickered in his eyes as he slowly drew the blanket away. A white rectangle covered a four-inch square above my left breast. He reached out, but instead of touching the bandage, he touched me.

Was it an accident? At the time, I thought so. The way he snatched his hand back, though not too far, and caught his breath, the way his startled, almost mortified gaze flicked to mine.

Later, of course, I knew better, but then, everything seemed so innocent, a product of the moment, of us. We'd almost died. It made perfect sense we should desperately want to prove that we lived.

The loss of his touch was more painful than a talon through the heart, and without thought, I arched, the movement causing hand and breast to collide again. Of its own accord, his wrist—now healed—turned, and my full weight glided into his palm. The next instant he was kissing me, or maybe I was kissing him.

He tasted like the night, cool and dark, even as his skin beneath my fingers seemed to burn. I'd touched him in my dreams a hundred—no, a thousand—times. Yet every stroke was a revelation. As if I were coming home to a house that still smelled new.

I tugged on his shoulders, and he dropped the towel, then slid onto the bed without ever lifting his lips from mine. His hands explored, learning the curves at my breast, hip, and thigh.

"Soft," he murmured, then moved his mouth across my jaw to my neck, where he worried a fold of skin between his teeth. "Sweet."

I laughed, and the sound was low, throaty, sexy, not at all like me. Then again, I practiced glamour. *Me* could be anything at all. Since Jimmy seemed to like this version, I let her stay.

He nuzzled my breasts, laved a nipple, and I caught my breath as the sensation shot through me. He lifted his head; his eyes glittered auburn in the firelight. "You like that?"

"Mmm," I agreed, and he lowered his head to give me more.

"I've been wanting to do this since you opened the door in that robe."

He drew me into his mouth, suckling hard, and I curled my fingers into his hair. He teased me with his teeth, then blew on the moist, taut peak.

"Did you know I could see the outline of these?" He lifted my breasts to his mouth, tonguing first one then the other. "They were so beautiful, I couldn't think of anything but you all the way to Mount Taylor."

"Good at hiding it," I managed.

He rolled on top of me, pressing his erection right where I needed it the most. "Not anymore."

I licked the trail of that droplet of water, across his chest to his nipple. Before I could close my lips around it, he plunged.

He was young—who wasn't compared to me?—but he also

wasn't completely human. He lasted longer than I thought he would.

I set my hands on his hips, gave him the rhythm, lowered my palms a few inches, and showed him the depth. His tongue echoed our movements. My breasts skimmed his chest with each thrust. He stilled, shifted, and did something amazing that made lights go off in the sky, on the ceiling, all around, or maybe just in my head. By the time I remembered my name, he was raining kisses across my damp cheeks and moving within me once more.

He was so beautiful, he made me ache. I couldn't help but reach up and touch him. When I did, he lowered his gaze, and what I saw there made my stomach jitter and dip. Was that expression merely a reflection? How could he love me so soon? Then again, I'd loved him before he'd even been born.

"Jimmy," I began.

"Shh," he murmured, and kissed me, making me forget whatever I'd been about to say. Right now, all that mattered was this. The two of us all tangled up in each other, warm and safe for the moment, a memory I already had come to life.

His movements became faster, harder, I didn't mind. He couldn't hurt me.

Or so I thought.

When he pulsed to the beat of my heart, the tandem of that pulse made another start in me. I caught my breath in shock and wonder, crying out as the world again fell away.

I clung. I couldn't help it. We couldn't be together every minute. I couldn't be in the right place at the right time *every* time. Sure, I'd made a deal, but the one I'd made it with lived on lies and had reneged on bigger deals with better angels than I.

Jimmy lowered his forehead to mine, his hair brushed my cheek an instant before his lips touched my nose, then he rolled to the side, taking me with him, folding me into his arms and flicking the blanket over us both.

His breathing evened out; I thought he was asleep when I whispered, "I dreamed of you."

As consciousness fell away I could have sworn he whispered, too.

I know.

I awoke alone, which at first didn't bother me. I couldn't remember the last time I hadn't. But I stretched, and the bed was warm everywhere, as if someone other than I had warmed it.

Then I remembered. Jimmy. Me. Us.

I hugged myself and went over every minute we'd shared, beginning with the expression in his eyes that had looked like love.

Then I heard his voice, and I leaped from the cocoon we'd made. When you lived a life like ours, a conversation in the middle of the night was rarely a good thing.

I paused, listening. He wasn't in the cottage, so I glanced out the window. Jimmy stood beneath the stars, having a talk with his cell phone.

"Mission accomplished," he said.

It wasn't until I heard Ruthie's answer—through the glass, across the distance, on a phone that wasn't anywhere near my ear—sure I was a fairy, but even I had limits—that I realized I was dreaming.

"Any problems?"

"What problem would there be? You've seen her."

Seen who? What problem?

"Did she suspect?"

"That this was a setup?" Jimmy blew a derisive breath through his lips. "I know what I'm doing, Ruthie. It would have been nice if you'd mentioned that the sorcerer was one of ours."

"Telling you would have defeated the purpose of the test."

"That was a test?" Jimmy asked. "And here I thought it was just one giant clusterfuck."

"Watch your mouth, boy."

"I could have died."

"Summer wouldn't let you. Why you think I made you take her along?"

"I know exactly why you made me take her along."

Silence reigned for a few seconds before Ruthie murmured, "It had to be done."

"That doesn't mean I have to like it."

"Considering what I usually send you out to do, I wouldn't think seducing a pretty woman would be such a hardship."

Suddenly the warmth of the room wasn't quite warm enough.

"She isn't a woman." I stopped breathing even before he continued. "She's a damn fairy."

"Not damned," Ruthie murmured. "Not yet. Besides, she could have been Satan's little sister, and the mission would have been the same. Count your blessings."

"This wasn't a blessing, it was a—" He turned, and saw me standing in the window. "Nightmare," he finished.

I woke up with a gasp, arms flailing, tangling in the covers as I tried to breathe but was unable to through the pain in my chest. I felt like I was dying even though I was well aware that I wouldn't.

I was at the cottage, alone in the bed, in the room. Outside, the low murmur of Jimmy's voice.

"Mission accomplished."

Ignoring the shimmy of déjà vu, I dressed, taking clothes from the owner's closet. Considering she was no longer here, and neither was whoever belonged to the man's clothes in a second closet, I figured the chupacabras had eaten them.

The missing woman was bigger than I but nearly everyone was. I glamoured everything until it was exactly the same thing

I'd worn before—fringe, boots, hat, and all. I didn't bother to cross the room and listen to Jimmy's conversation. Once had been enough.

For several lifetimes.

I thought back on all the occasions I'd thought he was hiding something, those prickles of unease with Jimmy, Ruthie, the entire situation. But instead of pushing for an answer, I'd been dazzled by him. How could I not be? I'd been waiting for Jimmy Sanducci for centuries.

The door opened. Jimmy saw me sitting on the edge of the bed and smiled. He almost looked as if he meant it.

"You're good," I said.

His smile faltered. "Thank you?"

"I actually believed you cared."

Confusion flickered across his face, then he glanced through the open door, at the window, and again at me. "You heard?"

I shrugged. I had, just not the way he thought.

"Let me explain—"

"I'm sure Ruthie had her reasons." She always did. "Although I'd think the Leader of the Light would be above pimping for the greater good."

"It's a long story. I—"

I zapped him with fairy dust, and he stopped talking. I guess what he'd been about to tell me wasn't merciful. More about making *him* feel better than making me not want to dive into a fresh patch of rowan or stab myself in the throat with the nearest cold, sharp steel.

Had Ruthie wanted us to bond? Had she needed me to protect him? She could have just asked. There was something more to this, but right now, I didn't want to know.

"Listen," Jimmy said, and that he *could* speak meant I should. "Bad things are coming. We're going to have to do whatever it takes to win the coming war."

The hair on my arms lifted. "Armageddon?"

"It's almost here."

I closed my eyes. The last war. The only one that mattered.

Who would win? Our Book said one thing. Theirs said another.

The universe craved balance. God versus Satan. Angels versus devils. Good versus evil. Us versus them.

I'd seen so many things in my sleep. I opened my eyes and stared into Jimmy's all-too-familiar face. I'd seen him die. But I'd also seen him live.

Because of me.

I loved him. Did it matter if he loved me back? Perhaps my love wasn't real, just a fantasy manufactured by our side so that I would protect him. But it felt real, and it wasn't something I was going to be able to magic away. I'd tried.

I'd promised everything I had, everything I was, to keep him safe. And looking at him now, even knowing what I did, I knew I'd promise the same damn thing again tomorrow.

We needed him. Without Jimmy Sanducci, the side of good, of light and right would not survive. I wasn't certain of much, but I was certain of that. I had to be.

"There will be demons," Jimmy said. "Scores of them. And the only thing that can stop them is us." He held out his hand. "You with me?"

Since being with him was all I'd ever wanted, I took that hand, and I kept my promise. It wasn't easy.

But, then, deals with the devil never are.

★ ★ ★

Author's Bio:
Lori Handeland is a two-time Romance Writers' of America RITA Award winner and the *New York Times* bestselling author of the paranormal romance series, The Nightcreature Novels, as well as the urban fantasy series,

The Phoenix Chronicles. Lori lives in Wisconsin with a husband, two sons, and a yellow Lab named Elwood.

"There Will Be Demons" takes place in the world of The Phoenix Chronicles. For more adventures with the same characters, as well as many others, start with Book #1, *Any Given Doomsday*.

For more information on Lori or her books, please go to: **www.lorihandeland.com.**

CHERRY KISSES

by ERICA HAYES

The blond vampire lounging against the mirrors had been ogling me for the past five minutes, the way a shark cruises for tasty meat. Designer jeans, diamond ear studs, dark eyes sunken with hunger. A perfect mark.

I tossed him a flirty smile, twisting a purple-dyed curl around my finger. Dark music throbbed in my blood, the raw metal of guitars and drums. Around me, dancers writhed, a snake pit of slick rainbow limbs, glowing fairy wings, the scarlet flash of vampire eyes. The sultry air coated my skin, dusted with fairy wing-glitter and thick with the scents of sweat and sex. Unseelie Court at midnight, the hottest, coolest, most dangerous nightclub in town.

Glamours clashed and sparked, electric, the glass-spun veil of magic that hid the supernatural from ordinary human eyes. I fingered the woven-wire pendant around my neck. It was warm to the touch, spells pulsing. Thanks to my pendant, I could see through glamour, and unlike most of the club's clientele, my vampboy admirer was just what he appeared—hungry, horny, and impatient.

I touched up my cherry-cola lipstick and stalked over, sparkling a little spell-sweet seduction into my scent.

I'm not a bloodwhore, understand. If I had a card, it'd say *Lena Falco, troublemaker for hire, caster of petty hexes and spells, no job too crappy.* But I'd just spent my last twenty on a couple of stiff drinks—so sue me, I'd had a shitty day—and I had rent and protection to pay. When business is slow, you gotta broaden your skill set. The bloodsucking mobsters who run this town aren't known for their patience. And neither am I.

I tossed my hair over my shoulder, letting it shimmer under glitter-smoked lights, and my mark's gaze drilled me crimson every step of the way. Handsome brute, too, blond curls and dark lashes, muscles shining in sweat under his frayed shirt.

Good for me. Bad for him. A less confident guy will assume I'm conning him and ask how much, but the hot ones think it's perfectly reasonable when a violet-haired vixen in a shiny blue corset and black-leather hot pants makes a pass.

This guy? Mr. Tall-blond-and-screw-me-now? Easy mark.

I stopped a foot away, cocking my hip to show off my fishnet-clad legs. The mirrors reflected us both, vamp and human—I know, boring but true—and I made sure I gave him my sultriest smile. "Looking for something tasty?"

"Found it." The vamp grinned, fangs glinting. His cheeks glowed with feverthirst. When vampires don't feed, the virus slowly eats into their brains, and they get manic and greedy. This guy looked like he'd abstained a few days past his manners' expiry date.

"Then come get it." I traced a finger along his sweat-slick collarbone, and he wrapped my hair around his fist and pulled me in tight. His lips burned my throat, eager fangs already stinging hot. His heartbeat echoed in my blood. He pressed his tongue over my vein, making a soft spot to bite. *Eww. This so better be worth it.*

I laughed and twisted back. "Easy, big guy. Aren't you gonna kiss me first?"

He didn't need to be asked twice. His lips scorched mine, hot and hungry, the salty tequila taste of his tongue a bright shock. Hard body pressed into mine, hands and lips and swollen heat, fangs grazing my lip bloody. He was eager, this one.

Pity it'd do him no good.

I kissed him harder, full contact. His eyelids fluttered closed, and with a soft sigh, he went limp. All of him, I mean.

I eased the drowsy vamp down onto the couch. His sweaty hair smeared the mirrors, and his breath came fast and shallow.

I wiped my mouth and reapplied my lipstick. Cherry-cola, sweet, and sparkling with soporific spelljuice. I made it myself, from a vial of stolen fairy breath. Unless you were immune—like I'd made sure I was—one kiss would send you straight to la-la land.

Dirty trick? Yeah. But I don't have much of my own mojo, see. My hex pendant is great, but it mostly just wards off curses. To cast spells properly takes time and study, and remember what I said about patience? Technically, I'm not a witch, not yet. But I've still got a few tricks up my corset, and I don't mean my double-D cups.

Swiftly, I slipped the rings from his fingers, the flashy watch from his wrist, and the fat diamond studs (definitely not Swarovski, folks) from his ears. Cash in his pocket, too, a thick wad of crisp plastic notes. Thanks very much, fangboy. Glad to be of service.

Around me, the dance raved on, oblivious. He wasn't any-one important, not a high-up gang minion or a demon's thrall, and in a nightclub teeming with ravenous creatures of all colors and tastes, no one cared too much about this one.

Harsh? Well, that's the world we live in. At Unseelie Court, everyone is fair game. And he'd wake in a few minutes, groggy and horny and none the wiser.

I stuffed the loot down between my breasts. I had a fence in North Melbourne, a potbellied green spriggan with toilet-brush hair and sewer breath. He had wandering hands—I'm not averse to a bit of hot fae action, don't get me wrong, but claws and bad teeth just aren't my thing—but he generally gave me a good price. This little lot would keep the mobsters off my throat, at least for a while. Then, I guess, I'd be back in the game.

Beside me, on the dirty velvet couch, a drooling waterfae girl blinked at me sleepily, moisture dripping from luminous green wings. Sparkle dusted her nose, that wild fairy hallucinogen that monopolized the recreational drug market these days. She wiped it off and licked her knuckles, her watery eyes swirling. "You got any peanuts?"

Fairies were crazy, mostly, and some would screw you over in a heartbeat for giggles, but I judged this one pretty harmless. "Sorry, sweetie. Ask at the bar."

"Only pretzels. No peanuts. Peanuts smell better."

"Ain't life a bitch."

She wiped long-clawed hands on her dress, leaving a wet stain. "I like your shorts."

"Yeah?" Briefly, I considered trading with her. I can always use more fairy spells. And there were plenty more hot pants where these came from, which was generally the SHOPLIFT HERE! section of the local discount store.

Just as I was about to make a bargain, my message tone chimed. I dug out my phone. *Turn around.*

My skin prickled. Mysterious. No name, no number.

Another chime, and more words flashed up. *I have a job for you, Lena Falco. Turn around.*

Mysterious, nameless dude who knows my name. For all I knew, he was standing right behind me.

And here's where I had a choice.

Switch off, make my bargain with the fairy girl, and go home, with her dress on and a new spell in my pocket, all set for another petty score tomorrow night.

On the other hand, mystery means danger. Big danger means big payoff, and there's always the chance it'll be The Job. The big one that sets me up, so I won't need to worry about rent and protection for a long, long time.

I flicked a fifty from my new cash roll and tossed it at the bloodwhore who sauntered by in a red rubber dress and six-inch heels, the ring of dripping scars at her throat proclaiming her trade. I pointed at the unconscious vamp. "See this guy? He's fevertripping. Make sure he gets some."

She eyed me suspiciously, blonde pigtails bouncing. "Who the fuck are you, the Salvation Army?"

"Maybe I'm his mother. What the hell do you care?"

The bloodwhore sniffed, tucked the money away, and strutted over to him. My good deed for the day. I'm a thief, not a vamp killer.

And then, just like the man ordered, I turned around.

Easy to spot, even in this crowd. Big guy, black hair, black eyes rimmed with red. Green lights reflected on glassy cheekbones, lasering those midnight eyes with menace. Dark lashes stark against pale skin, exotic, luminous like he'd been out of the light for too long. He wore unrelieved black, like it was all he had in his wardrobe, and damn it if that suit didn't look good on him. He looked like a cross between a vampire mobster from Moscow and a model for the Armani Fall Collection.

Danger, Will Robinson. No real person—no *human* person—looked like that.

He leaned back, ankles crossed, elbows on the white neon-glass bar. He smiled at me, angelic, and sparks danced in his hair. *Come closer,* he mouthed, and my message screen typed the words along with him. He wasn't even holding a phone.

Yeah, this is my guy, all right.

I swallowed and walked over.

He pushed a drink along the glowing bar with one finger. "Vodka tonic, ice, no lemon. Right?" His voice was soft yet somehow carried over the nightclub noise. I didn't hear him so much as *feel* him, a warm and creepy caress, and against my throat the hex pendant pulsed in warning.

"Very good. Who are you?" I didn't take the drink. Spiking is one of my tricks. I don't trust anyone.

He leaned closer, and my mouth parched. A bitter, chalky

taste. Ash. Suddenly, I felt dizzy, and I inhaled on the stink of ozone.

Thunder. Ash storms. Not vampire. Demon.

But everyone knew Kane, the local demon lord. This wasn't he.

The demon grinned, dentist-perfect. "I think we've established who I'm not. You're still standing here. Does that mean you'll take the job?"

I studied him and decided the resemblance wasn't accidental. Kane was blond and baby-faced, where this guy was all darkness and sharp angles, but the eyes were the same. Black, shiny, empty. Dip Kane in soot and starve him for a few millennia . . .

So what was going down here? Kane was jealous and territorial, and he and his vampire mobsters remorselessly crushed anyone who crossed the line. Unlikely that he'd ask big brother here over for a playdate.

I leaned on the bar and buffed my purple fingernails, casual. Demon turf wars were dangerous, but they could be good for business. "Maybe. What's the target?"

The demon drummed his fingertips on the bar, and tiny flames licked the glass. "You'll fetch something for me. An amulet. From a strongbox."

My ears pricked. Magic trinkets ahoy. "Yeah? What kind of amulet?"

"The powerful kind. It has . . . something inside it that belongs to me. I'd recommend you don't break it."

"What's the security?"

He shrugged, heavy like granite. "I'm afraid I haven't visited in a long time."

"I can arrange a preliminary survey."

"Not possible."

"Always possible. For an extra fee, of course. How much did you say you were offering?"

Another smile, but this time his teeth sprang long and sharp, and ash drifted from his hair. "That depends on the condition it's in when you return. If you return at all."

I licked my lips, bitter. "Okay. Forgive me if I'm cautious. Where did you say this strongbox was?"

"Somewhere unpleasant."

I sighed. "Enough with the evasive answers. I guess this is a bad idea—"

"One favor, Lena Falco." The demon caught my hand, swift like a snake, and his touch rooted me to the spot. "Whatever you desire, large or small. No catch. No lies. Do you want the job or not?"

He stroked my knuckles, sparks dancing, and temptation licked my blood hot. Money. Magic. Whatever I wanted.

I closed my eyes on spell-sweet dizziness. He was playing with me. My fairy spells were useless. I wanted to sigh, press his palm to my cheek, lean in, and kiss him until I died. But my hex pendant buzzed angrily, the heat shocking me awake, and I blinked drunkenly and yanked my hand away.

The job sounded difficult. But I needed the break if I wanted to keep my blood in my body and not in a mobster's liquid lunch. Either that, or I'd still be running the lipstick con into my mid-thirties. Cherry-cola cougar. Pathetic much?

Innate warning squirmed in my belly, the prehistoric kind that's supposed to stop you getting eaten. *Demon! Bad! Run!* it shrieked, but I stamped on it. Sure, dealing with demons was dangerous. But I wasn't promising this dude anything in advance. If I did the work, I'd get the prize—and if I didn't like the outcome, I could simply cut my losses and walk away. Right?

I sucked in an ash-tainted breath. "Okay. Deal."

He held out his hand again, silent.

I took it. Shook. His palm was warm, dry, smooth like glass. For a moment, sharp claws stung my knuckles. And then they were gone.

He smiled, all charm again. "Thank you, Lena. Sure you won't take that drink?"

"No, thanks. Where's this amulet, and what's it look like?"

"You'll know it when you see it. It's in a private residence. In the strongbox." He leaned toward me, sniffing. "You've got cash. That's good. You'll need it to get where you're going."

Shit. Should have included expenses. "Why? Isn't it a local job?"

"Not exactly." He smiled again at my expression. "Oh, it's quite close. It won't take long."

"Enough with the doublespeak, hellboy. You hired me. Where's the damned amulet?"

"Not damned, technically." The demon licked pale lips, flames dancing in his hair. "Just hell-trapped. It's at my brother's place. In hell."

Twenty minutes later, I stalked down a grimy alley, spray-painted walls looming. Trash littered the concrete, the stink crinkling my nose, and rats skittered and chewed. A fat yellow moon glared, warped through a dry heat haze that sucked the sweat from my skin, and my throat was parched, my eyes gritty.

I'd retrieved the knives I'd checked at the nightclub counter, and the twin sheaths were strapped crisscross to the back of my corset under my leather jacket. Serrated blades, well weighted for throwing, but mostly slicing and stabbing weapons. The handles lay within easy reach, and I'd cinched the metal bracelets that tricked the blades into returning to me around my wrists. More fairy magic. I'd made them myself, from a pair of coiled-wire bangles and a metalfairy's sly magnetic kiss.

I had a pistol, too, but I'd left it at home, which was just as well. Ordinary bullets would do no good where I was going.

But I still had to get there, and my new demon employer wouldn't help me. Apparently, he wanted plausible deniability

with his pals in the demon court if I got busted. Typical politi-
cian, covering his ass.

At the alley's end, beside a rusted iron fence, a bunch of
skinny fairies crouched around a fire set in a broken oil drum,
their faces dripping rainbow sweat. Firelight reflected on their
damp, glittery wings. Against the fence, more fairies lay, drooling and twitching and fondling each other, asleep or insensible.

I strode up, clearing my throat. "Which one of you guys is
Toffee?"

A golden-skinned one stretched long double-jointed arms
and blinked at me, shirtless. Ragged orange hair stuck in knots
on his shoulders, and his pointy nose twitched as he tested the
air for my scent. "Toffee's here. Who's the pretty cherry girl?"

I didn't move closer. He looked harmless enough. But I don't
trust anyone, remember? "Vinny D told me you're holding," I
said, dropping the name of a gangvamp asshole who I knew had
it over these guys. "Helljuice, I mean."

Toffee flittered to his feet. His butterfly wings puffed cara-
mel dust, and he scratched his pointed ear and gave me a sharp-
toothed grin. "Mmm, Toffee's holding, to be sure. What's the
pretty got?"

"Cash. Two-fifty. That's it. No funny stuff."

He sniffed at my hex pendant and licked my collarbone. His
tongue felt rough, like a kitten's, and he smelled of burnt sugar.
"Toffee likes the funny stuff, tee-hee. Cherry-cola?"

"Forget it." I pushed his face away. "Cash. Three hundred.
Final offer."

He giggled and licked my palm, wrinkling his nose. "Yick-
yick, demon squick. The pretty wants to go to hell? Toffee's got
the juicy." And he dug in his tight jeans pocket and came up
with a long glass vial, filled with what looked like runny shit.
Dirty brown gunk crusted the cork, and the contents bubbled,
thick and lumpy.

My stomach churned. *Great. Can't wait.* But short of damnation or a demon's flashspell, drinking this stuff was the only way to get to hell.

Hell is like another dimension, lurking just beneath this one. Drink, and your body disappears in the real world. You spend the night in hell, wandering around until the helljuice wears off. Then you wake up, in the real-world equivalent of wherever you ended up.

Sadists and adrenaline junkies used helljuice for a sick high, because in hell, anything goes. You can kill, maim, rape, torture, play real-life death-match games with monsters and angry damned souls. Whatever you like. Just don't die, or you'll stay there forever.

But the stuff stank like what it looked like, and bile cooked hot chili in my throat. My demon pal's favor better be worth it.

I folded six fifties and held them out. Toffee dropped the vial into my hand, took the notes with a gleeful giggle, and promptly rolled them up and stuck them into his ears, hooting with laughter.

I shook my head. Fairies. The rest of us need alcohol to act like that. Must make for a cheap night out.

"Ta, sweetie. I'll put in a good word with Vinny for ya." The hell I would. The mobsters I paid not to kill me were Vinny D's enemies, and besides, Vinny was a fever-mad psychopath who ate anything that moved. But no harm in a little creative truth-telling.

I tucked the unpleasantly warm vial into my cleavage—summer's sexy new fragrance, anyone?—and walked away.

"I got mine for two-fifty. You should have bargained harder."

New voice. Not fae. Familiar. I leapt backwards, hand flashing to knife. With a rich chuckle, the shadows coalesced, and from the dark oozed Ethan Benford.

All six-foot-two, blond-and-blue of him. Lean and hardbodied, tanned, not a scrap of fat. Long ponytail slung nonchalantly over one shoulder, Japanese sword with a leather-wrapped grip over the other. He wore ripped jeans and a black, silver-buttoned shirt with the sleeves slashed off, and, as usual, he looked disgustingly good.

I tightened my grip on the knife. "What are you doing here?"

Ethan pulled a vial similar to mine halfway out of his shirt pocket to show me. "Same as you. Demon amulet, strongbox, trip to hell? Sound familiar?"

Shit. No way is he cutting in on my job this time. I scowled, my heart rate only gradually calming. "How did you find out about that?"

"Doesn't matter. You sure you know what you're doing?" He stepped farther into the light, and moonshine glinted on his bare arms, where faint dark lines of power traced the bronzed curves of his muscles like fine tattoos.

My hex pendant hummed sweetly in harmony, and sweat dripped from my hair down my neck. Fairy spells, like I make? Ethan doesn't need them. He subscribed to the *study-hard-and-you'll-get-your-own* school of magic—oh boy, had I heard about it—and infuriatingly, the smug bastard practiced what he preached. In all that spare time he had, between meditating, and training with that counterweighted sword, and getting his umpteenth-dan black belt in some obscure martial art, and climbing fucking Everest on the weekend.

He tried to mentor me once, years ago. But I liked pizza, late nights on the town, and sleeping till midday. He was insufferably healthy, a ridiculously early riser, and a militant pain in the ass about little things like hangovers and caffeine consumption. I lasted a week. Just one more reason I didn't like him.

Sometimes, mostly when I'd run out of spells and cash, I regretted my impatience. The rest of the time? Just glad I didn't have to put up with his shit.

I jammed my knife away. "This is *my* job, Ethan. Butt out."

"What did he promise you?"

"Isn't it past your bedtime?" I stalked back up the alley without waiting for him.

He fell into step beside me anyway, and as I glanced at him, so cool and fluid and in control, for the first time that night I wished that my hot pants weren't quite so . . . well, hot.

Not that I didn't look smoking in fishnets. I knew I did. And I was good at my job, damn it. Nothing to be ashamed of.

But if one thing on this earth never failed to make me feel like a cheap gutter con artist, it was Ethan butter-won't-melt Benford.

He caught my eye, his gaze ice blue but somehow warm. "C'mon, what was it? Money? Magic? You always took the easy way out, Lena."

Well, screw you, Ethan. "That's fine for you to say. You've got time."

Did I mention Ethan's immortal? As good as, anyway. He's human, far as I know, but he hasn't aged a day in the ten years I've known him. He says it's because he meditates on the meaning of life. Like I said: one more reason.

He smiled, and I wanted my sunglasses. "You've got time, too, if you want it," he said. "You just waste it—"

"—on boozing and blokes, yeah, yeah. I got it." Still, I wondered if he was sore that those blokes of mine never included him. He didn't have a girlfriend, and for a guy who claimed he didn't like me, he sure showed up a lot. And okay, I suppose he wasn't a total eyesore. His smile would blow a fuse. Totally crushable hair, if he ever wore it loose, which he didn't. And all those gymnastic workouts sure paid off . . .

I caught myself checking out his butt and dragged my gaze away. Me, dating Mr. Zen-and-the-art-of-holier-than-thou? A one-way street to inadequate. No way.

We emerged onto the main street, where at 1:30 A.M., the traffic had thinned to a trickle. Streetlights buzzed and glared, fighting the moon. A gleaming silver tram rattled down the hill toward the station. A motorbike zipped by, a trio of whooping fairies hanging on like long-legged barnacles.

I jammed my hand on my hip, tapping my foot. "I'm busy, okay? Any more pearls?"

"Yeah, now that you mention it." Ethan didn't fold his hands or fidget. He just adopted that easy stance, relaxed, alert, ready for anything. "You ever helltripped before?"

"Nope." True, actually. A night in hell wasn't my idea of a good time. "Have you?"

"I've been. It's not pretty."

"I can handle it, thanks." His tone gave me the creeps, but I shrugged it off. How hard could it be? In my experience, monsters were like the Predator: If they bled, I could kill 'em.

"The demon is Phoebus, Kane's kin. Kane won't appreciate him meddling. You really want to get caught in a demon pissing contest?"

Phoebus? Heh. With a name like that, I'd be pissed, too. "Obviously, you do."

"I've got my reasons."

"Yeah? What possible reason could you have for stealing a hell-trapped demon amulet, Ethan? And don't give me shit about knowledge being its own reward. There's gotta be something in it for you."

He shrugged, blank.

I grinned. "You are so busted, my friend. C'mon, fess up. Phoebus make you an offer you couldn't refuse? Or do you want this famous amulet for yourself, is that it?" A thought struck me, and abruptly I shut my mouth. *What if Ethan's working for Kane? What if it's his job to stop me?*

Ethan's mouth tightened. "You coming or not?"

"With you? You're kidding, right?" I tried to push past him on the narrow sidewalk. I didn't need his help. I didn't trust him not to double-cross me once we had the loot. And to be perfectly honest, the last thing I needed while I fought my way through hell was the distracting sight of his sexy ass in those jeans.

He stopped me with his hand on my shoulder. Not hard. Just a light touch, but as heavy with threat as a punch in the face. "I'm going after the amulet," he said softly. "Either you're with me, or you're in my way. Your choice."

I sighed and shook his hand off. When he put it like that, I had no choice at all, really.

He ushered me off the tram at the Domain Road junction, where leafy plane trees sprawled over the wide median strip, and traffic lights buzzed amid the nest of electric-tram wires. Across the road, tall buildings loomed in moonlit shadow.

We crossed twin roads to the park, where dead brown grass crunched under my boots. I shrugged my jacket comfortable over my knives, and Ethan adjusted his sword. He'd worn the weapon openly while we sat on the tram, the air slick and sparkly with his *don't-see-me* spell, and no one noticed a thing. Me, I just wore a jacket.

Kane lived in one of the more fashionable parts of town. We'd just caught the last tram, and it rumbled its doors shut and carried on, around the corner the same way we were going. "We could have ridden that all the way to Chapel Street," I grumbled, more for something to say than because I cared. "Did we have to get off so far away?"

Ethan tidied and refastened his ponytail, the long blond ends flicking his shoulder. "Actually, yeah. What do you think would happen if we flashed into hell right by Kane's front door?"

I scowled. He always had to phrase everything as a question, like he was teaching me. "Umm . . . I guess we'd get our asses chewed by demon rent-a-cops?"

That sunflash smile. "Something like that. Better to approach from a distance. Keep your eyes open, it's—"

"Yeah, yeah. A wretched hive of scum and villainy. We must

be cautious. Thanks for the heads-up, Obi-Wan. You ready or not?" I uncorked my poo brown vial and brought it to my lips, wrinkling my nose against the stink.

He grabbed my wrist, halting me. "Weapons first. Be prepared."

I sighed and whipped out a knife, just in case. And before he could offer to go first, I tilted the vial and chugged.

The foul sludge hit my tongue, and I gagged. Grit coated my mouth, burning, the taste putrid. My throat squeezed tight, refusing to let the filth in. But I had to swallow, and I sealed my lips shut and choked the feral hellbrew down.

It burned, and hit my stomach like an acid bomb.

Agony clawed my guts, and I screamed. Darkness blotted my vision like evil ink. My bones filled with fire, flesh tearing, tendons popping. Howling split my ears. I struggled, but nothing trapped me, and with a sickening vertigo lurch, I fell.

Concrete smacked against my chest, squashing my breath away. My skull bounced, jangling, and everything was still.

I cracked an eye open, and blood dripped into it. I blinked. Charred buildings, broken concrete, a scarlet-stained horizon beyond dead trees. Acrid smoke stung my eyes. I tried to crawl to my feet, only something heavy and warm held me down.

"Ethan, let go." I wriggled, and he helped me up, his arm steady around my waist. Even in hell, he smelled like herbal soap.

"You okay?" His murmur brushed my ear, reassuring.

"Sure." I pushed him away, flexing my fingers around my knife. Nighttime, but dry heat scorched me like sunburn. Ash drifted, but no breeze stirred the parched air. My tongue stuck to the roof of my mouth. Bloodstained clouds boiled low and threatening—how could there be clouds when it was drier than a witch's corpse?—and lightning cracked the sky, illuminating the street with an eerie flash.

I squinted. It looked like Domain Road after the apocalypse.

The same as the real world, only the trees were blackened stumps, the buildings scorched, the road cracked and tilted in chunks as if a mighty earthquake had split it apart. Broken glass and charred metal littered the ground. Thunder boomed, deafening, and across the street, a ruined office building burst into flame, filling the air with ash and the stink of burning flesh. Gunfire ricocheted, and from somewhere, I heard the clash of iron.

"Charming." I rolled my shoulders, trying to relax. Ethan just stood there, poised and calm. Damn it if I wasn't glad I hadn't come alone. "Now what—"

An almighty screech tore the air, and a bundle of leathery skin and claws landed on us in a cloud of fetid stink.

I staggered backwards, instinctively arcing up my shielding hex. My pendant shivered, and protective sparks crackled around me.

But the hellbeast just snarled, scaly snout slavering with six-inch razor teeth, and slashed my hex to smoke with curved claws. It gibbered, its rotting tongue mangling the sounds. *"Bith. Eeeyor meet, bith. Meeeet . . . yummm!!"*

I reeled, revolted. Those were words. I think I just got invited to dinner. And Mr. Ugly had opposable thumbs. Lips. Eyelashes. A mutant lizard-thing on two legs, a hybrid of reptile and man.

Steel sang as Ethan unsheathed his sword. The beast laughed, a thick, cancerous sound that made me retch, and spat a lump of festering filth. Ethan dodged, and the stuff boiled and smoked on the broken concrete.

I whipped out my second knife, but somehow I couldn't throw. I swallowed, sick. "It's human, Ethan. It's a fucking person!"

"Not anymore." Ethan whispered a charm, and the faint lines on his muscles glowed red. He circled away, and his movements blurred, faster than I could watch. "It's a corrupted soul, and it's hungry. You want to be dinner?"

No, actually, I didn't.

I muttered a poison curse and hurled both knives at once. The toxic blades carved a deadly arc, slicing into the beast's hide. Black blood sprayed, the stink of rotting meat. My bangles vibrated, and the knives ripped free and slapped back into my hands.

The beast howled, poisoned steam hissing from twin gaping wounds across its chest. It swatted at the burns, but they bubbled and spread like acid. I stabbed for its bulging eyes. It staggered back, and Ethan danced forward like a deadly ballerina on speed and slashed the thing's head from its body.

The head cartwheeled, blood splattering, and the twisted body slumped. I stared, catching my breath. "Is it dead?"

Ethan's glowing charm faded, and he nudged the body with his foot. It rolled over, lifeless. "For now," he said. "But the damned don't get off that easy. It'll rise again with the sun. Best we keep going."

"Kane's place?"

He nodded, up the street, and, for the first time, I noticed a blackened tower, looming stark in the distance against the red-stained sky. Lightning crashed, and smoke drifted from the sharp battlements, shimmering in deadly heat. Huge carrion birds—or worse?—flapped lazy orbits around its summit.

I blinked. "No way. Don't remember seeing Sauron's fortress last time I shopped in Toorak."

Ethan grinned. "Nor would you. Kane lives in a town house there. That"—he stabbed at it with his finger—"is a manifestation of his power status in hell."

I glanced around. *Any meaner, more gruesome-looking buildings? Of course not.* I sighed. "Demon dick-measuring. Great."

"Arm wrestling would be more accurate."

"Whatever," I muttered, "it's stupid macho bullshit." The town house would have suited me fine.

"It's just a pecking order. It works for them. Until idiots like us blunder in and screw it up."

Ethan shook black blood from his sword, and together we advanced up the broken street, shoulder to shoulder, only a few feet apart. He didn't sheathe. I didn't either. But it felt kinda nice to have him at my back.

At the road's edges, creatures snarled and paced, hairless hyena-things with skinny bodies pale like sides of meat. They watched us pass with beady red eyes, their throaty laughter unsettling. Sweat stung inside my corset, down my neck, between my fingers, sucked away to nothing by the hungry air. Scorched buildings threatened, their windows smashed and bloody or melted to dirty globs. Every sound made me jump. Frantic footsteps drew near, then receded, and gunshots cracked, the sounds of a running battle. Screams and insane giggles echoed through the side streets, leaping out at me like unseen foes.

I wristed damp hair from my forehead as we clambered over an upthrusting twist of asphalt that blocked the road from side-walk to sidewalk, ten feet high and littered with sharp rocks. "So how d'you know all this stuff?"

"I've been here." Ethan hopped upwards, sword still in hand, balanced and agile like a mountain goat.

I sheathed my knives to scramble over the rubble, and the hot rock scorched my palms. My boots slipped, and I scrabbled for a hold. "Really? Never would have picked you for a recreational user."

"I'm not. But if you want to grow, you have to face your fears." He straddled the broken top of the slab and reached down for me. "Allow me, madam."

I rolled my eyes and grabbed his wrist, and he hauled me up.

I sat facing him for a moment, catching my breath, my feet dangling. The stink of brimstone soured my mouth. I peered over the edge. Beneath us, where the road once lay, a chasm gaped, down and down into distant depths crackling with flames.

A fat green snake slithered from a crack in the rock, striking at my thigh with three hissing heads. I flipped out a knife and skewered it at the junction of three necks. Drew the other and sliced all the heads off in a splash of smoking venom.

"Mmm. Tasty." I flicked the squirming carcass off my blades into the pit. "Fears, huh. Didn't think you were afraid of anything."

Ethan watched the snake fall and gave it a mock salute. "Everyone's afraid of something."

"Like what?" I scoffed. "Death?"

"Yes. Aren't you?"

Wow. No evasion. No flip remark. That'll teach me. "Umm . . . yeah. I mean, I guess. Shit, look around us, dude. Knowing there's somewhere to go doesn't mean it's all roses after we kick it. D'you think . . ."

I hesitated, that prehistoric danger alarm growling deep in my belly again. *Truth alert! Hide!*

But I wanted to know. I took a deep breath. "D'you ever think about damnation?"

"Of course. Not everyone believes magic is good work." His glacial eyes warmed. "But you do, right?"

My heart did a little somersault. Christ on a double cheeseburger. No man should have such clear, sweet eyes. Not for the first time, I wanted to dive in and drown.

We hadn't had an honest conversation in years. I'd forgotten how much I liked it. "I guess. What do you think?"

He shrugged, candid. "Temptation's the easy way, Lena. That's why it works. If magic were a helltrick, I believe the demons would've made it a damn sight easier."

Was he mocking me? Or apologizing for being such an asshole back in the day? I fidgeted. "Guess so. Look, I'm sorry we never . . ."

My hex charm sizzled, and I let out a startled yell and hurled my knife at his foot.

The hairless hyena-thing howled and tumbled, blood spurting from its pale rump, and its ugly jaws snapped shut inches from Ethan's ankle.

Ethan leapt, and was on his feet before the knife thunked back into my palm.

I'd missed the killing shot. The hyena-thing was only wounded, and it grinned evilly at me with a hoarse, chuckling sound. Below us, a pack of its mates tittered and started to climb. The thing cackled—*nyi-hi-hi!*—and dug its claws into the rubble, ready to jump.

Ethan slashed at it, but it dodged and leapt at me, slavering. I threw again, shouting a whetting spell that curled my nails and set my teeth on edge, and this time the spell-sharpened blade speared right between the thing's glassy red eyes into its brain.

Mr. Chuckles flipped in midair, its momentum reversed by my throw, and hit the rocks like a sack of sniggering hellshit. Blood exploded, running down the rocks, and the chortling pack leapt on the body and tore it to pieces.

I flexed my wrist, and my knife landed in my palm, dripping rotten blood. Ethan gave me a surprised glance. "Thanks."

He looked impressed. That was a first. I shoved him, flushing. "Dinner doesn't look like it'll go around. Get moving."

He leapt, and landed lightly on the other side of the chasm.

Twelve feet. Sure, I can make it. Just don't look down.

I jumped, and landed with somewhat less grace. Behind us, flesh ripped, and Mr. Chuckles's new dinner companions grunted and laughed in triumph. *Bwa-ha-ha, I just ate my brother, and he tasted fiiine!*

I picked myself up and dusted off my grazed knees. Ethan steadied me, and we hurried on, weapons drawn, picking our way between rocks, over razor glass shards, around rusted steel girders twisted by the heat. As we neared the tower, the helljungle noises grew louder. Burning buildings smoked and collapsed by the side of the road. Creatures sprinted through the streets, ignoring us or hurling ripe curses that blistered my skin. Some just sat by the road and howled, and their anguish stained the heat-warped air with bitter ash.

But Ethan wasn't letting me off easy. "I mean it," he murmured, his keen gaze checking left and right. "Nice job. I didn't even hear that thing coming."

He looked sheepish, and I squirmed. I didn't want to tell him that I hadn't either, that the only reason I'd noticed was my stolen hex pendant giving me the red-hot-poker treatment. That I'd been too busy daydreaming about his eyes to pay attention. "Don't sound so surprised. What are those hyena-things, anyway?"

"Imps, hellslaves, wrathmites. Call 'em what you want."

A big, naked, hairy dude with raw pustules rotting his skin swung his scythe at us, blood and worms splashing from his mouth as he screamed. I ducked and slashed at his kidneys, and Ethan took him down and sidestepped as the head hit the concrete and broke open. The scythe clattered harmlessly away.

"That's a nice razorcharm you used before," Ethan persisted, as if we hadn't been interrupted. "You been practicing?"

Yeah, right. I'd stolen that one, too, a couple of wing-splinters I pilfered from a drunken glassfairy.

It disturbed me how much I wanted to lie, and I snorted to cover my unease. "C'mon, you know me better than that."

"Thought I did."

"What's that supposed to mean?"

He flashed me that smile. "That you're still a puzzle, Lena Falco. I just haven't solved you yet."

I frowned. *Enigmatic equals good, right? Or not? Shit. Who am I trying to impress, anyway?*

Still, I edged closer to him, my guts tightening. The tower's shadow darkened the street like a smoke pall. Heat scorched me deep, and it was sure getting crowded around here. Rotting creatures shambled like shopping-mall zombies. Others—the normal people, dazed and bleeding, mostly naked, mouths slack with terror—screamed and fled. Guess they were new here. Still others stalked in packs, agile and twisted, their mutated bodies sprouting scales or feathers or extra limbs. And everywhere, weapons, blades and spikes and ugly saws designed to maim.

I tried to keep focused, not to dwell on how harmless my knives were in comparison. "More cursed souls?"

"Yeah." Ethan's gaze darted, swift but controlled. "They all look different. Depends what kind of asshole you were in life."

"Heh. Look at that jelly-ass one, then. Big dripping pile of smug. That'll be you."

"Bite me."

Around us, the creatures closed in, and I held my knives at the ready, circling. Those huge carrion birds squawked and flapped, hellish vultures with razor-curved beaks and talons the size of my forearm. One dived for a screaming pack of starved bodies, and came up with one writhing in its grip. More birds descended, fighting to peck the victim's eyes out, and the screaming went on long after any living person would have fallen silent.

I stared, and Ethan nudged me. "Stay frosty, marine."

"Oh, I'm shivering. Just how good did you say I've gotta be to avoid this place when I'm dead?"

"Makes you think, doesn't it?"

Zombies shouldered us as they stumbled by blindly. A woman with her face peeled off leapt at me, clawing for my eyes, and I broke her rotting neck with a thrust of my elbow. Ethan slashed at a gaggle of half-man, half-worm things that writhed along the ground to snap at his ankles. Worm juice and body parts splattered the pavement, but they kept coming, their blind eyes cloudy and wet.

I took another step backwards, and Ethan's back pressed against mine, warm and reassuring. "I'm getting a bad feeling about this, Obi-Wan," I muttered.

"What do you want me to say? Use the force?" He took a deep breath, and with a *zing,* his magical shield shone around us, iridescent like a bubble. The worm people slapped against it, leaving wet smears. "Tower's a hundred yards away. Stay close. Don't let them drag you from the bubble. Okay?"

"That much I figured out for mys—" I gulped. "Uh-oh."

From across the street, a mutant spied us, his bloodshot eyes gleaming with delight. He had a huge, naked skull and droopy ears, and his sagging belly oozed blood from open wounds that hadn't healed.

He hollered, waving his rusty chain saw—I shit you not— and his subhuman buddies all screeched and jabbered and flailed their misshapen arms. And ran. Straight for us.

My hex pendant buzzed like a nest of angry wasps. My mouth dried, and I gripped my knives harder. "This isn't good."

Captain Mutant fired up his chain saw—*rnn-nn-nnn!*—and capered about like a drunken mummy. And his mutant army kept coming.

Ethan gave a feral grin. The lines on his skin glowed green, and he levitated a foot off the ground and crouched there like a bad-ass flying ninja, his blade glinting hungrily. "Bring 'em on."

"You're a real smart-ass, you know that?" But I couldn't hide a smile. Sometimes, even I had to admit that Ethan was dead cool. Still, bitterness stung my mouth that I couldn't do stuff like that. That'd I'd never had the patience to learn. "Last one there buys the whisky, okay?"

He somersaulted, carving the air a new one with his sword at least six times on the way around. "You know I don't drink."

I muttered a charm, and my twin blades dripped green poison. I spun them, loosening my wrists in readiness. "All the more for me."

And with a duet of blood-rotting yells, we plunged into the fight.

It seemed like a hundred hours later when we finally staggered over the tower's dark threshold and dragged the spiked-iron door shut.

The bar thunked into place. Angry mutants hammered and hurled curses, their slack flesh slapping on the metal. The hinges juddered, but it held.

I collapsed against it, breathing hard. Blood stuck my fingers together, and I unwrapped them from my knife handles with a wince. Beside me, Ethan coughed and spat red phlegm, his face splashed with hellish gore. His bubble had helped us, and we'd fought well together, but we'd taken serious damage. My head ached from blows, and my skin was ripped raw in a dozen places. I was covered in claw marks and cuts, and dripping with stinking black blood and bits of flesh. I'd nearly lost a finger. My legs hurt. My lungs hurt. Hell, my hair hurt.

Ethan wiped his nose with his sword hand, smearing blood. He was fitter than I was, but still his breath hitched. It had taken a lot out of him to keep those spells engaged, and once he'd let them slip, weariness lined his face. "Well, here we are, I guess. You okay?"

"Yeah. You?"

"Never been better."

I surveyed the room. Black and empty, caked with dust. A fire pit in the center threw leaping shadows on the walls. It stank of salt and blood. A broken iron staircase spiraled upwards, and hisses and moans crept from upstairs. No other way out. I craned my neck. Nothing up there but darkness. "You think Kane's here?"

"If he were, we'd be dead already."

"Good point. How long you think we've got before the helljuice wears off?"

"Not long." He breathed, in and out, centering his energy or opening his aura or whatever, and when he opened his eyes, they shone bright, refreshed. "Let's get on with it."

His equivalent of a stiff drink. I sure could have used one. Or even just a rest. But no time. I sighed and wiped sticky mutant blood from my knives onto my pants. "Old guys go first?"

Ethan snickered and crept onto the staircase, and as I followed, my aching muscles eased a little. It was good to hear him laugh. Good to hear any living human sound.

The staircase turned, and we climbed, and climbed, the steps corroded and sometimes crumbling. Firelight leaked in through cracks in the walls, like some gruesome hellpit burned outside, and screams and moans twisted in the air like ghosts.

I shuddered. My hex pendant burned, but it had been screaming at me nonstop for the last few hours, and it meant nothing new. My shoulder prickled, an evil, hot breath, and I whirled, but there was no one.

I sucked in a breath, trying to slow my racing pulse. "Why is there no one here?"

"Because it's a trap?"

"Wow, that's really comforting."

"You're welcome."

I tried to push ahead of him, to have him behind me, but he held me back with a rigid arm.

"Wh—ugh!" I stumbled back, twisting my ankle on the step, and, at our feet, a massive chunk of rotted iron shuddered and fell. Four or five spiral steps tumbled away into the dark, and though I waited several seconds, holding my breath, I didn't hear them land.

Ethan sprang up over the gap, landed lightly on the next unbroken step and held out his hand for me. Yeah, right. Impeccable balance, light step, wiry strength. Stuff I didn't have.

I sucked in a breath and jumped.

Evil laughter echoed, and thick darkness wrapped itself around my legs and *pulled.*

I yelled and flung out a desperate magical web, but it was too far. My guts hollowed. Sparks rained, hissing, and I fell.

But Ethan flashed out his hand, and a stinging whip of light cracked like electric current. My sparks coalesced in harmony, a glittering green cascade, and the whip lashed itself around my waist and yanked me upwards.

Ethan caught me against his chest, and the magic light dissolved. I scrabbled with terrified feet for a hold, and he steadied me. "Got you. You okay?"

I caught my breath, reeling. He felt warm and safe, his arms possessive, holding on for a bit too long. Almost like he gave a damn.

I pushed away, awkward, my heart still racing from the fright. "Yeah. Thanks. What was that thing you just did?"

"No idea. Never did it before."

"Oh, so who's the puzzle now?" I scoffed, trying to regain my ease.

He glanced away, avoiding me. "Must be your lucky day. C'mon."

We kept climbing and reached a smoky landing that was riddled with jagged holes. Massive iron urns lined the walls, and inside them, *things* hammered and yelled for help, desperate to escape.

My stomach churned. I coughed in the acrid smoke. "Tell me those aren't souls in there."

Ethan's face was pale, and he didn't answer.

I gripped his shoulder. Killing these things was one thing. Leaving them like this . . . "We have to let them out! Jesus, we can't just—"

"This is hell, Lena." He touched my hand, and his compassion sizzled on my skin, magnetic. "Where can they go?"

I shrugged, angry. I wasn't used to feeling helpless. What was the point of all this power if people still suffered and died? The sooner I found the amulet and got out of this place, the better.

He brushed my cheek with his thumb, a tiny caress, then he climbed on.

The staircase spiraled more tightly, the walls closing in. Sparks leapt from the cracks and stung my face. Landing after landing, narrower and darker, the air howling with ghostly pain and fear that iced my bones. Shadows jumped and thrashed, stretching like torture victims trying to escape. Dark *things* I couldn't see touched me, caressed me, slid hot wet lips over my skin until it crawled. I tore at my hair, batted at my face, careless of my sharp blades. "Ethan—"

"It's okay." His voice strained tight like wire. Around him, angry magic sparked, and the wraithlike *things* gnashed and hissed and shied away.

At last, we reached another landing, and the staircase ended. Above, the ceiling tapered to a jagged hole, and hell's red sky glared through, casting bloody shadows. On the wall, a rusted mirror warped our reflection, and in the shaft of light lay a dusty black metal box with a spiked padlock.

We halted, and I caught my breath, glad of the light even though it scorched my face with fresh heat. "Is that a strong-box?"

Ethan nodded. "I'd say so."

I frowned. "Did that seem too easy to you?"

"We're not finished yet." He inhaled, scenting for trouble, and crept forward.

I hesitated. Lightning flashed, the thunder shaking the walls, and a fine golden glint at thigh level caught my eye.

My heart skipped, and I grabbed Ethan's arm and yanked him back.

He lurched, and recovered his balance with a little jump. "What?"

I pointed. Smoke particles drifted in the light, around a hair-thin golden wire stretching across the floor. Together, we craned our necks upwards. Above, wicked curved blades glinted, waiting to slice us into salami.

Ethan grimaced. "You're kidding. Trip wire?"

"Crude but effective. Our demon pals have a sense of humor."

"Terrific. Watch out for banana peel and itching powder." He hopped over the wire, sword poised, and I followed.

The strongbox just sat there, black and boring. I eyed it suspiciously. Couldn't be this easy. Not like a job topside, where you just break in, take stuff, and run away. Surely?

Ethan lifted two fingers, and a soft breeze whistled, blowing away the smoke. Tiny sparks crawled over the box, testing, seeping into the crack between body and lid. He shrugged, and the sparks extinguished. "I get nothing."

"What? No alarms? No threats of imminent evisceration?"

"Not a whisper."

"Maybe what's inside is the kicker."

"You think? How are you with locks?"

I whipped a shard of glowing pink fairyglass from my corset—who says you can't use an ingredient for more than one spell?—and waved it at him. "Watch me and weep."

I bent closer to the barbed padlock, and now that prehistoric coward inside me was really getting her voice on. *Demon box! Eek! Run!* she squealed, and, for a moment, I hesitated.

Stealing a cursed amulet from a demon lord. Not one of my safer ideas.

I glanced at Ethan, who crouched, alert, surveying the creeping darkness for threats, blood still trickling from his nose. I still didn't get what was in this for him. Was this the part where he turned me over to Kane? Pity. I'd liked having him around. And working for a demon sorta . . . dirtied him. Ethan wasn't like me, doing anything for a living. He had standards, at least I'd thought so.

But Phoebus's whisper from the nightclub caressed my memory, tempting me reckless. *One favor, Lena Falco. No catch. Whatever you desire.*

This was my big prize. Whatever the risks, it was worth it.

I gripped the glass between thumb and finger and shoved it in the padlock.

The sharp wingshard sliced my skin. Blood seeped, and pink fairy glitter puffed, intoxicating, lulling the lock's tumblers into submission. I rooted around a bit, feeling for the springs. Click, one. The spikes on the lock jabbed into my palm. Click, two. Clickety click, three. And . . . clunk. Open.

Thunder rolled, threatening. Carefully, I eased the padlock from its socket on the strongbox, and laid it on the floor.

The box just hunkered there, menacing.

I glanced up, and Ethan shrugged. "Now or never."

I poked the lid experimentally. It didn't poke back, and I gritted my teeth against disaster and levered it up.

The hinges creaked, and it opened. Silence. Together, we peered inside.

Just a pile of ashes. And atop it, a dusty red gemstone the size of an egg.

A deep, velvety chuckle echoed in my ears. I squirmed, my belly warming. Were those flames, flickering deep inside the stone?

Something inside it that belongs to me, Phoebus had said. Maybe he meant something *alive.*

Whatever. I reached for it, but Ethan caught my wrist. "Let me," he said, and he darted forward and wrapped his fingers around the amulet.

And the world burst into flame.

My body slammed backwards, and my head hit the wall with a sick crunch. Heat scorched my lungs, sizzling my mouth dry. I shook my head, clearing my blurred vision in time to see Ethan get hurled across the burning room by some invisible force. The trip wire sprang, and huge blades scythed. But he'd already hurtled past and smashed into the wall, falling in a twisted heap. His sword clattered from his hand and spun away, which was just as well, because if he hadn't dropped it, he'd have sliced himself in half as he fell.

Flames licked up the rusted walls, ringing the room in glare. The gemstone skittered onto the floor, attached to a spiked-iron chain. Light pierced the stone, and against the wall sprang a dark, hulking shadow. A slavering beast in silhouette, four twisted legs, spiked tail, razor-sharp fins along its spine.

I scrambled away in fright, searching for the monster. It was nowhere in sight. Only the shadow, the evil black projection of whatever lived inside that amulet.

Hollow female laughter boomed, and the shadow-demon swelled in triumph. "Give up, puny human. You're too decent, and your little slut is too weak. You can't control me."

I coughed, spitting dry with dread and black humor. *Puny human?* Seriously. Next it'll say, *Soon I will be invincible!*

But Ethan lay gasping, bleeding, fighting to rise, and it speared hot anger into my belly. He might be immortal, but he wasn't indestructible. And damn right he was decent. He'd grabbed the amulet to protect me. Screw me if I'd let this demon cow insult him.

I hurled twin knives at the shadow, and they clanged harmlessly off the wall and arced back to me. "Bite me, hellbitch. We'll see who's weak once I've hauled your crooked ass back to your boss."

The shadow whiplashed and snapped crocodile jaws at me.

I dodged, scrambling to my feet. Ethan flung out his arm, sparks flashing, and his sword erupted in angry green flame and dragged itself across the floor toward his fingers.

But the shadow-demon kicked it away—no fair, a kicking shadow, it's just a shape on the wall, right? Wrong—and stomped a fat clawed foot on Ethan's forearm. Hard.

Bones snapped, and my teeth grated. Jesus in a jam jar, that must have hurt. Ethan gave a strangled gasp, and the sword's flames sputtered out.

Furious, I hurled myself at the monster, but the shadow just darted out of the way, cackling like a wart-nosed witch. "Dance with me, while I suck out his tasty-sweet soul," it sang. "You can't stop me." And it leapt on him and lunged with gnashing teeth for his throat.

He kicked, and fought it off with sparking fists.

My heart clenched. I sprinted for him, but the demon flung me away. Bad plan.

I picked myself up, teeth rattling, and dived for the amulet instead.

The spiked chain bloodied my palm. The pulsing red stone sizzled, and my skin melted, but I didn't care. *Don't break it,* Phoebus said.

Well, screw him.

I slammed the gemstone into the iron floor. It didn't break. I tried smashing it with my knife hilt. The demon just laughed at me. I jumped up and crushed it under my bootheel. The fucking thing wouldn't break. I flung my poison hex at it, adding some stolen sunlight for good measure, but it just bubbled and seared the toxic goo to steam.

I yelled in frustration, and my hex pendant burst into furious red flame.

My hair smoked, the acrid stink filling my nostrils. And I knew what I had to do.

I grabbed the bloody chain, careless of the ripping spikes, and dragged it over my head.

The red gemstone clunked against my hex pendant. I grabbed both and squeezed, and with a stinking flash of light, they melted together.

Electricity jolted my bones. My body jerked, muscles spasming. Current arced from my fingertips, piercing the shadow-demon like lightning.

My veins burned, light and liquid fire, power juddering through me. My thoughts danced. My reflexes glittered. My senses erupted, every scent and breath and whisper swelling large. I inhaled, and thunder answered, ozone tingling my nose. Blood rushed to my core, and my body moaned in pure pleasure.

I flung my palm outwards and let rip with another lightning bolt. The demon howled and let Ethan go. I crooked a flame-wrapped finger and pinned the wriggling shadow to the wall. "Don't move, bitch. You're mine."

The demon cringed, and when I laughed, the ground shook.

Magic. Power. What I'd longed for, all those years. My body springing alive, my senses reeling, my subconscious wishes a force of nature. Never mind that it came from a demon, a foul creature of hell that was surely eating me away from the inside. It was better than pizza. Better than sex.

Better, too, than a lifetime meditating and doing yoga with Ethan. This was what I was for. What I was meant to be. And caught fast by my amulet—the demon trap that now hooked itself with eternally hungry claws to my heart—the monster thrashed and shuddered but couldn't break free.

Beyond the tower walls, the tortured screams of the damned played me a cruel symphony. Hellish light poured over my skin, tingling with a lover's caress. The demon cried for mercy. I didn't listen. I clenched my fist, and, slowly, my amulet sucked the shrieking shadow inside. It stretched and tore, desperate to escape. But there was no escape. For either of us. And with one final *schllpp,* the shadow was gone.

And silence fell, but for Ethan's rasping breath.

The amulet burned heavy at my throat, whispering foul curses. I staggered, sick. Fever gripped me. Cramp stabbed my guts, and I fell to my knees at Ethan's side. He struggled to rise. Bile frothed in my throat, the rotten helljuice repeating on me at last, and I clutched Ethan's bloodied hand like a lifeline and descended into blacker hell.

Pain thrust deep into my bones, and the nightmare vomited me up.

Cool air, smooth fabric beneath my back. Someone had removed my jacket and boots, and I ached all over. I forced my eyes open, and my vision slowly cleared. White ceiling, a fan slowly circling. Gray quilt, books piled neatly, spotless carpet with not a mote of dust in sight. My knives shone clean on the bedside table. Sunlight streamed over me from the open window, and distant traffic hummed softly.

Back on earth. Alive. But my skin felt numb, my senses bereft . . .

I felt for my throat. Nothing.

Alarm rocketed my pulse. The amulet. My hex pendant. Both gone.

A cool hand stroked my hair, and I jumped. "Take it easy," Ethan murmured, perched on the bed beside me. "Rough night."

I sat up, pushing his hand away. He'd showered, lemon and herbal soap, and his damp hair hung loose, unbloodstained. His bruised face was clean, his broken arm wrapped and splinted. He'd healed himself, or was well on the way. "How did we get here? I mean, this is your place, right? Last I remember, we were in hell."

"The helljuice wore off. I, uh . . ." He bit his lip, oddly childlike. "I carried you home. You were in pretty bad shape."

I scrambled to my feet. "That was not bad shape, Ethan. That was the best shape of my life. Where is it?"

"Where's what?"

"Don't play games!" My voice squeaked, frantic. It didn't sound like me. But I'd lost my lifelong dream, and I wanted it back. "The amulet! Where is it?"

He dug it out of his jeans pocket to show me. The red gem glinted, still welded to my hex pendant. I leapt for it, but he stuffed it away before I could reach. "It's safe."

I stalked closer and leaned over him, threatening. "It's mine, Ethan. Give it to me, or I'll make you sorry!"

Christ on a cracker. Listen to me. This isn't right. This isn't Lena Falco talking.

But without my hex pendant, I was helpless. Worse than helpless. Ordinary. And for a few minutes, I'd felt like a goddess. I'd never wanted anything as much as I wanted that.

Ethan didn't lower his gaze. "Lena, you're not thinking straight. The demon has addled your mind. Let it go."

"But—" I sucked in a breath, trying to be calm. Maybe he was right. All that magic had felt so good, I'd fallen for the demon's temptation. I couldn't keep the amulet, not if I wanted to save my soul. Right? "But . . . I have to give it to Phoebus. A deal's a deal."

"No. We can't give it to Phoebus. We can't give it to anyone. It's too dangerous, Lena. You know that better than most. It has to be destroyed."

I stared. "What? You mean you're not working for Kane?"

"Don't be ridiculous. You know me better than that."

"So all along, you never wanted this thing? You just wanted to *destroy* it?" My guts twisted. I couldn't believe it. He'd lied to me. He'd let me think . . . well, he'd let me think what I wanted to think, which was that we were partners. Ha. What a laugh.

Ethan shrugged. "I'm sorry, Lena. I needed your help. If I'd told you the truth, I didn't think you'd—"

"Damn right you're sorry." My eyes burned, and I marched into the bathroom and slammed the door.

Cool white tiles gleamed, annoyingly spotless, and did nothing to ice my temper. I thrust my hands under the tap, splashing water on my flushed face until I had to come up for air.

Yes, it hurt that he'd lied. It hurt that I'd believed him, that I'd thought we might be good together.

But it hurt worse that he hadn't thought me worth the truth. He'd assumed I'd betray him for a chance at Phoebus's favor. Taken me for nothing but a cheap gutter con artist who always took the easy way out.

And hell, he was right. Wasn't he?

I leaned both hands on the sink and forced my gaze upwards. My reflection glared back. Her corset was stained, her purple hair wild. A livid burn shone at her throat where the amulet had hung. Her dark eyes glinted, shadowed with bruises and fatigue. Hard. Angry.

Was it so wrong to long for more? If I traded with Phoebus, I could have whatever I wanted. Wealth. Influence. Power.

Ethan, even.

My skin tingled. That shadow-demon had threatened him, and I hadn't stopped to think about what was in it for me. I'd just acted. Unselfishness. There's a first.

One word from Phoebus, and Ethan would forget he despised me. I'd have his respect. We could be equals. Friends. More, if I wanted, and after last night, I realized I did want. More than I ever had.

I stared into my own unforgiving eyes, searching for a way out. There wasn't one. The power or the man. I couldn't have both.

And here's where I had a choice.

Fight Ethan for the amulet, take it to Phoebus, and claim my prize, whatever I choose it to be.

Or prove to Ethan that I deserve his respect instead of tricking it out of him.

Blood clots stained my hair, and slowly I washed them away. Straightened my corset. Checked my face in the mirror. And opened the door.

Ethan jumped to his feet. "Look. I didn't mean—"

"No, Ethan." My voice sounded calm and clear. "I was wrong. I guess, all that power . . . it seduced me. I wanted it. But you were right, that's not the way. We should destroy the amulet. I see that now. I'm sorry."

"Don't be sorry. You saved my life." He touched my shoulder, hesitant. He wouldn't meet my eyes. "And you nearly killed yourself to do it. I . . . I don't know what to say."

Him, awkward with me. Imagine.

"I didn't want you hurt," I admitted, and I swear that husky break in my voice happened all by itself. "I couldn't see another way. I had to put it on."

"I know." He looked up at last, ice blue eyes melting to sunlit sky. "I screwed up, Lena. I was trying to shield you from temptation. The last thing I wanted was—"

"I know." I flushed. God, he really did have great hair. "It's over now. Can we . . . y'know. Be friends?"

That flashbulb smile. "Lena, despite what you might think, we've always been friends."

"That's not what I meant." I leaned closer and brushed his lips with mine.

For a moment, he was still, startled. And then he kissed me back, slow and spine-tingling, like we had all the time in the world. He tasted of herbs, the coppery cut on his lip only spicing up the flavor. His hair fell on my shoulder, so soft and crisp, and my skin sparkled hot. Wow. I slid my arms around his neck and opened my mouth, inviting him in, and he folded me in his good arm and pulled me closer. His lean body crushed against mine as we kissed, and he felt as good as I'd always known he would.

And then he sighed, gave me a disbelieving blue glance, and passed out.

I eased him onto the bed, and swiftly reapplied the lipstick I'd put on in the bathroom. Cherry-cola. Made it myself. Bet you never picked Ethan for an easy mark.

Blond hair spilled into his sleeping face, and I brushed it back with one finger and a regretful sigh. Damn. He was really nice. I'd have liked that.

But the Lena he wanted was a lie, no matter how much I wished for his sake that I could be her. I might lie about the little things, but in the end, you've gotta be true to what you are.

And what I am is a cheap gutter con artist. No amount of wishing's going to change that.

I dug into his pocket and pulled out my amulet.

Dried clots of my blood still crusted the chain. I brushed them off. The remnants of my hex pendant were buried deep inside, and the stone winked at me, inviting.

I winked back and slipped it around my neck. Power settled over me like a warm, sparkly blanket, and the demon purred and wrapped herself seductively around my heart. I was her mistress now. She wouldn't fight me anymore.

Will I take her back to Phoebus? Maybe. Maybe not. He'd offered me a favor. But I already had everything I wanted.

Sparks zinged from my fingertips as I zipped my boots on and rebuckled my knives. I shrugged into my jacket and took one last lingering glance at Ethan, sleeping peacefully on his perfectly made bed in the land of out-of-my-league.

Well, almost everything I wanted.

But there's always another game. Another con. And if Phoebus wants his amulet, he can come and get it. With my new friend on my side, I'll gladly take him on.

I flexed my fingers, and distant thunder rolled. That was very cool. Not strictly ethical, but cool. I may not be a witch—not technically—but I've still got a few tricks up my corset.

I smiled, and stroked my demon, and vanished.

★　★　★

Author's Bio
Erica Hayes is the author of the Shadowfae Chronicles, a dark urban fantasy/romance series. Set in a demon-haunted city infested with psychotic fairies and bloodthirsty vampire gangsters, her books feature tough, smart heroines and colorful heroes with dark secrets. She lives in Australia, where she drifts from city to city, leaving a trail of chaos behind her. You can find her on the web at www.erica hayes.net.

THE ARCANE ART OF MISDIRECTION

by CARRIE VAUGHN

The cards had rules, but they could be made to lie.

The rules said that a player with a pile of chips that big was probably cheating. Not definitely—luck, unlike cards, didn't follow any rules. The guy could just be lucky. But the prickling of the hairs on the back of Julie's neck made her think otherwise.

He was middle-aged, aggressively nondescript. When he sat down at her table, Julie pegged him as a middle-management type from flyover country—cheap gray suit, unimaginative tie, chubby face, greasy hair clumsily combed over a bald spot. Now that she thought about it, his look was so clichéd, it might have been a disguise designed to make sure people dismissed him out of hand. Underestimated him.

She'd seen card-counting rings in action—groups of people who prowled the casino, scouted tables, signaled when a deck was hot, and sent in a big bettor to clean up. They could win a ridiculous amount of money in a short amount of time. Security kept tabs on most of the well-known rings and barred them from the casino. This guy was alone. He wasn't signaling. No one else was lingering nearby.

He could still be counting cards. She'd dealt blackjack for five years now and could usually spot it. Players tapped a finger, or sometimes their lips moved. If they were that obvious, they probably weren't winning anyway. The good ones knew to cut out before the casino noticed and ejected them. Even the best card counters lost some of the time. Counting cards didn't beat the system, it was just an attempt to push the odds in your favor. This guy hadn't lost a single hand of blackjack in forty minutes of play.

For the last ten minutes, the pit boss had been watching over Julie's shoulder as she dealt. Her table was full, as others had drifted over, maybe hoping some of the guy's luck would rub off on them. She slipped cards out of the shoe for her players, then herself. Most of them only had a chip or two—minimum bid was twenty-five. Not exactly high rolling, but enough to make Vegas's middle-America audience sweat a little.

Two players stood. Three others hit; two of them busted. Dealer drew fifteen, then drew an eight—so she was out. Her chubby winner had a stack of chips on his square. Probably five hundred dollars. He hit on eighteen—and who in their right mind ever hit on eighteen? But he drew a three. Won, just like that. His expression never budged, like he expected to win. He merely glanced at the others when they offered him congratulations.

Julie slid over yet another stack of chips; the guy herded it together with his already impressive haul. Left the previous stack right where it was, and folded his hands to wait for the next deal. He seemed bored.

Blackjack wasn't supposed to be boring.

She looked at Ryan, her pit boss, a slim man in his fifties who'd worked Vegas casinos his whole life. He'd seen it all, and he was on his radio. Good. Security could review the video and spot whatever this guy was doing. Palming cards, probably—though she couldn't guess how he was managing it.

She was about to deal the next hand when the man in question looked at her, looked at Ryan, then scooped his chips up, putting stack after stack in his jacket pockets, then walked away from the table, wearing a small, satisfied grin.

He didn't leave a tip. Even the losers left tips.

"Right. He's gone, probably heading for the cashier. Thanks." Ryan put his radio down.

"Well?" Julie asked.

"They can't find anything to nail him with, but they'll keep an eye on him," Ryan said. He was frowning and seemed suddenly worn under the casino's lights.

"He's got to be doing something, if we could just spot it."

"Never mind, Julie. Get back to your game."

He was right. Not her problem.

Cards slipped under her fingers and across the felt like water. The remaining players won and lost at exactly the rate they should, and she collected more chips than she gave out. She could tell when her shift was close to ending by the ache that entered her lower back from standing. Just another half hour, and Ryan would close out her table, and she could leave. Run to the store, drag herself home, cobble together a meal that wouldn't taste quite right because she was eating it at midnight, but that was dinnertime when she worked this shift. Take a shower, watch a half an hour of bad TV, and, finally, finally fall asleep. Wake up late in the morning and do it all again.

That was her life. As predictable as house odds.

There's a short film, a test of sorts. The caption at the start asks you to watch the group of people throwing balls to one another and count the number of times the people wearing white pass the ball. You watch the film and concentrate very hard on the players wearing white. At the end, the film asks, how many times did people wearing white pass the ball? Then it asks, Did you see the gorilla?

Hardly anyone does.

Until they watch the film a second time, people refuse to believe a gorilla ever appeared at all. They completely fail to see the person in the gorilla suit walk slowly into the middle of the frame, among the ball-throwers, shake its fists, and walk back out.

This, Odysseus Grant knows, is a certain kind of magic.

Casinos use the same principles of misdirection. Free drinks keep people at the tables, where they will spend more than they ever would have on rum and Cokes. But they're happy to get the free drinks, and so they stay and gamble.

They think they can beat the house at blackjack because they have a system. Let them think it. Let them believe in magic, just a little.

But when another variable enters the game—not luck, not chance, not skill, not subterfuge—it sends out ripples, tiny, subtle ripples that most people would never notice because they're focused on their own world: tracking their cards, drinking free drinks, counting people in white shirts throwing balls. But sometimes, someone—like Odysseus Grant—notices. And he pulls up a chair at the table to watch.

The next night, it was a housewife in a floral-print dress, lumpy brown handbag, and overpermed hair. Another excruciating stereotype. Another impossible run of luck. Julie resisted an urge to glance at the cameras in their bubble housings overhead. She hoped they were getting this.

The woman was even following the same pattern—push a stack of chips forward, hit no matter how unlikely or counterintuitive, and win. She had five grand sitting in front of her.

One other player sat at the table, and he seemed not to notice the spectacle beside him. He was in his thirties, craggy-looking, crinkles around his eyes, a serious frown pulling at his lips. He wore a white tuxedo shirt without jacket or bow tie, which meant he was probably a local, someone who worked the tourist trade on the Strip. Maybe a bartender or a limo driver? He did look familiar, now that she thought about it, but Julie couldn't place where she might have seen him. He seemed to be killing time, making minimum bets, playing conservatively. Every now and then, he'd make a big bet, a hundred or two hundred, but his instincts were terrible, and he never won. His stack of chips, not large to begin with, was dwindling. When he finally ran out, Julie would be sorry to see him go because she'd be alone with the strange housewife.

The woman kept winning.

Julie signaled to Ryan, who got on the phone with security. They watched but, once again, couldn't find anything. Unless she was spotted palming cards, the woman wasn't breaking any rules. Obviously, some kind of ring was going on. Two unlikely players winning in exactly the same pattern—security would record their pictures, watch for them, and might bar them from the casino. But if the ring sent a different person in every time, security would never be able to catch them, or even figure out how they were doing it.

None of it made sense.

The man in the tuxedo shirt reached into his pocket, maybe fumbling for cash or extra chips. Whatever he drew out was small enough to cup in his fist. He brought his hand to his face, uncurled his fingers, and blew across his palm, toward the woman sitting next to him.

She vanished, only for a heartbeat, flickering in and out of sight like the image on a staticky TV. Julie figured she'd blinked or that something was wrong with her eyes. She was working too hard, getting too tired, something. But the woman—she stared hard at the stone-faced man, then scooped her chips into her oversized handbag, rushing so that a few fell on the floor around her, and she didn't even notice. Hugging the bag to her chest, she fled.

Still no tip, unless you counted what she'd dropped.

The man rose to follow her. Julie reached across the table and grabbed his arm.

"What just happened?" she demanded.

The man regarded her with icy blue eyes. "You saw that?" His tone was curious, scientific almost.

"It's my table; of course I saw it," she said.

"And you see everything that goes on here?"

"I'm good at my job."

"The cameras won't even pick up what I did," he said, nodding to the ceiling.

"What *you* did? Then it did happen."

"You'd be better off if you pretended it didn't."

"I know what I saw."

"Sometimes eyes are better than cameras," he said, turning a faint smile.

"Is everything all right?" Ryan stood by Julie, who still had her hand on the man's arm.

She didn't know how to answer that and blinked dumbly at him. Finally, she pulled her arm away.

"Your dealer is just being attentive," the man said. "One of the other players seemed to have a moment of panic. Very strange."

Like he hadn't had a hand in it.

Ryan said, "Why don't you take a break, Julie? Get something to eat, come back in an hour."

She didn't need a break. She wanted to flush the last ten minutes out of her mind. If she kept working, she might be able to manage, but Ryan's tone didn't invite argument.

"Yeah, okay," she murmured, feeling vague.

Meanwhile, the man in the white shirt was walking away, along the casino's carpeted main thoroughfare, following the woman.

Rushing now, Julie cleaned up her table, signed out with Ryan, and ran after the man.

"You, wait a minute!"

He turned. She expected him to argue, to express some kind

of frustration, but he remained calm, mildly inquisitive. As if he'd never had a strong emotion in his life. She hardly knew what to say to that immovable expression.

She pointed. "You spotted it—you saw she was cheating."

"Yes." He kept walking—marching, rather—determinedly. Like a hunter stalking a trail before it went cold. Julie followed, dodging a bachelorette party—a horde of twenty-something women in skintight minidresses and overteased hair—that hadn't been there a moment ago. The man slipped out of their way.

"How?" she said, scrambling to keep close to him.

"I was counting cards and losing. I know how to count—I don't lose."

"You were—" She shook the thought away. "No, I mean how was she doing it? I couldn't tell. I didn't spot any palmed cards, no props or gadgets—"

"He's changing the cards as they come out of the shoe," he said.

"*What?* That's impossible."

"Mostly impossible," he said.

"The cards were normal, they felt normal. I'd have been able to tell if something was wrong with them."

"No, you wouldn't, because there was nothing inherently wrong with the cards. You could take every card in that stack, examine them all, sort them, count them, and they'd all be there, exactly the right number in exactly the number of suits they ought to be. You'd never spot what had changed because he's altering the basic reality of them. Swapping a four for a six, a king for a two, depending on what he needs to make black-jack."

She didn't understand, to the point where she couldn't even frame the question to express her lack of understanding. No wonder the cameras couldn't spot it.

"You keep saying he, but that was a woman—"

"And the same person who was there yesterday. He's a magician."

The strange man looked as if he had just played a trick, or pushed back the curtain, or produced a coin from her ear. Julie suddenly remembered where she'd seen him before: in a photo on a poster outside the casino's smaller theater. The magic show. "You're Odysseus Grant."

"Hello, Julie," he said. He'd seen the name tag on her uniform vest. Nothing magical about it.

"But *you're* a magician," she said.

"There are different kinds of magic."

"You're not talking about pulling rabbits out of hats, are you?"

"Not like that, no."

They were moving against the flow of a crowd; a show at one of the theaters must have just let out. Grant moved smoothly through the traffic; Julie seemed to bang elbows with every single person she encountered.

They left the wide and sparkling cavern of the casino area and entered the smaller, cozier hallway that led to the hotel wing. The ceilings were lower here, and plastic ficus plants decorated the corners. Grant stopped at the elevators and pressed the button.

"I don't understand," she said.

"You really should take a break, like your pit boss said."

"No, I want to know what's going on."

"Because a cheater is ripping off your employer?"

"No, because he's ripping off *me*." She crossed her arms. "You said it's the same person who's been doing this, but I couldn't spot him. How did you spot him?"

"You shouldn't be so hard on yourself. How would you even know what to look for? There's no such thing as magic, after all."

"Well. *Something's* going on."

"Indeed. You really should let me handle this—"

"I want to help."

The doors slid open, and Julie started to step through them, until Grant grabbed her arm so hard she gasped. When he pulled back, she saw why: The elevator doors had opened on an empty shaft, an ominous black tunnel with twisting cable running down the middle. She'd have just stepped into that pit without thinking.

She fell back and clung to Grant's arm until her heart sank from her throat.

"He knows we're on to him," Grant said. "Are you sure you want to help?"

"I didn't see it. I didn't even look."

"You expected the car to be there. Why should you have to look?"

She would never, ever take a blind step again. Always, she would creep slowly around corners and tread lightly on the ground before her. "Just like no one expects a housewife or a businessman from the Midwest to cheat at table games in Vegas."

"Just so."

The elevator doors slid shut, and the hum of the cables, the ding of the lights, returned to normal. Normal—and what did that mean again?

"Maybe we should take the stairs," Julie murmured.

"Not a bad idea," Grant answered, looking on her with an amused glint in his eye that she thought was totally out of place, given that she'd almost died.

Down another hallway and around a corner, they reached the door to the emergency stairs. The resort didn't bother putting any frills into the stairwell, which most of its patrons would never see: The tower was made of echoing concrete, the railings were steel, the stairs had nonskid treads underfoot. The stairs seemed to wind upward forever.

"How do you even know where he is? If he knows you're looking for him, he's probably out of town by now."

"We were never following *him*. He's never left his room."

"Then who was at my table?"

"That's a good question, isn't it?"

It was going to be a long, long climb.

Grant led, and Julie was happy to let him do so. At every exit door, he stopped, held before it a device that looked like an old-fashioned pocket watch, with a brass casing and a lumpy knob and ring protruding. After regarding the watch a moment, he'd stuff it back in his trouser pocket and continue on.

She guessed he was in his thirties, but now she wasn't sure—he seemed both young and old. He moved with energy, striding up the stairs without pause, without a hitch in his breath. But he also moved with consideration, with purpose, without a wasted motion. She'd never seen his show and thought now that she might. He'd do all the old magic tricks, the cards and rings and disappearing-box trick, maybe even pull a rabbit from a hat, and his every motion would be precise and enthralling. And it would all be tricks, she reminded herself.

After three flights, she hauled herself up by the railing, huffing for air. If Grant was frustrated at the pauses she made on each landing, he didn't let on. He just studied his watch a little longer.

Finally, on about the fifth or sixth floor, he consulted his watch and lifted an eyebrow. Then he opened the door. Julie braced for danger—after the empty elevator shaft, anything could happen: explosions blasting in their faces, ax-wielding murderer waiting for them, Mafioso gunfight—but nothing happened.

"Shall we?" Grant said, gesturing through the doorway as if they were entering a fancy restaurant.

She wasn't sure she really wanted to go, but she did. Leaning in, she looked both ways, up and down the hallway, then stepped gingerly on the carpet, thinking it might turn to quicksand and swallow her. It didn't. Grant slipped in behind her and closed the door.

This wing of the hotel had been refurbished in the last few years and still looked newish. The carpet was thick, the soft recessed lighting on the russet walls was luxurious and inviting. In a few more years, the décor would start to look worn, and the earth tones and geometric patterns would look dated. Vegas wore out things the way it wore out people. For now, though, it was all very impressive.

They lingered by the emergency door; Grant seemed to expect something to happen. Consulting his watch again, he turned it to the left and right, considering. She craned her neck, trying to get a better look at it. It didn't seem to have numbers on its face.

"What's that thing do?" she asked.

"It points," he said.

Of course it did.

He moved down the hallway to the right, glancing at the watch, then at doorways. At the end of the hall, he stopped and nodded, then made a motion with his hands.

"More magic?" she said, moving beside him.

"No. Lockpick." He held up a flat plastic key card. "Universal code."

"Oh my God, if the resort knew you were doing this—and I'm right here with you. I could lose my job—"

"They'll never find out."

She glanced to the end of the hallway, to the glass bubble in the ceiling where the security camera was planted.

"Are you sure about that? Am I supposed to just trust you?"

His lips turned a wry smile. "I did warn you that you probably ought to stay out of this. It's not too late."

"What, and take the elevator back down? I don't think so."

"There you go—you trust me more than the elevator."

She crossed her arms and sighed. "I'm not sure I agree with that logic."

"It isn't logic," he said. "It's instinct. Yours are good, you should listen to them."

She considered—any other dealer, any *sane* dealer, would have left the whole problem to Ryan and security. Catching cheaters once they left the table was above her pay grade, as they said. But she wanted to *know*. The same prickling at her neck that told her something was wrong with yesterday's businessman and today's housewife also told her that Odysseus Grant had answers.

"What can I do to help?" she asked.

"Keep a lookout."

He slipped the card in the lock, and the door popped open. She wouldn't have been surprised if an unassuming guest wrapped in a bath towel screamed a protest, but the room was unoccupied. After a moment, Grant entered and began exploring.

Julie stayed by the door, glancing back and forth, up and down the hallway as he had requested. She kept expecting guys from security to come pounding down the hallway. But she also had to consider: Grant wouldn't be doing this if he didn't have a way to keep it secret. She couldn't even imagine how he was fooling the cameras. *The cameras won't even pick up what I did,* he'd said. Did the casino's security department even know what they had working under their noses?

She looked back in the room to check his progress. "You expected that watch, that whatever it is, to lead you right to the guy, did you?"

"Yes, it should have," Grant said, sounding curious rather than frustrated. "Ah, there we are." He opened the top bureau drawer.

"What?" She craned forward to see.

Using a handkerchief, he reached into the drawer and picked up a small object. Resting on the cloth was a twenty-five-dollar chip bound with twine to the burned-down stub of a red candle. The item evoked a feeling of dread in her; it made her imagine an artifact from some long-extinct civilization that practiced human sacrifice. Whatever this thing was, no good could ever come of it.

"A decoy," Grant said. "Rather clever, really."

"Look, I can call security, have them check the cameras, look for anyone suspicious—they'll know who's been in this room."

"No. You've seen how he's disguising himself; he's a master of illusion. Mundane security has no idea what they're looking for. I'll find him." He broke the decoy, tearing at the twine, crumbling the candle, throwing the pieces away. Even broken, the pieces made her shiver.

Then they were back in the hallway. Grant again consulted his watch, but they reached the end of the hallway without finding his quarry.

They could be at this all day.

"Maybe we should try knocking on doors. You'll be able to spot the guy if he answers."

"That's probably not a good idea. Especially if he knows we're coming."

"How long until you give up?" she said, checking her phone to get the time. The thing had gone dead, out of power. Of course it had. And Grant's watch didn't tell time.

"Never," he murmured, returning to the emergency stairs.

She started to follow him when her eye caught on an incongruity, because the afternoon had been filled with them. A service cart was parked outside a room about halfway down the hallway. Dishes of a picked-over meal littered the white linen tablecloth, along with an empty bottle of wine and two used wineglasses. Nothing unusual at all about seeing such a thing outside a room in a hotel. Except she was absolutely sure it had not been there before.

"Hey—wait a minute," she said, approaching the cart slowly. The emergency-stair door had already shut, though, and he was gone. She went after him, hauling open the door.

Which opened into a hallway, just like the one she'd left.

Vertigo made her vision go sideways a moment, and she thought she might faint. Shutting the door quickly, she leaned against it and tried to catch her breath. She'd started gasping for air. This was stupid—it was just a door. She'd imagined it. Her mind was playing tricks, and Grant was right, she should have stayed back in the casino.

No, she was a sensible woman, and she trusted her eyes. She opened the door again, and this time when she saw the second, identical—impossible—hallway through it, she stayed calm, and kept her breathing steady.

Stepping gently, she went through the door, careful to hold it open, giving her an escape route. Her feet touched carpet instead of concrete. She looked back and forth—same hallway. Or maybe not—the room-service cart wasn't here.

"Odysseus?" she called, feeling silly using the name. His stage name, probably, but he hadn't given her another one to call him. His real name was probably something plain, like Joe or Frank. On second thought, considering the watch, the universal lock-pick, his talk of spells, his weird knowledge—Odysseus might very well be his real name.

"Odysseus Grant?" she repeated. No answer. Behind one of the doors, muted laughter echoed from a television.

She retreated to the original hallway and let the door close. Here, the same TV buzzing with the same noise, obnoxious canned laughter on some sitcom. She could believe she hadn't ever left, that she hadn't opened the door and seen another hall-way rather than the stairs that should have been there. This was some kind of optical illusion. A trick done with mirrors.

The room-service cart was gone.

She ran down the hall to where it had been, felt around the spot where she was sure she had seen it—nothing. She continued on to the opposite end of the hallway, past the elevators that she didn't dare try, to the other set of emergency stairs. Holding her breath, she opened the door—and found herself staring into another hallway, identical to the one she was standing in. When she ran to the opposite end of *that* corridor, and tried the other door there, she found the same thing—another hallway, with the same numbers outside the rooms, the same inane voices from the television.

Bait. The room-service cart had been bait, used to distract her, to draw her back after Grant had already left. And now she was trapped.

Casinos, especially the big ones on the Strip, are built to be mazes. From the middle of the casino, you can't readily find the exit. Sure, the place is as big as a few football fields lined up, the walkways are all wide and sweeping to facilitate ease of movement. The fire codes mean the casino can't actually lock you in. But when you're surrounded by ringing slot machines and video poker and a million blinking lights, when the lack of windows means that if you didn't have your watch or phone you'd have no way to tell the time, when the dealer at the blackjack table will keep dealing cards and taking your chips as the hours slip by—you leave by an act of will, not because the way out is readily apparent.

More than that, though, the resort is its own world. Worlds within worlds. You enter and never *have* to leave. Hotel, restaurants, shopping, gaming, shows, spas, all right here. You can even get married if you want, in a nice little chapel, tastefully decorated in soft colors and pews of warm mahogany, nothing like those tawdry places outside. You can get a package deal: wedding, room for the weekend, and a limo to the airport. The resort makes it easy for you to come and spend your money. It's a maze, and as long as your credit card stays good, they don't much care whether you ever get out.

That, too, was a certain kind of magic.

Grant climbed two flights of stairs, the single hand on his pocket watch giving no indication that anything untoward lay beyond the door at each landing, before he noticed that the earnest blackjack dealer was no longer with him.

He paused and called down, "Julie?" His voice echoed, and he received no response. He thought he'd been cautious enough. He looked around; the staircase had suddenly become sinister.

One of the notable characteristics of a very tall staircase like this one was that it all looked the same, minimalist and unwelcoming. This landing was exactly like the last, this flight of stairs like the first six he'd climbed up.

The number painted on the door at this landing was five. He turned around, descended a flight, looked at the door—which also read five. And the one below it. Climbing back up, he returned to where he'd stopped. Five again, or rather, still. Five and five and five. Somewhere between this floor and the last, his journey had become a loop. Which meant he was in trouble, and so was Julie.

There were still doorways, which meant there was still a way out.

Five was one of the mystic numbers—well, any number could be mystic to the right person under the right circumstances. Go to the casino and ask people what their lucky numbers were, and every number, up to a hundred and often beyond, would be represented. But five—it was a prime number, some cultures counted five elements, a pentagram had five points. It was the number of limbs to the human body, if you counted the head. A number of power, of binding.

What kind of power did it take to bend a stairwell, Escher-like, upon itself? This magician, who'd orchestrated all manner of tricks and traps, was drawing on an impressive source of it. And that's why the culprit hadn't fled—he'd built up a base of power here in the hotel, in order to initiate his scheme. He was counting on that power to protect him now.

When turning off a light without a switch, unplugging the lamp made so much more sense than breaking the lightbulb. Grant needed to find this magician.

He pocketed his watch and drew out a few tools he had brought with him: a white candle, a yard of red thread, and a book of matches.

Julie paced in front of the doorway. She thought it was the first one, the original one that she and Grant had come through, but she couldn't be entirely sure. She'd gotten turned around.

How long before Grant noticed she was missing? What were the rules of hiking in the wilderness? Stay still, call for help, until someone finds you. She took out her phone again and shook it, as if that kind of desperate, sympathetic magic would work. It didn't. Still dead. She'd be trapped here forever. She couldn't even call 911 to come and rescue her. Her own fault, for getting involved in a mess she didn't know anything about. She should never have followed Grant.

No, that hadn't been a mistake. Her mistake had been panicking and running off half-cocked. This—none of this could be real. It went against all the laws of physics. So if it wasn't real, what was it? An illusion. Maybe she couldn't trust her eyes after all, at least not all the time.

She closed her eyes. Now she didn't see anything. The TV had fallen silent. This smelled like a hotel hallway—lint, carpet cleaner. A place devoid of character. She stood before a door, and when she opened it, she'd step through to a concrete stairwell, where she'd walk straight down, back to the lobby and the casino, back to work, and she wouldn't ask any more questions about magic.

Reaching out, she flailed a bit before finding the doorknob. Her hand closed on it, and turned. She pushed it opened and stepped through.

And felt concrete beneath her feet.

She opened her eyes, and was in the stairwell, standing right in front of Odysseus Grant. On the floor between them sat a votive candle and a length of red thread tied in a complicated pattern of knots. Grant held a match in one hand and the book it came from in the other, ready to light.

"How did you do that?" he asked, seeming genuinely startled. His wide eyes and suspicious frown were a little unnerving.

She glanced over her shoulder and back at him. "I closed my eyes. I figured none of it was real—so I just didn't look."

His expression softened into a smile. "Well done." He crouched and quickly gathered up the items, shoving thread, candle, and matches into his pockets. "He's protecting himself with a field of illusion. He must be right here—he must have been here the whole time." He nodded past her to the hallway.

"How do you know?"

"Fifth floor. It should have been obvious," he said.

"Obvious?" she said, nearly laughing. "Really?"

"Well, partially obvious."

Which sounded like "sort of pregnant" to her. Before she could prod further, he urged her back into the hallway and let the door shut. It sounded a little like a death knell.

"Now, we just have to figure out what room he's in. Is there a room 555 here?"

"On the other end, I think."

"Excellent. He's blown his cover." Grant set off with long strides. Julie scurried to keep up.

At room 555, Grant tried his universal keycard, slipping it in and out of the slot. It didn't work. "This'll take a little more effort, I think. No matter." He waved a hand over the keycard and tried again. And again. It still didn't work.

A growl drew Julie's attention to the other end of the hallway, back the way they'd come.

A creature huddled there, staring with eyes that glowed like hot iron. At first, she thought it was a dog. But it wasn't. The thing was slate gray, hairless, with a stout head as big as its chest and no neck to speak of. Skin drooped in folds around its shoulders and limbs, and knobby growths covering its back gave it an armored look. Her mind went through a catalog of four-legged predators, searching for possibilities: hyena, lion, bear, badger on steroids, dragon.

Dragon?

The lips under its hooked bill seemed to curl in a smile.

She could barely squeak, "Odysseus?"

He glanced up from his work to where she pointed. Then he paused and took a longer look.

"It's a good sign," Grant said.

"How is that a good sign?" she hissed.

"A guardian like that means we've found him."

That she couldn't argue his logic didn't mean he wasn't still crazy.

"Can you distract it?" he said. "I'm almost through."

"Distract it? How on Earth—"

"This magician works with illusions. That thing is there to frighten us off. But mostly likely it's not even real. If you distract it, it'll vanish."

"Just like that, huh?"

"I imagine so."

He didn't sound as confident as she'd have liked.

She tried to picture the thing just vanishing. It looked solid enough—it filled most of the hallway. It must have been six feet tall, crouching.

"And you're absolutely sure it's not real." She reminded herself about the hallways, the room service cart. All she had to do was close her eyes.

"I'm reasonably sure."

"That's not absolutely."

"Julie, trust me." He was bent over the lock again, intent on his work.

The beast wasn't real. All right. She just had to keep telling herself that. Against her better judgment, Julie stepped toward the creature.

"Here, kitty kitty—" Okay, that was stupid. "Um, hey! Over here!" She waved her hands over her head.

The beast's red eyes narrowed; its muscles bunched.

"Remember, it's an illusion. Don't believe it."

The thing hunched and dug in claws in preparation of a charge. The carpet shredded in curling fibers under its efforts. *That* sure looked real.

"I—I don't think it's an illusion. It's *drooling*."

"Julie, stand your ground."

The monster launched, galloping toward her, limbs pumping, muscles trembling under horny skin. The floor shook under its pounding steps. What did the magician expect would happen? Was the creature supposed to pass through her like mist?

Julie closed her eyes and braced.

A weight like a runaway truck crashed into her, and she flew back and hit the floor, head cracking, breath gusting from her lungs. The great, slavering beast stood on her, kneading her uniform vest with questing claws. Its mouth opened wide, baring yellowing fangs as it hissed a breath that smelled like carrion. Somehow, she'd gotten her arms in front of her and held it off, barely. Her hands sank into the soft, gray flesh of its chest. Its chunky head strained forward. She punched at it, dug her fingernails into it, trying to find some sensitive spot that might at least make it hesitate. She scrabbled for its eyes, but it turned its head away, and its claws ripped into her vest.

She screamed.

Thunder cracked, and the creature leaped away from her, yelping. A second boom sounded, this time accompanied by a flash of light. Less like a lightning strike and more like some kind of explosion in reverse. She covered her head and curled up against the chaos of it. The air smelled of sulfur.

She waited a long time for the silence to settle, not convinced that calm had returned to the hallway. Her chest and shoulders were sore, bruised. She had to work to draw breath into complaining lungs. Finally, though, she could uncurl from the floor and look around.

A dark stain the size of a sedan streaked away from her across the carpet and walls, like soot and ashes from an old fireplace. The edges of it gave off thin fingers of smoke. Housekeeping was going to love this. The scent of burned meat seared into her nose.

Grant stood nearby, hands lifted in a gesture of having just thrown something. Grenade, maybe? Some arcane whatsit? It hardly mattered.

She closed her eyes, hoping once again that it was all an illusion and that it would go away. But she could smell charred flesh, a rotten taste in the back of her throat.

From nearby, Grant asked, "Are you all right?"

Leaning toward the wall, she threw up.

"Julie—"

"You said it was an illusion."

"I had every—"

"I trusted you!" Her gut heaved again. Hugging herself, she slumped against the wall and waited for the world to stop spinning.

He stood calmly, expressionless, like this sort of thing happened to him every day. Maybe it did.

She could believe her eyes. Maybe that was why she didn't dare open them again. Then it would all be real.

"Julie," he said again, his voice far too calm. She wanted to shake him.

"You were right," she said, her voice scratching past her raw throat and disbelief. "I should have stayed behind."

"I'm glad you didn't."

When she looked up, the burned stain streaking across the hall and the puddle of vomit in front of her were still there, all too real. Grant appeared serene. Unmoved.

"Really?"

"You have a gift for seeing past the obvious. You were the kid who always figured out the magic tricks, weren't you?"

She had to smile. For every rabbit pulled out of a hat, there was a table with a trapdoor nearby. You just had to know where to look.

"You *are* all right?" he asked, and she could believe that he was really concerned.

She had to think about it. The alternatives were going crazy or muddling through. She didn't have time for the going-crazy part. "I will be."

"I'm very sorry," he said, reaching out to help her up. "I really wasn't expecting that."

She took his hand and lurched to her feet. "You do the distracting next time." She didn't like the way her voice was shaking. If she thought about it too much, she'd run, scream-ing. If Grant could stand his ground, she could, too. She was determined.

"I was so sure it was an illusion. The players at your table—they had to have been illusions."

"The guy from yesterday was sweating."

"Very good illusions, mind you. Nevertheless—"

She pointed at the soot stain. "That's not an illusion. Those players weren't illusions. Now, maybe they weren't what they looked like, but they were *something*."

His brow creased, making him look worried for the first time this whole escapade. "I have a bad feeling."

He turned back to the door he'd been working on, reaching into both pockets for items. She swore he'd already pulled more out of those pockets than could possibly fit. Instead of more lockpicks or keycards or some fancy gizmo to fool the lock into opening, he held a string of four or five firecrackers. He tore a couple off the string, flattened them, and jammed them into the lock on the door.

Her eyes widened. "You can't—"

"Maybe the direct approach this time?" He flicked his hand, and the previously unseen match in his fingers flared to life. He lowered the flame to the fuse sticking out of the lock.

Julie scrambled back from the door. Grant merely turned his back.

The black powder popped and flared; the noise seemed loud in the hallway, and Julie could imagine the dozens of calls to the hotel front desk about the commotion. So, security would be up here in a few minutes, and one way or another it would all be over. She'd lose her job, at the very least. She'd probably end up in jail. But she'd lost her chance to back out of this. Only thing to do was keep going.

Grant eased open the door. She crept up behind him, and they entered the room.

This was one of the hotel's party suites—two bedrooms connected to a central living room that included a table, sofa, entertainment center, and wet bar. The furniture had all been pushed to the edges of the room, and the curtains were all drawn. Light came from the glow of a few dozen red pillar candles that had been lit throughout the room. Hundreds of dull shadows seemed to flicker in the corners. The smoke alarms had to have been disabled.

The place stank of burned vegetable matter, so many different flavors to it, Julie couldn't pick out individual components. It might have been some kind of earthy incense.

A pattern had been drawn onto the floor in luminescent paint. A circle arced around a pentagram and dozens of symbols, Greek letters, zodiac signs, others that she didn't recognize. It obviously meant something; she couldn't guess what. Housekeeping was *really* not going to like this.

Two figures stood within the circle: a man, rather short and very thin, wearing a T-shirt and jeans; the other, a hulking, red-skinned being, thick with muscles. It had a snout like an eagle's bill, sharp, reptilian eyes, and wings—sweeping, leathery—bat wings spread behind it like a sail.

Julie squeaked. Both figures looked at her. The bat-thing—another dragonlike gargoyle come to life—let out a scream, like the sound of tearing steel. Folding its wings close, it bowed its head as a column of smoke enveloped it.

Grant flipped the switch by the door. Light from the mundane incandescent bulbs overpowered the mystery-inducing candle glow. Julie and the guy in the circle squinted. By then, the column of smoke had cleared, and the creature had disappeared. An odor of burning wax and brimstone remained.

The guy, it turned out, was a kid. Just a kid, maybe fifteen, at that awkward stage of adolescence, his limbs too long for his body, acne spotting his cheeks.

"You've been summoning," Grant said. "It wasn't you working any of those spells, creating any of those illusions—you summoned creatures to do it for you. Very dangerous." He clicked his tongue.

"It was *working,*" the kid said. He pointed at the empty space where the bat-thing had been. "Did you see what I managed to summon?"

He was in need of a haircut, was probably still too young to shave, and his clothes looked ripe. The room did, too, now that

Julie had a chance to look around. Crumpled bags of fast food had accumulated in one corner, and an open suitcase had been dumped in another. The incense and candle smoke covered up a lot of dorm room smells.

On the bed lay the woman's purse with several thousand dollars in casino chips spilled around it.

"I think you're done here," Grant said.

"Just who *are* you?" the kid said.

"Think of me as the police. Of a certain kind."

The kid bolted for the door, but Julie blocked the way, grabbing his arm, then throwing herself into a tackle. He wasn't getting away with this, not if she could help it.

She wasn't very good at tackling, as it turned out. Her legs tangled with his, and they both crashed to the floor. He flailed, but her weight pinned him down. Somebody was going to take the blame for all this, and it wasn't going to be her.

Finally, the kid went slack. "It was *working,*" he repeated.

"Why would you even try something like this?" she said. "Cheating's bad enough, but . . . this?" She couldn't say she understood anything in the room, the candles or paint or that gargoylish creature. But Grant didn't like it, and that was enough for her.

"Because I'm underage!" he whined. "I can't even get into the casino. I needed a disguise."

"So you summoned demon doppelgängers?" Grant asked. Thoughtfully, he said, "That's almost clever. Still—very dangerous."

"Screw you!"

"Julie?" Grant said. "Now you can call security." He pulled the kid out from under Julie and pushed him to the wall, where he sat slouching. Grant stood over him, arms crossed, guardlike.

"Your luck ran out, buddy," Julie said, glaring at him. She retrieved her phone from her pocket. It was working now; go figure.

Grant said, "His luck ran out before he even started. Dozens of casinos on the Strip, and you picked mine, the one where you were most likely to get caught."

"You're just that stupid stage magician! Smoke and mirrors! What do you know about anything?" He slumped like a sack of old laundry.

Grant smiled, and the expression was almost wicked. The curled lip of a lion about to pounce. "To perform such summonings as you've done here, you must offer part of your own soul—as collateral, you might think of it. You probably think you're strong enough, powerful enough, to protect that vulnerable bit of your soul, defending it against harm. You think you can control such monstrous underworld creatures and keep your own soul—your own self—safe and sound. But it doesn't matter how protected you are, you will be marked. These creatures, any other demons you happen to meet, will know what you've done just by looking at you. *That* makes you a target. Now, and for the rest of your life. Actions have consequences. You'll discover that soon enough."

Julie imagined a world filled with demons, with bat-wing creatures and slavering dragons, all of them with consciousness, with a sense of mission: to attack their oppressors. She shivered.

Unblinking, the kid stared at Grant. He'd turned a frightening, pasty white, and his spine had gone rigid.

Grant just smiled, seemingly enjoying himself. "Do your research. Every good magician knows that."

Julie called security, and while they were waiting, the demon-summoning kid tried to set off an old-fashioned smoke bomb to stage an escape, but Grant confiscated it as soon as the kid pulled it from his pocket.

Soon after, a pair of uniformed officers arrived at the room to handcuff the kid and take him into custody. "We'll need you to come with us and give statements," one of them said to Julie and Grant.

She panicked. "But I didn't do anything wrong. I mean, not really—we were just looking for the cheater at my blackjack table, and something wasn't right, and Grant here showed up—"

Grant put a gentle hand on her arm, stopping her torrent of words. "We'll help in any way we can," he said.

She gave him a questioning look, but he didn't explain.

The elevators seemed to be working just fine now, as they went with security to their offices downstairs.

Security took the kid to a back room to wait for the Las Vegas police. Grant and Julie were stationed in a stark, functional waiting room, with plastic chairs and an ancient coffeemaker. They waited.

They only needed to look at the footage of her breaking into the rooms with Grant, and she'd be fired. She didn't want to be fired—she liked her job. She was good at it, as she kept insisting. She caught cheaters—even when they were summoning demons.

Her foot tapped a rapid beat on the floor, and her hands clenched into fists, pressed against her legs.

"Everything will be fine," Grant said, glancing sidelong at her. "I have a feeling the boy'll be put off the whole idea of spell-casting moving forward. Now that he knows people are watching him. He probably thought he was the only magician in the world. Now he knows better."

One could hope.

Now that he'd been caught, she didn't really care about the kid. "You'll be fired, too, you know, once they figure out what we did. You think you can find another gig after word gets out?"

"I won't be fired. Neither will you," he said.

They'd waited for over half an hour when the head of security came into the waiting room. Grant and Julie stood to meet him. The burly, middle-aged man in the off-the-rack suit—ex-cop, probably—was smiling.

"All right, you both can go now. We've got everything we need."

Julie stared.

"Thank you," Grant said, not missing a beat.

"No, thank *you*. We never would have caught that kid without your help." Then he shook their hands. And let them go.

Julie followed Grant back to the casino lobby. Two hours had passed, for the entire adventure, which had felt like it lasted all day—all day and most of the night, too. It seemed impossible. It all seemed impossible.

Back at the casino, the noise and bustle—crystal chandeliers glittering, a thousand slot and video machines ringing and clanking, a group of people laughing—seemed otherworldly. Hands clasped behind his back, Grant regarded the patrons filing back and forth, the flashing lights, with an air of satisfaction, like he owned the place.

Julie asked, "What did you do to get him to let us go?"

"They saw exactly what they needed to see. They'll be able to charge the kid with vandalism and destruction of property, and I'm betting if they check the video from the casino again, they'll find evidence of cheating."

"But we didn't even talk to them."

"I told you everything would be fine."

She regarded him, his confident stance, the smug expression, and wondered how much of it was a front. How much of it was the picture he wanted people to see.

She crossed her arms. "So, the kind of magic you do—what kind of mark does it leave on your soul?"

His smile fell, just a notch. After a hesitation, he said, "The price is worth it, I think."

If she were a little more forward, if she knew him better, she'd have hugged him—he looked like he needed it. He probably wasn't the kind of guy who had a lot of friends. At the moment, he seemed as otherworldly as the bat-winged creature in that arcane circle.

She said, "It really happened, didn't it? The thing with the hallway? The . . . the thing . . . and the other . . ." She moved her arms in a gesture of outstretched wings. "Not smoke and mirrors?"

"It really happened," he said.

"How do you do that? Any of it?" she said.

"That," he said, glancing away to hide a smile, "would take a very long time to explain."

"I get off my second shift at eleven," she said. "We could grab a drink."

She really hadn't expected him to say yes, and he didn't. But he hesitated first. So that was something. "I'm sorry," he said finally. "I don't think I can."

It was just as well. She tried to imagine her routine, with a guy like Odysseus Grant in the picture . . . and, well, there'd be no such thing as routine, would there? But she wasn't sure she'd mind a drink, and a little adventure, every now and then.

"Well then. I'll see you around," she said.

"You can bet on it," he said, and walked away, back to his theater.

Her break was long over, and she was late for the next half of her shift. She'd give Ryan an excuse—or maybe she could get Grant to make an excuse for her.

She walked softly, stepping carefully, through the casino, which had not yet returned to normal. The lights seemed dimmer, building shadows where there shouldn't have been any. A woman in a cocktail dress and impossible high heels walked past her, and Julie swore she had glowing red eyes. She did a double take, staring after her, but only saw her back, not her eyes.

At one of the bars, a man laughed—and he had pointed teeth, fangs, where his cuspids should have been. The man sitting with him raised his glass to drink—his hands were clawed with long, black talons. Julie blinked, checked again—yes, the talons were still there. The man must have sensed her staring because he looked at her, caught her gaze—then smiled and raised his glass in a salute before turning back to his companion.

She quickly walked away, heart racing.

This wasn't new, she realized. The demons had always been there, part of an underworld she had never seen because she simply hadn't been looking. Until now.

And once seen, it couldn't be unseen.

The blackjack dealer returned to the casino's interior, moving slowly, thoughtfully—warily, Grant decided. The world must look so much different to her now. He didn't know if she'd adjust.

He should have made her stay behind, right from the start. But no—he couldn't have stopped her. By then, she'd already seen too much. He had a feeling he'd be hearing from her again, soon. She'd have questions. He would answer them as best he could.

On the other hand, he felt as if he had an ally in the place, now. Another person keeping an eye out for a certain kind of danger. Another person who knew what to look for. And that was a very odd feeling indeed.

Some believe that magic—real magic, not the tricks that entertainers played onstage—is a rare, exotic thing. Really, it isn't, if you know what to look for.

★   ★   ★

Author's Bio:
Carrie Vaughn is the bestselling author of a series of novels about a werewolf named Kitty who hosts a talk-radio advice show. Odysseus Grant is a recurring character in the series. The ninth installment, *Kitty's Big Trouble,* was

released in 2011. She also writes young adult novels (*Voices of Dragons, Steel*), contemporary fantasy (*Discord's Apple, After the Golden Age*), and many short stories that can be found in various magazines and anthologies. She lives in Colorado and has too many hobbies. Learn more at **www** .carrievaughn.com.